UNTIL THE DAY I DIE

ALSO BY EMILY CARPENTER

Every Single Secret
The Weight of Lies
Burying the Honeysuckle Girls

UNTIL THE DAY I DIE

A NOVEL

EMILY CARPENTER

LAKE UNION
PUBLISHING

Text copyright © 2019 by Emily Carpenter
All rights reserved.

Published by Lake Union Publishing, Seattle
www.apub.com

Amazon, the Amazon logo, and Lake Union Publishing are trademarks of Amazon.com, Inc., or its affiliates.

ISBN-13: 9781503904217
ISBN-10: 1503904210

Cover design by Faceout Studio, Lindy Martin

Printed in the United States of America

For Kevin,
who helped me survive

MARCH

1

Perry's Journal

<u>Friday, March 1</u>

TO DO:
- Take Shorie for ice cream
- Pick up wings, beer, pinot gris
- Work on Shorie's letter
- Shorie's new Jax budget for school
- DO NOT OPEN SLACK OVER WEEKEND!!
- (except latest <u>Error Message</u>—kick to Scotty?)
- (and Global Cybergames guy—kick to Sabine?)

March's Oulipian constraint—N+5

> How do I love thee? Let me count the weddings.
> I love thee to the design and breaker and herb
> My southeast can reach, when ferrying out of silence.

> Elizabeth Barrett Browning, "How Do I Love Thee?" N+5

AUGUST

2

Erin

I was the one who insisted on the going-away party. Surprising exactly no one, I'm sure, because of how colossally bad an idea it was.

In fact, I have no doubt they discussed the issue behind my back in the days leading up to the dismal event. Just another instance of me forging blindly ahead, I'm sure they all agreed, trampling underfoot good sense, prudent measures, and the basics of self-care.

Proof positive that I was in dire need of a break.

Case in point: Shorie, my daughter, didn't even want to go away. Instead of accepting her scholarship and going to college—fulfilling her late father's wishes—she wanted to stay home and work at our tech company, Jax.

Additionally, the venue left much to be desired. For cost and conveniences' sake, I'd planned to have the party at Jax's office. Our startup, which launched a personal budget app, is run out of the funky loft space of a defunct department store in downtown Birmingham. The building is located smack-dab in the middle of the Birmingham Civil Rights Heritage Trail, and all day, you can see groups of tourists retracing the steps of Martin Luther King Jr. and the protests he led. Possibility and hope fill the air.

At least they used to before Perry died. But now—five months later—the place never fails to put me in a dark mood. When I'm there, I feel like a scuba diver trapped underwater, desperately trying to fight my way to the surface, all the while knowing my oxygen is running out. I love my job, but I hate the daily reminder of what I've lost.

So, not the best place to have a party.

In my defense, no one tried to talk me out of it. Sabine, my ever-loyal best friend, assured me everything would be fine. "Shorie will have a great time," she said in that soothing yoga-instructor voice she uses to persuade me to do things I don't want to do. "She may be the CEO's daughter, but we all consider her family."

I believed her and relaxed. Sabine has that effect on me. Behind my back, people call her the Erin Whisperer. A somewhat embarrassing but fair assessment. Truthfully I don't know how I would've survived Perry's death without her. She's been a lifeline for me, at work and with Shorie.

Sabine sent out the e-vites and ordered all the food, enough for the fifteen Jax employees and the handful of friends and family Shorie was inviting. Sabine said decorations were no big deal, just some flowers and Auburn swag to spruce things up. She even offered to take Shorie shopping for a new outfit.

I tried, I truly did. I plucked my unruly eyebrows, made sure to pick up my old workhorse black dress at the cleaners, and got my nails done, fingers *and* toes, for the first time in months. I had Shorie's gift cleaned and wrapped, a delicate band of emeralds that my mother gave to me when I went away to Auburn.

And then, the afternoon of the party, I unraveled.

It wasn't a Chris Stapleton song or the smell of an Altoids mint on somebody's breath or the way some man's light-brown hair curled up against the edge of his starched white collar. This time it was fast food.

I had popped into the hole-in-the-wall where Perry and I used to sneak off to revel in the forbidden glory of a chili slaw dog. In the shoebox-size space, I ordered what my Jax app had suggested to me—*Have Sloan's Special Dog, only $5.99!*—and found a table near the door, being careful not to smudge my newly glossed black nails as I sat. Then the vortex descended.

Perry lay on the hospital bed in the shadowy emergency room. In the curtained area, I could barely look at him, he was so bloody and still. He'd been driving from Columbus, Georgia, to meet us at the lake for a family camping trip, first one of the season. On 73, between Waverly and Roxana, he'd fallen asleep at the wheel, the police said. Veered off the narrow road and smashed his car into a pine tree. He hadn't been wearing a seat belt, that idiot.

After his meeting in Columbus, but before he'd gotten on the road, he'd met someone for drinks. A friend from college, Roy. Roy later swore to me that Perry only had one beer. The doctors did a blood test and didn't find anything to warrant concern, but what did it matter anyway? This motionless body covered in blood was not my husband. My husband was gone.

How to explain grief to someone who's never experienced it? It's like a cross between a panic attack and a case of acute appendicitis, only it happens all over your body. It never goes away, and it permanently alters who you are. There is no escape, only temporary reprieve. That afternoon, I raced out of the hot dog place without my food. At home, I vomited into the kitchen trash can, then locked myself in the guest room. The room had the only bed I could sleep in, one without any memories hiding between its sheets. I crawled under the blanket, fully clothed, and immediately fell asleep.

I awoke to the sound of someone tapping gently on the guest bedroom door. It was Sabine, who must have let herself in with her spare key. It was 9:30 p.m. Thirty minutes before Shorie's party was scheduled to be over.

3

SHORIE

The party's going okay, I guess. However parties are supposed to go. The nineties mix Sabine put on is playing so loud, it's making my heart keep time all the way down in the last cubicle.

I'm with one of Jax's yearlong, paid interns—Hank?—who has the darkest hair and palest skin I've ever seen on a human. Not *with* with; I'm just showing him some of the inner workings of the proprietary GPS program Jax uses. The way my dad used conditional constructs— the *if-then-else* statements of programming—to tailor it to a typical Jax user's needs.

I love tinkering like this, digging up the bones of a program, so to speak, but the truth is I have ulterior motives. Hank's skills seem pretty basic—rudimentary, if I'm being polite—and I'm hoping if I show him something cool, he'll give me something in return. Maybe tell me what Ben, Jax's lead developer, has him working on. Possibly send a problem or two my way when I'm at school. Just something on the sly for me to mess around with. He could obviously use the help, no offense.

As I type, I tell him about one of our former interns, a doofus who actually used the password *password* for his admin account. The story makes Hank (or is it Henry?) laugh. That trips me up, and my fingers freeze momentarily. I'm not used to making boys laugh.

And then Mom rushes into the cubicle, ruining the moment.

"Oh my God, Shorie, I'm so sorry." She's not wearing yoga pants, thank God, but her makeup looks kind of half-assed, and the tag is sticking up from the back of her dress. She's also got that glassy, confused look in her eyes. The look that's become all too familiar in the past five months—she's just woken up from a nap.

The intern snaps to attention at the sight of his boss. "Hey, Erin."

"Hello, Hank." Mom's face looks strained. "Mind if we have a minute?"

He doesn't even glance at me before fleeing the cubicle, and she moves to the desk. Taps her fingers on it. "Shor, I feel terrible."

I wait for the explanation to follow.

"I was out, running errands, and I went home. I was just going to lie down for a second. But I was feeling kind of off, and I must've fallen asleep—"

I push out of the chair. "It's okay."

She pulls at the neck of her dress, and I reach out and straighten it for her. It's the same one she wore to Dad's funeral, which pisses me off but at the same time makes me want to cry. How could she do that? Wear that dress again? And at my party?

But I don't cry or yell. What's the use? It's easier to be Robot Shorie—which is what my best friend, Daisy, called me one time in ninth grade when I refused to fight with her.

I do wonder what Mom's been doing all day. Not helping Sabine and me set everything up, that's for sure. I wonder if it occurred to her that she might not want to take a nap right before my going-away party. I want to slap her, then comfort her, then demand she apologize. All those emotions make me feel so nauseated, I could throw up.

"You look nice," is all I say.

She doesn't answer, just bites her lip.

When we rejoin the festivities, Daisy rushes up and presses a flute of what she pointedly announces is sparkling apple juice into my hands. I look around. Somehow Mom's already got a drink in her hand, real champagne, and is tipping it back.

"That guy likes you," Daisy says, her eyes like lasers on mine. "That intern, Hank."

I take a sip and make a face. She's smuggled me the real deal. I prefer the apple juice. "Yeah, I don't think so."

She shakes her head. She's been doing this for me since we met in fifth grade at robotics club—telling me which guys are interested in me. I never seem to be able to figure it out on my own.

"But if he does, maybe he can put a good word in for me with Ben."

She lifts her brows. "Oh, Shor. Forget all that. You're going to love school. It's going to be so much fun."

"Not as much fun as staying home and working at Jax," I retort, feeling bolder already. I'm kind of a lightweight when it comes to alcohol. And, no offense, but Daisy doesn't really understand where I'm coming from. She's 100 percent thrilled about heading off to Georgia Tech, where her parents went. She's basically been packing for college since she was in diapers.

I head over to talk to Gigi and Arch, my grandparents. They're all decked out for the party—Gigi in a green dress with a giant diamond starburst brooch on her shoulder and Arch in a natty suit and his favorite Yale tie, blue with little bulldogs all over it. He makes another crack about me going to Auburn instead of his la-di-da alma mater, and Gigi shushes him. But I'm glad to hear him joking. Ever since Dad died, he's seemed so sad. When I look around for Mom again, it appears she's melted away. Just then Sabine taps her glass, and the room quiets.

"I'd like to thank everyone for coming," she says. "We really appreciate every single one of you showing up to wish Shorie success in the next phase of her life. Before we say good night, we'd like to invite you to make a toast. One sentence, short and sweet." She winks at me. "I promised not to embarrass her."

"Me first," Ben says, raising his flute and clearing his throat theatrically. "An ode to Shorie. Looks like her daddy, codes like him too. But don't think you can have her. She's mine, Yahoo."

Someone shouts, "What's Yahoo?" and everybody laughs. Half of me feels suffused with happiness. The other half wants to run down the stairs and out into the street and never return. I really don't enjoy everybody looking at me like this.

"Okay, that was three sentences," Sabine says. "And nobody owns Shorie." She casts Ben a reproving look, but he just grins and points at me. I try to smile back. If he really wanted me, though, he'd talk Mom into letting me stay home and work. I've known him since I was a baby, and I love him like family—I even used to call him Uncle Ben before I figured out he wasn't really related to me—but I'm furious at him too.

Layton Marko, Jax's lawyer, raises her glass next. "You may be the smartest person I know, Shorie Gaines, but you never rub our noses in it."

Somebody yells, "Not true!" and breaks everybody up again.

"And comp-sci degree aside," she continues, "you can still go to law school afterward, like the cool kids."

I lift my glass to her while everybody hoots and hollers.

"My turn," Sabine says. She dabs at her nose, and I can see she's gotten misty-eyed. My heart twists a little. "You take our hearts with you, Shorie . . . so promise you'll come back."

Right then, I see Mom. She's standing beside Ben, who's got his arm around her. It isn't that abnormal; they're both huggers and have been friends forever. But for some reason it irks me. Mom catches my eye and raises her glass. Ben lets his arm fall away.

"Mine isn't one sentence either . . . ," she begins. The room quiets immediately, which is a thing that always happens when my mom speaks. "But first I'd like to say, I'm sorry for being late tonight. I lost track of time."

I gaze down at my sandals and my lemon-yellow toenail polish. It looked cheery in the nail salon, but under the fluorescent office lights, it makes me look like I've got a kidney condition. How is it even possible that the room just got quieter?

"That said," Mom continues, "I want you to know I am in your corner, one hundred percent, no matter what. Woo-hoo, Shorie!"

Ben's arm pops back up to Mom's shoulders, and he gives her a squeeze. But, at the same time, I see him and Sabine exchange glances. They're not falling for Mom's falsely upbeat tone.

"Anyway. I will always be here for you. I love you. Go get 'em, kiddo."

The guests clap. It might be my imagination, but the applause seems subdued, polite, like everyone senses there's something wrong with Mom. They know. I do too.

When Dad found a bug in Jax, there was a simple protocol. He would just assign the problem to someone, and they would work on it until the issue was fixed. If only we could deal with people the way we deal with computers. Mom needs to be fixed. Maybe it's not that simple with a human being, but I don't know. I think finding someone smarter than me—a professional with experience—is worth a try.

Because clearly something is very wrong with my mother. And tonight, for the first time, I'm afraid if it doesn't get fixed, something terrible is going to happen.

4

ERIN

Two days after her party, Shorie and I are hauling her bright-yellow Huffy cruiser up three flights of stairs in Amelia Boynton Hall—the dorm for all incoming freshmen with engineering scholarships—when she abruptly announces that she's tired and stops dead on the landing.

"We should keep going," I say, just as a fresh wave of kids and parents surge into the narrow space, filling it up and pressing us back against the wall. They must've let in the next group on the schedule, or else someone ahead of us is maneuvering an entire three-piece living room suite through one of the doorways, slowing the traffic. Whatever it is, now we're in a bottleneck to end all bottlenecks, and I'm reconsidering our decision to bypass the long lines for the elevators.

Lines of kids file slowly past us in both directions, ants bearing armloads of twinkle lights, rugs, microwaves, and coordinated bedding. The girls let their long hair hang down their backs, even in the ruthless, soul-crushing Alabama humidity.

I told you so vibrates through every cell of my body. *Gigi's stupid bike from 1990-something is not a substitute for a car.* But Shorie didn't want a car; she wanted her grandmother's bike. And insisted we haul it to her room until she can get the right kind of lock for it. I know I can handle getting a rusty, grease-coated bike up a set of college dorm stairs, but there's no rule book for leaving a daughter at college who distinctly, desperately, *angrily* does not want to be left. Or maybe there is a guide, and I just haven't paused long enough from working to google it.

This was always Perry's area—the delicate handling of our prickly daughter. If he were here, he'd whisper some inside joke in Shorie's ear, cajole and comfort and coax until she was laughing and charging up these stairs. I can't help but think the least he could've done was impart his secrets. But there was no time for a letter from my husband. And now there is just a big blank negative space where he used to be.

I still haven't gotten used to this new jagged anger that emanates from my daughter. It started when Perry died. Every once in a while, it shoots out in violent electrified bolts toward me, always taking me off guard, paralyzing me, making me hurt in ways I never expect. It stays constant, a low hum droning on and on underneath any other sound.

I have lost my husband. I am losing my daughter.

The urge to cry is sudden, sharp, and overwhelming, so I turn back and aim a huge grin at my daughter. "Come on," I say cheerfully. "Let's make a dent in the universe." I yank up my end of the bike, charging up the steps. I can feel her behind me, tripping to keep up.

We're almost to the fourth floor when Ben catches up to us. "Y'all should've waited for me." He's his usual happy, open-faced self, loaded down with a couple of plastic trunks full of clothes from the truck. He continues past us, then is back in less than a minute. He hoists the bike over one shoulder and takes the stairs two at a time, Shorie and I falling into line behind him. A crowd of girls presses up behind us, and I find myself jostled closer to him, so close I can smell sweat and soap and whatever detergent he washed his T-shirt with. His back is a really nice one—long and lean and muscled—and it tapers down into loose-fitting jeans.

I focus elsewhere: the dorm doors decorated with whiteboards and name tags and Auburn posters. I've known Ben (and Sabine—there was never Ben without Sabine) for thirty years. In those years there have, admittedly, been a handful of times when I considered what it would be like to be with him. There would be this flash between us, a moment that only lasted half a second, and a thought would flit through my head—*There's something . . .*

But those flashes were like the impulses you got when you stood at the edge of a cliff and felt that illogical urge to step over the edge. Easy enough to ignore. Especially when Perry was alive. Now that he's gone, they fill me with shame. I may feel lonely, but I'm appalled at the idea of even touching another man, much less my best friend's husband.

In Shorie's room, Ben swings the bike against the wall, claps his hands, and rubs them together gleefully like he's never had so much fun. "That's your grandmother's old bike?" he asks Shorie. "Damn thing's a millstone."

"It's a beach cruiser," she says.

I resist the urge to compare the bike to Perry's mother, Gigi, mill-stonewise. I'm the adult here, after all. It's up to me to keep things positive, even if it kills me.

"Bathroom's through that door," I say to Ben. "Knock before you go in."

Shorie, Ben, and I take turns washing up, edging politely around each other. When Ben says he's heading back to the truck for another load, Shorie turns to her bookshelves. She should be tossing confetti and dancing in circles around Ben. He canceled whatever weekend plans he had—work, hanging out with Sabine—and volunteered his truck. His reward? Being treated to a teenage girl's icy silence in the back seat of the cab the two hours down to Auburn.

"Do you want me to make up your bed?" I ask.

"Okay." She flips open the top of the bin with all her books.

I lay the foam pad over the thin mattress and wrestle the purple Pottery Barn comforter out of its plastic bag.

"Hey, where are the sheets?" I ask.

"The what?"

I breathe deeply. "The sheets. For the bed."

"I don't know. Didn't you pack them?"

I rummage through a couple of boxes. The sheets are stuffed into an actual suitcase, crammed beneath Shorie's collection of Converse sneakers, clearly stuff *she* packed. I decide not to think about the germs.

"When's Adelia getting here?" I ask.

"I'm not sure."

"She didn't say?"

"I never called her."

I straighten. "Shorie. She's your roommate."

"I was busy. You get that, Mom, right? It's hard to do all the stuff you should do when you're busy, busy, busy."

She slams a couple of books onto a shelf. I snap the top sheet over the bed. So many unspoken words simmer between us, but if I speak up now, it's going to turn into a battle. This is one topic we've covered thoroughly.

In March, after Perry died, his share of Jax's stock reverted to me, along with the new weight of major shareholder, and shifted everything into high gear. Granted, for a startup, we were doing well—making enough money to cover salaries and also roll some cash back into the company. But we were nowhere near millionaires, not yet. We always needed to be raising more capital to safeguard our income—and it was technically still my job to attend these startup pitch events and scout potential investors. But, honestly, a lot of what I was doing was unnecessary.

Ben brought up the subject, once, of my taking a break. But after I pointedly changed the subject, he never mentioned it again. At Jax, as I mapped out some wild monetization or scaling model for the next five years or reported on the latest habit loop design or A/B split testing at another meeting I'd called, I'd notice my partners' faces soften with pity. It was obvious they were placating me, showing up and sitting with polite smiles on their faces while I made up new reasons not to hand over the reins.

And then, early this summer, it occurred to me what I was doing. The goal I had been unconsciously moving toward ever since Perry's death. I was getting the company ready to sell. Preparing to let Jax go.

This is why Shorie's extra mad at me, as is Ben, even though he's doing a pretty good job pretending he's not. And I understand. None of us had planned on selling this soon, but none of us had planned on Perry's dying either. And we made a pact. We agreed that when we sold, we'd all move on.

I want Shorie to start fresh too. She's already on her way, with a full ride from National Women in STEM, along with career and mentorship opportunities that the organization will provide. She's got a chance to really make something of herself and her talents—if she'll just trust me and fly on her own.

But if she won't fly, I'm going to give her a push. As I see it, that's my job as her mother. And once I've done that—once I've gotten everything at Jax squared away and the company sold and my daughter launched into the world—then maybe, at last, I can focus on other things.

Like how I am going to survive the rest of my life without my husband.

5

SHORIE

Ben Fleming wants to sleep with my mother.

Sorry, no—I should just say it right out: Ben Fleming wants to fuck my mother. And OH MY GOD, just thinking those words makes me feel like I need to take a thousand scalding showers and then lock myself in a sensory deprivation chamber.

At first, I thought I was imagining it because of all Mom's other strange behaviors. The blank way she looks at me, her forgetfulness, the constant working—and when she's not doing that, the constant sleeping. But now that I think about it, these past couple of months, it does seem like Ben and Mom have gotten . . . tighter. I watched them the whole ride down from Birmingham from the back seat of Ben's truck. They chatted and laughed and periodically touched each other's arms. *Oh, my goodness, look! There's a deer on the side of the highway eating grass! How amazing! I must touch your arm for the hundredth time!* I wondered if Sabine would've minded if she'd been there.

Anyway, just add it to the list of suck: my dad is dead, my mom is making me go to college instead of letting me stay home and work at Jax, and now there's uncomfortable parental flirting. That last one, the flirting, doesn't just suck; it actually fills me with Hulk-level rage. That the two of them can joke and laugh like one didn't just lose a best friend and one a husband mere months ago infuriates me. And do they not care that I'm right there, watching them? It's fucking disrespectful is what it is.

Now, standing in my new dorm room, organizing my books, I am so knotted up with fury and fear and homesickness that I can't open my mouth. And even though the thought does occur to me, briefly, that I may possibly be overreacting to this Ben-and-Mom thing because I'm actually angry at Mom about other stuff, I shut it off and slam books onto the shelf instead.

Coincidentally the one I'm putting up now is my copy of *The Emotional Dictionary*. It was a graduation gift from Daisy's mom. Clearly she was trying to tell me something. Like that I'm maybe emotionally constipated or something. Which I'm not at all. Just because our culture expects girls to emote all over the place, that doesn't mean we should if we don't feel like it. I have emotions, plenty of them, and I can show them anytime I want. I cried when I learned about Euler's Identity, as a matter of fact. Right there in the third row of Ms. Blaylock's trigonometry class.

Just to prove to myself that I'm perfectly comfortable with my emotions, I list out the ones I happen to be feeling right now. For each one, I slam another book on the shelf. *Melancholy*, BAM! *Despondency*, BAM! *Misery*, BAM!

Don't get me wrong. I love my mother. And I know what I'm think-ing about my own maternal flesh and blood is disgusting and offensive, but it's the truth. It's not that hard to tell when a man wants a woman. Well, correction: as long as I'm not the woman in question. That, I'm not so good at.

And there's this: My mom is more attractive than your average suburban mom. She has long Disney-princess dark-brown hair and the bone structure of a runway model. Unfortunately she happens to dress herself like a color-blind toddler. And puts her hair in one of those mid-level, mom-style ponytails, scraped back and twisted with a scrunchie. She may be old (forty-eight?), a mad workaholic, and annoying as crap, but she would be a catch for any man her age. I guess. But it's way too soon for her to even think about moving on. Way too soon for flirting. Especially with Ben Fleming.

And I don't even know where she finds scrunchies anymore.

I load more books onto the shelf. BAM! BAM! BAM! I shouldn't be here, moving into this dorm, wasting my time going to dumb-ass English comp classes that I could literally sail through even if I were in a coma. I should be in Birmingham, working at Jax, doing what my dad did, taking care of everything he used to take care of. Isn't that the point of college anyway? To figure out your future? My dad already gave me my future.

My senior year, instead of playing lacrosse after school, I went to Jax every day and shadowed him. He showed me everything: the back and front end stuff, the database of all Jax's users, and the way the servers keep the whole show running smoothly. He explained Scrum, the work-managing system they followed to build Jax. And Slack, the software they used for assignments.

Dad also had his own quirky organizational system. He didn't use the calendar on his phone, or any other kind of personal-assistant app. He carried around a journal, slim and bound in coffee-colored leather, where he kept a record of everything—every problem he encountered, every to-do list, even ideas he had for new features. He jotted little poems to me and my mother in it, sometimes those dumb motivational quotes. He got a new one every month, and at the end of the month he put the old one on the shelf in his office at home.

He had me sit down for at least one afternoon with every single Jax employee for a Q&A session. I got to endlessly test every new feature of the app, even the long shots the more motivated interns were working on. He even set up the email server to automatically forward his daily event report to me so I could understand how he spotted problems.

I still check the report religiously at six fifteen every morning, right after I wake up, just like he used to do, even though I haven't told Mom. She wouldn't like it, guaranteed.

I haul another armful of books out of a box. BAM! BAM! BAM!

But here's what makes me nervous. My mom is not in the right head-space for making good decisions. I mean, if Ben is dumb enough to make a move on her, I worry she may go for it. I've never really been able to predict how my mother will react to things. But since Dad died, it's gotten worse. She'll work for, like, two days straight, then sleep for the next two. I never see her eat anything more than a cracker or half a banana. And she just kind of floats around the house like she's stoned. And then randomly snaps over something stupid like Foxy Cat shedding on her laptop case.

Once, when I was trying to convince Dad to let me enter this international hacking competition called the Global Cybergames, he commented that I didn't need it. He said social engineering was the biggest issue in cybersecurity. In other words, humans become the weakest link in any system by sharing their passwords or using their computers' automatic log-in function for email and unsecured websites. I probably shouldn't think this—it sounds cold—but sometimes I think my mom is the weak link of Jax.

I happen to know that Ben, Sabine, Layton, Arch, and Gigi have met secretly a couple of times to discuss what to do about her. I stumbled onto one of those secret meetings one Sunday night, when I dropped by Arch and Gigi's house to see if I'd left a magazine there, one of Dad's old copies of *Journal of Mathematics and the Arts*, that had an article I wanted to finish reading. I'd let myself in the kitchen door, and I could hear someone, on the other side of the swinging door to the dining room, talking. It was Sabine.

". . . could be just the rest she needs. A gentle push to encourage self-care. It's an incredible place."

I'd found the magazine and crept back out to my bike without anybody seeing me, then rode away as quickly and quietly as I could. What was strange was how not upset I felt. Yeah, I was shocked that the rest of the adults were talking about my mom like she was a problem. What outweighed it was the relief that somebody was going to take care of the situation.

But now that feeling of relief is disintegrating. If something happens between Ben and my mom, especially if Sabine finds out about it, surely that will be the end of Jax. And what's left of our family.

I chuck a final armful of books onto the shelf and head to the desk to arrange Arch's old cigar boxes and beer stein from Germany that I decided to use for decoration. I arrange the items methodically, positioning each exactly three inches from the next. I like things just so. Dad was the same way.

"You're lucky you STEM kids get to move in on Wednesday," Mom says. "I heard the other freshmen don't get in until Friday. They only get the weekend before they have to start school."

I grunt noncommittally and pull out my phone.

"Did everything allocate properly?" Mom asks, and it takes me a minute to realize she's talking about Jax.

"Mm-hmm," I say.

"The automatic deposit went through?" She cranes her neck, trying to get a glimpse. But the fact that she's asking the question proves that she's restrained herself from logging on to my account and stalking, which is a little surprising.

I know I should play nice and let her see, but I twist away instead. "It's all good, Mom."

"Just checking," she says lightly, and it occurs to me for the first time that maybe I'm taking the wrong approach to this whole school vs. Jax thing. Maybe my best strategy is to play along with what she wants and find another way to get what I want.

6

Erin

What the hell is keeping Ben?

Shorie's moved on to hanging her shirts and jeans in the closet, and I'm draping a string of twinkle lights across the window frame. Right now would be an excellent time for him to show up and inject a little levity into this putrid mother-daughter tension stew. But he's nowhere to be seen.

And then, a tall girl with bright-red hair appears in the doorway. She's struggling with a minifridge but, after a beat, lets it crash to the floor.

"Shorie?" Her voice sounds professional, like it's coming out of a TV, and she's wearing a ton of gorgeous, complicated-looking eye makeup. She's so big and beautiful that I'm rendered speechless. She fills the room with a delicious vanilla smell too.

Shorie fixes her smile. "Adelia."

"Dele." The tall redhead thrusts out her hand. "Like *Let's Make a . . .* , you know? I mean, you probably don't. Nobody our age does. It's just a thing my mom always used to say to her friends. I don't even know why I said that. I'm nervous. Anyway. Unbelievably excited to meet you."

Shorie nods. Smiles. *You can do it,* I think.

Dele continues. "You didn't bring monogrammed pillows, did you? My mom was like, you're gonna get the girl with monogrammed pillows, and she's going to fucking hate you because all you're bringing is the fucking Harry Potter sheets and a Hermione shower curtain." Dele turns to me and claps a hand over her mouth. "Oh my God. Sorry. My mom didn't actually say it that way. Cleanup on aisle Dele."

I wave her off. "You're good. All pro-Hermione here. I'm Shorie's mom. Erin."

"Sorry I haven't been more in touch," Shorie says. "I wasn't sure I was actually coming to school."

"Oh, no. I get it. No worries," Dele says. "Glad you decided to come."

Our eyes drag and catch. Dele and I have been surreptitiously emailing for the past couple of months. I feel guilty for not telling Shorie— and for being such a capital-*H* Helicopter Mom—but I know from experience how important your freshman-year roommate is. I was the only kid from my small Tennessee town who attended Auburn. Alone and nervous, I was lucky enough to have a roommate who insisted on dragging me everywhere she went.

Sabine and I pledged a sorority together, we attended football and baseball games, and she introduced me to her high school friends, Perry and Ben. My life was forever changed because of her friendship, and I want to make sure my daughter gets the same chance. So, sue me. I took matters into my own hands.

"I love your name," Dele says to Shorie. "Mine's from an old soap opera my grandma used to watch. Adelia Kent, *The Lighthouse.*"

"I used to watch that show," I say, but Dele doesn't look at me.

Shorie takes a deep breath. "Shorie was my mom's mother's name. She was Margaret Shore, but everybody called her Shorie."

I smile encouragingly at Shorie.

"Shorie Shore," Dele crows. "I love it. You know, my grandma from Eclectic, Alabama, had a friend named Poo-Poo. Poo-Poo Buchanan, I kid you not. And nobody even cracked a smile when they said it. *Poo-Poo, you got a cup of sugar I can borrow to make this peach cobbler? Poo-Poo, do you take this man to be your lawfully wedded husband?* His name was Lumper, by the way, the husband. Loony southerners. Just one step away from tripping and falling out of their Faulkner novels."

Dele then segues into a story about how even though she's not an engineering student (she received a journalism scholarship), she managed to personally strong-arm the housing department into letting her move into Amelia Boynton, where the atmosphere will supposedly be more studious. Her move-in time isn't technically until five, so her parents won't be here for another couple of hours. She then asks Shorie if she wants to go to a party at the Lambda Chi house with her that night. When Shorie actually agrees, I literally have to smother a yelp of joy.

Presently, Ben shows up loaded down with a hodgepodge of backpacks and old Trader Joe's bags stuffed with HDMI cords, back issues of Perry's *Journal of Mathematics and the Arts* magazines, and God knows what other useless odds and ends. After a whole new round of introductions, Ben leaves again, and Shorie and Dele sort through the bags. I can see my daughter has way underpacked. There are no picture frames or corkboards, only the twinkle lights that I packed at the last minute and have already hung and the Kristin Kontrol poster from her bedroom that she tacks up over her desk.

"You like the Dum Dum Girls too?" Dele asks her.

"Yeah, but Kristin's solo stuff is more eighties. Different."

"Cool."

I reach over, snag Shorie's phone, and hold it out for her to type in her passcode. "A few final motherly instructions, that's all."

She frowns but complies. I take back the phone and start swiping. "Don't forget to do everything through Jax, so we can keep up with what you're spending and keep it in your profile."

"Okay," Dele says. "I'm just going to go ahead and say it right now. I know Jax is your family business, and I just have to tell you, I'm a total fangirl." She lets out a whoosh of breath, her eyes shining. "I mean, how totally amazing is that? You created something millions of people love. I mean, that must feel incredible, you know . . ." She throws up her hands, awestruck apparently.

"It's covered, Mom," Shorie says.

"I love Jax," Dele goes on. "I use it all the time." She looks at me. "Maybe I could interview you for one of my classes. Is that weird, that I just asked you? You probably talk to, like, *Forbes* or whatever." For the first time, she looks abashed.

"I'd be happy to give you an interview." I put the phone down, and I can feel Shorie stiffening across the room, waves of unhappiness rolling off her. We're almost finished unpacking, and the resistance has become palpable, a living force, a psychic, full-body *no* emanating from her very pores. Such wasted determination. Think what my daughter could do if she focused this energy into something really useful.

Dele doesn't seem to notice. "Oh, Shorie. I'm supposed to meet my friend Rayanne. I'll bring her by later and y'all can meet, if you want."

"Okay," Shorie says.

When she's gone I turn to Shorie. "I just want to say one more—"

She interrupts. "There's nothing left for you to say."

She heads into the bathroom, shutting the door behind her, and I hear the water running. I sit on the newly made bed, sensing the vortex in the air above me. It's about to descend again.

When Ben comes up with the last load of plastic crates, I ask stiffly for his keys. In the parking lot, I climb in his hot truck and finally allow myself to burst into tears.

7

Shorie

After Mom leaves, Ben offers to set up my extra monitor, speakers, and printer, even though he knows I'm perfectly capable. He tries to make conversation—"What classes are you taking?" "Dele seems nice." "How many girls do you have to share that bathroom with?"—but I freeze him out with one-word answers. After he's finished tightening up the wobbly legs on my bed, he stands by the desk, flipping the wrench around his thumb and staring through the window's janky plastic blinds.

"You know your mom loves you."

I roll my eyes. "Thanks. Had you not told me, I would've never realized." I know I'm being a huge brat, and yet I can't stop myself. I'm so miserable and filled with rage, I can't form a civil sentence.

He goes on. "And I know this is hard."

I bite my lip fiercely to keep from crying. I'd rather die than cry, yet again, in front of Ben.

"Your dad—"

"Don't," I say. "Do not. Dare. Say another word. I should not be here."

"I know."

I can't help it; my eyebrows shoot up practically to my hairline.

He glances at the open door, like maybe Mom is lurking out in the hall, eavesdropping on our conversation. "But she's afraid if you don't do this now, take the scholarship, you may never come back. She thinks you'll regret it . . ."

Dele comes back in the room, a new girl in tow—she's tall like Dele but with a blonde pixie cut. Dele introduces her as Rayanne, and the two head to Dele's bed, where they start giggling and rummaging through some of her stuff. Ben and I go quiet, busying ourselves with other tasks. On their way out, Dele looks hard at me, like she's expecting a distress signal.

"You okay?" she asks.

I nod vigorously. "Fine."

"You want to grab pizza later, before the party?"

I've been thinking I'm going to bail on the party, but I probably should just bite the bullet and go. At least pretend to take part in the college experience.

"Great," I say. And with that, the two girls are gone.

I fold my arms and address Ben in a low voice. "What I'll regret is not being allowed to work at my parents' company before it's sold to some giant conglomerate. I want to be home. I want to be doing what Dad used to do. Finishing my father's work." My voice cracks on the word *father's*.

To my surprise Ben lets out a sympathetic laugh. "Believe me, I have said those exact words to your mother, more than once."

I can't hide my surprise. "You have?"

He shuffles his feet. Drops his hands deep in his jeans pockets. "I told her you should take a gap year. That the school would probably hold the scholarship for you, under the circumstances, if that was what you wanted. I told her that you could stay home and work at Jax. That she could travel or just hang out with you."

I don't know what to say to all this. Ben Fleming being on my side is not a situation I've anticipated. Then, before I can process the strange turn of events, he smiles at me. A slow-growing half smile that lights up his face and makes him look kind of . . . I don't know, trustworthy. And then I remember how he acted with my mother in the car.

"Shorie?" he says. "I'm going to take care of your mom. Because your father asked me to, and I swore to it. I know what you've been thinking about me—I can see it in your eyes. But that's not how it is. It's not why I'm here right now."

"Then why are you here?"

"Because your dad wouldn't have missed this day for the world, and I know I'm not him, but I hope I'm somewhere in the vicinity of the next best thing. I care about you, Shorie. But . . ." He nods, like he's trying to convince himself to go on. "I'm worried about your mom. She promised me and Sabine and your grandparents that she would take a break, but she hasn't. She just keeps going and going. Showing up every day, working until late like the early days."

I don't reply.

"She's slipping, Shorie. You see it, I know you do. She's scattered. Whenever anybody talks to her, she misses half the conversation. Our Monday meetings are a mess. She zones out, messes up numbers, lets important stuff slip through the cracks."

I think about the constant napping. Her awkward speech at my party. Maybe whatever is wrong with my mother is much bigger than I thought.

"I told her that she was in no shape to make the decision to sell," Ben goes on. "But your mother is . . . it seems like she's not in a place where she can take advice. From any of us. We've been talking. Me, Sabine, Layton, and your grandparents. Discussing the possibility of getting your mom to go somewhere. For a rest."

I stare at him. Hearing him say it out loud, directly to my face, is a whole other deal from eavesdropping. I feel shaky just thinking that my mom might be unwell in some way I haven't fully considered.

"Do you love her?" I say.

Ben's face flushes. Even the whites of his eyes seem to redden. I'm shocked the words just came out of my mouth, that I actually went there. But I'm not exactly sorry.

He plants his hands on his hips. "We've known each other a long time, your mom and I." He stares at me, and his face looks so guilty, I almost wish I hadn't said anything.

"You can't even lie to me about it."

He raises his arms. "I don't see the point in lying to you, Shorie. You're like a human polygraph. I do love your mom, yes, but in a different way than I love my wife. And I promise you, I'm not going to do anything shady." He scratches his head. "Here's a secret about being an adult, okay? Relationships are work. There are times when you may feel like there's a wall between you and your spouse. Or that you're not close the way you want to be, the way you used to be. But you don't just give up. You don't look for an out. You take responsibility. You look at yourself and say, What can I do better? How can I make this marriage better?"

I can't think of what to say.

"What matters is your mom is safe with me, okay? Because I care about her as a friend. And if I think she's in trouble and needs my help, then I'm going to be there for her. I'm going to do what's best for your mom, no matter what." His eyes seem really tired. Sad and tired. They are green, burning like neon in the slash of light from the blinds.

"Like an intervention, you mean?" I ask. I can't believe I'm saying this out loud too.

He blinks at me. "Maybe something like that, if the situation calls for it. Just her friends and family asking her to take care of herself. Nothing dramatic."

"Whatever you do, I want to be included. I want to be there when it happens."

"Of course. Of course you'll be included."

We stare at each other.

"But hopefully we won't have to do anything like that. Look, Shor, I'll talk to her, okay? Maybe you can come in over the winter break and work at Jax. And definitely over the summer, if we haven't sold by then."

It wasn't the answer I wanted to hear. "Okay."

He holds my gaze. "You're a good daughter, Shorie. A good, lovely person."

I grimace. I'm not a good, lovely person—I'm a human dumpster fire, and I've acted like a monumental shit today—but I don't argue with him. The truth is, even though I don't fully understand how he feels about Mom, I'm grateful that he's here and that he's looking out for her. I hadn't realized how heavily it had been weighing on me until just now.

Before he goes, he hugs me and tells me that he'll check in on Foxy Cat from time to time. I'm suddenly surrounded by his manly scent. It reminds me so much of Dad that I have the urge to leap backward out of his arms.

Grief, loneliness, confusion . . .

When he's finally gone, I grab my laptop, settle on my narrow twin bed, and pop on my headphones. I let the music blank me out, and while I wait for my email to load, I take a deep breath, hold it, and look at my phone. Gingerly, I touch the top right corner of my home screen. The app with the mustard-yellow icon featuring half a white *j*.

Jax: get the jump on your taxes.

"Hi," I say to the home page, like it's an actual person. But that's what Jax kind of is to me—an old friend with whom I've shared most of my life. And I feel things when I see that familiar mustard yellow page. So many things.

Sorrow, comfort, delight . . .

Or maybe the feelings are because of the single message in my unread private message queue. The last message Dad sent me before he died. The message I've never had the courage to open.

8

Erin

Perry, Ben, Sabine, and I dreamed up Jax one Christmas almost four years ago.

For the first time in our friendship, the four of us had found ourselves restless at the same time: Perry and Ben had spent a couple of decades working at various app development companies but had grown weary of making other people's ideas happen. Sabine was treading water, managing a chain of successful yoga studios for a company out of Atlanta.

Years earlier I'd quit my job at the management consulting company to focus on restructuring and filling Shorie's time, something her elementary school didn't seem capable of doing. But then, in middle school, she signed up for a string of advanced classes, joined the lacrosse team, and didn't seem to need me in the same way. I was okay with it, honestly. I was itching to get back to the world of adults.

That Christmas night, after all the wrapping paper and ribbon had been cleared away, Ben and Sabine dropped by. The five of us gathered around the tree that Perry and Shorie had decorated with purple-striped candy canes and silver spray-painted pine cones, drinking whiskey (Shorie, hot cocoa) and throwing out ideas for a new app. Some of them were okay; some were completely off-the-wall. But it was Perry's idea that made us all go silent.

An app that would keep people on the financial straight and narrow.

It would do everything for even the most budget impaired: deposit and allocate every paycheck into the proper categories, then, for the remainder of the month, tell customers what they could and couldn't spend.

And here was the clincher: Perry had figured out a new way to connect merchants, banks, and credit card companies with our system to pull all the necessary data on the fly—something no one had been able to do up to that point.

After the fire burned down and Shorie wandered upstairs to try out her new watercolors, we continued to brainstorm. There was a growing feeling of giddiness in the room. A kind of premonition of something so big and transformative just around the corner. We all knew what was happening without even saying the words aloud. *This was going to be* it. The idea that would change our lives.

We had two to build (Perry and Ben) and two to manage and sell (me and Sabine), and we agreed to split the ownership of the company equally between us four. Perry called his father, Arch, who had owned a trio of successful shopping centers out in Texas since the eighties. Over the phone, he agreed to kick in $650,000 to get things off the ground. A loan with no fixed repayment schedule, and he didn't even want ownership. I wasn't so sure I wanted us to be indebted to my father-in-law, especially with the uneasy relationship Gigi and I already shared, but Perry insisted we'd be able to pay him back within the first few years.

Then Perry had suggested the pact.

"This is our brainchild," he told us. "We build it together, and when we sell, we sell together. None of this splitting-up, edging-each-other-out stuff. For this thing to work it's got to be all of us or none of us. Agreed?"

Everyone agreed. We'd seen enough friendships shredded by a failed venture that we were wary. That was not going to happen to us—or our company. I had to admit, the whole pledge thing got me a little teary. When Perry and I finally collapsed into bed that night, I told him that our promise made me feel as if I were in one of those kids' books where the gang makes a blood pact to always stick together. I'd never felt a stronger feeling of belonging. He smothered me in a hug, and we fell asleep.

It was like a dream, how Jax just *worked*, right from the start. Our business model might've looked slapdash on paper compared to a flashier Silicon Valley outfit, but the four of us were strong on substance, not optics. With Ben's GPS experience and Perry handling his proprietary middleware stuff, we only had to pull in a database person, server administrator, and a few testers for extra support. I was CEO, raising additional capital and mapping long-term strategies. Sabine was COO, handling day-to-day details, staffing our cadre of paid interns, and generally running the office.

When Shorie wasn't at lacrosse practice or hanging out with Daisy, she'd tag along with us to the office and do her homework or play Ping-Pong with whoever needed to take a break. She even used to bake pumpkin muffins and zucchini bread for us in the tiny office kitchenette.

Perry, Ben, Sabine, and I worked twenty-four seven, including holidays. We ate all our meals in the office and slept there so many nights I lost count. Even Shorie moved in a cot to help out at the end. And finally, at the end of two crazy months, we had a lean "minimum viable product"—a version of Jax ready to launch. Our salaries were just enough to get by on, but after one year, we were able to pay Arch back in full.

Three years later, we had expanded the features, had over 1.3 million users with an 80 percent retention rate, and had been valued at close to six million dollars. Which, to be clear, isn't the same thing as getting six million actual dollars, just a guesstimate of worth. We weren't rich, not yet, because we hadn't monetized the app. But if everything went as planned, there was a chance we could hit the jackpot.

I sit in Ben's truck in the broiling parking lot of Shorie's dorm with my eyes closed. The left side of my head throbs. After all the emotional conflict with Shorie, now I just feel wrung out and only just slightly pissed.

What the hell is taking Ben so long? Are he and Shorie discussing how to handle me? How to get me away from Jax before I make a huge mistake, blow it up, and ruin all their lives? There have been other behind-my-back conversations, I'm fairly certain. Meetings where I was the subject at hand. Maybe because I've been less than on top of things. But more likely because of my recent announcement that I wanted the partners to sell Jax.

I dropped the bomb in June. Gigi and Arch, Ben and Sabine, and Shorie and I were all gathered for a Father's Day brunch at a funky downtown bistro called Red Mountain Grill. When dessert came, I told everybody that after Perry's death, I'd tried to keep up with my duties, but I'd not been able to. Without him there, I was overwhelmed. And the company had become an albatross, weighing me down in ways I hadn't expected and couldn't fully articulate, even to myself.

The bottom line: I was ready to invoke our pact. Perry was gone, and even though that wasn't what he'd meant when he originally suggested it, continuing on without him felt wrong. I wanted to sell.

We would need to hire an outside firm eventually, but for now Layton, our in-house lawyer, could handle the prep. The payout wouldn't be as big, not after only three years and with only a fraction of the users we could amass if we had two more years. And when some other firm bought us, there was no doubt we'd be forced out as shareholders. My partners might be disappointed we hadn't achieved the ultimate dream—a $100-million-dollar buyout by a Facebook-size company—but our prospects weren't exactly shabby. We could possibly get $10 million—$2.5 million for Ben and for Sabine, $5 million for me—and that wasn't bad. But my bottom line was the same no matter how much we made. I was finished with Jax.

They were all stunned, naturally, but said they understood. With the exception of Gigi. On our way out of the restaurant, she pulled me aside and informed me that she and Arch had been hoping to purchase some stock in the company now, before we sold in a couple of years. Arch had lost so many tenants recently, he'd had to turn over two of his shopping centers to the bank. The one in Houston that he still owned was doing well for now, but who knew what would happen? I had apparently ruined their retirement plan and was being horribly selfish for not safeguarding their future. *Like my son would've wanted,* she said, her pupils expanded to large black pools of hatred.

I realized the real estate crash must've had an effect on Arch's shopping centers, but he'd never mentioned it. To me, the whole thing smelled suspicious. My mother-in-law was notorious for not knowing the nitty-gritty of her personal finances. I wasn't about to get roped into changing my mind on something this important based on her tenuous grasp of her husband's business.

I removed my arm from her grip and spoke calmly. *Perry left me everything he had, including his shares of Jax. He trusted me to do what was right for our family.*

We're family too, she said, with a look that was anything but familial.

Back in the parking lot of the dorm, the driver's side door opens and I'm jolted back to the present. Ben slides in, angles his body toward me, and smiles sympathetically.

"Does she hate me?" I say.

"She does not hate you. And she would rather throw herself off a cliff than admit this, but I think she's excited."

Throw herself off a cliff. Interesting choice of words.

"It's called the 'dizziness of freedom,' you know." I stretch my neck, but my head's still pounding relentlessly. "That impulse you get when you're standing on a cliff, to throw yourself off."

Our eyes meet, but I look away.

"Are you okay?" he asks.

"Not exactly the way I envisioned the day I dropped my daughter off at college going down." I force a laugh, and we both check our phones at the same time. Layton's texted me.

How's the move in going? Is Shorie okay? Are YOU okay?

"Sabine's grabbing dinner with Layton." Ben taps his phone. "She says no reason to rush back."

I text Layton. I don't know. I hope so. I add a grimacing emoji.

"You want to get a drink? Debrief?" Ben asks.

"Oh, *hell*, yes."

"And if Shorie's having a rough time or needs you, you'll be close by. That's what the bag you left in the back seat is for, right? Because you were thinking you might spend the night?"

"I'm being ridiculous, aren't I? Every mom cliché rolled into one giant human helicopter."

"Erin. This is a big deal, to leave your only kid at college." He doesn't say *without her father*, but I know he knows. That's the hardest part of all this.

"It is a big deal, isn't it?" I ask.

"It is."

"Okay, then . . . what would you think about us getting a couple of rooms at the Conference Center? Just to make sure everything's okay with her?"

"I think it's a good idea." He maneuvers the truck around the line of minivans and pickups and U-Haul trailers. "I'll let Sabine know."

9

SHORIE

For a moment, I let my finger hover over the unread Jax message that Dad sent me. He sent it in mid-March, right after the STEM scholarship was finalized and he'd set up my budget for college. The day before he died. It starts *Shorie, my sweet,* just like all his messages to me. But I'm not ready to open it and read the whole thing. I may never be.

I close my eyes.

It's hard to explain why I don't want to open it. I guess it's like a wrapped present under the Christmas tree, shiny and beautiful and full of promise, and once I unwrap it, the anticipation will all be over. It will be the last communication—letter, phone call, text—I ever get from my father.

In my rational mind, I know reading it won't make me feel any less miserable. In fact, the opposite seems true. I have the distinct sense that I'll feel even worse if I do read it. It's the law of energy conservation. When energy flows from one place to another, it may change forms, but it's never destroyed. It's the same with sadness, I've discovered. You can't get rid of it.

I swipe back to my home page, and my allocations pop up, neat little bubbles all over the screen. Food, household, medical, personal, transportation, gifts, fun, savings. In addition to covering tuition, a meal plan, and books, the scholarship I've been awarded also gives me a little bit of living expense money. The school deposits that cash directly into my local bank account, which Dad connected to my Jax. Along with the extra money Mom's put in, I should have no problem hitting my budget goal every month.

So here's Jax in a snapshot: It's a comprehensive personal budgeting app that captures all your purchases, and it sorts and automatically files them into categories for you using your bank's bill-pay platform, the app's proprietary digital wallet feature, and your phone's GPS. It compiles authorized data from our retail and bank partnerships, scrapes a bunch of random public data plus our merchant partners' information, and then, using a bunch of algorithms, tells you how much money you can spend on a given day at a given location.

If you choose, your transactions can be shared with some or all of your connections, making them, in effect, public. Most people opt out of that feature; it's really there for parents keeping tabs on their kids or companies monitoring their employees' work-related expenditures.

The best part is, when tax time rolls around, Jax connects to your particular filing platform. Then all you have to do is electronically sign in a couple of spots and voilà, your taxes are done. After that it automatically adjusts your budget for the next year, helps you keep up with your spending, and gives you updated suggestions on how to manage future expenses.

I know. Genius.

Just then, a banner drops down on my phone with a text from Gigi.

shorie darlin have you spent your cash yet love gigi it is a thousand

I laugh. Funny how, in spite of the fact that her son created the world's first automatic budgeting app, my grandmother insists on using cash. Mom has always bitched about it, the fact that Gigi doesn't use Jax, but she and Mom rarely see eye to eye on anything. When it comes to me, though, Gigi's always been a big squishy cupcake. A cupcake that gives me lots of cash gifts and sends me all these hilariously unpunctuated, improperly capitalized run-on texts, all sent from a 2003 BlackBerry.

The air conditioner kicks in, and I straighten, letting the lukewarm stream of air wash over me. My grandmother slipped me ten one-hundred-dollar bills the other night at my going-away dinner. She asked if I wanted more, and I told her I'd let her know if anything came up. Mom would be pissed, but whatever. Gigi thinks Mom doesn't spend enough on stuff like nice clothes and fancy meals.

I jump off the bed and pluck the huge gangster roll of graduation money from the back of the closet shelf. I peel off a hundred-dollar bill and drop it into my purse, just in case there's something I want to buy that I don't want Mom to know about. Which reminds me. I haven't checked Jax's daily server report. Which should cheer me up. Definitely get my mind off being stuck here at school.

I settle back on the bed and move my laptop closer, already feeling a little bump in my mood. The daily server report is essentially a health check, a dashboard with data on the system processes, the drives, the memory, and any errors that might've cropped up over the last twenty-four hours. There are also log files attached to the email, in case you need to access more info.

The dashboard itself is really cool, a typical Dad design. It's an elegantly constructed, colorful one-sheet with columns and pie charts and graphs. Just looking at it makes me think of Dad and feel happy. Not many things make me do that these days.

I scan the report, and an error message catches my eye.

A database error occurred.
Source: Microsoft SQL Server 2016
Code: 0984 occurred 1 time(s)
Description: Transaction (Process ID 3168) deadlocked on
lock resources with another process and has been chosen as
the deadlock victim. Rerun the transaction.
Context: Application 'serve..search..queries..over..help..content'

Huh. Interesting.

I look over it again, nibbling at my thumbnail. The truth is, I could dig into this, but I'm not supposed to be messing with the servers. In fact, if Mom got wind of me poking around in Jax, she'd be pissed. Also, the server admin, Scotty, gets these reports, and he could already be on the case. But still . . .

I open one of the logs. Nothing looks out of the ordinary in the long columns. Not that I know what I'm looking for exactly, but sometimes things jump out at you. Time stamps, frequency, etc. I just can't get over the fact that, since I've been checking these reports, I've never seen an error message like this.

It could just be a glitch, some weird anomaly that will never happen again. There's also a chance it's a bug. Which is not that big of a deal; it just means somebody has to fix it.

But there is a third option. A remote one, but an option nonetheless. The glitch could indicate that there's a process running in Jax that wasn't set up by Dad and is conflicting somehow with the basic software. Which is concerning.

I know it's none of my business, but I can't help myself. The thought of somebody screwing around inside Jax's processes bothers me, but it excites me too. And the thrill of solving a problem could definitely take my mind off all the things that suck. So, before I can reason myself out of it, I shoot off a quick email to Scotty, asking him if he saw the error report and what he thinks it might mean.

Please don't mention I said anything to Mom or Ben, I write at the end, then hit "Send."

Dad would want me to do this, I tell myself.

10

ERIN

Something is happening. Whether it's happening for real or in a dream is hard to say.

Outside the car window yellow and red and green streak past in smeary underwater slow motion. Sound is low and garbled too. That Dolly Parton song "Here You Come Again" is a tinny earworm playing somewhere just above the water's surface. Soundtrack to my quest.

It's night now, but I've forgotten what came before this point. A lot of things seem tangled right now. Too difficult to tease out. I know I can't possibly be underwater because I'm driving a car. No, not a car, a truck. Ben's truck. I can smell him on the seats and in the air conditioning streaming over me.

Someone called me earlier. It was a woman, a girl, I think. She said Shorie needed me. That's all I needed to hear. I am going to my daughter.

All of a sudden, there's a loud *chunk*. I'm thrown against the wheel, then back onto the seat, and everything is still. I close my eyes, just for a second, just to rest a minute. My breath sounds like a roar. This is how Perry died, in a car accident. But I'm not dead. I'm not even hurt.

I stagger out of the truck and see that I've only just barely tapped one of those low poles. But also that I've arrived at my intended destination. Or close to it. I'm in a parking lot next to a brick-and-columned house with elegant landscaping lights and Greek letters over the door. Where Shorie is.

Next step: Find my girl. Tell her how sorry I am. Tell her I love her. Make everything right again. Somehow.

~♉~

It's not Dolly anymore. Now it's relentless reggae that's so excruciatingly loud, I feel like my brain is melting.

There are so many kids in this place too. They're jammed in the hallway and up the stairs, spilling out of rooms and windows. It's insane that they choose to gather in these tiny spaces. Can't they just find someplace to spread out? Don't they believe in personal space?

I squeeze between the kids, but they take up so much space with their yelling and dancing and drinking, it takes every ounce of strength I have. I feel like I'm swimming again, doing those water aerobics Perry and I got roped into once on that budget vacation we took when we were first married. My tongue is thick, and I can feel myself wanting to find a horizontal surface to lie down on, but I don't. I've become one of those cadaver dogs, nose to the ground, hard on the scent. *Shorie, Shorie, Shorie.*

I ask a few kids if they've seen her—but they just stare at me with their blank faces and mascara-fringed eyes. They are all so young and dewy and beautiful, I want to stop and touch them. Stroke their long, impossibly shiny hair. Press my palms against their tight, unlined cheeks and tell them to enjoy this moment. They have no idea of all the things to come.

Next thing I know, I'm being propelled down the hall, through a swinging door, and into a grimy-looking kitchen, and miraculously there she is. At the sink, pouring something out of her cup. She glances over her shoulder, and her mouth turns into a frown.

"Mom!" she shrieks.

"You called me."

"No, I didn't."

"Somebody called me. Dele, I think?"

"You're in your pajamas."

I look down at my pink flamingo–clad legs. "Yes."

"What are you doing here?" she says.

I blank for a second. Why am I here? Why was I driving Ben's truck again, past all the smeary lights to the tune of Dolly's lament? What is it that I want?

What do I want?

I want my husband back.

I want my daughter to be a little girl again.

I want us all in our house around the kitchen table, laughing and eating Thai takeout.

"I can't go home," I say, because I'm finding it impossible to translate my thoughts into words.

Shorie grabs me by the arms and shakes me. "You have to leave," she hisses. "Where is Ben?"

"He's back at the hotel." I push my hair out of my eyes.

She grimaces. "The hotel?"

I know what the look on her face means. Before I can explain that she's misunderstanding the situation, she pulls me out the back door, across a rickety porch, and down some concrete steps. I stumble over a garden hose. It's the first time I realize that I'm barefoot.

"I came to Auburn for you," she growls. "Because you forced me to, because you said it was what Dad would've wanted. And now you're telling me you can't go home?" She squints. "What's wrong with you? Are you drunk?"

"No," I say. But I don't think it's true. I actually do feel drunk or something very close to it. I'm those words the kids always use—*smashed, hammered, wasted.* The question is, How did I get this way?

"I want to say I'm sorry. I want to say . . . that I only want what's best for you . . ." My voice trails. My brain has meandered off into another plane. I have no idea what I mean to say next.

Her face is so open and vulnerable, it makes me think of five-year-old Shorie, asking me if we can go pet the kittens at the Humane Society. It stops me cold for a second, and I can't seem to find my bearings. My baby, my girl . . .

I try again. "I wanted to talk to you, Shorie. I wanted to make sure you weren't mad at me."

"Oh my God. Yes, Mom, I am mad at you. I am very, very fucking angry. I can't even believe you would . . ."

She's talking now, words piling up on words, sentences into paragraphs, and I know it's important—crucial, even—that I listen, but I can't seem to home in on the waves of sound bending the air. And even if I could hear, I don't think I could grasp the words' meaning. My head feels squeezed, front and back. *Reeling,* I think. This is what they call *reeling.*

Reeling with grief.

Reeling with confusion.

Reeling with some sinister substance I've never felt in my body before. It makes me feel light and heavy all at the same time. It makes the real unreal.

But I can fight it.

I interrupt her. "I want to tell you something," I say, feeling more focused. "I know you all think I'm making the wrong decision. I know you think you can take his place and everything can keep going. But I can't let you do that. I can't! You're just a kid, and you're not ready for that kind of pressure . . ." Now I'm sobbing, my insides feeling like they've been gouged out. But the crying does something—it makes me focused, able to finally speak my feelings. "We made a pact. A pact." It's all I can manage to say. And people are staring at us now.

Shorie grabs my arm. "We should call Ben—"

I wrench loose. "Nobody knows what it's like for me. To have to go into that office every day." I stagger toward her, but she ducks, and I stumble forward, over a chair or the hose or something. All I know is I'm on my hands and knees staring down at the dirt and a crushed red Solo cup.

I have done something irreparable, and I don't even know how I managed it. I quiet myself. Close my eyes. It's time for me to go. Way past time. I just need a moment. A moment . . .

"Mom!" It's Shorie who's screaming now.

Maybe it has something to do with the sensation that I'm heading back under, back to the place where everything is quiet.

11

SHORIE

Just like I thought, something terrible happened. Mom lost her shit—in a pair of flamingo pajamas, no less—at my first fraternity party. I've never been so embarrassed. I've never been so scared.

Now it's seven in the morning, and Layton is waiting in her red Mini Cooper in the deserted parking lot outside my dorm. She's going to drive me back up to Birmingham, and they're going to confront Mom. We all are, I guess, since, true to his word, Ben is including me in the process. I'm wondering now if I should just leave it to the adults. My stomach is churning in a sickening way.

I toss my backpack behind the seat and slide into the tiny car, glancing over. As usual, Layton looks like she's just come from the world's most important conference meeting, impeccable in a navy sheath with a matching blazer and black stilettos, the charm bracelet on her arm jingling.

I feel like a rumpled mess next to her. It doesn't help that I only slept a few hours last night. After I called Ben, and he came and collected me, Mom, and his truck, he dropped me off at my dorm. I don't think he wanted me around Mom anymore. Didn't want me to see her all groggy and weird. I don't know where they went after that, but honestly, I kind of didn't care. But then he texted me at six thirty this morning that Layton was picking me up. *For the meeting,* he'd said. The one I'd asked to be a part of.

As we pull onto 280 West, Layton points to the coffee in the cup holder. I sip it gratefully, and we exchange pleasantries. She's quiet for a moment after that, then speaks.

"I should tell you—and I'm not trying to scare you—but I think your mom could really benefit from psychiatric help." She glances at me. "Everybody has moments of crisis. Everybody could use someone to talk to. I see a therapist from time to time. It's really not that big a deal, I promise. You could see one too, if you wanted. I could get you the name of a doctor who works with young people."

"Thanks, but no."

"I apologize, Shorie, I know sometimes I can be blunt."

"It's okay."

She hesitates. "There is something else I wanted to mention. Something I wanted to ask you."

"Okay."

"Can you tell me how long the drinking has been a problem?"

"The drinking?" My voice squeaks in disbelief.

"At your going-away party, she had more than a few glasses of champagne."

I hadn't really noticed. "Are you sure?"

"Yes."

"Well, I mean, maybe. But we were celebrating."

She nods, but it feels like she's placating me.

"It's not a problem," I add quickly. "It hasn't been."

I'm telling the truth—Mom doesn't drink much around me—but the reality is, I don't exactly watch her every move. This summer I haven't been around a lot, at least not at night. I've been riding around town with Daisy or barricaded up in my room, playing video games. For all I know, she could have been spending those nights alone, getting smashed.

"Because a lot of people are very smart about hiding their alcohol consumption," Layton says.

A current of annoyance ripples through me. Who is she to be tossing around opinions? Assuming Mom is hiding some addiction. It's not like she's a doctor. And being so . . . *matter of fact* about it all.

Then she hands over a slick trifold brochure. I unfold it.

"Hidden Sands," I read. "Innovative. Individualistic. Intuitive." I stare at the colorful shots of a tropical island resort, then glance over at her. "What is this place?"

"It's a spa. But also kind of a low-key rehab."

"Rehab?"

"They call it restoration. Kind of a mellower approach to recovery. Not everybody goes for drugs or alcohol. Some people—people like your mom—just need a space to rest. And to work some things out."

I sigh.

"You're going to need to trust us, Shorie," she says. "We've been talking about this for a while." She pats my knee a few times. The rest of the way, Layton takes work calls while I distractedly scroll through my phone, trying to find something that'll take my mind off my mom and the impending intervention.

Another error message in today's server report, identical to the previous one, does just that. I study it for a second, chewing my lip, then see Scotty's email. *The error's probably nothing more than a glitch with one of our new functions,* he's written, *which we're NOT going to discuss because you have other things to do. Like college. Remember, Shorie, I agreed to "forget" to remove your email from the daily report list, but you need to focus on school or the deal's off. Got it?*

Shit.

As soon as we get to the house, I'll slip into Dad's office and have a look at his journals. If there's some top-secret new Jax feature that he started testing before he died, he definitely would have written about it in one. And if the glitch happens to be more than that, if it turns out to be an actual problem—there's a chance Dad could've noticed it before he died and written about it.

We're the first ones to arrive at our house. Layton parks down the street so we don't freak Mom out when she gets home, and I let us in the back door with my key. The house smells so familiar—cool and minty, with just a whiff of Foxy Cat's litter. I kind of shiver with delight. It feels so right to be back here, but at the same time all wrong. I'm not back home the way I want to be, not really. I should probably be back in my dorm, sleeping off a hangover, like Dele probably is.

Layton, on another call, heads to the kitchen. I slip through the dining room and enter the tiny side porch that my parents remodeled for Dad's office. Even though Mom's taken a lot of his files back to the office, she hasn't cleaned out any of his personal stuff. His brown leather journals are still lined up neatly on the small bookshelf beside his desk. Exactly thirty-nine of them, representing the thirty-nine months he'd helped run Jax.

I pull out the last journal on the right, running my fingers over the gold stamped lettering on the cover. *February 2019.*

But wait. The last journal should be March. Dad died on March 20—the first day of my senior year spring break—and he would have already filled out a little over 50 percent of the book. Or 0.612903 to be exact.

I check the previous years. Then this year's journals. *January, December, November, October, September, August* . . . The rest are here, in perfect order, only there's no March. I tear through his desk and the console behind it. In the living room, I look in the drawer in the coffee table and in all the nooks and crannies of the antique secretary. No journal.

I run upstairs, two steps at a time. My heart is thumping now. It has nothing to do with the error message; that I can handle, even if it gets me in trouble. I just don't like the idea of my dad's last journal, containing the last words he wrote, being lost.

I fly into Mom and Dad's bedroom, check the dresser, nightstands, closet, even under the bed. Nothing. The bathroom's clear too. I walk back out into the hall. I can hear a car door slam behind the house. Arch and Gigi. Or maybe Sabine.

And then I remember something from that terrible March night.

A nurse had taken Mom and me from the waiting room at the hospital in Alexander City to a smaller room down the hall. About a half an hour later, the doctor had come in and told us Dad hadn't made it. But before he came in, while they were still trying to save him, a young female police officer had stopped by. She told Mom that an officer would have Dad's car towed anywhere she chose. Then she held out a white garbage bag full of items they'd collected from the car.

On our way back to Birmingham, I sorted through the items. A windbreaker with the Auburn logo, an insulated coffee cup, a beige umbrella, his duffel, a little stuffed spider Beanie Baby. The spider Beanie Baby had been a gift for me, I knew. An inside joke referring to the time a spider bit me. I'd taken it out of the bag and slept with it that night. But there was something else in that white bag.

His March journal. I remember it clearly.

"Shorie, darling," I hear Gigi call from downstairs. "Come help me clean up this mess!"

12

ERIN

I wake as Ben wheels the truck into my driveway and push matted hair off of my sleep-swollen face. I try to put the events of last night into some kind of order, but I can't. My headache has morphed into a massive body ache, my mouth tastes bitter, and my brain seems only to be able to recall flashes of things. Shorie's angry face. Loud music. Me screaming about Jax. Nothing hangs together the way it should. Did I really drink that much? It doesn't seem possible.

I focus hard on our white mission-style stucco house with its chestnut trim and leaded glass windows. There has never been such a welcome sight. Perry and I bought this house when Shorie was two, a quirky fixer-upper in a south Birmingham suburb called Hollywood. Like in its namesake, stately stone English Tudors and Spanish missions line the shady streets. We'd loved it in this house with its uneven, creaky oak floors, thick plaster walls, and every staircase, door, and banister built to last forever. We would have lasted forever too, if we'd had the chance.

The weather-warped door of the detached garage just beyond the house catches my eye. Perry always meant to upgrade to one of those doors that looked like real wood. He never got around to it, and I sure as hell won't be doing it anytime soon. Anyway, who gives a shit about what your garage door looks like? Only people who've never had to deal with any real problems.

"Erin." Ben clears his throat, and I snap back to the present.

"Here we are," I say absently and gather my purse and the tote with my toothbrush and clothes from yesterday. I'm still wearing the flamingo pajamas and an Auburn Tigers T-shirt.

This morning, I woke in the hotel room to the sound of someone knocking on my door. When I opened it to Ben, he said it was almost checkout time, then asked if he could come in. Something had happened last night, he said, didn't I remember? When I said no, he filled me in. I'd taken his truck, abandoned it in a parking lot next door to a fraternity house, and gotten into some kind of an altercation with Shorie. He'd received a call from Shorie and Ubered over to us.

I drank the water Ben handed me, then downed a cup of coffee. *How could all that have happened without me remembering?* He said blackouts are something that can just start happening to a person, especially someone who's been under a great amount of stress, anytime, with no warning, and I should be careful. He seemed worried.

None of it sounded right to me, but I was scared, very scared, and so I meekly let him drive us home. Now, as Ben swings the plastic tubs we emptied at Shorie's dorm out of the bed of the truck and stacks them, he seems totally shut down.

"Just leave them here," I say.

Ben holds on to the tubs. "I can bring them in."

"I don't want them inside." My voice is an exasperated growl. "We keep them in the garage." Then I realize I said *we*, and there's no "we" anymore. There's only me. I am alone. My resolve breaks, and I dissolve into tears. Down go the tubs, and I feel Ben gently touch my arms. "I'm so embarrassed," I sob. "I'm so sorry. I don't know what's wrong with me. I really appreciate everything you did. I'm sorry for whatever . . . whatever it is I—"

I close my mouth. Talking's not going to do me any good anyway, not like this, when I'm so strung out. I need a shower, a huge glass of water, and then bed. *The guest bed.* Tomorrow. Tomorrow, I'll sort things out. Tomorrow, I'll pull myself together and be the mom Shorie deserves.

Ben pulls me into a hug. He feels warm and comforting, and without even thinking, I rest my head on his shoulder. My lips accidentally brush against the salty skin of his neck, and like a jolt of electricity, something inside me responds. I've almost forgotten what skin tastes like.

I'm so tired, it happens like a reflex, my arms lifting and circling his neck, my body moving to his. But then he makes a groaning sound, and it sounds so open, so vulnerable, that I keep going, raking my fingers up into his hair, letting him nudge my face up to meet his.

Next thing I know, we're kissing. Only it can't be a real kiss, can it? Because even though it's lips and tongues and our hands on each other's faces and in each other's hair, it's Ben. *Ben.* And something else. This kiss can't be real because it is very, very good. Soft and gentle and moving with that secret choreography that only the best kisses have.

And then, as quickly as it began, the moment is over. The atmosphere around us changes into something heavy and dark. A storm cloud of bad ideas and unwise decisions descending. We pull apart and stare at each other in stunned, horrified silence.

"Ah." His voice is a rasp.

I feel like I want to disappear, like it might be better if I could just die.

"No, no. I'm sorry—" I say.

"I didn't—"

"Me neither—"

"It was just—" He glances through the leaded glass of the front door, his expression pained. Then he grips his forehead in one hand. "I hope the neighbors didn't see."

I look around uncertainly. Jesus. *The neighbors.*

"I'm sorry," I repeat numbly.

"I'm sorry too," Ben says. "That was . . ."

My fault. So stupid. Wrong.

"Yes," I say. "Left field. But it's over. Moving on, okay?"

"Okay. Yes. Moving on."

"I'll see you tomorrow, at the office." I unlock the door. He doesn't move.

"The tubs," he says. He seems forlorn.

I need to get inside. Away from Ben. Away from myself with Ben. "Just leave them," I say firmly, step inside, and shut the door behind me. I stand in the foyer, eyes squeezed shut, like it will somehow stop the disastrous tape from running. Like I have the power to force this cataclysm I created into nonexistence. But I can't. It's too late, and I know it and the helplessness makes me want to wail out loud. To scream until I'm hoarse. Oh my God. I have done a thing that can never be undone.

Reality: My husband is no longer the last man I've been romantic with. It's only been five months—*months*, not years, for God's sake—and I kissed someone. Like a goddamn horny teenager. And it wasn't just someone. It was Ben. Ben! Perry's friend. My friend. Sabine's husband. I did a monumentally stupid thing, and now our friendship is irrevocably changed. Forever. *Shit.* Shorie—what would she think if she knew? She would be devastated. She would kill me. She would kill Ben . . .

I force my brain to stop looping through the bombarding thoughts. Order it to start at the top. Proceed calmly.

Say it, Erin.

Reality: I've fucked up.

Challenge: Unfuck it all.

If that's even possible.

I open my eyes. Force myself to take in my surroundings. The hallway is cool and comfortably cluttered with Shorie's things: two pair of boots, and a couple of her jackets that I never got around to putting away last winter, still hanging on the hall tree. In the chipped ironstone tray on the chest, a pair of earbuds that the cat chewed. I run my hands over her pink fake fur coat and watch as bits of the fur swirl to the ground. I forbade her to wear it past the front hall because it shed worse than Foxy Cat. But she looked so glamorous in it, her shiny light-brown hair cascading over it, hazel eyes sparkling, and the dimple flashing just under the corner of her lip. My daughter looks like Perry grew her in a petri dish all by himself, but I don't care. They are the two most beautiful human beings I have ever laid eyes on.

I pull my T-shirt over my head and let it drop to the floor, then hook my thumbs in the pajama pants and step out of them. I feel better in my sports bra and underwear, but in the hallway, I still push the thermostat down to seventy. I should start a load of laundry. And get some water, and aspirin, before I head upstairs. I snatch up the clothes and head back to the living room.

"Foxy," I call. "Foxy Cat. Where are you?"

The room is dark and quiet, strewn with signs of Shorie's last-minute, late-night packing. A bag from Urban Outfitters on the slouchy sectional sofa. Ripped tags and receipts on the glass coffee table. Empty hangers and a suitcase she decided she didn't need after all. I gather it all up and dump it in a corner near the back door, then stop, staring out the windows that look into the backyard.

There's a car in my back driveway—a black Escalade. Arch has an Escalade. But why would Perry's father be here on a Thursday? Clutching the T-shirt and pj's against my chest, I tiptoe into the dark kitchen.

In the low light, I can see the whitewashed cabinets and tile countertop have been wiped down. The dishwasher is gurgling away, and the perpetually stacked-up drainboard beside the farmhouse sink is empty. Foxy slinks along the legs of the table, rubbing up against something in addition to the table legs. Human legs. Instantly I'm hit with a very distinctive smell. Chanel Coco perfume. Gigi.

Extra chairs have been pulled up to the table, and five people are seated around it. Five people I know and have loved and trusted until just this very second.

Gigi, Arch, Sabine, Layton, and Shorie.

Each one of them looks at me, face grim, back straight, hands folded.

And now suddenly, the kiss with Ben feels even more horrifying and wrong and shameful than it did a few minutes ago. Because, of course, he knew. He's a part of this. There are two empty chairs at the table.

I turn and run out of the room.

13

SHORIE

Mom runs out of the kitchen, and pity rises in my throat. She looked so shocked when she saw us. So vulnerable, standing there in her underwear, covering herself with those wadded-up pajamas. I will be okay if I never see my mother look that caught off guard again.

We all sit in silence—Gigi, Arch, Sabine, Layton, and me. Gigi and Arch look like they always do—tan enough to be healthy and dressed like they're on their way to a cocktail party at the country club. Sabine, with her wavy blonde hair falling out of its messy bun, wears loose-fitting ripped jeans and a yoga top with a crisscross network of straps that reveals her thin, muscled shoulders. Naturally Gigi's already given her a sniff of dismissal, but she thinks people should wear pearls and gloves to scrub a toilet, and I'm sure Sabine doesn't give a rip. In fact, she doesn't seem worried at all. Like always, she seems slightly separate from whatever's going on, like she's floating in her own bubble of serenity.

I am not so serene. Confronting Mom is nerve-racking enough, but now I can't stop thinking about Dad's missing journal. Where could it be? Why would it even be missing in the first place? I tell myself not to freak out. There's got to be an explanation. Maybe Mom took it back to his office at Jax, in case she needed to use it there.

Soon enough, Mom's back in the kitchen, Ben by her side. She's put the flamingo pajama pants and T-shirt back on and retwisted her scrunchie. But she still looks terrible. Her face is yellowish, and she's got these puffy purple bags under her eyes. And she looks scared, the way she looked right after Dad died. I don't like seeing her that way, so I focus on the plaque on the far wall, the one I painted for her birthday a couple of years back.

Put a dent in the universe.

It's some inspirational bullshit Steve Jobs said once. Or that Pinterest said that he said. Let's face it, Cookie Monster could've said it, for all I know. But the phrase looked cool painted in silver lettering against a starry blue sky. I focus on the silvery swoop of the letter *d* on the plaque and tell myself to breathe. That we're going to be done with this soon and Mom will be taken care of and I can find Dad's March journal.

"What are you doing here?" Mom says. I flick a glance at her but don't answer. The adults told me to leave the talking to them until they got through the main part.

Ben puts a hand on Mom's back. "Erin. Let's sit down. We want to talk to you."

She pushes away his hand and sits. She looks like she wants to kill us. Then, "Thanks so much for coming," she announces to the room, like it's a party or corporate event or something. "Say what you've come to say, and then I'm going upstairs to bed. It's been a long couple of days."

"We came here to talk to you, Erin," Arch booms. "And you're going to do us the courtesy of listening."

We all stare at him. He's a quiet man, kind of disconnected, actually. Not exactly what you'd call warm. But, I don't know. Maybe the situation is just so mega-uncomfortable that he thinks he should get aggressive. That makes me extra nervous, the sound of Arch being loud. The thought of a fight breaking out.

Gigi cuts in. "We know what happened in Auburn last night. We've talked to Layton and Shorie, and we know everything."

Mom looks at me, a question on her face.

"You were drunk," Gigi says. "And you made a scene at a fraternity house. Shorie was terrified. Here's her mother, taking a car that doesn't belong to her, drunkenly barging into a party. Making a fool of herself. Passing out on the ground outside, in her pajamas."

Mom looks really hard at me. "That's what I did?" I don't answer, and our eyes meet. Hers immediately turn red and fill with tears. Then mine do too.

Ben speaks. "We're worried about your well-being, Erin. We just want to suggest pushing the 'Pause' button."

Mom gives him about the nastiest look I've ever seen her give anyone. My heart starts to race uncontrollably.

"At a top-notch rehabilitation facility," Gigi cuts in. "For people who need help pulling themselves together. Arch heard about it from a friend of his."

Everybody lets that one pass because we're all used to my grandmother's little digs at my mother. The unfortunate truth is my grandmother can be a colossal bitch at times. I just wish she'd throttle it back right now.

"Hidden Sands is a great place to rest," Sabine says gently. "To regroup."

"They call it restoration," Ben says. "For people who are overworked or stressed or have mental health issues. And yes, addictions too."

"Restoration." Mom's voice drips with sarcasm. "How interesting."

I pipe up. "It's on an island. There's a beach. And yoga."

Mom gazes at Sabine. "I'm impressed with how quickly you were able to find this place. Seeing as how all this just happened last night."

Sabine folds her hands. No one says anything.

Mom looks around the table. "So how long have you all been talking behind my back? How long have you been plotting to send me away?"

The way she says it, I have the feeling she knows.

"You need help, Erin," Layton says.

"We've been worried about you for a while now," Sabine says.

Mom zeroes in on me. "I'm sorry, Shor. I'm so sorry for humiliating you like that. I don't know what happened. But you know me, I barely even drink. You know that."

I clear my throat. "You didn't tell me you weren't driving back home after moving me in. That you and Ben were going to check into a hotel instead."

The room gets really quiet. Sabine looks down. Gigi emanates grandmotherly disapproval.

"I wanted to hang around, just in case Shorie needed me." Mom turns to me. "Then later that night, you called—or your roommate called, I don't remember exactly. I just know whoever it was said you needed to see me."

"Well, then you should've called an Uber," Gigi says. "Even I know how to call an Uber." She glances around, like she expects congratulations on living in the present-day world.

"How did you get the keys to Ben's truck?" I ask.

"He's always had one of those magnet things under the bed of his truck. That must've been how I did it." Her expression is so vulnerable again. So sad. The contrast with her earlier anger is so pathetic, I almost can't stand to look at her.

"Erin, it's okay," Sabine says. "We really sympathize with what you're going through. We all miss Perry so much. But you . . . well, it's different for you. I think maybe we haven't taken into account how deeply his death affected you. I've heard sometimes these things—blackouts and breakdowns—can happen when someone has undergone a trauma like this."

"So why didn't anyone call 911?" Mom asks. "Or take me to the hospital?"

Ben interjects. "Well, no one wanted to . . ."

"We thought you were drunk," I say.

"But I wasn't. I could've been roofied," Mom says.

"What?" I say. But it seems like I'm the only one who thinks this sounds crazy. Everybody else is just sitting there like it's no big deal. "Who would want to roofie you?" I demand.

"I don't know. No one specific. It happens. But if I'd gone to the hospital and had my blood tested, we'd know. Now it's probably too late."

"I'm sorry," Ben says. "Taking you to the hospital didn't occur to me. I thought maybe you'd been drinking back at the hotel, in your room. I didn't want what happened to get out, to embarrass you publicly . . ."

There's a beat of uncomfortable silence.

"Very exclusive place, Hidden Sands," Arch interjects, like we haven't just been talking about someone dosing my mom's drink when she wasn't looking. "Only the best food, amenities. Spa services. Golf, if you want it. Tennis. Therapy, which is optional, of course."

I love Arch, but oh my God, is he clueless.

"Nobody to bother you for a whole month," he continues. "All the time in the world for you to rest and relax and get back to normal. So you can decide how you want to proceed."

"How I want to proceed?" Mom echoes, a quizzical look on her face.

"He means if you still want to sell Jax," Sabine says.

"Me selling Jax has nothing to do with whatever happened last night," Mom says.

"We think it might," Ben says.

"How?" She places her palms on the table. "Look, I'm very sorry for involving Shorie—"

Gigi interrupts. "What's a child supposed to do in a situation like that—you getting drunk and following her? Embarrassing her in front of all her new friends at school. What kind of mother are you? What kind of example—"

"Felicia," Arch says, and lifts his hand. Miraculously Gigi shuts her mouth.

"Erin," Layton says. "Whether we sell the company next month or in two years, the issue is still the same. A CEO's responsibility is to make their team feel safe and at the same time make potential buyers comfortable and confident. I think you'll agree, this behavior falls short of that."

I clear my throat. "You have to admit, Mom, you haven't been . . . yourself since Dad . . ."

"I know," Mom says slowly. "I realize I've been a little erratic. But I swear, it was one glass of wine. But somebody could've put something in my glass." She looks around the table, her eyes pleading. "Please understand how hard this has been. I'm trying—" She looks like she's about to burst into tears.

Layton puts a hand on Mom's arm. "Are you currently in contact with any buyers, privately? To do my job properly, we can't have any secrets. We all deserve to know."

Mom shakes her head, but now there are tears slipping down her cheeks. She wipes them away and presses the back of her hand to her nose. Sabine passes her a box of tissues.

"You can tell us the truth, Erin," she says.

"The truth is the most important thing," Arch says.

"You don't have to pretend to be strong," Ben says.

"You have to *be* strong," Gigi interjects. "You're a mother. You're all Shorie has, and you . . . you act like an unstable—"

"Stop," I blurt out. "All of you. Can you all just shut up for a second and tell her about Hidden Sands? That's why we're here. Not to make her feel like shit!"

Gigi collects herself and swipes at the berry-colored lipstick gathered in the corners of her lips. Ben pushes the brochure toward Mom.

"It's in the Caribbean," he says. "A small island called Ile Saint Sigo, just off the coast of Saint Lucia, privately owned by Erdman International. They own boutique hotels all across the world. Hidden Sands is one of the most exclusive, private spa retreats there is. They'll look after you."

"Innovative. Individualistic. Intuitive," Mom reads. "What's *L'Élu?*"

"It's this trek they take everybody on," Ben says. "Kind of a short-term vision quest challenge the guests have to complete. After you've been there for three weeks or so—resting, relaxing, whatever—the final step is the L'Élu. You get a certificate that proves you've satisfied Hidden Sands' requirements, and then you're released."

"Released." Mom nods. "So that's how it is?"

He and Mom gaze at each other over the brochure, and we all wait. It's like we're being locked out while a series of secret communications passes between them. I wonder if it bothers Sabine as much as it bothers me.

Mom flips open the brochure and peruses the shots of the wide white beach, turquoise water, and lush, leafy jungle. The modern spa, its serene lobby featuring an indoor stream running through the center of it. The luxurious monochromatic bedrooms with glass-and-steel walls, and teak-paneled yoga studios. Rich-person rehab, where movie stars and pop singers go to dry out.

"You really don't have a choice, my dear," Arch says. "Whatever it is that you took—"

Mom looks around the table. "I would think one of you—somebody—would care about *that* instead of plotting against me, behind my back. For months. I mean, for God's sake, maybe I need to go to the doctor. Maybe there's something wrong with me. Maybe I'm sick. Maybe someone did this *to* me—"

"Enough with that roofie nonsense!"

We all swivel to face Gigi. Her face is slack and pale, and I've never seen such hatred shooting out of someone's eyes. "You almost ruin your daughter's chance at a college education, and all you can do is think of ways you're not to blame. It's not only about last night, Erin. It's about the way you've been ever since he died. You work all the time. You don't come to dinner when I invite you. You wouldn't even answer your phone. You've shut us all out for months—"

"I am doing the best I can!" Mom shouts back at her.

The air seems to crackle. Everyone's still, and Mom's eyes are huge and full of hurt. I'm trembling.

I stand up, almost toppling my chair. Everybody stares at me. "That's enough, Gigi. Not another word. From any of you."

The room is quiet, all except for the gurgling of the dishwasher.

"Not another word." I jut out my chin. "She just needs some rest. To get away from Jax, from all the pressure, from everything for a little while so she can reset. That's it. That's all."

No one answers me. I guess they can tell I've had enough. Mom is still staring at me.

"I'll go to this place . . . to Hidden Sands, if Shorie promises to stay in school," she says quietly.

"I promise," I say.

"Who's going to take Foxy Cat?" Mom says. She sounds resigned.

Layton pipes up. "She'll be fine at my house if you're okay with that. I've been thinking about getting a cat, so this'll be good practice."

Sabine slides a printed-out boarding pass toward Mom. "All the arrangements have been made. Go upstairs. Shower and change, then get some rest. Your flight leaves at seven tomorrow morning."

"Impressive work, you guys. If only I could get this kind of performance when I need something done at Jax," Mom says coolly. She brushes her fingertips over the ticket. Her lips are pursed in that super annoying way she has when she's mad. In a heartbeat, she's turned into my mother again. Gigi's pushed back from the table. Arch is shaking Ben's hand. Sabine and Layton are up too.

"We'll look after Shorie," Arch says to Mom in his gruff grandpa voice, and gives her a hug. "Don't you worry. She'll be just fine, you can count on that."

Layton touches my back. "Shorie, Ben said he'd drive you back to Auburn."

Mom is drifting toward the living room, Ben tracking her every move. Layton glances at Ben and snaps shut her briefcase. A little too forcefully, in my opinion.

"Call me if you need anything, okay?" Layton says to me. She crosses the room to Ben, touches his arm, and leans to whisper something in his ear.

The dishwasher hums in the background. Gigi and I loaded it together while we waited for Mom. She told me about the time she took Dad to a birthday party and the kid's parents had hired a clown. She said the party was a disaster; most of the children were frightened and cowering behind their mothers' skirts. Apparently Dad marched right up to the clown and kicked him, right in the shin, bringing him to his knees. The clown had cussed out the birthday boy's parents, then screeched off in his crappy car, never to be heard from again.

My dad, Perry Gaines, everybody's hero, even at age six. I miss him so much.

Ben approaches me. "Ready to go?"

"Can we drop by Jax first? I left something in Dad's office."

"Sure." He throws a look over his shoulder, and at first, I think he's checking on Mom, but then I realize Layton's still standing by the door. I wonder if I missed his signals, and it's really Layton he's interested in.

"We should go," I say in a cold tone. Our eyes meet, and I'm pretty sure he gets my message. *Whatever you're up to, I'm watching.*

"Hey, babe?" he calls to Sabine. "We're heading out."

Sabine blows me a kiss. "Good luck at school, Shorie." The light slanting in from the breakfast room window haloes her, making her hair spun gold, her face like a Madonna in a painting. I wonder what she thinks about everything that happened last night. I wonder if she has questions about her husband. I wonder if she knows how he feels, or felt, about Mom. I wonder if she sees the way he is with Layton.

"Thanks," I say to her, then flash a smile at Ben. "Let's go."

14

Perry's Journal

<u>Sunday, March 3</u>

TO DO:
- REI: tent, 2 sleeping bags, air mattress
- Beanie Baby spider for Shorie— (funny? hope so, probably not)
- Schedule lunch with Dad—$$
- Shorie Jax budget
- Shorie letter

I know after the excitement and intensity of your Jax assignments, college work may feel boring. But core classes, while not difficult or time consuming, are still important. They provide a structure that'll be good practice for you to navigate. Constraints are good things, Shor. They actually give freedom. And just think, you can use the extra time to socialize! Ha, ha.

Take a cue from your mom. She works social events like a boss—master of the three-minute small-talk personality assessment. She's never misjudged an opponent . . . or failed to target an ally, not that I've seen. You two are different, but you can learn so much from her, Shor, if you'll just give her a chance . . .

15

ERIN

I sleep a fitful eight hours, wake to Sabine's phone call, and am whisked to the airport by Ben. They're quite the magicians, my friends. Able to make me disappear in the blink of an eye.

The first flight to Miami, the seemingly endless second leg to Saint Lucia, and the ferry ride to Ile Saint Sigo happen without incident, but I barely register any of it. I'm too shaken from the intervention—but also Ben's incessant apologizing on the way to the airport. He jabbered the whole way, saying he was the worst kind of douchebag, explaining why he'd done such a shitty thing like kissing me (he "didn't know what the hell he was thinking"), and repeating how terrible he felt for taking advantage of me when the intervention was literally about to happen just on the other side of my front door.

Mostly to shut him up, I told him that I forgave him. But, really, I do forgive him. I mean, I'm an adult who makes my own decisions. And I put my arms around him, there on my front stoop, kissed him, and pressed my body against his. It would probably behoove me to examine the reasons why. Right now, however, it's all I can do to think about how my life has gotten away from me so quickly. One minute, I'm seeing my daughter off to her freshman year of college. The next, I'm on my way to rehab.

Excuse me. *Restoration.*

It's late afternoon when the driver meets me at the ferry terminal—if you can call the rickety wooden shack at the edge of town that houses a tiny ticket booth and a row of turquoise-painted benches that. He's driving a sparkling town car, this freakishly good-looking guy in his twenties with a head of artfully mussed hair. And he's dressed in khaki board shorts and a spotless white polo with a Hidden Sands logo embroidered in navy right over the swell of his perfectly proportioned pectoral muscle.

He's Grigore from Moldova—my concierge, he says—and as he shakes my hand, his silver flat-link bracelet flashes in the bright sun. His hands and smile are warm and reassuring. I'm not exactly unappreciative. He's cute. I guess this is one way of disarming your clients, preparing them for the regimen ahead.

After Grigore loads my duffel in the trunk and settles behind the wheel, he asks if I'd like a quick tour of this side of the island before we head inland to the resort. I agree, and as we embark, he gives me the rundown. Ile Saint Sigo, eight nautical miles off the east coast of Saint Lucia and a total of five miles square, shore to shore, boasts a total nontourist population of roughly four hundred. In the eighteenth and early nineteenth centuries, it was a thriving sugarcane plantation, until after emancipation, when it fell into disrepair. The islanders who didn't head for Saint Lucia in search of work subsisted on fishing and sporadic tourism until the early eighties.

That was when hotel magnate Edwin Erdman, wintering at his personal compound on Saint Lucia's Jalousie Beach, spotted the tiny paradise during his morning helicopter ride. He built Hidden Sands and purchased three-quarters of the island, all owned under the Erdman International banner. When his daughter Antonia came of age, he handed the reins of the resort—and island—over to her. The town basically exists to support Hidden Sands, although there are still a few fishermen and farmers continuing to scratch out a living.

Oh, and there's a volcano, way up at the northernmost tip of the island. Apparently there's a collapsed crater where, heated by magma, springs boil at upward of 350 degrees Fahrenheit.

"The actual crater is off-limits to Hidden Sands guests," Grigore says at the conclusion of his spiel. "There was an accident a few years back."

He switches on the music. I toss my purse aside, sigh, and rest my head on the seat. It's kind of ironic. Here I am at rehab, and even though I'm normally not much of a drinker, I'm craving the taste of rum. It must be the tropical heat and humidity and gorgeous spicy smell hanging in the air. My brain's switched over into vacation mode.

"Water? Fruit juice?" He checks me in the rearview mirror.

"No thank you. What's that smell?"

"Incense. They make it from the sap of the lansan tree that grows in the interior of the island. They burn it in the church over there."

As he rambles on about the wide variety of exotic vegetation on the island, I look at the humble plaster church we're rumbling past and think of the priest who swung the smoking incense at Ben and Sabine's wedding. Perry and I have never attended church. He didn't like the formality, and I was on the fence myself about all things religious, so we used our Sundays for rest and play.

Maybe that's part of my problem—instead of believing in God, I fastened all my hopes on the frail, imperfect humans around me. Or rather, one human. And when he left me, I was lost.

I think back to this morning, after I'd gotten out of Ben's truck and called Sabine. *Talk to Gigi,* I'd said. *Find out where she was when I was in Auburn.*

Seriously? Sabine said. *You think Gigi went out to the mean streets of Mountain Brook, scored some GHB, then drove to Auburn and put it in your drink? Without somehow attracting all the attention in the room to her? That woman can't set foot inside a restaurant or a hotel without demanding to see the manager. You know that.*

Well, it could've been Ben, I guess, I snapped. *He certainly was there.*

It was an unkind thing to say to his wife, to my best friend, and she didn't bother answering me. But I knew what she was thinking—that it was the stress talking. That Perry's death had finally pushed me into the land of paranoia. To a place where I imagined my friends and family were organized against me.

And maybe Sabine saw the truth. Maybe I really was losing it.

Grigore drives us through a small town, which consists of several paved roads that meet at a large stone fountain that seems to have been dry for a very long time. The roads are crammed with tiny shops and restaurants and open-air stands selling trinkets and produce. People fill the narrow sidewalks. Locals, it looks like, not tourists. Down a few alleyways lined with brightly painted houses, I spot children running and riding skateboards and electric scooters.

We drive down a few more streets, then abruptly we are in the thick, leafy jungle. The dirt road winds and winds for what seems like an eternity, and my exhaustion envelops me. My eyes shutter, and instantly I am lost to sleep. Sometime later, I awake to the sound of the trunk popping open. We've drawn up under a portico constructed of huge wood beams, rough-hewn and stained a dark coffee color. To my left, a tall, clover-shaped fountain, this one working, splashes arcs of water onto lily pads and some kind of extravagant orange blossom. To my right, a pair of massive wood doors banded by iron and set in a pristine white stucco wall are being held open by two young men wearing the same board shorts, polo, and sunglasses as Grigore. They have the same haircut too.

Welcome to Hidden Sands. My really expensive ascetic rehab complete with eye candy.

Grigore opens my door, a dazzling, sexy smile on his face. His teeth are straight and a blinding shade of white (like everything else here), and suddenly, irrationally, inappropriately, I think of kissing him. Which brings to mind what I did with Ben on the front stoop of my house less than twenty-four hours ago—with Sabine sitting mere yards away in my kitchen.

I burn with shame all over again. How could I have done that to Perry? To his memory?

If I had been the one who died, he would never have done such a thing. He wouldn't have dreamed of it—running to Sabine for comfort. Lacing his fingers through her hair. Opening his mouth on hers . . .

What the hell kind of person am I?

Maybe Gigi was right. Maybe I really can't manage my life.

"Remove your shoes, please."

Grigore has shouldered my duffel. It's all Hidden Sands allows their clients to bring to the island: personal toiletry items and underwear. The rest—clothing, pajamas, workout wear, shoes—the brochure said they would provide. It was a psychological tactic, probably. Deny you the comfort of your own clothing and make you dependent on them. Prime you for compliance.

I blink at him, then slip off my flats and hand them over. On our way to the double doors, we're immediately swept aside by a phalanx of handsome, tousled-haired men and gorgeous, impeccably groomed women who are heading inside too. They are all clad in the Hidden Sands uniform and flank a thin brunette woman who's got a phone pressed to her ear. A black silk scarf holds her hair back, massive gold-rimmed aviators rest on a perfectly pert nose, and her designer jeans threaten to fall off her tiny frame. I recognize her immediately—an actress, with at least a dozen multimillion-dollar-grossing films under her belt, who's now starring in a wildly popular TV series. She sweeps by me, and I catch a whiff of a very particular, spicy scent. One I haven't smelled since I was a much younger woman.

What the . . .

"Fucking Antonia," she snaps into the phone. "L'Élu was a nightmare the first time I did it, and she's going to make me do it again. I will tell you this, if she doesn't let up with this *Survivor* bullshit, I'm never coming back."

She stops just short of the door, pirouettes, and catches my eye. Her mouth twists into a snide grin, and she winks, like we're sharing some kind of secret. Then she glides through the double wood doors, her entourage swarming behind her, bearing bags and totes. No single-duffel rule for movie stars, I guess.

"Shall we?" Grigore gestures toward the open doors.

The lobby—an architect's dream of concrete, glass, steel, and white plaster—is blessedly frosty and smells like cucumber and mint. Enormous bamboo fans whir overhead, and at my feet, a deep, pebble-lined stream stocked with koi ripples through the center of the room, powered by some unseen pump. Concrete ledges extend out into the indoor stream, providing stepping stones across the space.

The room itself has just the slightest green tint to it—a soothing glow coming from some light source I can't see. And there are flowers everywhere. Not just tropical flowers—roses and peonies and lilies and ranunculus and foxglove and even sprays of hard green blackberries budding from the stalk. They must spend a fortune shipping them in.

More staff—male and female—glide across the room. A couple of them smile and murmur welcomes to me. They're all in their twenties or early thirties, all easy on the eyes. Like, improbably so. I try to avoid eye contact; not that I have anything against attractive people, but so much pretty in one place is striking me as peculiar.

I wonder how much my friends and family know about Hidden Sands. How much research they did before shuttling me off here to Supermodel Island to get fixed.

"This way." Grigore puts a glass of water in my hands. There's a tiny purple blossom floating on the top, and the water tastes like the room smells. Suddenly overcome with thirst, I chug most of it, flower and all. At a desk tucked in an unobtrusive corner sits a lovely (of course) woman. She's dark skinned, with close-cropped platinum-dyed hair and a narrow gold ring in her nose. A silky white sarong is knotted under her arms. She smiles at Grigore.

"Un, deux, ou trois?"

Grigore nods at her. "Trois. Erin Gaines."

The woman smiles and extends her hand. "Ms. Gaines, welcome to Hidden Sands. To body, soul, and spirit restoration. Anything you need during your stay, anything at all, if you'll just leave a handwritten note on my desk, I'll take care of it." She waves her hand behind her. There's a stack of notecards and a glass of pens. No computer or phone that the guests could use. "I trust you had a pleasant flight and ferry over?"

I nod. "Yes."

"Cell and bag, please." She eyes my purse, and I hand them over. She deposits the phone in a drawer, and after a quick inspection, returns my bag. "Your phone will be locked in a safe for the duration of your stay. You aren't on any medications, correct?"

I shake my head. "No."

"We have a roster of experts at your disposal: a naturopath, iridologist, hypnotherapist. In our Ayurvedic spa, we offer Reiki, acupuncture, and volcanic mud facials."

"Straight from your own personal volcano," I say.

She smiles. "That's right. Additionally, for a more in-depth Hidden Sands experience, may I suggest our Life Odyssey program? It's an immersive—a three-day alternative course of curated experiences, based on ancient techniques and modern clinical practices, designed and supervised by our owner, Antonia Erdman."

"Sounds fun."

The woman laughs. "More like life changing. And if you're wondering, no, it's not described in the brochure. Many of our experiences aren't. We use the brochure—and the website—as more of a way to draw people in, people who might feel skittish about rehab."

"So no tennis or golf?"

"We believe restorative work is best done in a competition-free environment."

I'm nodding and smiling, resisting the urge to laugh in disbelief. If Jax lied on our advertising like that, we would catch all kinds of trouble, but it appears down here in the crazy Caribbean, nobody gives a shit.

"Sound good?" She gently removes the empty glass from my hand.

"Yes." And then, like a reflex, I think of all the ways it's not going to be good. And I don't feel like laughing anymore.

The woman says something to Grigore in French—*demain* is all I catch—and hands him a key.

"What did you just say about tomorrow?" I ask. They both stare at me. I guess they're not used to guests asking questions. "Sorry, I only have a little bit of French."

The woman laughs. "No problem. I just said you'll be beginning your personalized program tomorrow."

"Oh. Okay."

"Grigore will show you to the prep station and then your room." She sweeps her hand toward the rear of the building. "Dinner's at eight thirty in the dining hall."

We traverse the clear rippling stream with a series of skips across three floating concrete pads. We head down a long hall and stop at a set of frosted glass doors. The word **PREP** is etched in the glass. We enter a dim, quiet room with wood-paneled walls and a smooth concrete floor. Piped-in music plays, a soothing classical guitar. Another woman behind another desk smiles warmly at me.

"Erin Gaines, trois," Grigore says.

"Hello, Erin," she says. "Ready to shower?" She pulls a bundle from under the desk, and Grigore scoops it up.

"This way," he says.

I follow him down another hall that ends in another frosted glass door. He hands me the bundle and takes my purse.

"This is your regulation Hidden Sands clothing. After undressing, leave your clothes in the bins. The staff will launder and hold them until the day of your release." He unzips my duffel, allowing me to pull out a fresh set of underwear, then zips it back. "Several more outfits are in your room, where I'll leave your purse. I'll be back for you in fifteen minutes."

My hair cascades down my back and, startled, I turn. Grigore is holding my scrunchie, and I can't help but stare at him. The last person who touched my hair was Ben. On my front porch when we were kissing. And I can still feel the pressure of his fingers. Why does that particular gesture feel so invasive? So intimate?

"No hair ties," Grigore says simply. "Antonia asks her clients to wear their hair natural."

I shake my head to clear the memory and snort. "Okay. For argument's sake, we'll call this natural."

His gaze doesn't waver. "It's lovely," he says in a gentle voice, which makes me feel about a hundred different ways I don't want to feel. *Foolish. Needy.*

Alone.

"It's a psychological tactic, right?" I say. "To make us feel vulnerable and uncomfortable, so we're more malleable? So you can break us."

"See you in fifteen" is all he says, then he spins on his heel and heads back down the hall.

I head toward the shower room. On the other side of the door, I pause, pinch the bridge of my nose, and tell myself there's nothing to do but roll with it. With whatever this place throws at me. I'm on a mission—to get done whatever it is I have to do to obtain my release. Get back home, to my daughter and my company.

The shower room is a cavernous tiled space with rainfall shower-heads and shower curtains that encircle each stall. Right now the room is empty, all the curtains pushed back. I shed my clothes, step inside a stall, and pull the curtain. I turn the lever. When the torrent of steaming hot water shoots out, I duck under and groan in delight.

After I've stood there for probably longer than I should, I remember to lather up with the minty body wash and shampoo. White suds stream into the drain at my feet, and for the first time, I start to feel calm. Then I hear the door to the shower room open, and what sounds like a group of women enter the room. No one speaks, the only sound the shucking of clothes and shoes. I peek from behind my curtain.

An assortment of clothes—mud-caked shorts and T-shirts, hiking boots, and underwear—lies heaped on the floor. Four women surround it—two white, one black, and one Latina. They're all coated in the same filthy brown dirt, hair matted and greasy. I see the way the naked skin of their bodies contrasts with their grime-streaked arms and faces as they move toward the showers. The Latina woman is young, in her early twenties, short and round. She wears glasses and is limping.

She enters the shower next to me. The minute I hear the spray of water, she yelps.

"Agnes? You okay?" one of the other women says.

"*Sí,*" she says.

I stay motionless under my shower. And then I hear a low murmuring. One phrase repeated over and over again, in a quivering voice, barely audible above the sound of the water.

"*Dios te salve, María . . . llena eres de gracia.*"

There's maybe less than a foot separating my curtain from hers, and a bit of a slope to the floor, and after a few seconds her runoff water streams across the tile, pooling around my feet and gurgling down into my drain. I back away, toward the wall, my eyes wide. There's something red mixed in the dingy brown water.

Blood.

16

SHORIE

Friday night, after a few attempts to talk me into going to eat then to a party at this house on Gay Street, Dele gives up. She says goodbye, and she and Rayanne finally leave me alone.

It's not that I dislike Dele—I like her just fine, actually—but there's no way in hell I can hang out with a bunch of people tonight. I'm miserable, and I'm not one of those people, like my mother, who can fake happy. Parties aren't my thing anyway. Flirting and dancing don't exactly come naturally to me.

I stretch out on my scratchy lavender comforter that will probably smell like the inside of a Pottery Barn until time is no more and stare up at the blank white ceiling of my dorm room. The journal wasn't in Dad's office at Jax. Ben waited in the car while I ran up and turned the office upside down with no luck.

I roll over and smoosh my face into my faded yellow pillowcase I brought from home. My pillow is just the right amount of flat and smells heavenly, too, just like our house—a combination of the laundry detergent Mom uses, that citrusy floor polish, the rosemary candles she burns, Dad's shaving cream, and a whiff of Foxy's litter box tang.

That's what does it, interestingly enough. The thought of Foxy, her white fur and single black spot right on top of her head. Her trusting green eyes blinking up at me. I start wailing and sobbing into my pillow, and all the while a part of my brain remains detached, floating somewhere up against the ceiling.

When will this pain stop? my brain thinks, looking down at me. *When I'm dead too?* But there is no answer, and I keep crying. Eventually the tears dry up, and my body lets out a final shudder. I feel like one of those cicada shells in the daylilies beside the garage. Empty. But also very calm.

I haven't checked today's server report so I open my email to see if the error message has shown up again. Today's is clear, interestingly. And when I download the log, the only activity I see is not by an admin, but by a user. It looks like from the 128-bit universally unique identifier, a regular Jax user has logged on the same way an administrator does.

Okay, that's highly unusual.

I jot the UUID down and stare at it. Somebody's up to something, messing with the servers. And it appears they fixed the deadlock issue, which is not the way things work at Jax. Only admins get on the servers and fix things.

The frustrating thing is there's no way for me to know who this person is. As a digital wallet app, Jax has to follow really strict FDIC rules about privacy. All our user accounts are anonymized with these UUIDs. This person could be any one of the millions of people who are using Jax.

There is one way to gather more data from this UUID, although it's not an entirely legal one. It would involve uploading a basic surveillance software program to my phone, then doing some minor reconfiguring of the setup. Installing spyware on this person's Jax account, in other words. Which is terrible and all kinds of wrong and really not what I should be doing. But I'm curious—okay, nosy—and it's the only way I'm going to figure out what's going on. If I ask Scotty, he'll just bump me off the report list.

I grab my laptop and start digging.

An hour and a half later, I realize two things. I'm starving, and there's no food in our room. Well, Dele has some peach yogurt and grapes and Little Debbie Swiss Rolls in the fridge, but I haven't had a chance to go to the store yet, so I don't have anything. I check the school's app and see there's one cafeteria open until nine. I flash to an image. Me, sitting at a table, choking down a sad, limp sandwich, while a couple of other kids—who either didn't know how to find their way to parties or were too stubborn or anxious to go to the ones they were invited to—notice with pity my puffy red cry-face. *Ah, the homesick girl.*

What I really want is a Davenport's black olive and onion pizza and a large root beer over mounds of flake ice, but that's not going to happen, so I better get my butt in gear. I do a quick check in the mirror, then grab my wallet and room key. The idea of hunting for a meal in the fresh air sounds strangely invigorating. Something concrete to focus on.

I head toward where the new-student guide said there are some food trucks, in one of the fields where they let the RVs park on game days. Sure enough, in the center of the field there's a semicircle of food trucks, all but one of them shuttered. I check my app. Great. Not officially open until school starts. But there is that one . . .

It has a pita wrap painted on the side of it with the words **SHAWARMA-RAMA** below. It may not be a black olive and onion pizza, but the window's up and the trio of picnic tables beside it is deserted, so it'll have to do. I break into a trot, actually salivating and waving my phone around in the general direction of the truck. No menu or price suggestions pop up on Jax. Then, when I'm about half a block away, the awning slams shut. I slow, hot and wilted, my feet throbbing from all that running in my slides.

I rap tentatively on the pink metal. "Hello? Would you mind selling me . . . well, whatever you've got left? Leftovers? I've got cash." There's no answer. "I'll pay you double. Whatever you've got. Please, I'm starving."

Nothing.

I glare at the truck. There's somebody inside, I can see that, but now they're hiding from me. It's completely silent in there too. Instead of cleaning up, like he should be doing, that asshole is holding his breath, waiting for me to give up and go away.

"Great customer service, buddy," I shout, then sit. I can outlast this guy. He has no idea.

The sun's going down, a hot, messy egg yolk, spilling every shade of orange there is across the horizon and then trails of pink and blue and purple. Prettiest sunset on the plains, Dad used to say, and he's not far off. This was his alma mater. He majored in computer science, like me, joined a fraternity, and played intramural football. Also he was a Plainsman, which is basically like the official host of the school who has to wear an amazingly ugly orange blazer and striped tie. But it was a big deal, and I've seen pictures of him at games. He looked a lot like a young Paul Newman.

Which is not a thing I would say, except that Gigi used to say it a lot. Once I googled Paul Newman, and he was a straight-up babe, for sure, but nobody likes to think of their dad that way. I just think Dad looked cute and happy, hugging my mom under the spreading branches of an old oak festooned with toilet paper.

I check my phone. It's been exactly fifteen minutes. And I guess I can hear a few thumps from the truck, but the Shawarma-Rama guy hasn't had the decency to show his face or collect the napkin dispensers from the picnic tables. I pick up one of the dispensers and hurl it at the truck.

Instantly the door to the food truck slams open, and the guy thunders out.

Holy Paul Newman.

This guy really does look like him. Or maybe not him—but he's movie star good looking, so much so that my mouth goes dry and my face suddenly feels like I've just slathered on a molten lava facial mask. I wish desperately I hadn't thrown his napkin dispenser at his food truck. I wish desperately that I had bothered to brush my hair. And also my teeth.

"What the hell," he says, looking me up and down with his squinty, sexy movie star eyes. He's wearing jeans and a pink T-shirt that says **SHAWARMA-RAMA** with the same horrific drawing of a pita with meat spilling out of it that's on the side of the truck. I don't really care about the shirt because his jaw is covered with stubble the color of warm cinnamon that I immediately imagine rubbing my nose against.

"What did you do that for?" He picks up the dispenser and puts it on the steps of his truck. It looks like I've dented it.

I stammer out an apology as he gathers the rest of the dispensers from the picnic tables. But he can't open the door with his arms full.

"I'll get that." I jump up and open the door. He stomps past me, letting the door slam behind him. I wait, not sure if he's coming back.

Then the door opens a foot or so, and a sinewy arm covered with cinnamon-colored hair holds out something wrapped in foil. It smells fantastic, and I take it quickly, before the door shuts again. I eat the whole thing standing up, in about four bites, tahini sauce and chicken juice dripping all over my tank top. It seems Paul Newman's made up his mind to hide in his shawarma truck, so what the hell. Why shouldn't I go for it?

But then, just as I'm wishing I'd torn a few napkins from the dispenser before I chucked it at the truck, the door opens and he clatters down the steps. I execute a surreptitious wipe of my chin on my shoulder.

"Sorry about that," he says gruffly.

"Me too. I'm sorry too." I dip into my wallet for my hundred and hold it out to him.

He squints at it, then laughs. "I don't have change for a hundred. But don't worry about it—it's on me."

I stuff it back in my wallet. "I mean, I don't blame you for not wanting to serve me. It's late. I can't imagine what it's like to be a student and have the responsibility of providing those amazing pitas to twenty-eight thousand students and faculty, give or take. That's really intense. And classes haven't even started yet. I mean, whoa."

I mean, whoa? Could I sound dumber? Not to mention, I can't believe how much I just said to this guy. I don't talk this much to people I've known for years.

"You have no idea," he says.

I blink at him. He and I are the same height, approximately, about five feet five. The physics of kissing this guy would be perfect, requiring just a minimum amount of effort. *Just the slightest angling. The slightest push to enact the logic of Newton's third law . . .*

"You want to get a drink?" he asks.

I do, but I'm feeling overwhelmed by the idea of objects colliding from equal and opposite forces—and then kissing.

"You don't like beer?" he says.

I don't, but I'm not about to tell him that. And I really want to go with him. So, so much.

"I'm eighteen," I say.

He makes a *pfftt* sound. "I know a place we can go. It's no problem."

"You're legal?" It's a dumb question, but, aside from the spyware thing I just did back at the dorm, I'm generally a rule follower, and my brain needs all the facts. Especially if I have to factor in a potential ride in the back of a police cruiser.

"Hell no." He grins, revealing nothing more than a set of regular teeth and gums and slightly chapped lips. But somehow, together it's more. Together it forms this magical, incandescent something.

"I'm Rhys." He offers his hand. "Not *R-e-e-c-e. R-h-y-s*. It's Welsh."
"You're Welsh?"
"Grandfather is."
"Nice to meet you. I'm Shorie." We shake.
"Oh." He looks slightly confused, like everyone else who hears my name for the first time. "*S-h-o-r-i-e?*"
Oh my God. *We are spelling names. Equal and opposite forces.* "Yes. Exactly."

I think about a couple of things: No one knows where I am. I have no idea who this guy is. He is extremely good looking, but good genes and symmetrical facial features do not preclude the possibility of someone being a killer and/or rapist. But also, they do not preclude the possibility of someone being Mr. Right. Someone who spelled my name correctly on the very first try.

Also, Mom made me take self-defense classes my senior year, in preparation for going away to college. Not only did I not hate them, I ended up being kind of good at getting wrist control over an opponent. Especially one just my height.

"I should probably let my roommate know where I'm going," I say. There's a little tremor in my voice, which makes me blush. Good thing it's getting dark.

"Sure." He glances at my shoulder, my clavicle, where the yellow lace bra is creeping out of my shirt, then looks over at the truck and ruffles his cinnamon hair. It sticks up adorably, and I want to smooth it so badly. "I'll just lock up."

He disappears while I text Dele.

I met a guy and we went out to get beers. I'm safe so don't worry. Shorie

The text reads like I'm a forty-year-old woman instead of a bubbly college freshman reveling in her boundless new freedom. But truth be known, I've never been bubbly or reveling or any way most girls are. I've been myself for eighteen years. I guess there's no reason to stop now.

Dele's reply zooms back to me. Three lines of smiley faces with heart eyes. I put my phone in the pocket of my pants as Rhys clatters down the steps and locks the door.

"All set?" he says.

I nod.

"You feel safe?"

I gaze into his eyes. They are the most beautiful shade of caramel, fringed by lashes the same color as the hairs on his arms. He is cinnamon, caramel, and a dozen other dessert-themed colors that I can't think of right now because my brain has switched over to some unknown frequency. I am in danger, I think, just not in the way he's talking about.

"Yes."

He drives a beat-up orange VW van with the grungiest seats I've ever seen. He brushes McDonald's wrappers, water bottles, and about a pound of crumbs off onto the floorboard, and I climb in, trying not to think about the community of germs my butt is nestling into. He connects his phone to the radio and Run the Jewels plays. Okay, that works. I sit back (gingerly) against the seat and try to relax.

We head out of Auburn—past Toomer's Corner, and over the train tracks. Eventually all the signs of modern civilization have disappeared, and we're out in the country. Stands of towering pines then cow fields flank both sides of the blacktop, and now there are so few streetlights I can see actual stars forming a canopy over the rolling hills.

We drive and drive, talking about where we're from and where we went to high school. I've just about made up my mind that if I have to be kidnapped, at least I'm being kidnapped by probably the single best-looking offender in FBI Most Wanted history, when Rhys pulls the wheel and guns it up a gravel drive.

We park in the grass alongside a bunch of other cars, in front of a ramshackle farmhouse on the crest of a hill. The house is lit up with more string lights than any house I've ever seen, even at Christmas.

There are white ones and multicolored ones, so many, in fact, that I can see the house is painted light blue with white trim. There's music blaring, too, the Death Grips, and there are people everywhere. And a guy nestled into a hammock on the screened-in front porch.

We climb the rickety steps. Even though five-eighths of the windowpanes on the front of the house are patched with cardboard, I can still see inside. The place is teeming. Rhys yanks the door, which seems to be stuck, and holds it open. I smell beer, weed, and something else. Something electric. The way it used to smell at Jax, back in the beginning.

I turn to him in wonder. "What is this place?"

He sighs, his face grim. "My office."

17

ERIN

With all the *trois* this and *trois* that, I expect to be staying in cottage three. But I'm actually in number twelve. This, it occurs to me, encapsulates the way Hidden Sands makes me feel. Like I'm out of the loop. I guess that shouldn't come as a big surprise. I'm used to being in charge, and when I'm not, it throws me off-balance.

My cottage is painted in what I'm quickly coming to think of as Hidden Sands White, a shade I'm pretty sure is going to end up giving me a splitting headache in this blinding Caribbean sunshine. The cottage is perched on a high ledge above the crescent beach and overrun, quaintly so, with a lush purple blooming vine. Inside, the small bedroom/sitting room combo smells of lavender-scented cleaner. My duffel and purse sit on a luggage rack, and I do a quick check. Wallet, passport—everything's there, not that I'm going to need any of it. But it does make me feel better. Like my extra jeans and T-shirt from home would make me feel, if they weren't banned.

To be fair, the clothes they gave me aren't bad. Three pair of unbelievably soft, beige drawstring pants made out of some stretchy-silky cotton blend. Three luxe white tank tops with the most spectacular barely there built-in bra. And this drapey, lightweight cardigan that I'm already planning to smuggle home in my tiny duffel.

No shoes. Everyone goes barefoot, because, as Grigore explained, those are the rules. To me, it's just another psyops-style tactic. Also, I wonder what will happen if there's some sort of natural disaster—a landslide, earthquake, or jeez, I don't know, volcano eruption? How will we all escape? Town cars and golf carts, I guess.

I assess the single room: white plaster walls, wood floor, no blinds or curtains on the windows. The only furniture a downy-looking king-size bed, low dresser, and one nightstand with a lamp. Everything is so clean it practically sparkles. There's a tiny attached bathroom, the entirety of which I can see from where I'm standing. When I venture inside the cramped space, I notice something amiss.

"What happened to the shower curtain?" I ask.

"I'll have housekeeping take care of that right away," Grigore says from the room.

Upon closer inspection, I see that there's also no rod. The shower curtain is the kind that attaches with Velcro to the ceiling. I've seen pictures of these before. They're used in psychiatric and correctional facilities. To prevent ligatures.

I scoot out of the bathroom in time to see Grigore slide open the balcony doors. By now, the humidity has made my hair grow ten times its normal size. I'm starting to feel like I'm Medusa, strands slithering into my eyes and mouth and down my neck. But the breeze feels nice.

I join Grigore at the iron rail. "The balcony's accessible anytime," he says, gazing out over the leafy hill that drops gently down to the curved white beach lapped by turquoise water. The sun's already gone down, but there are still streaks of pink and orange and lavender spilling out over the horizon.

"Should I feel the need to jump," I say.

He smiles. "If you did, you'd just roll down the hill and end up with a couple of bruises or a twisted ankle, tops."

I note that, on either end of the sandy crescent, high cliffs block any view. In spite of the string of cottages that line the ridge on either side of mine, I feel isolated. Perfectly and completely alone in this place. No one's on the beach below my balcony, not one sunbather, not even a yoga class. I am suddenly filled with longing for Shorie. I wonder if Dele is looking after her. I hope so.

"Perhaps you could meditate instead." Grigore gestures to the nearby cottages.

From my vantage point, I can see the balconies of the other cottages, and on at least half of them are women, dressed in the Hidden Sands uniform, their hair loose. Their eyes are closed, expressions serene, doing their thing. It looks peaceful. Bees swarm the purple blooms creeping up the side of the balcony and up onto the overhang. I close my eyes too. Their music fills my head. Even then, it doesn't drown out the memories.

When Shorie was young, she was deathly afraid of bees, especially the fat kind that didn't sting but dive-bombed her head every time she went outside. One day, after swimming at the neighborhood pool, Perry pointed out a lilac bush that had just bloomed. *Mom loves lilacs. They're her favorite flower,* he told her. Which was true, even though I'd only mentioned it once, back when we first met our freshman year at Auburn. Perry always remembered those kinds of things—the small details that other men usually forgot.

Shorie was terrified, but she'd always been willing to do anything for Perry, and a little bit later they came home with armfuls of the fragrant purple blossoms. That night when we were in bed, Perry pulled up a video on his phone.

Shorie, hair wet, shivers in her beach towel next to the lilac bush at the end of our street. Her eyes are closed, freckles standing out on her snub nose, brown lashes fluttering because she's concentrating so hard on standing still.

The bees swarm her and swarm her, and after a moment or two, a slow grin transforms her face. She's blissed out. "They're singing me a song," she says, then tilts her face back and starts to giggle. The shot tightens on her face. Shorie laughs and the bees laugh and my handsome, loving, big-hearted husband laughs with them all, making the camera shake so much that he loses Shorie altogether and it's just a series of quick pans of a lilac bush and the grass and the blue, cloudless summer sky . . .

And then I think of Shorie's face, looking at me across the kitchen table yesterday afternoon. I've failed her in so many ways. Messed everything up so badly that now I'm at a rehab facility, for the love of God. How did I let things get so out of hand?

When I open my eyes, Grigore has vanished. And so has his golf cart. I pad back into the bare room and sit on the bed and wonder what I'm supposed to do next. The tropical vibe makes me want a fruity rum drink or maybe to order up room service and watch movies in bed. But this isn't vacation, and there's no TV or bar in my room. There's nothing here but my own crowding, guilt-inducing thoughts about Perry and Shorie.

I amble out onto my cottage's miniscule front patio. The sun's already set, but there are lights everywhere—lanterns on the cottages and rows and rows of blazing iron tiki torches. I look to my right, down the line of cottages that stretches along the jungle path, maybe as far as the cliffs. It's hard to say; the darkness and the leafy tangle obscure my view. To my left, there are at least a dozen cottages separating mine from the main building. I set off in the direction of the spa—no locking the door, as they don't believe in keys around here, apparently. There's about forty-five minutes before dinner, and since Grigore didn't leave me with any instructions, I'm guessing I'm free to explore the place.

I keep to a narrow grass path, which is soft and spongy under my feet. I only notice it now—all the landscaping around here is reversed. The paths are grass; the beds, gravel sprouting with palms and birds of paradise and frangipani. The message is clear. Stay on the paths.

I sense someone behind me and jump.

"Sorry. Didn't mean to startle you." It's a woman, tall and pretty in that aging cheerleader way, with a perfectly highlighted blonde bob, sharp eyes, and a husky voice. Her face is lined—delicately so, probably from hours on the tennis court—but something about the twist of her lips and the no-bullshit light in her eyes raises my antennae. She's either an entrepreneur or an executive, has to be.

"I'm in cottage nineteen. Deirdre," she says. "Are you new too?"

"Twelve. Erin Gaines. Just got here a couple of hours ago." We shake and start back down the path side by side. "Did your guy, your concierge, give you a schedule or a map or anything?"

"Nope," she says. "Too busy strutting around, flexing his arms, trying to give me a lady boner."

"They are all strangely good looking," I agree. "Are you un, deux, ou trois?"

"Trois. I think it's the people without major drug or alcohol addictions." She eyes me, and I suddenly realize how awkward it's going to be here, trying to meet people without prying into their lives.

"Sounds about right. I'm here just to take a break from work."

She grins. "Ah, work. The ultimate addiction."

"You've got that right."

We arrive at the main building, and the doormen open the doors for us. The lobby is the same as it was an hour ago. And yet somehow different. Still deliciously cool and fragrant and buzzing with insanely attractive staff, male and female. And then it hits me. The light is no longer green. It's salmon colored—the gentle pink-orange of a sunset.

No one's manning the concierge desk, and as we navigate our way over the stream and down one of the corridors, none of the staff takes notice of us. Halfway down the hall, we find a frosted glass door with the word **YOGA** etched into it.

I can just make out the dimly lit wood-paneled room on the other side, hear the flute music playing in the background. The instructor, an ethereal-looking redhead, so pale the veins in her neck stand out like tattoos, holds a graceful tree pose, arms overhead. Her eyes are closed, face lifted, nostrils flared. Tendrils of damp hair encircle her neck; tufts of reddish hair fur her armpits. The class follows her lead, a dozen or so women in the room, every size and shape of glistening body completely naked.

"Oh dear," I whisper.

"I am *so* doing that," Deirdre says.

"I am *not* doing that," I say simultaneously.

Suddenly the door, which is automatic, apparently, and which I've activated, slides into its pocket with a neat *shunk*. Deirdre and I are standing in full view of the whole class. The teacher opens her eyes, and a couple of the students twist around.

"Join us, ladies?" the redhead says.

"No," I practically scream.

"Later, for sure," Deirdre says.

"Sorry to interrupt," I say.

We slink away, giggling like a couple of preteen girls. Behind us, I hear the automatic door hiss closed. "That better not be mandatory," I say and head for another door labeled **WELL SPA**. I wave my hand, and the door obligingly slides open. Deirdre slips in, beckoning me with a conspiratorial grin.

This room is a perfect jewel of rose-veined white marble—walls, floor, and ceiling—and plush, low-slung leather chairs. The whole length of wall facing us is a waterfall, running over green glass tiles, foamy and white. Every other wall is lined with planters overflowing with varieties of succulent and vine and fern. It smells like a combination of rosemary and lavender and jungle.

From one of the back rooms, we hear a woman shriek.

Deirdre's eyes go wide. "What the hell?"

"Somebody getting a massage?" I whisper.

I imagine myself on a table, naked under a sheet. Letting someone dig into the knots in my neck and shoulders and lower back that seem to have formed and made themselves a permanent part of my body in the past five months.

What would it feel like to let go of them after holding on so long? Would I wail like that? I feel a rush of panic, and I'm suddenly bathed in sweat. I don't know how I'm going to make it through an entire month in this place.

There's another wail. Not a scream exactly, something more subdued. Then the woman starts to sob. Deirdre and I exchange wide-eyed glances.

"Jesus," Deirdre breathes.

Then we hear a woman's voice, low and controlled. "Agnes, talk to me."

"I don't want to talk," comes the subdued reply. "I just want you to let me go home."

"You know I can't allow you to do that. Your family sent you here, and they insist you not return until you've earned your L'Élu certificate."

More sobs.

The woman continues. "Agnes. What you need to understand is that L'Élu is not just a physical challenge. It's a vision quest. A chance to shut out all the noise of the world—all the things that distract us from what's most important—and accept what the universe is trying to tell us." A beat, then the woman speaks again, slowly. Deliberately. "The universe is trying to tell you something, Agnes. Can you hear what it's saying?"

There's no answer, only the sound of crying.

"It's saying that your life is not your own. But that you are part of a family and must subjugate your desires to the greater need. It is saying your father has found a wonderful opportunity for you, to marry a man who can take care of you for the rest of your life. It is saying you need to gratefully accept the opportunity. Do you understand, Agnes?"

A muffled, "Yes."

"I've spoken with your father and told him that, instead of kicking you out, I'm willing to give you one more chance. I'll be sending you on another L'Élu. Not L'Élu un. L'Élu trois—have you heard of it?"

"No."

"I think it's just the right experience for you, Agnes. So you can get to the heart of what's bothering you. Sound good? You'll leave tomorrow morning, so I suggest—"

"Ladies?"

Deirdre and I spin to face a young woman—Filipino, I think, another ten, with a slicked-back ponytail and white sarong. She's standing behind us and smiling. I wonder how long she's been there.

"It's almost time for dinner," the woman says smoothly. "Would you like me to show you the way to the dining hall?"

"Sure," Deirdre says with just enough snark in her voice to show she's not buying into this whole Hidden Sands thing and can't be bossed around, even by a beauty queen in a sarong.

I'm not quite as plucky. After hearing the conversation down the hall, I feel distinctly sick to my stomach. Something is definitely wrong with this place. And I do not belong here, no matter what Sabine and Ben and the rest of them think.

But, "Thank you," I say, because I can't exactly make a run for it now, and the beautiful woman escorts the two of us out of the marble waterfall room.

18

SHORIE

Not only is this Rhys's office, but apparently he's the boss. I know this because when we walk in, a kid yells out, "Hey, boss!" Then another one says, "Hide the cocaine!" and the rest of the room bursts out laughing. Rhys does not look amused.

There's music playing, but no one's partying. Instead, they're sitting around on the tattered furniture, tapping away on computers or talking in groups in hushed voices.

"Um, everybody," Rhys says. "This is Shorie. Shorie, everybody."

Everybody—which, as far as I can tell, is just a bunch of college students—looks up and smiles and says, "Hi, Shorie," in unison. I murmur a hello, and they go back to what they were doing.

Rhys steers me into a dark hallway. Before we can get to wherever it is we're going, though, a lanky guy with a mop of blond hair, green frames, and unbuttoned shirttails that flap over a worn NASA T-shirt blocks our way. He's holding up a brown bottle, some kind of craft beer I don't recognize. He offers the beer to Rhys with a hat-tip flourish, even though he's not wearing a hat.

Rhys hands the beer to me. "What the hell is going on in here, Low?"

"Campus Wi-Fi melted down. I told everyone to come here and we'd do a verbal. Get through it super quick. Tristan and Mackenzie brought snacks, and we had some of the stuff from last time, but you have no idea how hard it's been to keep them out of your stash. I had Carly hide it in her . . . in the . . ." He suddenly takes note of my presence. "Oh, good! Are you the new comp girl? My God. You're so pretty. You sure you're not lost?" He guffaws.

"She's not the new comp girl, Lowell. But could you . . . could you just excuse us a minute?"

Lowell grins a toothy grin. "I'm Lowell. Rhys's assistant."

"Shorie Gaines."

His eyes widen, and he shakes his head. "Oh! Right! Of course." I glance at Rhys, but he's staring at Lowell with great intensity. Lowell and I shake, and Lowell does the goofy hat-tip thing again, this time at me. "It's a pleasure, Shorie. Really. Welcome aboard. And well done, my man, if I do say so myself."

"Okay, off we go." Rhys grabs my hand, tugging me down the hall.

"Get her to fix our lame-ass website, while you're at it!" Lowell calls after us, just as Rhys kicks open a slightly crooked door and hustles us inside a dimly lit room. He moves to shut the door behind me, but I catch it before he can. Our eyes meet, and I flash to a memory.

My dad, chasing five-year-old me through the house in a game of hide-and-seek and chanting a song: *Eeny, meeny, miny, mo. I will find you wherever you go . . .*

The creepy way he used to sing it as he prowled around always scared the shit out of me. So much so that at one point, I decided to turn it around on him. I hid in a closet and waited until I saw the doorknob just begin to turn. Then I shoved open the door and jumped out at him, letting loose with a high-pitched little "boo!" The plot had its intended effect. I don't think I'd ever seen an adult scream like that.

Now, standing here in this guy's bedroom, I'm overcome with all the same jittery hide-and-seek feelings. I have no idea what's going to happen next. What I do know is that I'm the one who holds the power of "boo."

I stand as straight as I can. "Does that guy know me?"

"No . . . ," Rhys begins, flustered.

"He sort of acted like he did. And he congratulated you like you just bagged a trophy elephant."

"That's not what he meant, I swear. His social skills are rudimentary, at best. He's like the antithesis of a wingman. He repels women away from his friends."

He didn't answer the question, and whatever that nonsense was that he did just spout, I'm not buying. But I don't say anything, because I'm basically struck speechless at the sight of his room.

First of all, it's huge. With a mega-expensive-looking platform bed on top of an antique rug. Persian, I think. There's a painting on the wall—a tiny abstract oil of some kind of still life with oranges and a milk bottle on a rumpled tablecloth that looks like something you'd see in a Dutch museum. Up against the wall is a giant desk topped in black marble that looks like it belongs in a CEO's office. Three huge, 4K monitors on the desk display elaborate-looking spreadsheets. Rhys must see me taking it all in because he moves to the desk and claps shut his laptop. The monitors go dark.

"What the hell was that?" I ask.

He sits in the chair—a black plastic futuristic thing that leans back with a sleek pneumatic whoosh. "It's my business."

"Shawarma-Rama?" I draw closer, magnetized by the information that just vanished from the screens.

"No. That's where my buddy works. He was doing something for me, so I filled in for him."

"He was doing something for you?"

"For my business." He does a kind of half-hearted gesture at the computer screens.

"That's your business? And all those kids out there?"

He swallows, and for the first time, it occurs to me that he seems nervous. Which is kind of a surprising development. Usually I'm the one feeling awkward in situations like these. Not that I've ever been in a situation quite like this.

"So," he starts. "Here's the thing. Lowell does know who you are. I do too."

"Okay," I say slowly.

"Shorie Gaines. Freshman, Amelia Boynton Hall, roommate Adelia Foster. Majoring in comp sci and software engineering. Full academic ride, with all the trimmings. Meal plan, books, box seats for home games."

I cross my arms over my chest, feeling suddenly very shaky. And deeply regretful that I've just followed a boy I don't know back to his house at the end of a gravel road in the middle of a field in the country. At night.

"How do you know all that?" I ask in a faint voice.

"It's something I do for my business. For recruiting purposes."

I feel like I can't move. This guy researched me? For his business?

"I swear, it's not as creepy as it sounds," he adds lamely.

"Wait. Are you a student? How old are you?"

"On and off. I'm twenty. Just turned."

"And you knew who I was when I walked up to the food truck?"

"Yes."

"So why didn't you pitch me on your business thing then? Why did you close the window?"

He clears his throat for a really long time. "I guess I didn't feel like I was ready. I'd seen your pictures and all. But when you walked up to the truck, it was like . . . you weren't what I expected." He looks flushed, embarrassed. "And then you threw the napkins, and I thought it was really . . ." He seems uncertain. "I thought that was pretty feisty, so then, I decided what the hell."

Okay, I'm definitely confused. For a second, it seemed like Rhys might be nervous because he liked me. But now he's telling me he thinks I'm feisty. Which, I'm not sure, may be code for bitchy. So here I am, hanging out with a guy in his oddly grown-up-looking bedroom, alone. A guy who knows about me for some strange, stalker-y reason, who brought me back to his bedroom. Where we are now hanging out, just the two of us. In the semidarkness.

I put down my beer. "I should go."

"We would've met eventually anyway," he goes on quickly. "We usually try to arrange it so the pitch is more natural, though. Through a friend of a friend. Or at a party."

"I'll call a car." I move to the door. "I can wait out on the porch."

"Hold up, okay," he says, and like a fool, I do. It's the caramel and cinnamon thing he's got going on, plus probably his way with chicken shawarma. A lot to resist. He stands, approaches me cautiously. "I'll tell you everything, lay it all out, and then, I guess, it's up to you to say yes or no."

"Yes or no?" I give him my feistiest glare. *Wrist control,* I think. *The power of boo.* If I have to, I know I can get myself out of here.

He opens the laptop, and the monitors light up again. After a few taps, I see the spreadsheets.

He points to the screen on the left. "This is the class of 2023, *a* to *z*. The ones on academic or athletic scholarships are highlighted in yellow." He points to the middle rainbow-coded table. "This is my available pool of freelancers—sophomores, juniors, seniors. Some working on advanced degrees. The ones shaded in pink can take your English Comp I or II for you and earn you a ninety or above. Purples, the same for any core history class, including tech and civ. Greens do core social sciences and Core Science Sequence I and II. Brown, any math."

"And the screen on the end?" That one is different; it has a graphic of outer space behind all the rows and rows of text.

"Oh." He looks super flustered and clicks off the monitor. "That's *Eve Online*. My fleet data."

I laugh in spite of my nerves. "And that's the screen you're embarrassed for me to see?"

He flushes. Inhales. "So here's the deal. I started this company last year. I'm a junior . . . and change. Not enrolled this semester because fall is always busy. For a reasonable fee, I can have someone—a surrogate—take one or more of your core freshman classes, freeing you up for endeavors that make better use of your time."

I blink slowly, taking it in. I'm not sure exactly what he's talking about, but it sure sounds an awful lot like cheating.

"Some kids' majors are just total grinds, right? And their parents have no idea that if they actually finish it in the four years required, they'll wind up drooling in a drain ditch somewhere or jumping off the roof of Haley Center. So they can take additional classes and get ahead without stressing so much. And then there are some kids, the really brilliant ones, who are already being pursued by top companies. They use the time to freelance because they're gonna make way more than what they pay me. And then there are the rest."

"The rest?"

"They just want to get stoned all semester."

"So which category do I fall into? Because obviously you've heard of Jax. And you know who my parents are."

He scratches his jaw, then plants his hands on his hips. For some weird reason, it makes me think of my dad.

"I mean, I've heard of them, yes," he says.

"You said you memorized everything about me. Well, surely you know that, along with being awarded a four-year full ride from National Women in STEM, my parents created Jax."

"I know. But our recruiting lists are just educated guesses about who might be interested. I didn't know which category you fell into. If you fell into any of them." His eyes meet mine. "You seemed like somebody who really liked school."

I move closer to the monitors, studying the columns. There are scores of names, reams of student ID numbers, phone numbers, class locations, and teachers. And there's a final column labeled *Tiger Card*. So the guy has to provide fake student ID cards or apps or however he does it, on top of everything else. This operation makes the Russian mob look like kindergarten.

But, honestly? In an odd way, it kind of excites me. The same way downloading that spyware on the anonymous Jax user excited me. This is not the kind of person I used to be—sneaking and conniving—but, I don't know, things change, I guess. I mean look at how everything's changed since Dad died. Why shouldn't I change too?

"How much do you charge?" I ask.

"That's not why I asked you over here, Shorie. For real."

"But you were planning to, eventually. Run into me at lunch somewhere, or a party. Right?"

"Yeah. I guess."

I think of Mom, stretched out on a chaise on the beach, drinking some kind of health smoothie. Rhys is definitely the kind of person she'd be intrigued by. And, putting aside the illegal aspect of what he's doing, she'd definitely want to hear about his business. She never passes up opportunities to hear about innovative ideas.

I take a deep breath and lock eyes with him, Mom style. "So pitch me the deal."

Then my phone chimes, alerting me of a notification from the spyware I installed. I've received my first screenshot from Mr. or Mrs. 323a456-a97e-12d3-b654-829625410000's Jax account. Holy smokes.

"One second," I say to Rhys, and click on the alert, holding my breath. In the time I've been here, I've gotten three of them. The first is a private message, sent to the monitored account from a user who's named his profile "Yours."

I miss you. Thinking of you naked.

And the reply from my anonymous friend, Don't message me here.

Ew. I make a face then turn away from Rhys so I can think. Yours has to be a guy; a girl wouldn't send a message like that, would she? Naked messages typically originate from guys, I think. Which leads me to believe my anonymous user is probably a female.

On the other hand, I could be basing this on a false assumption—a stereotype I've derived from my own prejudices. What if girls text guys that they're picturing them naked all the time, and I'm the weirdo who's never heard about it? It wouldn't surprise me. Half the time, I feel like a runtime error in human form.

I check out the second screenshot, the allotment balances, which include categories like housing, insurance, and debt reduction. So, she's older. An adult, with monthly budget categories that total roughly fifteen thousand dollars. Pretty well-off individual, this Ms. X. In the top 5 percent, easy. Everything else looks pretty normal.

I move on to the next picture, another screenshot of the allotments.

"Holy shit," I croak.

"What?" Rhys asks.

I'd almost forgotten that I was standing in a cute guy's room. "Uh, just an unexpected email. Hold on."

I study the shot again. From a mere thirty minutes earlier, the allotments have all gone up, each category's balance having risen substantially. I do the math. Roughly $162,000 just got dumped into this person's account.

My brain is clicking away, moving the facts around, considering alternatives. Ms. X doesn't want her sext buddy to contact her over Jax. Probably because she's meddling in Jax's servers anonymously without an admin identifier, fixing a weird-looking deadlock that I've never encountered in all my years of shadowing Dad. There's something going on with this account, that's for damn sure. Something illegal, maybe.

A brand-new thought occurs to me, something I've never considered, not once in my whole hardworking, straight-arrow, do-what-you're-told life: Sometimes breaking the rules isn't just for fun. Sometimes it's an absolutely, utterly essential move so you can find other rule breakers.

And that's my responsibility, isn't it, while my mother's gone? One greater than going to class or making good grades or meeting cute guys. To find out who's messing around with Jax?

I click off my phone and turn back to Rhys, who's fiddling with his keyboard. "So how much?" I say.

"What?"

"How much would you charge me if I wanted a surrogate to take all five of my fall semester classes?" I'm thinking fast here. It's going to take time to track down the journal and to monitor the activity on this Ms. X's account. Time to figure out how all these elements fit together, if they fit together at all. And Rhys happens to be someone who can give me that time.

"All five?" he says. "Even Intro to Engineering?"

"Yes."

"Six hundred and fifty per class, plus five hundred for the new Tiger Card, that's—"

"Thirty-seven fifty. How do you take payment?"

"Cash. But classes start in three days—"

"What? Is it too late?"

"No," he says slowly. "No. I have a lot of people on call." He hesitates. "Do you want to get out of here?"

I smile.

19

ERIN

The lobby's changed colors. It's now a soft twilight lavender, and there's not a soul in sight. The Filipino woman leads us beside the rippling indoor stream and toward the back.

A series of columned arches opens up into a large wood-paneled room scattered with round tables. The only sound is the muted clink of cutlery against china. About thirty or so women, dressed in the Hidden Sands outfit, have already started the meal. Heads down, they all chew in silence. Deirdre and I exchange glances.

"Bon appétit," the Filipino woman says and leaves us.

At the buffet, we heap salad, a vegetarian couscous concoction, and grilled fish onto plates monogrammed with a gold *HS*, then sit at a table with three other women.

"Hi," I say, nodding all around. The women jerk up their heads and stare. Deirdre bursts into laughter.

Bang!

We look up to see a tall, red-cheeked woman, dressed in chef's whites, standing at our table. She's just thwacked the table with a huge metal cooking spoon. Her eyes narrow at Deirdre.

"Honor the food," she says. "Engage all the senses as you eat. Be mindful. Start with the salad. Small bites, ten chews before swallowing. At the bell, move on to the entrée."

A laugh wants to bubble out of me, but at the woman's stern look, I stifle it.

"No talking," she repeats, and spins on her heel.

"I'm calling that one Aunt Lydia." Deirdre shoves a mountainous bite of couscous into her mouth, chews loudly a couple of times, and then swallows it down.

From the lavender glow of the main reception area, a woman appears beneath the arch. Her gaze sweeps over the room; then she spots us and strides toward our table. Up close I see that she's young, closer to Shorie's age than mine. She stops at our table.

"Hello." She has a cherub's face, sunny and makeup free. Her white-blonde hair is woven in a complex system of braids forming a crown around her head. Her nose is just pert enough to give her a childlike, innocent look. She's wearing the same thing as Deirdre and me—the pajama pants from heaven, tank, and cardigan. Underneath she's got a knockout body.

She smiles warmly at us. "Newcomers, would you follow me, please?"

We leave our plates, and outside in the shadowy reception area, she clasps my hand in hers. "Erin Gaines, it's such a pleasure to finally meet you. I heard you arrived later this afternoon, after the morning orientation. I'm Antonia Erdman, the owner of Hidden Sands." She glances at Deirdre. "And Ms. Galliani, of course. So happy to have you both here."

In the lavender light, the woman looks like a teenager. It seems hard to reconcile that somebody so young could possibly own a huge resort like this. But of course, as Grigore said, her wealthy father gave the place to her. A playhouse to keep the princess occupied. Must be nice.

Antonia sneaks a glance into the dining hall, then tilts her head in the other direction. "Would you two like to come back to my office and eat with me? Where we can talk in private?"

"Absolutely," Deirdre says.

"Sure," I say.

In a few minutes, we're through the lobby and down another shadowy corridor that leads us to Antonia's office. The space is expansive, all blond wood and Hidden Sands White and filled with expensive modern furniture. At one end of a floating credenza sits a tidy collection of bottles—high-quality scotch, rye, and bourbon, ringed by a set of crystal tumblers. I almost do a double take. A rather unexpected sight in the office of the owner of a rehabilitation center.

We sit on either side of an impressive acrylic-and-wood structure that looks more like a piece of art than a desk, and I examine the room. A cluster of silver-framed photos sits on the credenza behind her desk— the Erdman family on a sailboat, and the elder Erdman, about Arch's age from the looks of it, and his gorgeous, much younger, blonde wife at a formal event. There's also a photo of teenage Antonia, arm in arm with another teenager, a tall boy in sunglasses and a blue baseball cap.

I check out the walls. A series of four small paintings hangs on one wall. Jagged black slashes of paint, cut with random splotches of gold and pink.

"You're familiar with Tachism?" Antonia asks.

I shake my head. "Not really."

"Oh, you should look into it. It's such an unbridled expression of freedom."

A spectacularly good-looking young man (of course) delivers a stack of silver trays. I'm starving, and the meal looks like a delicious departure from the rabbit food they were serving in the dining room. Rare filet mignon, mashed potatoes, asparagus drizzled with hollandaise. Dessert is some kind of complicated fruit parfait. I try not to shove it in my face all at once, but by the time I'm halfway through the potatoes, I look up and notice that Antonia is watching me.

I send her a sheepish smile. "I guess I was hungrier than I thought."

"No, that's great. Go for it." She nods at me. "I wholeheartedly approve of the female appetite, in every way."

Okay.

"What do you think so far? Of Hidden Sands?" She's directing the question at me.

"I think it's amazing. I just . . ."

Antonia smiles encouragingly. "Go ahead. Say it."

Where to start? The bizarrely attractive staff? The grossly misleading brochure? The ever-so-slightly threatening private lecture happening in the spa? If I'm being honest, I want explanations for all of it, but I know better. This woman holds my immediate future in her hands. I need to keep things friendly.

"I'm a little surprised that somebody so young owns all this," I say.

Antonia's bright expression doesn't waver. "Yes. A lot of people look down on me because I didn't earn my position the bootstrap way, the way they like their one percent to get rich, but I can't help that. Caring what other people think is the fastest way to get yourself stuck. And what I lack in years I've made up for in personal experience. I struggled with addiction for a couple of years, when I was younger. Got into some trouble and spent some time in juvenile detention."

"Oh. I'm sorry."

"Don't be. I learned so much through the whole experience. That's why I keep those liquor bottles out. Every day those bottles and I fight a battle. And every day I win."

Not exactly your conventional twelve-step program, I think. And maybe unwise, having alcohol sitting out in the open like this in a place swarming with addicts. But it's not a mistake. Antonia Erdman may be young, but she strikes me as being far from careless.

"My addiction gives me a certain level of understanding of human nature," Antonia continues. "The tendency we have to use people. To gain power over others in our fight for survival."

She pushes aside her plate, the steak and potatoes untouched. She digs a spoon into her parfait, slides it into her mouth, licks it. "My father inherited a boutique hotel company from his father, and back in 1983, he bought this place. It was his favorite because it was so isolated. So pristine. He ran it personally for many years, then . . . well, after I ran into a little bit of trouble—for the third or fourth or fifth time—he decided I needed something to keep me busy, and he turned it over to me." She practically glimmers with pride. "I expanded the program far beyond what my father ever expected. Hidden Sands is one of Erdman International's highest-earning assets."

"It's a beautiful place," I say. "I've never seen anything like it."

"That's why I call it a restoration facility rather than a rehab. We have traditional rehab services for those who require them, but truthfully, we're here for anyone, at any point in their life. For any reason whatsoever. You choose your poison. So to speak." She grins. "I know you won't have your official tours until tomorrow, but in the meantime, is there anything you'd like to ask? Anything you're curious about?"

"My concierge's relationship status," Deirdre says.

"Actually, yes," I cut in. "Who were those women who came in earlier, into the shower? They looked really . . . beat up."

Antonia dips her spoon into her parfait again. "Ah, yes. They're our latest L'Élu group. Our wilderness survival experience. After a certain number of days at Hidden Sands—enough time to assess if you're ready—you partake in the experience."

"One of them was bleeding."

"It can be an intensely challenging experience. Accidents happen."

"Can we do something else?" Deirdre asks. "Naked yoga for a week?"

"No. Everyone has to complete a L'Élu at the end of their stay to officially graduate from the program."

I lean forward. "You said 'a certain number of days.' Does that mean we could get out of here sooner than a month?"

"Well, it all comes down to satisfying the family's request and occasionally a court order, but, all things being equal, yes. A few women who really want to dig into their recovery can attempt one sooner to try for early release."

Early release. The words ring out like the chime of a church bell. I hadn't realized that was a possibility, but now my head pulses with images: An early flight from Miami to Birmingham, the quick drive down to Auburn. A dinner out with Shorie, during which I apologize for being Mom in absentia for the past several months and invite her to tell me exactly how she feels. Ben too. Maybe not a dinner, though. A talk at the office.

The point is, with both of them, I would own up to my lack of self-awareness and fragility in the wake of Perry's death. I would apologize—thoroughly and completely—for all my failures.

Swear to do better. To *be* better . . .

Beside me, Deirdre groans softly and pushes her tray back. Antonia leans forward, a look of concern on her face. "Deirdre?"

"Ouf. My apologies. Something just hit me."

"The food?"

"Oh, no. The food was perfect." She clutches her stomach. "Probably just the travel."

"Would you like me to dial the nurse?" Antonia says. "We have a fully outfitted clinic if you need anything. Holistic treatments for any ailment."

Deirdre waves her hand. "No, I'll be fine, I'm sure."

Antonia stands. "Hold on," she says, and disappears behind a door.

"Are you okay?" I ask Deirdre.

She moves to the credenza, expertly slides the bottle of bourbon under her wrap and into the depths of her yoga pants, then returns to her chair. I almost laugh at how smoothly she does it, and how outrageous a move it is.

Shortly Antonia reappears with a bright-pink bottle. "The good stuff. From my private stash."

Deirdre shakes her head. "I can't take your Pepto."

Antonia waves her off. "I'm fully stocked. Take it, and we'll see you in the morning." She attends to something on her computer, and in a flash, Deirdre's through the door. My heart thunders, as if I were the one who just swiped a bottle of liquor.

Antonia turns from her computer and smiles at me. I smile back.

"Did you see that?" she asks me. "She took the whiskey."

I hold my breath. I don't know Deirdre well, but I'm not sure I want to rat out a fellow guest to the owner of the spa. It feels like stepping into a minefield.

Antonia flutters her hand. "My best guess is she's taking that bottle right back to her cottage, where she's going to share it with her concierge. Which is fine, as she's not here for a drinking problem. Or a sex addition, that I'm aware of."

It takes all my self-control to keep my mouth from dropping open.

"Have you met Dimitri?" she asks.

"Ah, no."

"An interesting young man. Handsome, of course, as they all are. Pleasant disposition. Smart-ish." She leans back in her chair. "He's nowhere close to as interesting as Deirdre's husband, though, in my opinion. Did Deirdre tell you anything about him?"

I shake my head, dumbfounded at the turn in the conversation.

"His name is Michael. Forty-four, freelance writer and college journalism professor. Doesn't make a lot of money, not the kind Deirdre wants. But he works around the clock, and he loves her. Hard to fathom preferring Dimitri over a man like that. But I guess we all make our choices, don't we?"

A strand of her white-blonde hair has come loose from the braid, the tendril framing her face. Shock has all but immobilized me. I am stunned at everything she's just said. Has this woman ever heard of a breach of confidentiality? What the hell kind of rehab is this?

One surrounded with a cadre of waving red flags, that's for sure.

Her lips part, and a tip of pink tongue darts up over her top teeth as she leans forward, templing her fingers. "I know you're dying to ask me. Don't you want to know why Deirdre's really here?"

I can't look away from her. I'm stunned at her behavior but also, in a strange way, mesmerized. I feel like I've woken up in some alternate universe.

"Of course, it's none of your business. And normally, this kind of information is for my eyes only. But you're an exception, Erin. I really respect you . . . and would be interested in your perspective. Rest assured, this conversation would be just between you and me."

It feels all kinds of wrong, but her words have ignited my curiosity, and it's quickly overtaking my caution. I take in a measured breath.

"Okay. Why is she here?"

She stares at me over the peak of her fingers. "She's in the rub-and-tug business. Our lovely friend, Deirdre Galliani, who lives in Boston with her devoted husband, Michael, and her two young children, happens to run a wildly successful massage operation in a high-end community in central Florida. Dozens of employees, beautiful young women, working their way through college mostly. Three locations, all rental houses in exclusive neighborhoods. She's made a lot of money for years, all tax free, of course." She winks. "Been lying for years about the business to her family back in Boston. Told them she was in the importing business." She lets out a delicate little snort. "Why do they always say that? That they're in the importing business? It's so obviously a cover."

I shake my head. "I don't know."

"They just found out—her husband, parents, and children. Saw all the dirty details, pictures, documents, the whole nine yards. So her husband sent her to Hidden Sands to reconsider her life. To decide whether she wants her family—her life with them and position in the community—or the business."

She hesitates, her voice slow and girlish and just the faintest bit shy. "I have a confession—I was hoping she would take the alcohol so you and I could chat alone." She leans forward, eyes sparking. "I know who you are, Erin. What you and your late husband did with your friends— creating a breakout app thousands of miles away from Silicon Valley. I've got to say, I admire you so much. In fact, I'm kind of starstruck just to be sitting here with you."

It's a line—utter bullshit—but her words send a small thrill of pride up my spine anyway.

She flushes, stammering a little. "As a businesswoman, you are such an example to me. To all young women. Starting a business in your forties."

"Well, I didn't do it alone."

"Of course not. Who does? I'm just saying that what you did do is really inspiring to me. You know"—she lays one delicate hand on her chest—"as a person who other people would like to write off."

"Write off?"

"You know. Young, privileged daughter of a wealthy man. I've got the fancy degree and all the right connections. I'm the person everyone loves to hate. So when I heard you were coming, I just felt . . ." She puts her hand over her heart again. Her nails are manicured in an intricate black and pale-pink ombré that I can't tear my eyes from. "I'm obsessed with Jax. Of course, Hidden Sands uses a modified merchant budget. And when anyone starts to work for me, I insist they sign up for Jax as well. It's really the foundation of all good financial decisions."

"You've got to stop," I say. "I'm going to start crying or self-deprecating or something."

"Oh God, not the dreaded self-deprecation." We both laugh, and she sends me a shy smile. "I hope I didn't make you feel uncomfortable."

"No, not at all. I'm flattered."

Flattered, I think, *just not fooled.*

"Erin." She pushes aside her tray, filet still untouched. "In your own words, why exactly are you here?"

I shift in my seat. "The night I dropped my daughter off at college, I had an episode. I blacked out, apparently borrowed a friend's car without asking."

"Do you have a drinking problem? Because that's not what your intake file says."

"May I see it?" I ask.

Antonia cocks her head. "How about I summarize it for you instead? You haven't been taking care of yourself properly since your husband's death. You've been working around the clock, but not fulfilling your responsibilities in an adequate manner. Sleeping a lot. Neglecting your daughter and the rest of your family."

I swallow down the lump in my throat. "Okay."

"Do you think you needed rehab for that, though? Why couldn't they have just sent you on a luxury Mediterranean cruise? Or at least something a little less rigorous than this place? I mean, come on." She laughs.

I want to agree, but I'm wary. I just watched this woman set up Deirdre, right in front of me, then break all kinds of confidentiality rules. And although I realize the whole episode was just a bit of amateur theater so she could show me who was boss, I don't trust her. She's got a chip on her shoulder and something to prove. And people like that can be dangerous. I'm thinking the smartest thing for me to do is to let Antonia Erdman scratch her dominance itch—and then, hopefully she'll feel like expediting my L'Élu and early release.

I shake my head. "I guess my friends and family thought I was on a destructive path. That I was about to make an unwise decision."

"Oh? What decision?"

"I'd rather not say."

She studies me. "Fair enough. But let's talk about how you feel. Do you think you belong at Hidden Sands?"

"I think I can get something out of the experience."

"Diplomatic answer. A person like you, a smart person, can get something out of any experience. I am a firm believer in the therapeutic model we've developed here at Hidden Sands. But I don't think it's for everybody. And I don't think it's what you need right now."

I wait.

"You've been through a terrible trauma, Erin. And the way I see it, you could really use a break. An opportunity to drop all your cares and worries and responsibilities and just let go."

I think about that kiss with Ben on my front steps. The feel of his rough cheek against mine. The easiness of being in his arms. It had felt so good to let down my guard, to not be sad about Perry or guilty about Jax or worried about Shorie. It had been such a relief just to *be*.

"It sounds wonderful, actually," I admit.

"It can be therapeutic to escape," she says. "From the days that keep marching by. The relationships that weigh us down with so many expectations. A break can allow you to let down your defenses. Heal the way your psyche wants to."

I feel like the conversation has taken yet another turn. One I don't fully understand. *Jesus. What is it with this woman?*

"I'd like to offer you another Hidden Sands experience," Antonia says evenly. "The VIP experience. There is a second L'Élu group. L'Élu II. It's strictly off the books—an alternative program we offer to a select few who do not wish or do not need to go through the traditional L'Élu I."

She's watching me expectantly, and now not only red flags are waving, but also flags of every other color of the rainbow.

"In a nutshell, for a substantially higher fee, you'll spend five days of absolute freedom at an undisclosed location on Ile Saint Sigo—to do whatever you want, with whomever you want, enjoying the kind of privacy and discretion only afforded by Hidden Sands' top-notch staff."

I stare at her. She waits.

"You mean," I finally say, "like, *whatever*."

She smiles. "In terms of the legalities of the particular activities you may choose to indulge in, we're a mostly privately owned island, under the jurisdiction of the Royal Saint Lucia Police. But they aren't known to take much notice about what's going on here." She lifts her eyebrows. "I do what I want on the island. And what I want is to offer you five full days and nights to do what *you* want—even if that's just Netflix and nap."

I level my gaze at her. "So, you're telling me, while my friends and family think I'm completing some kind of arduous, vision quest–style recovery program, really I'm sitting in the sun, drinking wine, and watching movies?"

"If that's what you choose, yes." She leans back in her cushy chair. "And at the end of the five days, you still go home with an authentic, verifiable Hidden Sands L'Élu certificate accepted by any doctor or court in the States."

I laugh in disbelief. *Netflix and nap.* Spooky how she knows exactly what I'd want to do if I had free time. I definitely underestimated this woman.

She continues. "We can access your account immediately. I take wire transfers through Jax, as it happens."

I shake my head. "I don't understand. Why would you offer me this?"

"I like you," she says simply. "And I admire what I've read about you. Other women I've liked and admired have appreciated the chance to experience L'Élu II. So much so that after they returned home, many chose to partner with Erdman International, in one way or another."

She regards me from across the desk. I smile.

Ah, yes. Here it is. The catch . . .

"I think we might work well together," she says. "I think I could add value as, I don't know, maybe a board member, or a consultant."

"Uh-huh."

"For example, have you considered who sent you here, Erin? Is there any reason they might have to want you out of the picture for a while? So they could have full and free access to Jax while you're gone?"

I haven't considered that. Not really. Not until just this second.

"Because I thought of it. And I think it's only right that I should mention it to you. You deserve partners who are going to look out for your best interests."

"It's not an issue," I say, but that's a lie. The intervention in my kitchen felt like a pile-on. Like it had been planned for a while, and Ben and Sabine and Layton and the rest of them were just waiting for me to mess up in a big enough way so they'd have their excuse. Like Antonia suggested, could there now be something going on back at Jax? Some kind of coup?

"Look, I want you to succeed, Erin. But I think you should do it on your terms. And, as someone who admires you greatly, I've got to be honest. I don't think you belong at Hidden Sands."

I don't either, I want to shout. For the first time in months, I feel like someone understands that I'm neither okay nor a wreck. I'm just somewhere in between. And now there's a way for everybody to get what they want.

But how will Shorie react if she discovers I paid extra to take some kind of shortcut? To cheat? She'll be furious. And I don't know if I can deal with that. I've already let her down in so many ways. Not to mention Ben and Sabine.

Goddammit. No. I refuse to give any of them the satisfaction of saying I didn't finish what I started. I refuse to let them win. So I'm going to take my medicine with a big, fat smile on my face.

I stand. "I appreciate the offer, Antonia. I really do. But I think I'm going to stick to the traditional experience. I may regret this, but I think I'll just complete the program, like everybody else."

She stands too and extends her hand, like I've just opted to skip dessert. "Of course. Whatever you prefer. I just wanted to put the offer out there in good faith."

And yet, somehow, this whole conversation has felt miles and miles away from good faith.

"Thank you for dinner," I say.

She gestures to the door. "Have a wonderful night, Erin."

When I find myself standing in the now midnight-blue lobby, Grigore is there. He tells me he can give me a ride in his golf cart, which is wedged into the gleaming line of town cars under the portico. While we wait for the caravan to move, four women spill out of the heavy wooden doors. Their knot tightens as they embrace one another. It's the L'Élu group I saw earlier in the showers, only now they're clean and dressed in civilian clothing.

Antonia appears in the portico, says a few words of farewell to the women, and kisses each of them on the cheek. All except one woman—the young Latina woman with glasses who showered next to me. Agnes. The one who was crying in the spa services room. The woman who failed her L'Élu because she didn't want to marry the man her father selected for her.

I wonder what it means for me. Would Antonia still give me my L'Élu certificate even though I turned down her offer to come on board at Jax? And would there be any other repercussions? Our conversation in her office had felt like a trap, maybe even a touch threatening—but maybe it had just been nothing more than two businesswomen talking.

After Antonia disappears, the three departing women load into the town car in front of our cart. A blond concierge takes Agnes's elbow, and she hobbles beside him down the path. A white bandage peeks out from below the hem of her yoga pants.

As Grigore maneuvers the cart past her, I notice a bottle of Veuve Clicquot nestled in the compartment behind the seat. I turn away, though, steeling myself. It's probably being delivered to the mysterious L'Élu II, that hush-hush bacchanal somewhere up in the shadowy hills of Ile Saint Sigo. What I wouldn't give for a phone right now. To tell Ben and Sabine and the rest of them that they've sent me to the sketchiest rehab in the Caribbean.

They probably wouldn't believe me. I barely believe it myself.

I climb out of the cart and catch Grigore's eye. "You wouldn't want to come in, would you? Open that champagne?"

He's very still for a second. "I don't think so."

I feel my face heat up. "Right."

"It's just that . . . it's a trap, you know."

"Beg pardon?"

"I don't mean you. I mean that"—he lifts his chin back at the bottle—"is a trap. Antonia's little sadistic treat. You drink it tonight, what comes in the morning is that much more painful."

"Oh, right. I should've known." I give him a look. "So what's coming in the morning?"

"Can't tell you that. But, trust me, I'm doing you a favor."

Well, at least there's one person on the staff of Hidden Sands who's a straight shooter. That's certainly refreshing.

"What time should I wake up?" I ask.

"Don't worry about that. Everything's taken care of." He waves and unlocks the brake. I watch him go, observing the cart's quiet journey down the path and to who knows where after that.

20

PERRY'S JOURNAL

<u>Friday, March 8</u>

TO DO:
- Dorothy McDaniel Florist—lilacs for Erin
- Ask Scotty to keep an eye out for similar Error Message or any other deadlocks/potential glitches in the servers
- Spider Beanie Baby—eBay? Etsy?
- WORK ON SHORIE'S LETTER
- Send Shorie message re: new Jax budget
- Globalcybergames.org

License my roving hands, and let them go
Before, behind, between, above, below.

John Donne, "To His Mistress Going to Bed"

Until the Day I Die

My roving happinesses
My roving harbors
My roving hardwares
My roving harms, harvests, hazards . . .

21

SHORIE

The Alabama night is soft and thick with humidity and hungry mosquitos. Toomer's Drugs is closed, so we get Cokes at the Draft House and amble down College Street. We talk and brush enormous, bloodthirsty creatures off each other's arms and faces, which turns out to be a surprisingly romantic activity.

After a while, I surreptitiously check my email. Sure enough, there's a new screenshot, another message from Yours to Ms. X.

I think about you all the time.

"If I may," Rhys says, "what do you have planned this semester that classes would interrupt?"

I slide my phone into my pocket. The question is so formal. And sweet, like he's one of those *Downton Abbey* dudes come to inquire as to my availability for courting. No way I can tell him what I'm doing. Jax's business is need to know only; Dad taught me that.

"Probably the same stuff as your other clients," I say vaguely.

He gives me a doubtful look. "Hmm."

"What?"

"It's just that lying on the sofa, bingeing on *Game of Thrones*, and eating pot brownies doesn't seem your style, to be honest."

"Actually, I've got a job," I say.

"With Jax?"

I nod. Again, no need for full disclosure.

"Oh. That's awesome. Really cool."

I nod again, and we walk in silence, cutting past the art building on the way to my dorm. I wish I didn't have to lie to this guy. I really like him. Plus, I kind of suck at lying. But at this point, I barely know him, so talking about Jax—the deadlock, the crazy balances, and the private messages—is really out of the question.

"I'd be okay without a degree," I say. "I know what I want to do, and I can learn whatever I don't know on the job."

He nods. "I have a friend who took a gap year in the Caribbean two years ago. Well, not a gap year exactly. He was on academic probation, and his parents thought it might do him some good to work for a semester. They got him a job as a lifeguard at this ridiculous five-star resort, and he liked it so much he never came back. Chucked college altogether. Pissed his parents off so much. Anyway . . ." He trails off, going dead silent.

I wonder why.

Then a charge sizzles up the back of my neck. "What island?" I ask casually.

"Huh?"

"What island is your friend on?"

He shrugs. "The Canary Islands, I think. One of them."

"You said it was in the Caribbean." I suddenly feel a jolt of panic. Was there some reason he changed his story? Could it be that his friend is on the island where my mom is? He knew who I was without ever having met me, he knows about Jax, and he runs a company that encourages fraud. What if he has something to do with the error messages I've gotten? What if Jax is the real reason he wanted to meet me . . .

He gives me a strange look. "Did I? Aren't the Canary Islands in the Caribbean? Or maybe not. I suck at geography, FYI."

"Okay." *Breathe, Shorie. Slow down. No reason to go spinning into crazy land with your conspiracy theories quite yet.* God, this server thing has got me way too wound up.

At my dorm, kids are streaming in and out. We stand off to the side, just on the edge of a pool of light cast by floods.

"I read about your dad," he starts. "What happened."

"Oh." I hesitate long enough that I can tell he's starting to regret bringing it up.

He tries again. "I just wanted to say I'm sorry."

"Thanks."

He looks up at the bright dorm windows.

"I don't mind talking about it—" I start. "It's just that it's really—"

He catches my eye. "Personal."

"Fine," I say. "I mean, it's fine. But also, I'm fine. I don't really need to talk about it."

We stare at each other, our conversation at an awkward impasse. I'm struck with how beautiful his lips are, really full, both of them, top and bottom. Excellent lips for kissing. And the way Rhys runs the rest of his life, I bet he would give kissing 100 percent.

Passion, lust, elation . . .

I feel off-balance—and super tired. This wave after wave of conflicting emotions is starting to drain me. So what do I do? Keep an eye on this guy because he may be connected with Jax? Or because his lips look perfect? I really have no idea. And right now either reason seems perfectly valid.

"So, the money?" he says. "For the classes."

"Oh right. It's, ah—" My mind has gone blank.

"Thirty-seven fifty," he says. "Broken down into monthly installments, if you need to. You can Jax it to me directly, unless your mom would see it. Most kids can't since their parents watch their expenses pretty closely their freshman year. If they're on Jax, they'll typically slide it through their food or a miscellaneous category, saying they hired a tutor or, I don't know, paid up front for yoga classes or something. If they have enough credit cards, they'll pay for their friends' meals, gas, whatever and get the cash that way."

"I still have some cash from graduation." Although, I'm pretty sure it's not enough.

He smiles. "I just need the first installment by next week. Maybe . . ." He angles his body toward me in such a way that I think, with some panic, that he might try to kiss me right here, right now. "Maybe we could hang out again. Get pizza or something."

My phone buzzes against my hip, and instinctively I reach for it. My fingers close around a small card instead, a punch card from this ice cream place near home, Caldwell Creamery. Mint green with a hand-drawn four-leaf clover logo in one corner, edges soft from having once been run through the washer. Eleven of the twelve boxes have been punched out.

"What's that?" Rhys asks.

I hold the card up to him. "It's for an ice cream place my dad and I used to go to together. He gave it to me so my friend and I could get the free cone. I forgot about it."

Specifically, Dad had given it to me in March, right before he died. Spring had come early. It was warm out, in the seventies already, with thick, hazy skies over blooming tulips and daffodils and determined birds. One Friday afternoon, after Daisy and I had been hanging around Jax for hours, Dad said we should go treat ourselves. We'd ended up going to the skate park to watch some guy Daisy had a crush on instead. I must've stuffed the card in my pants pocket.

And then my father died, and it rained for two weeks straight, the sun hiding behind the wall of white sky. The birds seemed to sense the season's earlier false start and went quiet too. The world without my father was a desolate place. Who would go for ice cream?

Rhys interrupts my thoughts. "What's your friend's name?"

I'm staring at the card, willing myself not to cry. "Daisy. She goes to Georgia Tech. She's majoring in materials engineering. Like polymers and metals and stuff." Rhys is staring at me now, and I know I'm rambling. Acting prickly and difficult and weird. It makes me miss Daisy even more.

"I should go," Rhys says.

My heart squeezes. I've probably run him off.

"I'll text you later," he says. "Good luck with your job."

When he's gone, my good sense finally, belatedly, kicks in. And starts lecturing me, Dad style.

I may want to see Rhys again, but it's a bad idea. The guy's researched me. He knows about Jax, even about my father's death. Put that together with the fact that most people think I enjoy the life of a privileged princess, and I'm sure he sees me as a target. And then there's that Caribbean/Canary Islands thing too. Maybe he's in on whatever's happening at Jax and with Mom. He may even be connected to the error messages.

Frustrated, I pull out my phone and text Daisy.

How's everything going? I miss you.

I stare at the screen, willing an answer bubble to pop up. Or at least the dancing ellipses. Nothing. She's probably out, having fun. It's Friday night. With a heavy sigh, I check the latest email of screenshots. One of them shows the monthly balances. They've all gone back down to where they were this afternoon.

I blink, like I'm seeing things, and do a quick mental tabulation. That's exactly $161,772.96 Ms. X moved in and out of her account in less than four hours.

22

ERIN

The banging on my door seems unnecessarily aggressive. But it achieves the intended result. Even before I crack open my eyes, my heart has shifted into high gear.

It's still dark out; I can sense it even before I see it. And not just predawn dark—pitch-black, middle-of-the-night dark. I'm trying to remember what's happening, and why the hell it's happening so early in the morning, but I've got nothing. Other than the rush of gratitude that Grigore wouldn't share that bottle of Veuve Clicquot with me. Bless that guy's sweet Moldovan heart.

The knocking stops, there's a beat, and the door slams open.

"Up and at 'em," sings out a man's voice. Without even thinking, I obey.

In the dark room, he looks about eight feet tall, a monster with shoulders as broad as a house. When he flips on the lamp, I see he's tall, broad enough across the shoulders, but by no means a giant. He's more like a surfer guy, in his early thirties, with long, sun-bleached hair pulled back in a curling ponytail and a faint scar bisecting one eyebrow.

He's dressed differently from the other staff too—in dirty shorts and a threadbare red-and-yellow Mexican Baja hoodie. A hippie-looking guy. Kind of cute, actually—but, of course, what else would I have expected?

"What time is it?" I ask him meekly.

"Time to get dressed." He grins slightly and tosses a string sack at me. In the bathroom, I change out of my Hidden Sands pajamas and into underwear, sports bra, nylon cargo shorts, and a white moisture-wicking T-shirt. When I walk back out, he points to a pair of hiking boots and socks on the bed. I sit and put them on, then stare at his ponytail wistfully.

"Could I have something to tie my hair back?"

"Sorry, no." He swings open the door. "Move out."

Outside my cottage, three women huddle in the bed of an idling pickup truck, all of them dressed in the same shorts and T-shirts. One is Deirdre, who manages a quick grimace at me. Not surprisingly, her pale, puffy face resembles three-day-old scrambled eggs. There's also a black woman I haven't seen before. And Agnes, crouched in the far corner of the truck.

Behind her glasses her eyes are round with fear. I can't imagine why. I get that the early-morning wake-up call is just another way to throw us off-balance, but the guy seems nice enough.

We all cling to the sides of the truck as he drives us down the lane, past the cottages, and into the jungle. As we hit a patch of rough road, overhung with a leafy canopy, I berate myself for not sticking my mouth under the water faucet when I was in the bathroom. And for not peeing.

I'm longing for coffee—dying for it—but I'm getting the distinct impression there's not going to be any chance of getting it. Or a bed or warm breakfast, for that matter. The farther we get away from the resort, the more I start to wonder if what is happening here isn't, in fact, the start of my L'Élu. But that seems strange.

Why would Antonia fast-track a couple of newcomers like Deirdre and me? Is it because I refused her offer of the special VIP L'Élu II, and she wants to inflict some kind of punishment on me?

Agnes could probably provide some context, seeing as how she's already done one of these things, but she's put her head down, and I'd have to yell over the truck engine to be heard. And anyway, it doesn't make any difference. Whether Antonia is acting out of revenge or just changed her mind, the bottom line is, finishing my L'Élu means I get to go home. This is what I wanted. I need to focus on the task at hand.

We climb a hill, ford a stream, then climb another hill, the truck ramming its way through thick brush. In the back, we cower to avoid the stinging lash of branches. Deirdre vomits the sour-smelling contents of her stomach over the side. Some sloshes down into the grooved bed of the truck, and the other three of us lift our butts and crab walk around the perimeter to avoid it.

"I'm so sorry," she keeps saying. She's weeping now, tears and snot streaming down her face. A tide of foreboding rises inside me, and I turn away from her so I don't choke. If this is our L'Élu, she's in for a world of hurt.

We finally pull off the side of the road, and Ponytail jumps out, banging the side of the truck. We climb out, and higher now in elevation, we huddle together, arms folded against the chill air. There's a smell here—a dank, mossy aroma of old soil and decaying fish. The light between the dark silhouettes of the trees has turned gray. The sun will be up soon. And I've still got to pee.

"I'm Lach," he says, arranging the strap of a canvas bag full of water bottles across his chest. "Welcome to your L'Élu."

In the predawn gray, I can't help but notice his eyes. They're the lightest I've seen on a human. Blue, probably. And he's deeply tanned and wearing faded leather flip-flops, like he's a surfer headed out to the waves instead of leading a group of women through the tropical rainforest. I look around the group. Agnes is scowling. So is the black woman. Deirdre looks like she wants to die.

He stares off into the distance. "We're now going to embark on a quest," he says. "The heart of your Hidden Sands experience. It's meant to be a physical challenge, but, be aware, it is a spiritual one as well."

We all exchange glances. Whatever Tony Robbins, self-help bullshit this is, we can handle it. We all just want to get through this.

"On a L'Élu, you've got to think and feel at the most basic level," he continues in his tour-guide monotone. "You must get away from your self-centered, first world mindset so you can become more fully, completely yourself. While the external focus is on survival, problem-solving, and teamwork, the internal focus is on forging a new way of seeing yourself."

How should I see myself? I think. *If I'm not CEO of Jax, not Perry's wife, what am I?*

He sighs. "Anyway, you get the gist. You're about to do a hash, okay? Anybody other than Agnes know what that is?"

No one says a word. He reaches into the canvas bag, pulls out a handful of flour, and sprinkles it onto the ground. It's in the shape of a circle with an X inside.

"A hash is a running challenge, a social activity, where you get to drink beer at the end. Only we drink water, not beer." He gives us a slight sardonic smile. "The hare—that's me—runs ahead and leaves a trail for the harriers—that's you—to follow. A normal hash is part treasure map, part obstacle course, but ours is a little different. Ours is not a game. If you find the trail and follow it correctly, you get food and water. If you don't, there's a consequence."

Nobody asks what the consequence is. He produces an old-fashioned wind-up alarm clock and balances it on the edge of the truck. "I get a twenty-minute head start. When this thing goes off, you go off. Got it?"

We all stare at him, dumbfounded.

"Hello?" he says, and we all nod. "All right. Namaste, my little chickadees." He turns, takes off at a jog, and in seconds, has disappeared into the jungle. I scoot around to the other side of the truck and furtively relieve myself.

When I rejoin the group, the black woman claps her hands. "Okay, bitches. Let's go." She speaks with a New Orleans accent, rich with Cajun undertones, and now that the sun's up, I can see she's a little younger than me and a lot fitter, with killer cheekbones and a set of excellent eyelash extensions. This woman had the right idea; she looks ready to conquer the jungle. To kick this L'Élu's ass in style.

She starts up the road, Deirdre padding after her like a puppy.

"Hold up," I call out to them. "Don't you think we should wait for the alarm?"

They stop. "No," the black woman says.

"What's he going to do?" Deirdre says. "Punish us?"

"I don't think we should antagonize him," I say. "Not right off the bat. We should play by the rules. Wait for him to get ahead of us, like he wants us to. We can use the time to make a plan. He literally told us nothing. If we go running into the woods—"

"Jungle," the black woman says.

"—the jungle, without a plan, we'll die."

"She's right," Agnes says from behind me. "It's dangerous out there."

We all turn to her.

"I was kidding, actually," I say.

"I'm not."

"That's right. You got hurt on your first L'Élu." I nod at her bandaged leg. "How did it happen?"

She presses her lips together. "A few of the guides like to mess with your head. Make you think you're in mortal danger. I didn't appreciate it."

"Do you actually think they take chances they shouldn't? That the L'Élu's unsafe?"

"I think," Agnes says flatly, "that this whole island is unsafe."

I want to ask her more, but the clock is ticking. Literally. And we need a plan.

"We should get organized," I say, then catch myself. I'm on Jax autopilot, marshaling the troops, meager as they may be, to meet the challenge.

"Organize us, then," says the black woman.

I turn to Agnes. "You've done this before. Is there anything you can tell us? Any advice we could use?"

"Well." Her eyes dart from the jungle back to the road. She's nervous about something. Really nervous.

"Agnes?" I prod.

She picks up a stick and draws a circle. "He didn't tell you any of the signs. This means wrong path." She draws three parallel lines. "This means go back to where you came from. There are signals you yell to each other, and you'll see them written, too, if he's being nice. The words *on-on* means one of you found the right direction. *On-in* is the trail's end. Which is important, because Lach may not be there, and if you keep going, you could get lost or hurt."

I survey the group. "We should get each other's names, so if one of us gets lost, the others can find them. So we can stick together. She's Agnes. I'm Erin."

The black woman pipes up. "Jessalyn. Jess." She looks at Deirdre, who's pinching the bridge of her nose and looks like she may have drifted off to sleep even though she's still on her feet. "Hangover. What's your name?"

"Deirdre."

"Quick question, Deirdre," Jess says. "Where'd you find booze at a rehab?"

Deirdre turns away.

"Try to stay dry, if you can." Agnes finishes braiding her long hair, then dips a hand in her bra, pulls out a little piece of square blue plastic, and fastens the end of the braid with it.

"What's that?" I demand.

"Bread tie."

"Smart," Jess says. "Do you have an extra one?"

"Sorry." Agnes plants her hands on her hips. "Also, you should try to find a weapon."

"A weapon?" I say.

Her eyes meet mine for a brief moment. But she doesn't elaborate.

"You guys," Deirdre says. "I totally think Antonia set me up. She did this to me. She let me drink on purpose." As if to punctuate the statement, she then vomits all over her hiking boots.

"Good Lord," Jessalyn says. "Honey, no offense, but you did that to yourself."

I check the clock. We've got roughly six more minutes before the alarm goes off. Six minutes to see what we can salvage for the days ahead. I fling open Lach's truck door and check the floor. "Bingo." I hold up two stray rubber bands.

"Oh, me, me, me!" Jessalyn says. I hand her a band and twist my hair up into the kind of topknot bun thing Shorie does. It feels like heaven to have my hair off my neck. Jessalyn and I also find a couple of extra rubber bands, which we pop over our wrists, a stick of gum, and a half-empty pack of cigarettes.

Then the alarm goes off, and we all stare at each other. Jess shuts it off, and that's when I realize Agnes is no longer with us. She's gone.

23

SHORIE

I wake up a little before nine on Saturday morning and lie in bed, strategizing. I'm still $600 shy of the $3,750 I owe Rhys. I consider withdrawing the money from my personal budget allocation—there's enough extra in there that it wouldn't exactly be a hardship. But even though I know Mom doesn't have her phone or computer at Hidden Sands, I'm worried it'll somehow get back to the school or someone at Jax. And I can't risk that.

For a split second I wonder how much the emerald band Mom gave me would bring. But no. That would be beyond shitty.

I consider seeing if I can get Dele and her friend Rayanne to agree to eat someplace nice tonight, maybe order steak and dessert and let me pick up the check in exchange for cash to at least get me started toward the six hundred. But then I think of something better. I call Gigi.

She's up, of course, making Arch's daily oatmeal. I tell her I've decided to take her advice and trade my trendy wardrobe of sweats and T-shirts from Goodwill for a few classic, well-made pieces—including but not limited to a cashmere coat for winter, an expensive leather bag, and some wool trousers and cashmere sweaters, maybe even a status pocketbook.

My grandmother practically dies of happiness. In fact, Gigi's so excited about my deciding to dress like a Junior League member she doesn't even question me when I ask her if she can wire it to me, since my roommate wants to drive to the mall in Montgomery first thing this morning. Shockingly, she agrees, and I send her phone kisses, promising to text pictures of me in my new old-lady clothes.

When we hang up, I only feel a tiny twinge of guilt. I love Gigi, but she was so mean to Mom at the intervention, and in a way, that feels a little like my fault. It's hard to untangle all the threads of blame. But I'm not changing my mind about the money. Or about letting one of Rhys's surrogates take my classes. This is what I want to do. What I have to do.

Dele's still asleep, so I get dressed and brush my teeth as quietly as possible. Out in the hall, the floor is quiet; in fact, the whole dorm is silent as death. Seems like everybody was out late last night but me. It's depressing, being awake when everyone's asleep, asleep when everyone's awake. Just another way it feels like I'm constantly out of step with the world.

I haul my Huffy into the elevator, down to the first floor, and head out toward the Winn-Dixie on College Street. The cash safely stuffed in my purse, I pedal over to Mama Mocha's, where I gobble a bagel with cream cheese, nurse a cappuccino, and slowly flip through a local real estate brochure like a middle-aged person. I'm wondering if 11:07 a.m. is a reasonable, nonstalker-y hour to text Rhys when I hear a voice behind me.

"Investing in some real estate?"

Rhys is dressed in black gym shorts and a dingy blue T-shirt. He's holding a zucchini muffin wrapped in a napkin and a paper cup of coffee, his adorably mussed cinnamon-colored hair flipping out from under an Auburn cap.

"Oh, hi," I say. "I was just . . ." For the life of me, I can't think of a single lie.

He sits and breaks his muffin in half. His arms are hairy in a nice way, and look warm. I try not to stare.

"Did you just happen to be passing by?" I ask. Now I sound like an episode of a *Masterpiece* show. But still. It's kind of strange that he's here.

"You mentioned liking this place last night, and I was hoping to run into you."

I want to scream with happiness. But I don't. There are other things I remember from last night. Like him saying that he has a buddy, one who lives on an island and works at a five-star resort. Maybe or maybe not in the Caribbean. Where Mom is.

He crams half the muffin into his mouth. "Oh my God. I was craving this so bad. You want half?"

I shake my head, and he smiles at me, his mouth full.

"You were hoping to run into me?" I ask.

"Yeah. For the fee." He smooshes a couple of crumbs on his thumb and pops them into his mouth. "Not that we have to do it in person. But, it's more fun that way." He smiles.

That smile, my God. I quietly die a rapturous death.

"You want to Venmo me?" he asks.

I shake my head. "You know, at my house, Venmo's kind of a dirty word."

"Ah. My apologies. You know, Lowell was joking, but we really could use a revamping of our site. Like a program that would help me with all our surrogates. If you want to barter."

Even though the idea of writing a program—and all the puzzle solving that entails—does kind of fire me up, I shake my head. "I should probably just pay you, like everybody else."

"Okay, cool." The other half of the muffin goes in his mouth. Amazing how somebody can eat like a total pig and still somehow come off looking completely adorable. I'm hit with the memory of how it used to drive Mom crazy when Dad would mix up all the food on his plate. He would do it with the grossest stuff: spaghetti with salad, or eggs and sausage and hash browns. He'd swirl it all up into one lumpy mountain, then attack the whole thing at once, while she howled in disgust. I wonder, though. Had she thought it was cute when they were dating?

I reach for my purse, but he puts a hand on my arm. "You don't have to pay me right now. Do you want another coffee?"

"Okay, sure."

Moments later he's back with two steaming mugs.

"Thanks," I say, and gulp it down black. It burns the back of my throat.

"Can I ask you a personal question?" He cradles his mug, and I study his hands. They're rough-skinned, perfectly proportioned, with knobby fingers and squared-off nails.

"Sure." I steel myself, thinking he's about to ask me where I got the money to pay him. If we're rich because of Jax.

"Before your dad died, did he . . ." He hunkers closer to the table. "Did he give you anything special? I mean, like a graduation gift or something that felt important? Like, I don't know, meaningful to you in a way that you knew you would keep it forever?"

I stare at him for a second, thinking about the plastic bag Mom and I got at the hospital.

I swallow. "No." *Just a Beanie Baby spider.*

He nods thoughtfully. "It's weird, you know? I think about stuff like that a lot. That I wish my father had given me, like, an old knife of his, or a watch or something. So I would have something concrete to pull out and look at any time I wanted to remember him."

"Your father died?"

"Cancer, yeah. It was the worst. He was in hospice for about six weeks. He handwrote this five-page letter to me, on notebook paper, the kind you tear out, with the fringe . . ." He flutters his fingers, but

I know what he means. "He didn't put it in an envelope or anything. He just handed it to me one afternoon. I took it up to my room and stapled the pages together because I was so afraid of losing any of it. But I didn't read it for the longest time."

Envy stabs at me from the inside out, tiny pinpricks in my heart and gut. It shocks me how bad it hurts. How instantly resentful I feel. I mean, yes, I have one unread message on Jax, but it's not a goodbye letter; it's just instructions about school and Jax. Nothing like what Rhys is talking about.

"I hope you won't take this the wrong way, but you seemed—I don't know—a little wrecked last night about the ice cream card."

"I guess I was." I manage a smile. "Pretty pathetic. Getting upset about something like that."

"Not at all. I get it." He hesitates. "I was eight when he died. So maybe I was just a dumb, ungrateful little kid who wanted a cool knife instead of a letter."

"I'm really sorry about your dad."

He shrugs but doesn't say anything. I get it. Talking doesn't really help; sometimes it feels like it just diminishes the whole experience. I toy with my mug. The coffee looks oily to me now, and my stomach turns.

"You're lucky about the letter, though," I say.

"Well, your dad wanted you to have his freebie cone. That's pretty touching too."

I grin. "I guess."

What I really want to ask is what Rhys's father had written to his son, but I can't force the question out of my mouth. It's none of my business, first of all. But the main reason I don't ask is because, if it turns out he wrote something really wonderful and perfect and life-changing, I may start crying.

Rhys shifts in his chair. "So, the fee."

I lean down and dig into my purse, crestfallen and glad for the opportunity to hide my face. I hand over the padded envelope full of cash. He doesn't look inside to count it or anything, just tucks it in his messenger bag and drums his fingers on the table.

"Okay, you've got my top woman all ready to go for the main four: English comp, tech and civ, Calculus I, and core science. For Intro to Engineering, I had to cast a wider net."

"Is there a problem? Can the other girl not do it?"

"No, apparently once she got a B in it, and—"

"Yeah, no."

"I already found another girl. Same height, same hair. Pretty—"

I freeze.

"But that means I'm going to have to get two Tiger Cards, so—"

"The price goes up," I finish for him and then feel my face warm. *He thinks I'm pretty.*

"It's no problem, Shorie. It's my cost. You don't have to worry about it."

"No. I've got it." I open my purse and plunk down five more hundred-dollar bills. He sweeps the bills off the table, fast, then we return to our coffee.

"So what's your job at Jax?" he says. "I mean, if you're paying me a shit ton of money to get out of your first semester of college, it must be a great company to work for."

Now I'm not just warm, I feel hot all over, and my eyes water a little bit. It's none of his business, and yet part of me is wildly grateful that somebody's asking, that someone's interested. But I just can't tell him the truth. Not until I know more.

"It is."

"You know," he says slowly. "If you ever want to talk about your dad, you can hit me up anytime."

I so desperately want to tell him about my dad: *He was a brilliant, goofy, fun nerd. He liked poetry and science and coding. He hiked with*

143

my mom and me, and followed this group of French mathematicians and poets called Oulipo, who wrote entire novels without the letter e *or made up stories that follow mathematical problems like the knight's tour of a chessboard. He learned the songs from* Wicked *and sang them with me. He called me "Shorie, my sweet." And I scared the shit out of him every time we played hide-and-seek . . .*

But if I say all that I'll probably start bawling like a baby, and I'm sure not ready to let this guy see me ugly cry. Besides, I have plenty of stuff to sort out already—getting to the bottom of this glitch at Jax, finding my dad's missing journal—without dumping my entire personal emotional dictionary on some random dude I just met.

So I just nod.

When he finishes his coffee, he gives me a hug, and we say we'll see each other around. Then I ride my bike down to the drugstore for the most formidable-looking combo lock I can find.

24

ERIN

The hash is slow going. Besides the fact that Lach's flour marks seem to be immediately absorbed into the damp, mossy jungle ground, we keep having to stop while Deirdre is sick all over the same damp, mossy ground.

The checkpoints appear roughly every half mile or so. At each one, we find and guzzle the tiny mini water bottles Lach has left, then attempt to decipher the next set of flour signs, most of which are designed to purposely mislead us. To find out which mark is the one to follow, we have to split up and explore each trail. I don't like that part. The way it forces us to separate. Most of the trails dead-end, and we wind up yelling for each other, echoing back and forth through the trees until we can locate each other and start all over again.

The air has a weight to it, a suffocating heat that's intensified by the thick canopy of trees and bushes that wrap their muscular arms over the land. Alabama is hot, but this is a whole different universe. Also none of us has eaten since the night before. By afternoon, Deirdre has begun dry heaving.

Jessalyn plops down on a rock. "I'm not doing this anymore," she says, ripping the rest of a torn fingernail off. "I don't give a shit if I fail the test and have to stay here another month. I'm done."

"I'm going to die," Deirdre announces then leans against the trunk of a knotty tree.

"We have to keep going," I say. "There's food at the end." I have no idea if what I'm saying is actually true, but I feel compelled to keep everybody's spirits up. The CEO in me, probably. I'm also legitimately worried about Agnes, by herself in the jungle. She clearly had her reasons for cutting out on the L'Élu, but I don't know if not telling anyone was the right thing to do.

In fact, as we've been leaping over fallen branches and roots, splashing through streams, and slogging up muddy hills, I keep seeing the fear in Agnes's eyes. Hearing her tell me to find a weapon. What the hell was she implying?

After I give Jessalyn and Deirdre my best mom/cheerleader/CEO routine, they seem to rally. An hour later, we've made it to the big flour *on-in* checkpoint where we get (hooray!) full-size bottles of water. Just on the other side of a clump of bushes, we find our camp. It's a simple space, a generous-size clearing matted with ferns and encircled by four small tents and a fifth, larger one. A neat campfire bordered with rocks crackles in the center. Off to the side, a picnic table loaded down with plastic containers of sandwiches and cookies and chips and fruit beckons. I have no idea what time it is, but the sun is low in the sky, and it's cooled considerably.

I want to cheer. I want to cry. I want to lie down on the ground and sleep for three consecutive days.

"Chickadees." Near the campfire, Lach's slouched on a folding chair with his ankle propped on his knee, flip-flop dangling. He's changed into a fresh T-shirt and a light-blue bandana holds back his hair. His tent must've been fully stocked beforehand. He holds up a bottle of tea, beaded with condensation, and waves it at us. My mouth waters in response, then I see his eyes cloud. "Where's Agnes?"

"She opted out," Jessalyn says.

"She what?"

"She opted out of the *experience*," Jess enunciates. "By which I mean, she bounced."

Lach straightens. "Which way did she go?"

"Back in the direction of away from here."

He addresses me. "Where?"

I shake my head. "I don't know. We didn't actually see her leave."

"Jesus. Oh, shit." He starts pacing in tight circles, scratching the back of his head. He gestures toward the picnic table. "Get some food and wait for me. I need to make a call." He pulls a phone out of his pocket and walks to the edge of the campsite.

"Dude's going to get fired," Jess says.

"I don't know. But I do feel bad," I say.

"Me too," Deirdre says. "But not for him." She jerks her thumb toward the tents, a couple of yards beyond the campfire. "It's naptime, chickadees."

Jess and I settle at the picnic table, where we descend on a stack of turkey wraps. They're warm and limp from sitting in the sun, but I don't think I've ever tasted anything quite so delicious.

"I wonder what Antonia's going to do about Agnes," I say. I can't forget Agnes's prayer in the showers. Her crying in the spa as the woman—Antonia, I assume now—berated her. *The universe is trying to tell you something, Agnes.*

Jess plucks a cluster of grapes from a plastic bowl. "I don't know, but truth? Not our problem."

"Yeah." I check out Lach pacing at the edge of the clearing. He's still on his phone and gesticulating in earnest now.

"We should probably put some food in Deirdre's tent," Jess says. "And a bottle of water." "Who knows when we're going to eat next."

"Aw, look at you. Having a heart."

She grins just as Lach trudges past us back to his chair.

"Everything okay?" I ask.

He sits heavily. Takes a swig of his tea. "She made it back to the resort. So that's good."

Jess and I exchange brief looks.

"What's going to happen to her?" I ask.

"Oh, Antonia will probably put her on the first flight back home." He settles back into his chair. "Some people don't want to be helped. Nothing you can do."

After we're finished eating, Lach informs us that the rest of the afternoon and evening are ours. He grabs his walkie, phone, and a backpack from the picnic table, then disappears into the jungle.

"That was bizarre," Jess says.

"What?"

"I think he was lying about Agnes. I mean why didn't Antonia just send her right back up here to finish the challenge?"

"You heard what he said. Maybe she's cutting her losses."

Jess shrugs. "I don't know. That part could be true. I heard Agnes pulled a shiv on her first L'Élu guide."

I gape at her. "What?"

"One of the women from her L'Élu told me their guide—not Lach, some other guy—wouldn't give them food after they'd been hiking all day. Agnes lost her shit and stabbed him."

"Are you kidding me?"

"She stabbed him with the broken end of a plastic spoon, supposedly. But still. I heard the dude wrestled her to the ground in front of her whole L'Élu group."

"Jesus."

"I know. It's ridiculous. You'd think after an altercation like that, somebody would call the police."

"You know, my concierge said there had been other incidents. Well, accidents, actually. At the volcano."

Jess laughs. "Oh my God. Please tell me you're making this up. There's a volcano?"

"Apparently." I dig into my aching arch. "Antonia told me the Saint Lucia police basically leave the island to her. I think she's the only law around here."

"Really comforting. God."

I think about the fear in Agnes's eyes this morning. "I heard Agnes's family wanted her to marry somebody she didn't want to marry. So they sent her here."

"What?"

"That's what I heard."

"I cannot believe that shit still happens. Don't folks know it's the twenty-first century?"

I don't reply. I'm dying to know what brought Jessalyn to Hidden Sands, how exactly she's going to fit into the dynamic of our little three-woman survivor team, but that's the manager in me talking; it's actually none of my business. I need to remember that, basically, everybody has a virtual "Do Not Disturb" sign hanging around their neck. But I can't help connecting the dots. Deirdre, Agnes, and I all seem to be in this group for reasons other than addiction. Maybe that's what makes us trois, the common thread that ties us together.

Jess shakes her head. "Do me a favor: if I look like I'm about to stab that guy, stop me. I do not want to have to go through this all over again. Or get sent home."

"Speaking of getting sent home . . ." I glance at Deirdre's tent. "Maybe we should help her out."

We unzip Deirdre's tent flap and slip in a bottle of water, a wrap, and a couple of cookies. I can hear her soft snoring and feel a pang of sympathy. Despite her slowing us down this morning, we have to stick together. It's the only way we're going to get through this.

Back at the fire, Jess pushes the smoldering remains with a stick, and the wood rekindles, spitting sparks into the soft navy-blue sky. My gaze drifts off to the darkness beyond. Who knows what animals are hidden behind the cover of trees, burrowing into holes, nestling into beds of cool leaves? Maybe they're dangerous. Maybe they bite or sting or shoot quills of deadly venom.

I guess I should add them to the list of challenges I'm unprepared to meet out here. I'm not used to failure, but Agnes certainly looked capable—healthy and fit—and she had to repeat her L'Élu. What if I fail to meet the challenge, and they never let me leave this place? What if this is some kind of nightmarish, Sisyphean challenge where I have to relive this torment every day, hoping to survive?

"So. You going to ask me why I'm here?" Jess asks.

"No. I didn't want to pry. And, also? I didn't really want to talk about why I'm here."

She laughs. "I hear you. But I'm pretty sure this is what they want us to do. Why they set up this whole vision quest thing. To get us to face why we've come here. So, if we want to get the certificate, we should give them what they want."

I smile. "Okay, Jess. Why are you here?"

"I wanted things that I wasn't allowed to have. And even though certain people didn't like me wanting them, I couldn't help it." She lifts her face to the stars, lets her eyes flutter closed.

"You're not going to stop there, are you? You're killing me."

She adjusts her position on the log. "I used to want to be the CEO of a Fortune 500 company. You know, there's only been one of us in the Fortune 500 since 1999. One woman of color to attain that title. And only fifteen black men."

"And you never made it?"

"No. No sir, I did not." She gives me a wry look. "Full disclosure—I drink large quantities of vodka, which may have had something to do with the disappointing career advancement."

I eye her. Some instinct tells me she's only revealing part of the truth. But that's okay. I have no right to this woman's secrets.

"Also full disclosure—I already know who you are. About your company, Jax, and your husband. I read that Business Insider article."

I sigh. "Oh, yeah. That."

"Is that why you're here?" she says. "Because of what happened to him?"

I'm not the kind of person who spills her guts at the drop of a hat, but I don't want to be rude. We're a team, and we're going to need each other to get through the next several days. I have to say something.

"It's been harder than I thought it would be," I admit. Which is a massive understatement, but true, nonetheless.

"What was he like?" she asks.

"My husband?"

"Yeah."

He was a good man. Unafraid of failure or of looking foolish. Most importantly, he was not afraid of me. Headstrong, stubborn, always dialed up to ten . . .

"It's okay," she says. "It's hard talking about someone you've loved then lost." Her eyes have gone a little out of focus.

"Now that he's gone," I say, "I don't know—I'm just adrift. I don't belong at work, I don't belong at home. I can't seem to figure anything out."

I go quiet and immediately regret saying as much as I have. Not because Jessalyn doesn't seem like a perfectly reasonable person to talk to, but because this is the first time I've verbalized these particular feelings to a fellow adult. It makes me feel vulnerable.

"So what do you think he wanted you to do?" Jess prods. "Your husband. I mean, did y'all ever talk about it? What you'd do if something happened to one of you?"

"We have wills, of course, but we didn't stipulate anything about Jax, other than this pact we had with our partners, a kind of Three

Musketeers thing. But Perry and I never talked, not about anything specific with Jax. It just didn't seem . . ."

. . . like death should be in the ten-year plan.

Just then, Lach appears out of the jungle and tells us it's time to turn in. I'm glad. Jess could be 100 percent on the up-and-up, but I've interacted with enough people who are trying to get something for nothing—information, money, a leg up on some deal they want in on—to know I've said enough. For now, anyway. And, truthfully, Antonia's pitch still has me somewhat rattled.

Later that night, I lie awake in my tent. I feel grimy all over, sweaty from the day's hike, still wearing the same clothes, and I never got to wash my face or brush my teeth. I've camped before. Perry and Shorie and I used to spend a few weekends a year at Wind Creek on the lake, sleeping in tents, hiking around the lake, roasting marshmallows at night. But there was always a community bathroom with hot showers and toilet paper, and the only animal was a friendly dog from the next campsite over.

Those weekends seem like a lifetime ago. Suffused with a kind of sepia light and blurred at the edges. They were so fun, especially the hikes. We'd circle the undeveloped shores of the lake, and Shorie would belt out the entire soundtrack from *Wicked*. She was obsessed with that show. Perry knew every single word to every song and joined in enthusiastically. My contribution was more along the lines of humming.

On one of the trips, when Shorie was fourteen, we noticed what we thought was a mosquito bite on her calf, just below the back of the knee, but turned out to be a brown recluse bite. Within two days the spot swelled and turned purple, then blistered and scabbed black, leaving an oozing ulcer. She spent two days in the hospital, pumped so full of fluids her normally thin face looked as plump as it had when she was a toddler. She didn't develop any particular fear of spiders. I, on the other hand, declared that to be our last camping trip ever. Obviously I was voted down on that one.

But this situation is altogether different, in more ways than one. There's no running water, no toilets—just rolls of paper stacked on the picnic table. There are no marshmallows, no singing, and God-help-me-please, no spiders. I try to think back if I've ever seen a nature show on Caribbean arachnids. Maybe it's best I can't remember. If they're crawling on this island, they're probably exotic and deadly and horrifying, and it really wouldn't do me a bit of good to know.

I tell my mind to calm, to try to focus on sleeping, but I can hear noises. Or at least I think I do. Whispering, maybe. Or an animal rooting around for scraps of food.

I pull on my boots, unzip my tent, and creep out into the clearing. The fire is smoking, the picnic table loaded with plastic tubs of more food—the next couple of days' rations, most likely. I have no idea where they came from. I didn't hear anyone come into camp and drop them off after we'd gone to bed, but that had to be what happened.

Towering trees form threatening silhouettes in the dark. The jungle is surprisingly loud at night. It buzzes and whistles and shrieks with the songs of insects and frogs. Over by Deirdre's tent, there's a different kind of rustling, which must be what I heard.

I creep closer. The flap of her tent is unzipped, giving me a perfect view inside. A perfect view of Lach and Deirdre, naked on top of her sleeping bag, legs twined together. Their bodies grind in unison.

I gasp audibly, but they don't hear me. I know I should leave, stop intruding on this private moment, but I can't seem to move. It's the sounds they're making. Their breathing quickening together, their inhaling and exhaling in dramatic, drawn-out moans. The sound of it shoots arrows through my gut. I used to make sounds like that when Perry touched me. When he held me. Kissed my neck. Explored my body with his hands and mouth.

I miss him so much. I miss him so much it's a physical pain.

All of a sudden, Deirdre cries out—a series of soft yelps—and I'm finally shaken from my trance. I retreat to my tent and stumble back inside, zipping myself back into my sleeping bag. But I don't go back to sleep, not for hours.

25

ERIN

In the morning, I wake to the smell of coffee brewing. When I approach the crackling campfire, I see I'm the only one up besides Lach, who's kicked back in his lawn chair again. I sit on a log near him, and he offers me a protein bar, but no coffee. He whistles while he slurps from his own steaming mug.

"Sleep well?" he asks.

"Yes, thanks."

He grins at me. "Never a better night's sleep than one under the stars."

"Agree to disagree," I say.

Just then his phone dings. He points at the coffeepot before answering. "Off-limits."

I nod—miffed that we don't even get a small cup of coffee to ease us into the day—and he saunters a couple of yards away, talking in French on his cell. I only catch a few words. *Rivière . . . attendez . . . volcan.* Wait at the river? What's that supposed to mean? And *volcan*? Volcano, maybe? I have no idea.

Deirdre doesn't make an appearance until later that morning and doesn't make mention of anything that happened last night. She does, however, look fresh and dewy and pretty. Like she's slept twelve hours in a king-size bed at the Ritz-Carlton. Lach takes the three of us on a hike to a meadow, where he teaches us how to build a fire and construct one-man shelters at the tree line. He props himself against a towering tree laden with green bananas to watch us toil away but is generous enough with the water and granola bars. I catch him gazing at Deirdre a couple of times, but what the hell? Maybe it's not a bad thing that he's hot for her. Maybe their hookups will make the going easier for all of us.

That night, after we return to camp and eat, Lach sends us off in different directions to find a place to meditate. I suspect that he and Deirdre take advantage of the opportunity to indulge in another tent rendezvous. Which I'm not judging, okay, but I do hope there's more to her plan than just getting laid. I hope she actually does have a plan. I'm not trying to be petty here, or misogynistic, but if she's going to get the royal treatment for screwing the guide, she should really leverage that to see that her teammates benefit as well.

On day three—Monday, I remind myself, thinking if I keep the days straight in my head, I'm somehow better off—we embark on another hike. This one is to a waterfall farther inland than we've ventured thus far. It's a long way. And on the way, Deirdre and Jessalyn pull ahead, leaving Lach and me walking together. I decide to strike up a conversation.

"My husband would've loved this. He was an avid hiker. Loved camping too. We used to take our daughter every summer down to this lake. Beautiful place. Not as exotic as this. But still, peaceful."

Lach doesn't reply to any of my random, vaguely disconnected statements, just glances briefly at me. But if I can get this guy talking, maybe I can forge some kind of partnership. And a partnership—an alliance—can end up being really beneficial. Beneficial, how? I have no idea.

"He died, in a car accident on the way to meet us at the lake," I continue. "Which is why I'm here. I haven't been able to deal with it. Been working night and day like that would fix things. Really messed up some of my relationships because of it."

I let the silence settle.

"I lost my son a couple of years ago," he finally volunteers. "He didn't die. I mean, his mother took him away. Disappeared. Went underground with him. The kid was five."

"That's awful. You haven't seen your son in two years?"

He shakes his head. "I asked my dad to find him. But I don't think he really tried."

"Pretty shitty of him, no offense."

"He never liked her, my girlfriend. Nobody in my family did." He points to the scar slashing his eyebrow. "I did this the night she took him. Put my face through a glass door."

I'm quiet for a moment. "Yes," I finally say. It's the only way I can think to reply.

Yes, sometimes loving someone is more than we can bear.

Yes, hurting yourself is sometimes the only way to survive.

Yes, there are scars.

We walk in silence a while longer, the tropical birds *chee*-ing around us. The proverbial dam breeched, Lach chats nonstop. He tells me about the species—Jacquot, bobolink, grackle—as well as the names of the trees—tamarind, kapok, strangler fig.

"Now would be the perfect time to quote a poem," I say. "I have a million of them in my head. But none with the right words."

Lach glances at me.

"My husband liked poetry, but he was a computer engineer, so he had a very particular way of enjoying it. He followed this French group that wrote using mathematical principles or constraints, like palindromes or lipograms or the knight's tour of a chessboard to play with the form."

Lach laughs. "I have no idea what you just said."

"They're just algorithm-based experiments, setting parameters on the writing. He said we all work within constraints to create anything, so we should embrace them. He said we're all just rats, building labyrinths that we plan to find our way out of."

"Huh."

I watch him. "I mean, that's what you and I and Deirdre and Jess are doing here, aren't we? We pay you to put us through a miserable five days that I will feel accomplished to have worked my way through."

"I guess so."

We walk in silence for a couple of moments before I speak again.

"The only poet he never rewrote was E. E. Cummings. He liked the way Cummings used experimental punctuation and syntax. The arrangement of the letters on the page. He said it reminded him of lines of code."

"Interesting."

I hear a hissing sound. It grows louder and louder until we crest the top of the trail, and a roaring column of rushing water comes into view. The four of us stop in respectful silence. The wall of water sheets from a high cliff of lichen-covered rock, white and foamy, into a crystal-blue pool below, and even as far back as we are, a cooling spray mists us.

I close my eyes and shiver, my damp skin going to gooseflesh under my T-shirt. Then I hear a shriek and open my eyes to see Jessalyn and Deirdre gazelle-leaping through the underbrush toward the pool.

I charge after the other two women, galvanized by an equal mix of joy and dread. The thick grass is matted, and my feet keep getting stuck and have to tear through it. I feel a wave of fear, that feeling you get when you're dreaming that you're stuck in mud and can't run from that shadowy man chasing you. Lach's not chasing me, but he is following, and I can feel my actual blood rushing through every part of my body.

I hate this place. The whole setup feels amateurish and unsafe. And I'm completely at the mercy of these people. I'm stuck on this island run by a two-bit hustler-princess in Louboutin pumps, and my own family blithely signed off on it without a second thought.

And there's something else. Like that old joke—"terrible food and the portions are so small." As miserable as the hash was, as annoying as it's been to sleep in that flimsy tent, to not get a morning cup of coffee and to hike for hours in the crushing heat, I expected more.

I expected more structure, more spiritual substance to the program. More *something*, to help me root out this sick, self-sabotaging thing in me that makes me do things like kiss my best friend's husband. But there's nothing. Well, nothing other than a day hike, activities like building the shelters, and unsupervised meditating at night. As much as I don't want to be here, I'm still disappointed. I had hoped in some way that this L'Élu would save me.

Maybe nothing will save me. Maybe Perry was the best part of me, and I just am what I am.

At the waterfall, I find Jessalyn and Deirdre stripped down to their sports bras and underwear, ducking in and out of the pool beneath it like a couple of kids. I kick off my boots and jump in the pool, clothes and all, surfacing to the sound of their laughter. Lach ambles up, pulls off his boots too, and settles on the edge of an overhanging rock.

"Get in!" Deirdre yells at Lach.

"Oh, no," he says. "I'm the lifeguard." He seems to be zeroed in on me, though, as I dunk all the way under the water. "Bad move, Erin," he says when I surface. "You never want to get your clothes wet in the jungle. Never know how long it's gonna take to dry them out."

But I don't want to take off my clothes in front of him. "I'll be fine," I say.

"Just looking out for you. Don't want you to have to do this all over again." He shoots me a half smile, but I avert my eyes, and through the clear water, study my hands as they sink into the black sand. Half of me—the stupid half—enjoys the attention; the other half of me thinks this is just his idea of a game of psychological chicken. Well, fine. If it is, it's wasted on me. I'm not that into tent sex.

Deirdre paddles up to us, leaning back in the shallow water, preening for Lach. "What's on the program today?" she asks. "Kill and roast a parrot? Make a sundial out of twigs? Scale the waterfall with our bare hands?"

"The last one," Lach says. "You're going to climb that waterfall."

She turns to ogle the sheer cliff rising up beside the foaming waterfall. "Jesus. Really?"

"No, you dim bulb," he says. "You think I'm going to haul your asses up there with no ropes or safety equipment? Not likely." He leans back, closes his eyes, and lifts his face to the sun. "I'm gonna sit here and let you ladies entertain me."

Deirdre giggles, but I keep my face down. It's then that I notice, on the sandy bottom beneath the warm, clear water, a blue plastic bread tie.

Water splashes me, and my head jerks up.

"Come on!" Jessalyn shouts at Deirdre and me, and splashes us again. Deirdre paddles back to her.

"Go have fun, Erin," Lach says. "You're too uptight." His phone rings, and he answers it with a "Yo, what's the word?"

I look down at the clear water. The bread tie is resting beside what looks like a small white bone with bits of something translucent and stringy clinging to it. I move my hand a centimeter closer, stirring the sand into a cloud under the surface of the water. A chicken bone, maybe, from someone's picnic.

When the sand settles, though, I see that it doesn't really look like a chicken bone. It's just the length of the last joint of my forefinger. And it looks human.

26

SHORIE

I spend Sunday messing around on the computer and trying to avoid Dele so I won't have to pretend I'm excited about school, and then, suddenly, before I know it, it's Monday, my first official day of college.

Of course, I'm not on my way to class. I'm hiding out in a booth at University Donut, watching backpack-laden students stream across campus and chowing down a Nutella old fashioned. I still can't quite believe I'm doing this, ditching school. I was never even late for any of my high school classes. Now look at me.

After I review the daily server report for the third time and determine it's clean, I check for an update on Ms. X. The balances in all her allotments look completely, frustratingly, normal. However, the next screenshot is another private message from Yours.

I wish we could be together right now.

The third shot shows one of Jax's mustard-yellow bubble suggestions: *Saks Fifth Avenue, The Summit, Birmingham, Chloé Quinty Leather Clogs, $795.00! Stella McCartney Slouchy Denim Boots, Preorder $995.00!*

I sit there, staring at my phone like it's a fucking Horcrux, and my heart does this jagged kind of dance inside my chest. I put down my half-eaten donut. I can see where Ms. X is—in Birmingham, shopping at Saks. Or at least walking past it on her way someplace else. But my hands are tied. I can't just start digging into Jax's servers or trying to crack the UUID number of this user. That's totally against FDIC regulations. What I'm doing, spying on them, is already bad enough.

But I can't help but think—if she's in Birmingham, and she's messing around on a server, it isn't a stretch to think she might be an employee at Jax. We only have three women executives. Mom, Sabine, and Layton. But there are at least five other female employees who might be capable of this. Most of them don't make the kind of money this woman does. Their salaries are nowhere near high enough to have allotments like this. Or maybe they have other income that I don't know about. It's possible.

It's also possible, for that matter, that Ms. X is a man. A man who's purchased women's shoes and who's in an illicit relationship. And he wouldn't have to work at Jax to hack into the servers. So really, I shouldn't rule out anything at this point. It'll prevent me from examining clues with a truly open mind. I stuff my phone back in my purse and finish my donut.

That evening I find myself back downtown, wandering around trying to decide what I'm in the mood to eat. It's entirely too early for dinner, but there's not a whole lot to do when you're a student who's not actually attending school. Jax is doing its thing—pushing a yellow bubble on-screen every time I pass a restaurant. *Have the chicken satay!* it chirrups when I near a Thai place, *$7.99 with a cucumber salad and a glass of hot green tea!*

I keep going, then duck into a Tex-Mex place and find a table near the back. The server brings me a water and menu and nods at my phone.

"My boyfriend and I just got on it," she says. "We love it so much. It's totally gotten me out of debt in, like, six months, and now it's helping us save for a wedding."

I hadn't realized I'd opened one of the screenshots of Ms. X's Jax account. I cover the phone with a hand. "Oh, cool. But . . . don't waste your money on a wedding. The entire industry is one giant scam. You should save it for a really incredible honeymoon instead. Or a down payment on a house in whatever neighborhood around you that has the fastest rising property values. Jax will tell you that too. Also, in the advanced settings, there's an allocation for eloping."

I shut my mouth abruptly. It's like my mother is talking through me. Like she's the ventriloquist, and I'm her dummy. Suddenly my eyes mist over, and I can't swallow.

"You're kidding me," she says. "I had no idea. I haven't really had a chance to explore all the extras."

I nod mutely.

"Do you want me to come back?" the server asks.

"No. Um, what do you recommend?"

She cocks her head. "Well, everybody makes a big deal about the fish tacos, but you know they raise those tilapia in tanks where they eat their own poop. So, if I were you, I'd get on that vegetarian train, you know what I mean?"

"Okay, yeah. I'll do that. And a tea as well, please."

When she's gone, I check my phone. To my surprise, this time there's a long chain of message screenshots.

I feel like you're slipping away, the first one reads. I can't go forward with everything—I won't—if YOU are not the reward at the end.

I'm not slipping away, comes the reply. I just don't want to talk here. I told you, not on Jax.

I want to see you, and not with a bunch of people. It's not enough.

I want to see you too, but we need to be more careful.

You know computers, you work for an app company. Can't you just erase this?

V funny. Not how it works.

I've got business in Sylacauga tomorrow morning. I'll be at Dally's BBQ in Childersburg, 4:30pm. Nothing fancy . . .

Nice change from a hotel room, tho. I'll try. xx

I sit back against my chair. *You know computers, you work for an app company.* So one of them could definitely be a Jax employee. And maybe both of them. Maybe that's what the text *not with a bunch of people* means. They both work at Jax, and they already see each other there. There are a handful of people at the company—Layton, for instance—who aren't programmers. Maybe the message was an attempt at sarcasm.

Anyway, whoever this is, they're definitely planning something together, doing something. *I can't go forward with everything . . .* that has to mean illegal activity. Probably related to the big chunk of money that made a brief appearance in Ms. X's account yesterday. They can't risk messaging on Jax—maybe because Ms. X works there, or Yours does, or both—so now they've set a meeting at a different location.

I've got to get to Childersburg tomorrow. But how the hell am I going to manage that? It's over an hour from Auburn. I could ask to borrow Dele's beater Honda, but I can't tell her about what's going on at Jax. I mean, don't reporters or journalists live for scoops like that? I can't risk it.

That leaves only one person. The only person I know who's got a car, who knows I'm skipping class, and who definitely won't judge me for hacking into somebody's private messages. Rhys is literally the only person in this town I can trust. But also somebody, like Dele, who I'm not sure I can trust, which confuses the hell out of me. So what in the world am I supposed to do?

The server is right about the veggie tacos. They're wrapped in warm corn tortillas and loaded with cotija cheese, and it takes me less than fifteen minutes to clear my plate. I pay the check with Jax, adding a nice tip, and immediately the app repopulates all the fields of my allocations.

But I don't get up from the table, because I'm doing some quick addition and not from my account, but from somebody else's. I can't quite believe what I'm seeing.

Another bump in Ms. X's balances. And the total is the exact same as the last amount—$161,772.96.

27

Erin

As we hike back to the campsite, the setting sun turns the scattered clouds into cotton candy shades of pink and orange and purple and blue, but I can't even take a moment to admire the spectacular sight. The blue plastic bread tie is tucked safely into my bra, and the puzzle pieces in my brain have begun to arrange themselves into a frightful order.

If the bread tie is the same one Agnes put in her hair, that means Lach lied to us when he said she made it back to the resort and was sent home. It means she's still somewhere on the island. I wonder if that's what he meant by what he said on the phone: *she's waiting at the river.*

On the other hand, the tie could be just a bit of random garbage from a group of picnickers who'd trekked out here to spend a day at the waterfall. Or a makeshift hair tie used by another woman on another L'Élu.

The bone I can't begin to explain. It can't have come from Agnes. Even if she got lost or drowned or something, bodies don't decompose

that fast. Unless, of course, an animal got to it. One of the many creatures of prey who live in this jungle.

I shake off the thought. Obviously Agnes isn't dead. I'm just being
dramatic, letting things get to me. Despite the L'Élu being less extreme
physically than I'd anticipated, being out in the jungle, with these
women, with this weird guy, was clearly messing with my mind.

On our way back to camp, there are a couple of times—once on a
muddy hillside and again over a stretch of precarious boulders—when I
stumble, and Lach offers his hand to help me along. His hand is strong
and warm and rough, and both times it feels like he holds on to me
longer than necessary.

Deirdre's back stiffens every time he touches me, her face set in a
look of supreme annoyance. But what the hell am I supposed to do? I
can't control what the guy does, and I'm not going to waste my time
trying to appease a grown woman who wants to play petty high school
mean-girl games. I have more important things to think about.

After we've eaten dinner, tidied up the picnic table, and settled
around the fire, I see Lach reach into a cooler and pull out a bottle of
beer. As he ambles back to the fire, I roll my eyes.

"I thought this was supposed to be a rehab," I say.

"Do you have a drinking problem, Erin?"

"No. But I heard there have been accidents up here. Maybe you
shouldn't."

"There's not going to be any accidents," he says. "And Deirdre's
okay with it. It's only Jessalyn here with the problem. But she has to go
back to the real world at the end of the month, don't you? Can't expect
to be treated with kid gloves then."

Jessalyn shoots him a nasty look. "I never asked for special treatment. You do what you want."

He settles back against a log, takes a swig, and nods at me. "Erin
doesn't have a problem with the bottle. She's here because she works

too much." He laughs. "If that's an addiction, my whole family ought to be sent off."

I shrug.

"So you can have a beer," he presses.

"My God." Deirdre gets up and saunters over to the cooler. "We'll drink with you, Lach, all right? Quit trying so hard." She comes back with two bottles, offering me one. A frosty bead of water runs down and splashes on my leg.

Jess dismisses me. "Go ahead. I don't care."

I hesitate.

"Drink the beer, Erin," she says. "I'm fine."

I take the bottle, clink it against Deirdre's, and gulp down a good quarter of it. Almost immediately, probably because of the day's strenuous exercise and the fact that I haven't eaten nearly enough, my body goes loose limbed and languid.

It feels so good. *Really good.*

A seventies southern rock song drifts out of a little wireless speaker Lach has set on the picnic table. I stretch my scratched, insect-bitten legs toward the fire and sing along. After a second, I realize I've got my beer raised like I'm at a concert. I glance over at Lach. He's laughing. And then he's not laughing; he's just watching me with those pale eyes. I shut my mouth and look away.

Jessalyn's up, holding his phone. "What's your password? I want to change the music."

"Try his name," Deirdre calls out.

Jess waggles the phone at him. "Password, chickadee."

"Lock," he says.

"*L-a-c-h* or *l-o-c-k*?" Jessalyn retorts. "The man? Or the thing on a door you stick a key into?"

"It's also one of those things on a dam," Deirdre says.

Jess taps at the phone. "Holy shit," she says. "Y'all. His password is actually *lock.*"

Prince's "Let's Go Crazy" starts playing.

"It's short for Lachlan, you dimwits." He grins at all of us.

"That's a homonym," Jessalyn says. "Which is different than a homograph. That's when two words are spelled the same but mean different things."

Deirdre laughs. "Like a fine . . . money you owe . . . and *fine*." She sways a little. "God damn. I've only had one beer."

I know what she means. The effect of one drink is much stronger than I expected.

Lach leaps up and grabs Deirdre's hand. "Dance with me." His voice has a wheedling tone to it.

She struggles loose. "Shouldn't we be meditating or working on our chakras or something?" She strides over to the picnic table and pops open another beer. "Didn't you say we were supposed to go beyond our first world mindset?"

Lach addresses Jess and me. "Okay, I'm calling an audible. You guys have done a great job this week, really worked your asses off. So we're going to take a time out from the official agenda and celebrate your successes." He glances at Deirdre. "Even if I have to force you."

"What does that mean?" she retorts, then turns away. "Asshole."

"You don't have to force me," Jess says.

He angles toward her. "You wanna dance?"

"Maybe." She eyes him coyly. I glance at Deirdre. She's glaring at them both.

But Jess slips around Lach and shimmies over to me. She crooks her finger. I laugh and shake my head but offer my hand. She hoots with triumphant laughter and pulls me up, grinding on me to the music.

"There you go," Lach says. "Look, Dee Dee. These girls know how to have fun."

As Deirdre settles back beside the fire, Lach corrals me with his arms. He pulls me in close, and I can feel her eyes on us. Under his ratty

T-shirt his chest feels like granite. He smells like campfire smoke and beer and sweat, and when his whiskery cheek brushes mine, I stiffen.

"Jesus, relax." He pulls me closer. "I don't bite."

I can't relax—but I'm not sure I want to make a big deal of pushing this guy away. I don't like the vibe I'm getting from Deirdre, sure, but more importantly I'm worried about Agnes. Really worried. And I'm starting to feel that Antonia didn't send her home like Lach said.

But bottom line, even if Agnes is lost in the woods, and Lach's been lying to us about it, playing innocent is the smartest move. At least until I can find out what's really going on.

Lach's hand has made its way from between my shoulder blades down to the curve of my lower back.

"So you're pretty famous, huh?" he says.

I kind of laugh and shake my head at the same time.

"You did that app that's worth a shit ton of cash, didn't you? People write stories about you."

"I'm not famous."

"You're rich, though. Really rich now that your husband died." He smiles, and I feel a chill run up my back. Prickle the hair on my scalp.

And then I feel his fingers flutter across my chest. My eyes fly open just as he plucks the blue plastic bread tie from where it had worked its way up from my cleavage and become stuck to my sternum.

He holds up the tie. "What's this?"

Fear rips through me. "I took it off the package of bread this morning. I wanted to use it to tie my hair back."

He glances at my hair twisted into a bun with what is clearly a rubber band.

"In case I lost the one I have now," I add quickly. "Or it broke. Can I please keep it? It can be our little secret."

He lifts his eyebrows. Studies my face. I can feel myself starting to shake under his gaze, but I don't look away.

"Okay." He gingerly tucks the tie back into my bra, pushing it slowly, purposefully too far down between my breasts. His eyes rise to meet mine, but I can't bear to hold his gaze. And, great. Now Deirdre's on her feet, scowling at us.

Lach's cell dings, and he releases me. He answers the call, spinning away from the campfire into the shadows. I drift away from the other two. The air is smothering me, and somewhere far away, thunder rumbles. I wish I could crawl in my tent and go to sleep.

"Come on, Dee, dance," Jessalyn says, but Deirdre doesn't move.

"I'm going to bed," she says.

Lach steps back into the firelight. "Chickadees! The party's just starting." He scoots up behind Deirdre and gives her a little hip bump. "Come on, darling." He runs a finger across her chest, down her arm, and to her hip. She doesn't stop him or pull away. She just stands there, letting him run his hands all over her.

The hairs on my scalp and arms prickle. Something about this night is starting to feel very wrong.

"I can't go back to them," she says vaguely. "They know it, and I know it."

Lach backs away from her, and Jess and I go quiet. For some reason, the jungle sounds have died too. The fire crackles between us, the only sound in the still, humid night besides Prince crooning about the rain.

"I don't even know what I'm doing all this for," Deirdre says. "I mean, my God, what's even the point?"

"Come on, Dee. Buck up," Lach says. "It's a party." He wanders around to the other side of the fire and plops back down on his log. He looks dejected.

"Okay, Lach, *honey*, I'll buck up," Deirdre snaps. "Anything to make you feel better." She sways toward him. "I'm just here to make you feel better. You and all the men of the world. Because God forbid any of you motherfuckers feels the least bit *insufficient*."

She pulls her shirt up and over her head and in her bra does a little shimmy for him. He watches her with his pale eyes. The firelight reflects off her skin.

"How's that?" she says. "Good enough? Because you know, it's my mission in life to make a man feel better about himself."

She drops her arms and stumbles to the far side of the fire.

Whoa.

But she's not finished. "I've been pulling down half a million a year, tax free, for *him*. Putting braces on my kids' teeth, paying for their anxiety meds, their private tutors so they won't get left behind at their private school my husband insists we send them to. But I'm the criminal here, right? Of course I am."

Her voice ratchets up a notch. "He gets to come home from his honorable job as a creative writing professor at a rinky-dink college and announce that we're going to the Vineyard for the summer. Oh, and that we've got to hire a trainer for the nine-year-old because the kid's showing some promise in soccer, and what if the colleges of America don't take notice? Do you know how much an ex–navy SEAL charges to make your nine-year-old son do push-ups in his own front yard?"

No one utters a word. We're all frozen.

"Half my savings, that's how much."

Jessalyn, who's now sitting on top of the picnic table and fiddling with Lach's walkie, speaks up. "That's the dumbest thing I've ever heard, getting a personal trainer for a kid. No dumb-ass kid deserves a trainer."

"Tell me about it," Deirdre says. She downs the rest of her beer. Her pale skin shines in the firelight.

"Okay," Lach says. "Let's get the dance party going again. Get up there and show me a Supremes thing." He's grinning.

Jessalyn doesn't budge from her spot. Her eyes are cold. "This is Prince. Somebody needs to explain the difference between Wendy & Lisa and the Supremes to you."

"What?" Lach says.

"Fuck you," Deirdre barks suddenly. Her eyes are like slits, zeroed in on Lach.

"Fuck me?" He presses a hand against his chest. "Why? What are you so mad about?" She turns away. "Don't be selfish, Deirdre. You can't get all the attention. Besides, you already got a husband, and Erin here, Erin's husband is dead."

I point at him. "You need to shut your mouth." My voice is unsteady, and I realize I'm quaking with anger.

"You know what—" Jessalyn starts to say.

Deirdre interrupts, pointing at Lach. "If you touch her. If you dare touch her—"

"Deirdre," I say. "Don't listen to him. He's messing with you. Being an asshole."

"You know," Lach says to Deirdre, "I told Antonia I was gonna save you till last. Play with you a few days. But she said no. She said you'd be a problem, which indeed you have turned out to be."

Deirdre cocks her head.

"Not a problem I can't deal with," he goes on. "But she called it, is my point. And that's why she's the boss, I suppose. So, I guess playtime's over."

The air between them crackles, but it's not because of the campfire. Even Jessalyn is quiet now.

"What the fuck are you talking about?" Deirdre says.

In answer, he pulls a gun from the back of his waistband—a gleaming black pistol that looks like something a cop might carry, except it has an extralong barrel. He points it at her.

"Antonia says all clear," he drawls. "All the mango and banana farmers are in their little houses, tucked into their comfy beds. We're finally alone."

"What the hell are you doing?" Jess says.

That's not a long barrel. It's a silencer. Instinctively I take a step toward Deirdre.

"*Bonne nuit*, Dee Dee," Lach says simply. Then one shot, a muffled thwack that sounds like nothing more than a firecracker, splits the air, and Deirdre drops to the dirt. I dart to her and fall to my knees, my hands out. Then I feel something warm and wet spurt onto me. It trickles down my chin, and I swipe at it, knowing what it is before I touch it. When I look at Deirdre I see blood arc up from her chest in short intervals. It's in time to her heartbeat, I realize, sick to my stomach. He hit her artery.

Everything around us slows—the droning of the jungle, the flames dancing under the moon, the sound of Jessalyn's voice. She's on her knees, too, on the other side of Deirdre, hands all over her, screaming something I can't decipher. My body is frozen and so is my brain, and now Deirdre's blood is spurting in lower arcs.

She's dying.

There was no one to watch Perry die. He was alone . . .

Lach points the gun at Jess. And then I hear a second thwack, and the screaming stops. She goes down, just like Deirdre.

I leap up and step back. One step, two, then three. The fire spits and hisses, and Lach's gun swings around to me. I think, *No, no, no, no, no,* and time stops. His pale gaze holds mine. He doesn't smile, only looks deep in thought.

A moan. He points the gun down at the ground just beside the fire, where Deirdre is lying. The third thwack makes me jump.

Then, in a flash, Jessalyn is scrambling to her feet, running toward me. She yanks my shirt, nearly pulling me over, and screams at me to run. I do. I run straight into the jungle, Jessalyn crashing through the trees beside me. Behind us I hear Lach's gun, firing shot after muffled shot.

28

SHORIE

"Let me get this straight. You noticed something off in your parents' company's servers, and so you installed spyware in a Jax user's account? And now you think they're stealing money?"

Rhys is studying my phone intently, his legs splayed out on a saggy oversize chair in the main room of his house. It's dark out, Rhys's living room lit by a lone lopsided lamp. Outside on the porch, moths party around the fanlights. As much as I like the idea of being alone with Rhys in his house at night, we're not. Lowell's back in the bedroom, tallying up the week's reports.

Back at the restaurant, I'd grappled with the idea of confiding in Rhys without any proof that he was trustworthy. It was a risk, no doubt. But ultimately—even though I wasn't completely convinced that Ben or Sabine hadn't hired him to keep an eye on me—I decided to go for it. I had a couple of reasons. One: he seemed like someone who could handle big situations. He reminded me a little of Mom in that way. And two: pheromones.

"Embezzling, to be more precise," I say. "I think it's an employee."

"Really? Who?"

"I don't know. We don't have access to identities on our servers, just anonymous UUID numbers."

"It's such a ballsy move," Rhys says. Which is something, considering what he does.

"You know," comes a voice from the end of the hallway. It's Lowell, dressed in an old bowling shirt and straw fedora. "Somebody did this with an Indian IT firm recently, the CFO. The technical word for it is *defalcation*. Basically, the updated version of a bank teller taking five to ten bucks from hundreds, even thousands of large customer deposits. Obviously, there's a bigger payoff with as many accounts as Jax has . . . but because they're microtransactions, hardly anyone notices."

Rhys hands back my phone. "Private conversation, Lowell."

"Sorry." He hands Rhys a sheaf of printouts. "Milady."

"Is that the only way they do it?" I say.

Lowell looks thoughtful. "They could also make up a fake company and charge small amounts through Jax that people don't notice when they go through their monthly charges. So many people don't review their charges carefully, especially if the balances are only off by a few cents."

"So who would do something like that?" Rhys asks.

"I'm not sure. Somebody who can code."

Lowell settles on the opposite end of the sofa from me, and a cloud of dust poofs up around him. "So, who on staff at Jax can code?"

Scotty. Or Ben.

I sigh. "Well, some better than others, obviously. But most everybody, to some extent." I think of Hank. "Some of the interns. The new database guy. For all I know it could be the guy who delivers lunch."

"Shorie, do you think your dad had any clue about this—before he died? About the skimming?"

"If he did, he would've made a note of it. In the last journal he kept, the March one. But it's missing."

Both of them bolt upright so fast, it's almost comical.

"Jeez!" Rhys exclaims.

"Why didn't you mention that earlier?" Lowell cries.

"I don't know."

"You think somebody might've taken it?" Rhys asks. "The people messing around on Jax?"

"I don't know," I repeat. "I've looked everywhere for it. But it doesn't make any sense. None. My father was never without his monthly journal. He wrote everything in it. Everything—his weekly plans, his to-do lists. Even poems he thought my mom would like. He couldn't function without his journal. I used to make fun of him." I feel my face grow red, my heart throb. "An IT guy, toting around his analog diary."

We fall silent.

After a moment, Rhys speaks. "If your dad noticed anything amiss in the servers, he would've made a note of it, right?"

"Maybe. Hard to say for sure. That kind of thing wasn't always important enough for him to deal with. A lot of times he'd get somebody else, another programmer or an intern, to deal with it. He might've even kicked it over to me, as an assignment." My stomach does a little flip. "Wait a second. The message. Maybe he mentioned it there."

"What? He messaged you?" Rhys says. "Through Jax?"

"Yeah, when he was setting up my budget. It was the day before he died, and I . . . I just couldn't . . ." I shake my head, embarrassed.

The room has gone silent, all except for the wheezing from the fridge back in the kitchen. I look down at my phone. Open Jax. Take a deep breath and click on the unread message.

"Shorie, that's a private thing," Rhys says. "The last message from your dad. You don't have to do this right now. Right here, with us."

"It's okay."

I hope I'm right. I hope I won't lose my shit right here in front of Rhys and Lowell. But even if I do, I've got to open the damn thing;

avoiding the inevitable is just becoming stupid. And it may reveal something I haven't thought of yet.

Dated March 19, the message starts the way all Dad's notes and cards and letters to me always do. Shorie, my sweet . . . And it's long. I take a deep breath, lightheaded, terrified, and exhilarated all at once. I scan the first part.

"He set up a couple of special allocations for me. Emergency, car, extra medical."

He'd also instructed me not to connect with men I didn't personally know—fairly standard Dad advice—and gave me a mini-lecture about birth control. But I wasn't about to reveal that.

"It's mostly details about Jax," I say. "Working on my budget—a college student's budget that includes a scholarship—has got him going back and tinkering with the original algorithm he created."

"Is that it?" Rhys asks.

"No," I say. There's more.

I feel myself going wobbly inside, and I order myself not to cry.

Shorie, my sweet, one last thing. I've been trying to write you a letter . . .

The air in my lungs whooshes out of me, so fast I nearly faint.

"Are you okay?" Rhys asks me.

I nod, inhale deeply, and read silently. . . . but I've been having trouble with it. I know at some point, I'll give up on trying to say the perfect thing to you before you leave home and go off to school. But the damn thing's like a wonky piece of code that I just can't get right, and you know how I am about those . . .

My vision is suddenly obscured. When I wipe my eyes, my fingers come away wet.

Anyway, one day I'll finish, but I wanted to tell you, if the letter is lame, it's because there's no way to express exactly what you mean to me. I'll keep trying. Love, Dad.

I sit quietly, staring at the message.

Rhys finally speaks. "Shorie?"

I look up. Unbidden tears swim up and spill out; then to make matters worse, my nose starts running. Rhys's expression changes, but I can't tell if he's feeling awkward or regretful that he didn't push me to wait—or if he's just remembering how much he misses his dad too. It doesn't really matter, I think. The only thing that feels important right now is what I just read.

"He was writing me a letter," I say. The tears are overflowing now, and I can't care. I just can't.

"I'm so sorry, Shorie," Rhys says. "But I'm glad too." And he does seem really sad and also glad. Not like someone who's been tasked with spying on me.

I start crying even harder.

Rhys touches my hand. "We'll help you figure this out. We'll do what we can."

29

Perry's Journal

<u>Sunday, March 10</u>

TO DO:
- Haircut—ask for Cindy this time, NOT GARRETT
- Mercedes Marathon with Layton?
- $5,000—transfer to Mom's bank account (Set up lunch or dinner with them to talk about finances)
- <u>New Error Message</u>—Shorie assignment—take a look at it and write up fix? New process? Glitch?
- WORK ON SHORIE LETTER!!

Drink to me only with thine eye-openers,
And I will pledge with minicab;
Or leave a kitty but in the curate,
And I'll not look for winning.

(for Erin—or Foxy Cat, Ben Jonson, "Song: To Celia," N+7)

I'll not look for winning . . . nice.

30

ERIN

I stumble forward on shaky legs, thrashing through giant banana tree leaves and furry vines, ordering my body—my mind too, while I'm at it—not to collapse. Jessalyn's close behind me. I can tell, because she won't stop crying. I think about turning and shushing her, but we can't afford the delay. Lach could be right behind us.

It's pitch dark, and even though there's a watery half-moon overhead, I still trip over or hit every root and branch in my path. Eventually we come to a clearing with tall grass. But my heart plummets when I take in the strangely familiar shape of the field. *Shit.* We've just been following the trail we used earlier today. The one that leads to the meadow with our shelters and eventually to the waterfall.

As Jessalyn runs past me, I grab her shirt and yank her off the path. She yips as I pull her deeper into the thick screen of leaves. A half dozen yards farther into the cover of the jungle, I push her down into a depression in the ground. We're hidden, but I can still see the path, and there's no sign of Lach. Not yet.

Jess is trembling violently, breathing too loudly. I put a hand over her lips, and she gulps, quieting. In the scant moonlight, I see her face is coursed with sweat and tears and flecks of blood.

Then I hear the crashing. I throw my arm around Jess, flattening us both into the dirt and rotted leaves, willing us invisible. I strain my ears, expecting him to continue past, but he stops, yards away from us.

I can't see him, can't hear him now either, but he's just standing there. I hold my breath, squeezing my eyes shut.

Go. Gogogogogogo . . .

I need to be thinking, planning a way out of here if this asshole spots us, but all I can think of is Shorie. My sweet, smart, stubborn Shorie, who painted a starry sky with the words *Make a dent in the universe.* Why do I always think I have to be the one out front, leading the charge? My daughter knew better than me. She didn't want to go to school. She wanted to stay home, with me, watching TV and eating ice cream and healing from the cruel blow life had dealt us.

What an idiot I've been. What a selfish, bullheaded idiot. If I'd listened to her, we'd be home now.

"Chickadees!" Lach calls out in a singsong voice, and a fresh wave of adrenaline washes over me again. Sharp, hot pinpricks, like I'm being electrocuted.

He's trying to figure out which way we went. Looking for footprints on the trail or broken branches or something. I don't know if the guy's any kind of tracker, but if he is, I'm hoping our signs are too hard to read in the dark.

We stay still, and after what seems like forever, he jogs away, back in the direction he came. I count three hundred *Mississippi*s, then shake Jess gently.

"Are you hit? Did he hit you?"

"No, he missed and I just dropped. But why did he shoot Deirdre? Why did he shoot me?"

I shake my head. "I don't know. But we need to stop and think about our next step. We don't know this island, but he does."

"Should we stay here? Or go?"

"Stay, I think. At least for a little longer."

We're in a good spot. Thick undergrowth obscures the small depression, hiding us from the path. I don't see a flashlight or hear any animal noises, only the distant rumble of thunder. It sounds like it's a ways off, but I don't know how fast storms travel across a tiny island in the middle of the Caribbean. We've had showers here, at least one or two every afternoon, but not a full-on storm. Yet.

"I almost forgot. I got this." Jessalyn fumbles with something, a green battery light glows, and then there's a crackle. Lach's walkie. "Hello? Hello? Is anybody out there?"

A voice crackles back. "Dimitri here. Who's this?"

She presses the button again, but I snatch the walkie from her and start searching frantically for the power button. "They can track these things," I whisper.

Where *the hell* is the goddamn button? I work in tech, for the love of God.

A female's voice comes through the walkie, low and modulated. "Jessalyn? Is that you?"

I freeze, and Jess puts her hand on my leg.

"Jessalyn?" Antonia says. "Is everything all right up there? Where's Lach?"

In the dark, our eyes meet.

I press the button. "Antonia?"

"Who's this?"

"Erin Gaines."

"Erin? Is everything all right?" Her voice is breathy. Light. I'm not fooled.

I suck in a long, deep breath and let it out. Jess sends me the smallest nod.

"No, Antonia. As a matter of fact, everything is not all right. But there's no time to go into it now. Right now all I'm going to say is you better get your goddamn ducks in a row—call your lawyer, shred documents, wipe hard drives—because this is the end of the road."

She doesn't answer. My fingers have begun to tingle.

"RJ for Antonia," comes a different voice.

"Go," Antonia says.

"What's your twenty?"

"Studio C."

"I'll meet you there in a second to pick up the yoga mats."

"Over."

And then she's gone. I stare at the screen, wanting to scream. To smash this stupid walkie to powder.

"Erin?" It's Jess. "You really think she planned this?"

I flash to Antonia's wide eyes and pink-flushed face. The privileged young heiress, given the world and the attending belief that she's above its rules. I sat there in her office, listened to her pitch, amused by the combination of her naïveté and boldness. And maybe impressed by it a little bit, too, if I'm being honest. Because I've always gravitated to ambitious women who prefer to apologize rather than ask permission.

But maybe she knew that. Maybe she was just flattering me. I've been reading people a long time. Spotting potential, knowing who's going to be a smart hire and who'll be a drain on the team. Determining which investor is leading me on and which is worth having one more drink with.

But she showered me with compliments, and I fell for it. In service of my ego, I overlooked the glaring breaches of privacy, the wildly inappropriate offer of the alternative L'Élu, and gave the princess a pass. But she knew what she was doing from the moment she came strolling into the dining room to fetch me. She knew.

Oh, hell yes. Antonia Erdman is the ringmaster of this circus.

"Erin?" Jess says.

I realize she's been waiting for my answer. "Yes," I say. "I think she definitely planned this." I tell her about Antonia's proposition to me in her office back at Hidden Sands. About finding the bread tie that Agnes used in her hair and the bone that could've been human. When I say that I think Lach probably killed Agnes, too, and that she wasn't the first, Jess scoffs.

"That's crazy. Utterly batshit crazy," she says. "Why would Antonia want anyone dead? Why would she want *us* dead?"

"I don't know." I think for a second. "But Deirdre was running a massage operation. Sex work. Her family gave her a choice—quit or lose them. But maybe she refused to stop. Maybe her family sent her here and paid Antonia to deal with her."

Jess doesn't comment. But I am suddenly, horribly, overcome by the truth: I am the major shareholder of Jax. And I just announced I want to sell, long before the big payday we all planned for. I screwed up everyone's plan to get rich. So someone must have decided to get rid of me—Ben or Sabine, Gigi or Arch, Layton.

One of them wants to kill me.

Jess speaks, her voice small and scared. "What are we going to do?"

"We're going to solve the problem," I reply numbly.

Because that's what I do. I solve problems. Lach may be a lecherous guy with a gun, but still, at his core, he is nothing more than a problem. Anything I've ever done as a businesswoman—positioning Jax, strategizing ways to ensure that the company survives the cutthroat world of technology—will be useful to me now. If I can just keep my fear under control.

"Okay," I say. "They can track this walkie. Which means we have to ditch it. But that'll help us. It'll be a decoy."

"Where?" she asks.

I don't answer right away. There's this thing you always hear in the startup business: "Build it and they will come." It's bullshit advice, for the most part; customers aren't going to go somewhere they don't want to go, use some service they don't really want. But the point is a lot of folks do stuff on reflex, and I think the concept might apply here. I think Lach might be that essentially uncreative person who will assume that we'll head someplace we've already been.

We stay off the trail, clambering through the underbrush and, after about forty-five minutes, manage to locate the meadow. On the far edge, set just inside the line of trees, three dark mounds rise up in the moonlight. Our shelters are still standing, which I guess means we did a passable job of building them. Up close, Deirdre's is the most impressive. I remember her weaving some palm leaves into a kind of decorative pattern and laying it out like a welcome mat at the opening.

She'd beckoned Lach with a crook of her finger, and he'd sidled closer to inspect her handiwork. As they stood beside her shelter, he'd let a hand touch her shoulder, then drop down to her bottom. The memory makes me sick. He'd known then that he was going to shoot her.

"Do it," Jess says.

Just as thunder rumbles over us, and the skies release a torrent of rain, I toss the walkie into Deirdre's shelter. Then I yell above the noise.

"Remember when we first got to camp, there was a bunch of supplies on the picnic tables? Supplies that Lach hadn't brought in? There's somebody else out here, maybe in another house or a warehouse or something, delivering food and equipment directly to the L'Élu groups."

Jess nods. "I was just thinking that. And there's no way they regularly bring up people who are really detoxing without some kind of access to a clinic or a doctor. Addicts who are in withdrawal would need some kind of real medical help. There's got to be a building close to us."

I grab her arm. "When I first arrived, my concierge told me there used to be a sugarcane plantation on this island. This field must've been one of the sugarcane fields."

"Okay."

"And if there was a plantation, there may be a house." I think for a moment. "It'll be on a high point. Maybe overlooking the other side of the island. A base camp for storage, communication, and medical supplies. Hopefully there'll be a phone or a computer there too. I want to contact my daughter, let her know what's happening, and warn her not to talk to anyone at Jax. Is there anyone on your end you trust?"

Even in the rain and dark I can see her face is grim, jaw set firmly. "No."

"All right, then, we'll try for Shorie."

The rain slows us down, and we walk for another half hour, tromping through the wet foliage, our feet sucking in the mud. I don't see any sign of any building, much less a house. Maybe we should rethink our plan. I don't say anything, but I know Jess is thinking the same thing, because when we come to a huge spreading kapok tree with thick branches and high, ridged roots like buttresses, she stops.

"We can try again in the morning," she shouts through the downpour and snags a broad leaf from a nearby banana tree.

We scramble underneath the kapok, then take turns funneling rainwater from the broad leaf into our mouths. After scurrying out into the rain to pee, we settle in for the night, huddling in the space between two sheltering roots. We press close, not so much for warmth, but more from some deep, primal instinct for survival. I don't think I've ever so keenly felt the comfort of another human body against my own.

"I just don't understand it." Jessalyn's head is against the massive trunk of the tree. "If we could just break it down . . ."

I shake my head. It's a simple question, just too horrifying to attempt to answer out loud.

A setup.

An execution.

My conversation with Antonia has come into unbearably sharp focus in the time we've been walking in the dark. Someone hired her, paid her, to have the four of us killed. But because I'm the CEO of a successful company, she saw an opportunity and offered me a better deal—L'Élu II, for a couple of thousand dollars more and the possibility of some kind of business partnership. Basically she was double-crossing whomever she'd done business with and didn't seem to be all that worried about it. But who was that person?

Ben? Sabine? Layton? Perry's parents?

Jess interrupts my thoughts. "So let me get this straight. There are three L'Élus—the real one, the fun one, and the one where you die."

"That's the long and short of it."

"What the Sam fuck . . ." She sniffs. "We sure drew the short straw, didn't we?"

"We're going to figure our way out of this, I promise you."

She doesn't answer. We both know I'm cheerleading, that words mean nothing in comparison to Lach and his gun, so I vow to keep my mouth shut until I have a real plan. The only sound now is the rain, and although I have a fleeting thought that one of us should keep watch, I don't say anything. Both of us will need sleep to keep going.

"Why are you here?" Jess says, out of the darkness. "Really?"

"I blacked out and stole a friend's car, then drove it to a college frat party where I passed out on the lawn."

Jessalyn shifts beside me. "You were drinking?"

"I had one drink."

"That's bullshit. Nobody blacks out after one drink."

"They said it could've happened because of stress. The next morning, my friends and family have miraculously organized an intervention where they tell me I'm going to Hidden Sands."

"Who led this discussion? Who found the resort?"

I shrug. "I don't remember. Who told you about Hidden Sands?"

"My father." She leaves it at that.

"The thing I can't get over," I say, "is I'm not a big drinker. I mean, yes, I may have had one or two more drinks than normal at a dinner or a party since Perry died. But nothing at all outrageous. It just seems so . . ."

"So what?"

"Convenient, I guess. The way it happened . . ." My voice trails off.

In the dark, I can feel her eyes on me. "You know what happened, don't you? You think somebody drugged you."

I inhale then blow the breath out slowly. "The night before I left, I was googling like crazy. GHB is the big thing now. Liquid ecstasy. It's really easy to get your hands on. I know it sounds ridiculous. But I do think that. I think somebody roofied me."

"That's interesting," Jess says. "Because before I came here, I think someone roofied me too."

31

ERIN

Jessalyn's body shifts against me, and I wake. The rainforest is transforming from inky black to grayish green. It's morning—Tuesday, I think. I didn't really sleep, just dozed a bit all night long, drifting in and out of wakefulness, like I was traveling through a horrible half dream. And now I feel like I've awoken in a nightmare.

I run my hands down my legs. They're covered in stubbly hair and streaked with mud. Mosquito bites pock the rest of me, even up in my most tender parts. But there are some positives: The rubber band is still holding back my hair. It stopped raining in the night, and under the spreading branches of the kapok tree where we slept, my shirt and hiking shorts dried out almost completely.

My only question is why Lach hasn't found us yet. Surely he knows every inch of this island. Is he waiting on something?

We crawl out from our hiding place to find the forest floor teeming with horned beetles and stick insects and narrow green lizards. Emerging from their hiding places, I guess, just like us, after the downpour. Some kind of birds—parrots maybe—whistle in the trees overhead. I look back at our tree. It's festooned with orchids, bright pink and white and dotted with dark-wine markings like a native warrior around pollen-yellow centers, sprouting out of every crevice. A fairy tree. A sight that would take my breath away, if I weren't being chased by a man with a gun.

The wind carries with it a whiff of a fire. Old or new, I don't know. But it does make me remember what Grigore told me. Erdman International owns Hidden Sands and three-quarters of Ile Saint Sigo. But there are a few people still living up here, farmers, he said, and fishermen. It sure would be great to run into one right about now. Unless, of course, they turn out to be working for Antonia.

We take turns peeing; then I take a minute, reorienting my inner compass. I notice Jess is looking at me with an odd expression.

"You've got blood all over your shirt," she says, her voice edged with horror. "And on your neck. It's her blood." She pulls out her shirt, then splays her hands out. "Oh my God. It's under my nails! He shot her in the heart!"

"Jess. We need to go."

She covers her face with her hands. I think she may be crying.

I touch her shoulder. "The more we stay on the move, the better our chances of avoiding Lach."

She wipes her eyes and gulps in air. "Okay. I'm good. Let's go."

We search for a path, but it turns out we don't need one, because almost immediately the jungle opens up to reveal that I was spot-on in my speculations last night. There is indeed a jewel in the crown of the former plantation that probably used to rule every social, economic, and political aspect of this island. The big house. From our hiding place under the tree, we'd been less than a quarter of a mile away from it.

An imposing white coral stone building with a red tile roof, the centuries-old structure is studded with balconies and porticoes and awnings. A series of stone stairs zigzag up the hill and then onto the foundation walls to the grand front entrance. The place looms over the surrounding fields, a vast, honest-to-God mansion, sun bleached and windswept. It's not pretty—it's actually kind of ungainly and forbidding—but I think that's kind of the point. It looks the way it does to send a message, one of uncontested privilege. Of timeless wealth and permanence. A worshipful monument to the horrors of colonial exploitation and entitlement.

Jess studies the place, arms folded. "Fuck this place."

I nod. "Yes. Absolutely. Fuck it times a thousand. But we need a computer so I can contact my daughter and the FBI and get the hell off this island, so we've got to go in."

She squints into the sun. "Do you think anyone's home?"

"No idea. Ten to one, though, whoever is in there is connected to Antonia. So we better be invisible." My gaze sweeps over the facade. The numerous windows opening into numerous rooms. The house is huge. I don't know how we're going to sneak through it undetected. Especially in broad daylight. But anything could happen between now and when the sun goes down. We can't risk wasting any more time.

We creep around to the back of the house in search of a more unobtrusive entrance than the grand front door. Sure enough, on the far side, we find stairs leading up to a back portico. I notice a small dish affixed to a railing. Satellite internet. Perfect.

A back door lets us into a wide central hall, and pressed against the back wall, we listen for activity. We're rewarded with the sounds of a door slam and the clacking of heels above us. Hopefully, they'll stay upstairs.

I take in our surroundings. The house, with its rows and rows of wavy-glassed windows, is sun drenched but only minimally decorated. A few antique sofas and tables line the walls of the wide hallway. A scarred, sun-bleached wood floor. Walls papered in faded golds and blues and greens. Carved cornices, heavy moldings, columns, and medallions adorn doorways and the soaring central staircase.

Jess and I creep down the hall, poking our heads into each room. One room, the floor-to-ceiling windows hung with puddling panels of blue silk, seems to be a living room. There's an old carved sofa, an inlaid wardrobe, a long wood table, and a few other scattered pieces of furniture. The room next to it is neatly stacked with clear plastic tubs, some empty, others filled with paper towels, toilet paper, and other sundries.

Jess pulls out a bottle of green bath gel. "Oh my God. Look at this." She touches the smears of blood on her neck and chest. "We could be in and out in five minutes. Just get the blood off."

"Jess, no," I say. "No shower."

I motion her to follow me down the hall. We find an improvised pantry, fitted with shelves stocked with every kind of canned good imaginable. We grab a couple of bananas and some jerky, and at the front door, loop around and check the other side of the hall, cramming our mouths with the food. At the end of the hall, we find a closed door. It's unlocked.

I peek in. It's empty. I give Jess a thumbs-up and whisper, "Keep an eye out, okay?"

She nods and I slip inside. The room's been converted into an office. There's a console with a printer and fax machine, as well as four modular desks. A sleek desktop computer sits on the desk near the window. It's playing soft jazz. Beside the computer sits a framed, autographed eight-by-ten glossy headshot. It's that actress I saw when I arrived at Hidden Sands. I read the Sharpie-scrawled inscription.

For Zara ~ love, light & limoncello!

Zara can't be far. In fact, that's probably her clacking around upstairs. I scoot behind the desk and wake up the computer. Instantly a series of spreadsheets fill the screen with columns labeled *Hidden Sands, L'Élu I, L'Élu II, L'Élu III.*

I stare at it for a moment, trying to make sense of what I'm seeing. Of the numbers and names all laid out before me. But really, I don't need to. I already know what I'm looking at. It's Antonia's three experiences, just like Jess described them last night. L'Élu I, the real program. L'Élu II, the fun fake for VIPs. And L'Élu III—the one where you wind up dead.

Right here in front of me, in black and white, are records of everything to do with every incarnation of Hidden Sands' "restorative experiences." Balances, vendors, lists of payers. The L'Élu I column for just this week is substantial: *Akin, Blanchard, Brock, Capone, Curry, Dhanial, Freeman, Haddad, Hardy, Kurkjian, Lawson, Oyinlola, Peterson, Pullen, Shelton, Zabicki* . . . There are lists of names in the L'Élu II and III columns too, but a lot fewer, and the cash amounts are substantially higher. Like, in the six-figure range higher.

I scan the length of the L'Élu III column, searching for the name of one of my friends or family—*Fleming, Gaines, Marko.* But all I see is a list of the participants' names. There are sixteen in all. Mine, Jessalyn's, Agnes's, and Deirdre's are at the bottom. There's not the slightest hint about who paid for our delightful, "one-of-a-kind" experience. But there are several tabs at the bottom of the screen.

I open one, incongruously labeled *Landscaping,* and another spreadsheet appears with a list of, no surprise, plants. Sixteen of them, which makes my body literally shudder in horror. This is it, it has to be. The plant names are links too, so I pick one near the bottom, *ginger lily.* It sends me to another page, one that appears to be some kind of deal memo from a company called *Cutstone, LLC,* purportedly located on the island of Providenciales in Turks and Caicos.

A fake, obviously. This is some shady offshore financial bullshit for sure.

Jesus. I press my fingers into my temples. This is what they mean by a paper trail, I guess. And if I had more time, I could follow it. Possibly even figure out who paid to send me here. But I'm working under the gun here. Literally. My top priority is to get a message to Shorie and get Jess and me the hell out of here before anybody sees us. This database will have to wait.

I minimize the windows and try to open the internet browser, but the screen won't direct. They must have installed blocks restricting full access to the internet. So Zara couldn't mess around on Facebook when she was supposed to be working, probably. If Perry were here, this wouldn't be a problem. If a computer could be compared to a woman, then Perry was Lothario, Don Juan, and Valentino all rolled into one. In other words, when he showed up, computers dropped their firewalls. I, on the other hand, am not that skilled.

I study the task bar at the bottom of the screen. All the basics besides the internet browser—photos, music, calendar, and the whole Office package. And then, a mustard-yellow square with a white lower-case *j* leaps out at me. *Jax.*

Whoever uses this computer has logged in to their personal Jax account.

It's like someone turned up a volume knob on me. My whole body starts to vibrate. My fingertips even tingle. Maybe Perry is here, in some way, after all, watching over me.

I hit the icon. *Hi, Zara!* the little *j* says at the top of the screen. Proving my husband's point that humans are indeed the weakest link in cybersecurity. Zara, in particular, has neglected to log out during her last session, allowing me full access to her account. I scan the allocations, a dozen clean columns of white. She doesn't make a whole lot, salarywise—she's using our basic budget, the "essential."

I log out of Zara's account and sign in to mine. In my private messages, a clean white bubble pops up. I click on it and type:

Shorie, it's Mom. Please se

There's a sharp knock on the door; then, from out in the hall, I hear a clatter of footsteps near the front of the house. I leap up, straining to hear where they're headed. My heart is doing such a good job of pumping its way out of my chest that it hurts. I need to get out of this office—fast—and try to find Jess.

I hear a woman's voice, high and girlish. "Ladies, welcome to L'Élu II," she trills. Sounds like she's near the front door. "May you rest in the knowledge, the *confidence*, that you are *the Chosen*."

Antonia.

Shit. It's Antonia.

Even though I haven't completed my message to Shorie, I hit "Send" and log off my account. Thanks to the computer's automatic log-in being enabled, I can hop back on to Zara's account. I check the desk to make sure everything's in order.

"You know and I know," Antonia continues from out in the hallway, "that we are more than the labels that people hang around our necks. Those labels are like nooses, and we refuse to wear them. We are artists; we are thinkers. Creators of solutions, when they'll leave us alone long enough to think of them . . ."

There's a wave of appreciative laughter. There's more than one person out there, that's clear. And this is definitely the fun L'Élu group, the by-invitation-only L'Élu that only special guests who part with a tidy sum of money get to experience.

I peek around the door into the hallway. The front doors have been flung open, and the group has congregated just outside on the wide front portico. Antonia, sleek in a black strappy sundress and stilettos, her white-blonde hair wound in braids around her head, stands in the open doorway before a small group of women. They're dressed in hiking clothes like our group, except these gals look infinitely more relaxed.

There's no sign of Jess.

Antonia surveys the group and laughs. But it's not that soft, girlish giggle I heard in her office that first night. It's deep and throaty. "We may love and appreciate those who sent us here, but we also know that they don't fully understand who we are. And who are we? We are the Chosen."

She lifts her phone over her head, and instantly music fills the house. It's instrumental, electronica over a slow, hypnotic beat.

"As those who have experienced L'Élu before know," Antonia announces over the music, "upstairs there is a series of rooms, each with its own theme. Each room with an open door contains within a variety of *gifts*. Of tantalizing treats."

Another wave of titters.

"Go explore, find your room, your pleasure, and share it with a friend. And tonight, after dinner, your concierges will be joining us. Don't be afraid of a little hedonism, ladies. It won't hurt you. In the words of Lord Byron, 'the great object of life is sensation.'" She steps back against the door and flings out her arm. "So go live life, ladies!"

As the women swarm into the hall, I dart to the stairs, joining them. I take the stairs two at a time, pulling ahead of the throng, but no one takes notice. The air is filled with excited chattering and giddy laughter.

In the huge hallway upstairs, I pause for a second, wildly scanning the opened doors before me. One is closed, though, all the way at the end of the hall. I run toward it and slip inside, shutting it behind me. There's no lock, and I curse softly, then survey the room.

It's large and sunny, with a bare wood floor and floor-to-ceiling windows with no curtains. It's mostly unfurnished, with only a giant four-poster bed that's draped with a gauzy white canopy and piled high with an array of silk pillows. On a far wall, a lone dressing table of burled walnut with scrolled legs catches my eye. And what's on top of it—an array of crystal decanters filled with every shade of liquid in the rainbow. Tumblers and goblets and flutes, delicate china trays of pills, and tiny jewel boxes.

I move to it and lift the hinged lid of one translucent blue box edged with gold leaf. There's a mound of white powder. So this is what L'Élu II is all about. The royal treatment the super-rich or celebrity guests get. A Marie Antoinette, let-them-eat-cake bacchanal. A bubble of laughter forces itself up and out of me. So much better than L'Élu III—that *alternative experience* in which you forgo your morning coffee, go on long forced hikes, then get straight-up murdered.

I realize I've been listening to the sound of running water coming from behind a door on the other side of the room. Jess. Oh, no. She must be trying to wash all that blood off. Not the wisest move, the house now crawling with people, especially Antonia.

I crack the door, and a cloud of steam hits me in the face. "Jess!" I whisper.

I push the door open. Inside the marble bathroom, the only window is cranked all the way open, and the sink is running. I shut it off and look into the basin.

There's a faint trace of red. Blood.

She was here, but now she's gone.

32

SHORIE

Dally's BBQ is in the heart of Childersburg, tucked between an auto parts place and an army surplus store. The outside is made of standard concrete block. Inside is basically an Auburn Tigers–themed armory. Old BB guns, shotguns, and rifles hang on brackets over every window. Whatever wall space is left has been made into a shrine to Pat Dye.

I showed Rhys (and Lowell) the screenshots between Ms. X and Yours of where they planned to meet. Without even hesitating, Rhys offered to drive me up here. I'm hoping I've done the right thing, confiding in him. He's all I have right now.

I've jammed an Auburn cap low over my eyes, so when we walk into the restaurant, nobody even glances our way. I'm not hungry but I order anyway. No reason to raise suspicion. The meal comes with a cornbread muffin, which I pick at then wash down with sweet tea, all the while keeping an eye on the door. Rhys orders a full chopped pork plate, "extra outside" with mac and cheese, fries, and collards. Head bent, arms cradling his plate, he wolfs the food down, and I try not to fall in love with this guy who knows the code words of barbecue so intimately.

"See anybody yet?" he asks, dredging a fry through ketchup and jamming it in his mouth.

"Nope."

"Who are the suspects again?"

"Pretty much all fifteen or so people who work at Jax," I say.

"What about the sexting?" Rhys says. "Does that tell us anything?"

"That criminals are horny, I guess?" He glances at me, and I flush.

Just then the restaurant door opens, and someone walks in. I can't see very well, as there's a coatrack festooned with about a dozen old football helmets in the way and a group of old men, the early supper crew, standing right at the door. My instinct is to rise up out of the booth, crane my neck so I can see, but they'd see me. I slump down, lower my chin under my cap, and lift my gaze up ever so casually. A server meets the person in the center of the room and points. He turns, spotting the table she's pointing out, and I see him . . .

Ben.

Ben Fleming, standing right in the middle of Dally's BBQ in Childersburg, Alabama. I involuntarily sit bolt upright in my seat and go hot all over. I want to scream, burst into tears, and vomit, all at the same time. I've misunderstood everything. Every single thing.

All the flirting with Mom, all that touchy-feely, nicey-nicey stuff—it was a big nothing. He wasn't after Mom—because he's having an affair with Ms. X.

Ben and Ms. X!

"Who is it?" Rhys hisses.

Calm down. Think.

I mean, it definitely fits. On move-in day, Ben all but confessed to me that he was having problems in his marriage. And now, as promised in the texts, he's in this out-of-the-way barbecue place to rendezvous with the other woman. To cheat on Sabine. And not only is this asshole a cheater, he's a thief. He's trying to wreck my parents' company.

I scrunch and twist around as far as I can without looking like a complete nutball. "It's Ben Fleming," I say to Rhys. "My mom and dad's partner at Jax. Their best friend. Oh my God, oh my God, oh my God."

"He's alone?" Rhys glances over his shoulder.

I motion for him to lie low. "Sh. Yes."

Ben's parked himself at a booth in the corner on the opposite side of the restaurant, and now he's studying the menu. The server is bent over him, pointing at a few items and grinning down at him. How nice of her, how helpful.

"What's he doing?" Rhys asks.

"Flirting with the waitstaff."

"Dirtbag."

But maybe it's more like she's flirting with him. I don't know. I can't tell. Let's face it, I'm not the best judge of those kinds of things. I didn't really think it was going to be Ben who walked through that door. I may have been suspicious of his intentions toward my mom and Layton, but I never actually believed he could do something criminal.

And what about Rhys? I don't even know the guy, and I've pulled him into this mess. What if he's just pretending he doesn't know what's going on? What if he's in on this with Ben, and I've fallen for it?

I drop my head in my hands. There's also the possibility that I'm being ridiculous, and Rhys really is just a nice, caring guy. And maybe it's me who's losing it.

We finish our meal in silence—well, Rhys finishes, and I pick at mine and obsessively check the screenshots of Ms. X's account even though the extra money is still there and nothing has changed. Eventually our server reappears. "Y'all want anything else?"

"Peach cobbler," I mumble.

The flaky, syrupy, bubbly peach cobbler and mountain of vanilla ice cream melting on top does nothing for my appetite. I push it around my plate and watch Ben from under the bill of my cap. For another forty minutes, nobody familiar comes into Dally's. No one joins Ben in his booth. And then, just as he's pulling cash out of his wallet, my cell rings.

Layton.

It rings again, a loud, clear jangle, and my heart stops.

"Answer it," Rhys whispers fiercely.

I put the phone to my ear. "Hello?"

"Hi, Shorie. What's up?" She sounds like she's driving with the window open. Or standing in a tornado.

"Uh. Just having lunch . . . dinner. With a friend." Rhys gives me a thumbs-up.

"That's fun. Where?"

"Where?" I make a face at Rhys. "Some barbecue place. I don't really know the name."

"Jax approved, I hope."

"Oh, yeah. I mean how expensive can barbecue be?"

"Right."

Maybe she was coming to meet Ben and spotted me and Rhys through a window or something. And now she's trying to figure out what's going on.

"I don't really know why I called, Shor," Layton says. "I guess I just wanted to check in after the dust settled and make sure you were okay."

"Oh. Okay. Well, thank you. I'm good. Doing pretty good."

"Foxy Cat misses you. But she's happy. Torn my sofa to shreds."

"Oh gosh, I'm sorry."

"No, it's okay. I was going to buy a new one anyway. Never spent my Christmas bonus."

On the other side of the restaurant, Ben plunks some cash on his table and slides out of his booth. He heads toward the door.

"Hey, Layton, can I call you back?" I say.

"No need. You go do your college thing. It's good to hear your voice."

"You too." I hang up. "Come on," I say to Rhys, but he puts out a hand. Closes it over mine.

"I want to look him in the eyes," I protest.

"I know, but maybe you should wait. I have the feeling this might be bigger than you realize."

An hour later we're all settled in Rhys's living room again—Rhys and Lowell and me and also some girl I recognize from the work party the other night. She's blonde and willowy and wearing a crocheted halter top that shows a double-pierced navel. I hope she's Lowell's girlfriend and not Rhys's.

"So who was it that didn't show?" I say for the millionth time.

"Well, it's obviously not Sabine," Lowell suggests. "So the lawyer? Layton? Maybe that's why she called you. She saw you and was trying to find out how much you know."

"It has to be somebody within the company," Rhys says. "There was that message about how she works at an app company. And Ben definitely could've written that program."

"Maybe," I say, rubbing my temples. My mind is such a jumble, I've got a headache now.

"Okay, let's back up," Rhys says. "We know Ben is involved, somehow. I think you should just sit tight, watch your Jax account for a little while, and see what happens. Back up the screenshots, all of them, online and maybe on a hard drive."

I open my email again and nearly choke.

"What?" asks the blonde girl, leaning forward.

"The screenshots. All the balances are back down where they were before," I say. "The money's gone again."

Lowell whistles. "How much?"

"Roughly one hundred sixty thousand dollars, just like last time. Which divides out to approximately twelve cents from every Jax user. That means whoever this is has now taken over three hundred twenty grand." They all gape at me. "Or more. Those are just the two times I've seen the money come in and go out."

"And this time it took longer for the balances to go down, right?" Lowell says.

"Yeah. Overnight," I say.

"She's varying her routine. She doesn't want to call attention to her account," Rhys says. Our eyes meet.

"It's really happening," I breathe. "They're stealing from Jax's customers."

Lowell shakes his head. "No offense, but it's kind of weird that you don't have any stopgaps in place. People are always looking for opportunities, you know? You got to stay on top of that kind of thing or you're pretty much asking for it."

I roll my eyes at him. "Thanks for the advice. I forgot who I'm talking to—the real professional criminals."

The blonde girl gives me a head wag. "That's rude. Aren't you one of Rhys's customers, though? I mean, aren't you paying to have somebody take all your classes for you?"

Rhys's face kind of freezes, and Lowell looks embarrassed. The blonde girl leans back on the couch.

"I'm not stealing from millions of people," I spit back. "It's not even close to the same thing."

"Look—" Rhys starts.

"You said it was, like, twelve cents from each person," the girl interrupts. "I've got three times that at the bottom of my purse."

I jump up and stalk to the door. On the front porch I drop into a swing and kick it into a furious sway. It squeaks, but the motion is calming, almost narcotic. I tip my head back, but there are no stars, just the cobwebby gray board-and-batten porch ceiling. I could sway here forever, the breeze wafting over me. The breeze that smells faintly like cow pies, but still. It's quiet.

The glider thunks as Rhys drops down beside me. He lays his head back like me too. "Holy smokes, that's a lot of spiders."

I can't help but smile.

"They could drop down on us at any time. Spiders on our faces. It's like a horror movie up there on my porch ceiling."

"You know, there are many spider heroes in ancient mythology. According to Islamic legend, a spider saved Muhammad from the people who were trying to kill him."

He gives me a sidelong glance, and I get the distinct feeling he knows this is one of the ways I deflect, going full-on nerd and dumping information on people. What I didn't tell him was that I got bit by a spider once, and ever since I've imagined that I became a hero myself, like Peter Parker. Imbued with all a spider's very best traits. Hardworking, solitary, aggressive when necessary.

I clear my throat. "I didn't mean what I said. Earlier."

"Sure you did. That's what I like about you. You tell it like it is. And so does Mackenzie. She's cool, I promise."

"If you say so." I sigh. "I didn't mean to come across so bitchy."

"It's okay. You were right. I'm . . ." He stares at the pasture beyond the house. There's one cow, a brownish-red one, that's staring back at us. "I know what I'm doing, and some days I'm less proud of it than others. They'll figure it out, what I'm doing, one day, and then . . . I don't know. I'm not a Bond villain. I'm just a kid who's terrible at school but good at making money."

"But your dad died. You have to make money."

He laughs. "Yeah, not really. My dad had a ton of life insurance. My mom lives in a huge house down in Florida. And my little sister goes to the most expensive art school in the southeast. I'm a privileged white kid, making money by scamming the system. I'm everything people hate. Everything that's unfair in the world."

"Then why don't you stop?"

He looks at me, studies me really, his brown eyes on mine. "I like feeling like I can take care of myself. Like I'm not a loser." He says it quietly, then breaks our gaze and folds his arms over his chest. I get the feeling he's telling me something he hasn't told anybody else.

The air has stilled on the porch, and I can hear something buzzing around us. A mosquito or yellow jacket or wasp. The sound reminds me of a kitchen timer, one the universe has set. It's like the minutes are ticking by, the possibilities narrowing, and if I let the moment go much longer, the timer will ding, and I'll be shit out of luck. I roll my head in Rhys's direction, meeting his eyes again. He's close; it would only take the slightest movement to cross the couple of inches between us.

And then, in one swift movement, he does it. His lips touch mine. Once, softly, then again. The third time he doesn't move, just leaves his lips pressed against mine, and our breath mingles, hot and speeding up.

Taking his time, he repositions his mouth on mine. It's like he's concentrating on learning the feel of my lips. His fingertips brush my jaw and move down to my neck. His breath smells like beer. And peach cobbler. And I decide it's time to quit thinking about my parents.

And then he breaks the kiss, yelping and leaping back and sending the porch swing into wild gyrations.

"What, what?" I scream, jumping off the swing too.

"Spider!" Now he's dancing around the dark porch, brushing and slapping at himself. I burst into laughter.

"You're scared of spiders?"

He gives me a defensive look. "They bite."

"I know," I say, and my heart suddenly brims with so much homesickness and longing and regret that I think it might explode.

"Do you see him?" Rhys asks.

"I think you either smashed him or scared the bejesus out of him."

"So I may have overreacted." He shoots me an endearing smile. "Anyway. It's getting dark. I should probably get you home."

All the wonderful kissing emotions drain right out of me. I know it's Tuesday, but I'd hoped maybe we were going to hang out. And do some more of what we'd been doing.

"Sorry. I've got work," he says.

I can't tell if he's making up an excuse or telling me the truth. Maybe Ben, that jerk, really did hire him to keep an eye on me. Or maybe he's just a guy, just a random guy who happens to be cute and who I like very much and who likes me back. Then why is he taking me home so early? *Shit, shit, shit!*

Rhys is quiet on the drive, and back in my dorm, lying on my bed, I stare at the blank white ceiling. But I'm too exhausted to name my emotions. It's a stupid thing anyway, labeling your feelings. Who cares if you're *rapturous* or *rankled*? What I need are answers. What I need is to talk to my mom, to tell her what I found out about Ben and Jax. But of course, she doesn't have her phone. And if I called the resort, I don't know if they'd even let me talk to her.

I hear her voice in my head: *What's the reality, Shorie? What's the challenge?*

I don't know what the reality is. Or the challenge. Surprisingly, without my mother here, I truly feel like I don't know anything.

I miss her suddenly, and it feels like a sharp, allover body cramp. The kind that hits you on the first day of the flu. It makes me feel even sicker to think that at some point soon, if Ben is involved in stealing from Jax, I may have to call the police. But what the hell am I supposed to say when I do?

I think maybe someone I know is stealing from my parents' company.
I can't trust anyone.
I'm afraid.

The thought of doing such a thing terrifies me. What if Ben comes after me? If he were angry enough about my telling the authorities, would he do something violent? I'm just a kid, but I don't know. But I don't feel safe now, not at all. It's like I'm standing just outside something vast and dark. A rocky cave, its yawning, jagged mouth the entrance to a monster's lair. And that monster—Ben, maybe—waits inside, a grin on his hideous face.

Because he knows I'm weak.

33

ERIN

I stand in the empty bathroom, steam wafting around me and out the open window. As the faucet drips a steady beat, I try to force my brain to slow down.

Think, Erin.

All signs point to a struggle, then Jess possibly wiggling out the window and dropping down to one of the faded red awnings. There's water everywhere. Bottles on the floor. The open window, big enough for a person to squeeze through. But when I peek out, the portico below is deserted.

Or—and the thought is admittedly crazy, but what's a little more crazy in an already senseless situation?—Jess could've messed up the bathroom herself. Set it up to look like someone, Lach probably, barged in here, fought with her before she was able to escape. But would Jess really do that? Could she really be somehow in on Antonia's plan? I saw Lach aim his gun at her and pull the trigger. I saw her sob with fear.

No. Jess hasn't betrayed me.

Lach's taken her.

I feel the blood rush from my head and steady myself against the counter. Out in the bedroom, the door slams open, and I jump so hard I nearly slip in a puddle. I move to the bathroom door and peer through the crack.

It's the actress—she of *love, light, and limoncello* fame. She's slung her backpack on the floor and shucked off her boots, followed by her shirt and shorts. She's wearing filmy sky-blue lingerie—definitely *not* Hidden Sands regulation—and she's thin but muscular and curvy all at the same time, which seems like something only a film actress could achieve.

As she moves to the windows, flings them up, letting the ocean breeze lift her hair, I order my thundering heart to slow. She has thick, impossibly shiny caramel tresses that fall around her shoulders like in a shampoo commercial. The gauzy canopy on the bed whips wildly, and she tosses her oversize sunglasses in the direction of her backpack. At the dressing table, she selects an opalescent jar and unscrews the silver lid. Plucking a straw from a crystal tumbler, she takes a dainty sniff with each nostril, then tilts her head back.

"Ahhhhhh," she says to the empty room. "Ah, yes."

Okay, way past time to get the hell out of Dodge. She'll probably see me, but maybe she'll be so high she won't think anything of it. What I really shouldn't do is stay in here so when she pops in to pee, she gets a surprise. That would be disastrous.

I push open the door and step out of the bathroom, and she seems to regain her senses, widening her eyes and locking on to me like a laser beam.

"What are you doing in my room?" she asks in a quiet, formal tone.

I freeze. "My friend is in trouble. We saw . . . we saw one of the L'Élu guides shoot a woman, and he shot at us too—"

"What the FUCK are you doing in my ROOM!" It's a well-modulated shriek this time, and I bolt for the door. But a key has materialized in the hole below the elegant crystal doorknob, and the door is locked. I pull on it like an idiot until she grabs my ponytail and jerks me back to face her.

"Didn't you hear what Antonia said?" she purrs.

"I—"

"She said take any room with an OPEN DOOR." The expression on her face is withering. Disdain mixed with utter contempt. I find it overwhelmingly effective.

"I'm really sorry. I got separated from another group, an earlier group. I didn't mean to . . ." I edge back toward the door. "I'll just go."

"This is unacceptable. Absolutely unacceptable." She glances at the bathroom door. "Were you using the sink in my bathroom?"

I gawp at her.

"You better not have rubbed your filthy hands on my clean towels, you sorry-ass, piece-of-shit stalker!" She's already unlocking the door to the hallway and flinging it open. Trippy music pours in. I try to duck out, but she blocks me with her arm.

"Antonia," she yells into the hallway. "Antonia, there's a stalker in my room!"

I pivot and head for the bathroom, bursting through the door and sliding across the marble-tiled floor. I focus on the window. If it was good enough for Jessalyn, it's good enough for me.

"Stop," the actress screams. "Get your ass back in here. Antonia! She's getting away!"

I manage to squeeze myself out the window, let go of the ledge, and slam down on the awning over the window below. For a moment, my vision pops and goes blotchy. I can't breathe, but I force myself to roll until my legs are dangling over the edge of the faded red canvas. I turn onto my stomach, then drop again, collapsing on the tile portico.

Above me, I hear the actress. She's screaming. And then, from somewhere inside the house, I hear pounding boots and clacking heels. Someone's coming—either Antonia or Lach or some other good-looking, deadly assassin-goon on her staff.

I stagger to my feet and limp toward the flight of polished limestone steps that lead down to the road. I don't know if anyone's coming after me, and at this point, I don't give a shit. All I can think of is Jessalyn, alone in the forest, and that ridiculous, half-assed message I sent to Shorie.

Shorie, it's Mom. Please se

Fantastic. Great work, Erin.

When I reach the bottom of all the stairs, I pause, turning one way, then another, trying to decide which way I should run. Should I try to get back to the campsite? It's possible Lach might try to take Jessalyn there if that was where he was supposed to kill us. Only I have no idea how to get there from here.

I peer into the sun and try to think. The campsite, from what I remember, was back in the direction of Hidden Sands. There has to be a pretty clear trail leading to it, because someone delivered food from this house, and they probably used a four-wheeler to do it. If I could find that road or trail or whatever, I'd be golden.

Eeny, meeny, miny, mo. He will find me wherever I go . . .

It was something Perry used to say, when he and Shorie played hide-and-seek. She did this thing where she'd jump out at him before he found her and try to scare him instead. But that won't work here. This isn't a game. I grip my head in my hands and close my eyes. *Just pick a direction, any direction, Erin. Find a road, a trail, a path. Anything. Just get away from this house.*

I suddenly feel myself lifted up, then slammed back down to the ground. My right knee buckles, and pain shoots all the way down my leg. I try to scream, but it comes out a pathetic "Ahhh" as I feel the air forced out of my lungs. Stars on a purple background—flashes of white and yellow and black—wink across my vision, and I lose where I am for a couple of seconds. The ground tilts.

I scream again. Or at least I try to, but I don't hear anything come out. Some time passes, I don't know how long.

And then, "Get up, chickadee," I hear someone whisper against my ear.

34

SHORIE

I wake up a little after eight. Dele's sitting at her desk, peering into her fancy makeup mirror. She applies under-eye concealer like an artist, and I watch her for a while, soothed by her process. I'm also a little aggravated by the mess of bottles and tubes and compacts scattered all over her desk, but I try not to think about it.

In the reflection, Dele sees that I'm awake. She starts telling me about this girl in her Mass Media Law class who invited their study group over to her house, which, as it turns out according to Google Earth, happens to be a mansion on Lake Martin.

I know I should be nice, but I can't muster the energy. I feel like there's a thick cloud wrapped around me. And now, thanks to Dele, I'm being pummeled by memories of camping at the lake with Mom and Dad. When we'd go on hikes, Dad used to sing the songs from *Wicked* with me. He knew the words but used to mess them up on purpose, just to drive me crazy.

"Do you want me to go pick up some breakfast for you before I go?" she asks. "I could get you an Egg McMuffin, or one of those vegan sausage rolls from Mama Mocha's."

I shake my head. My throat suddenly feels clogged, and I'm scared I'm going to cry. Which I don't want to do. Not in front of Dele.

Dele swings around in her chair to face me. She's shadowed one eye but not the other, and she looks like a spooky but beautiful supervillain.

"Can I ask you something?" she says.

"Sure."

"Where are all your books?"

I swallow. "My books?"

She stares at me. "Are you going to your classes?"

"Yes." I swallow again, but I can't get rid of the lumpy feeling in my throat.

She smiles. "Then where are your books?"

"There's only been two days of classes. I haven't bought them yet." I stomp over to the bathroom and slam the door. After I pee and wash my hands, I stare at myself in the mirror. She's waiting for me to come back out. I have the feeling she knows, but I haven't decided yet if I'm going to tell her. The thing is, I could use a friend.

I slip back in the room. Dele is working on her left eye.

"So, I'm not taking any of my classes," I announce. "I'm still officially enrolled, I'm just not going."

She spins in her seat, makeup brush poised in the air.

"Holy fuck balls," she breathes. "Really?"

I nod. "I paid a guy to have another girl take my classes."

"You did? What guy?"

"The guy I met at the food truck."

"Wait. Why don't you want to go to class?"

"Because something weird is going on with my dad's company. Jax. My mom's away . . . and I need to figure it out."

She's gaping at me now, shocked by what I've said. But I know I haven't told her the truth. Playing Nancy Drew is not the real reason I'm skipping. It's never been the real reason.

I take a deep breath. "I'm too sad and messed up to sit through class with a bunch of supermotivated brainiacs. I don't think I can do it. I'm scared I'll fail and wind up losing my scholarship." I meet her eyes and say it louder. "I'm afraid I'm going to let my father down."

She nods, wide eyed. "So you noped the fuck out."

I nod.

"You should've told me."

I bite my lip. After a moment, she climbs onto my bed, crosses her legs, and pats the space beside her. I join her and let the rest of it spill out: the server report error, the spyware, the money, and the missing journal. Rhys and I seeing Ben at the barbecue restaurant and my dad's message about the letter he wrote me. I even tell her my doubts about Rhys, my concerns that maybe he's connected to what's happening at Jax.

By the end of the story, she's looking at me like I'm Wonder Woman and James Bond all rolled into one.

"Also?" I say. "I kissed him. Rhys."

Her eyes widen.

"His dad died too. But that's not why I kissed him. It is maybe why I paid him more than four thousand dollars without really thinking it over too long. We have a lot in common."

"It's definitely a moral dilemma," she says. "But look, I think it's okay what you've shared with Rhys so far. But you don't have to tell him anything else. Not one thing. What you absolutely have to do is go to Birmingham, get into Ben's house, and find your dad's journal."

"You think?"

"Shorie! That journal is missing for a reason. It definitely has information in it, something your dad noticed about the glitch you saw or something else, I don't know—but that is definitely why that shit gibbon, Ben, stole it." She wags her head ominously. "The journal is evidence."

"Then he's probably already burned it or thrown it in a river or something." I pop my knuckles slowly, one by one.

"Or maybe he's trying to alter it somehow and will put it back in your dad's office later. That's why you have to try to find it. Shorie, I don't mean to stir up more drama than you already got going on, but I don't think you realize how big this is. Jax is a successful, well-known company. And an employee stealing from it—maybe even two employees—is going to be big news. Especially because of everything that just happened with your mom."

I blink, an animal in headlights.

"I mean"—she speaks carefully here—"don't you think it's a little coincidental that she had this random blackout and got sent away to a Caribbean island at the exact same time all this weird Jax money stuff was going down?"

My mouth opens but nothing comes out. Of course I knew that. I just hadn't heard anyone put it in such clear, concise terms. And now that Dele has, I'm really nervous. Super crazy nervous. And flooded with guilt.

And, Jesus. I just sat there, in our kitchen, at that table, and let everyone gang up on Mom. I agreed with them that she needed to be sent away. I let this happen.

Dele softens. "I'm not trying to be your grandma here—really I'm not—but I think there's a good chance that your life is about to go balls up, big-time."

I don't bother mentioning that Gigi, my proper southern grandmother, would never say *balls up* or, for that matter, condense and contextualize all the events that I'd just told her about in such an impressive way. Even as messed up as I am right now, I can see that Dele is gonna make one hell of a reporter. Which gives me an idea.

"If you'll drive me to Ben's house," I say, "I'll give you the story. You can have the exclusive rights, the scoop, or whatever they call it, to write about the whole thing."

"Nobody says *scoop* anymore, FYI," Dele says. "But that's really nice of you." She puts a hand on my knee. "I'm happy to drive you to Birmingham. But I just want to let you know, I'm not doing this for a story. I'm doing this because you're my friend."

35

Erin

I force my swollen eyes open, no clue as to how much time has passed. Wherever it is they've put me, it's bathed in low amber light. Jess is curled up next to me, her head resting against the wall. I can see blood dripping from a gash in her lip. We're not tied up, but that's probably because there's a huge wooden door bolted with iron fittings keeping us locked in this place. Our feet are bare. I guess Lach's taken our boots.

"I heard them talking before you came," she says, and I start. I hadn't realized she was awake. "Antonia told him not to kill us here, so we've got some time."

"What day is it?"

"Wednesday, I think. You've been out for a while."

As my eyes adjust to the light, I see we're in a wine cellar. It's wired for electricity and hung with gothic sconces in the shape of iron torches. Arched brick cubbies, cobwebbed and dark, line the walls. *Probably home to about a million spiders,* I think, and shudder. There are no wine bottles that I can see, but in the center of the room, on the stone floor, sits a wobbly wood table and two chairs. Someone's left peanut butter sandwiches and water. I help Jess to her feet, and we finish them off in seconds.

We're not so far down in the depths of the earth that we can't still hear the god-awful music playing on the main levels. The trippy, trance-like beat is driving me out of my ever-loving mind. I tell Jess about the run-in with the actress and the message—the half message, to be more exact—that I got out to Shorie.

My head throbs with every beat of the music. My knee's tender, too, but I keep bending it and stretching it. I think if I have to run, I'll be able to, even barefoot. These people, they're monsters. Although they're not the only ones. There's someone else—someone from my real life, back at home—who set this up.

Ben, Sabine, Layton, Gigi, or Arch. Or maybe all of them, working together, a well-oiled criminal conspiracy machine. I wonder what Antonia named them in her stupid code name, secret spy landscaping file. Poison ivy? Deadly nightshade?

We'll go with motherfuckers for now.

"It's up to your daughter, I guess," Jessalyn says.

"Except that I didn't give her any useful information. Or any information at all," I growl.

She pats my knee, and we both go quiet. It feels comforting to be with her here, down in the shit hole. She makes me feel stronger. More hopeful. I sigh and let my body relax against hers.

"Have you thought about how it'll be if we get out of this?" she says after a while. "I mean, somehow we dodge this asshole who's chasing us, hop a plane—me to New Orleans, you to . . ."

"Birmingham."

"What do we do then? Stroll up on our family or our friends who signed us up for Rehab, the Deluxe Version, and say what, exactly? 'I know you put a hit out on me, like you think you're some goddamn Tony Soprano. But—surprise, I slipped out the side door and now I'm home, so you wanna go get some mozzarella sticks and tell me why you want me dead so bad?'"

I regard her. "You said your father sent you here."

"He did." She wipes her eyes and sniffs. "Because I fucked up, big-time."

Just then, we hear the squeal of metal on metal, and the heavy door creaks open. Antonia strides in, glamorous and out of place in her black dress and heels. The door slams shut behind her and locks with a loud *chunk*. She looks down at us with an expression of thoughtfulness, and I realize I've dropped my eyes to the floor, the posture of the submissive animal. I lift them again and glare at her.

She addresses me. "I'm impressed with you, Erin. But then, I had a feeling from the start about you."

"What's the holdup, Antonia?" I say. "Why haven't you killed us yet?"

She sighs. "I think you know why. Witnesses who are high or drunk are, unfortunately, still witnesses."

"Okay," I say. "So, another subject. Who signed me up for this magical experience? This L'Élu trois?"

She blinks, surprised that I've put it all together, and I have to admit, satisfaction shoots through me.

"I think I deserve to know," I add.

"You deserve nothing."

"If you're not going to talk," Jess snaps, "why don't you go ahead and get the fuck up out of our dungeon?"

Antonia smiles. "Actually, I came here because I thought you two should know about each other." She addresses me. "Have you gals had a chance to get to know each other?"

Jess makes a dismissive sound.

"I could understand if you didn't want to lead with it, Jessalyn," Antonia continues. "It's delicate when you've just made a new friend. When you're thrown into a situation where trust is so crucial . . ."

Antonia gathers herself with a deep breath and a pat of her braids. "Anyway, what's done is done, and I have work to do with my upstairs group. So, au revoir, ladies. I leave you to Lach."

She vanishes, the door bolting behind her.

I turn to Jess. "What the hell was that about?"

Jess is picking industriously at her nails.

"Why would she want us to tell our stories to each other?"

Jess sends me a defiant glare. "I don't know. Because she's got some kind of competitive CEO thing going with you? Because she doesn't just want you dead; she wants to make sure you know she's won?"

"Maybe that's true. But, since we're here with nothing to do, why don't you tell me what I don't know about you."

"Are you fucking serious?" She laughs. "You're going to grill me just because that princess said so? This is just another one of her manipulations. You're too good to fall for that kind of thing." She attacks her hair, working it into a fresh bun.

"What are you hiding?"

She gets very still.

"Jess."

She sighs. "It's a long story, okay?"

"I got nowhere to go."

36

SHORIE

On our way to freshman parking, somebody cruises up behind us and honks their horn. Dele shouts, "Slow your roll, fuck boy!" but when I turn around, I nearly faint.

It's Rhys.

Not a coincidence, my brain tells me, Jax style.

Auburn is a small town, I argue back, but my brain is wise to probability theory, so I leave it at that.

"Hey," I say, and lift a hand. Rhys guns it and pulls into the lot ahead of us.

"Oh," Dele murmurs appreciatively. "Your moral dilemma is coming into very sharp focus now."

He intercepts us at Dele's Honda.

"I'm glad I ran into you," Rhys says.

Again, my brain adds helpfully.

He nods at Dele. "Hey. I'm Rhys."

"Dele."

They shake, and Dele flips her hair over her shoulder. I can't say I blame her. He'd make the *Venus de Milo* flip her hair.

"What's up?" he says.

Dele and I exchange glances.

"You're going to Ben Fleming's house to look for your dad's journal, aren't you?" He says it in such a matter-of-fact way, I want to laugh. But I don't. There's still that chance that he's involved somehow. I mean, the guy can code some. And he already admitted he likes easy money. What if he sees this as an opportunity to get in on the Jax scam? It would certainly explain why he keeps popping up at the most opportune moments.

Dele fixes him with a gimlet eye. "Rhys, I'm going to need you to tell the truth."

"Um, okay."

"Did somebody from Jax hire you to babysit Shorie? Maybe to keep her off their trail?"

I flush instantly. But, at the same time, I'm also glad she's grilling him. Something I'm clearly too chicken to do.

"What? No way." Now Rhys reddens too. "I'm one hundred percent on her side. I want this loser to pay. To get locked up for what he's done to her family and their company."

Dele stares at him.

"Okay." Rhys addresses me. "I will admit I've been . . . circling around the lot for a while. And . . ." He swallows. "I didn't leave after I dropped you off last night. But I swear it wasn't in a creepy way. I was worried that you would try to go to Ben's house alone, and I don't think it's safe."

Dele arches one brow. "Shorie can take care of herself."

"I can take care of myself," I echo, sounding 100 percent like I can't.

"I know, I know," Rhys says. "Look, I don't have to go or anything. You guys can handle it. I was just . . . I don't know . . ."

"Concerned," I say.

He shoves his hands in his pockets. "More than that, actually. I wanted to see you again."

My eyes meet his. "You did?"

"Yeah. I did."

I turn to Dele. "He could be the lookout, maybe."

She thinks for a minute, then sighs. "Okay. You're the lookout."

In Dele's beater Civic, ninety miles an hour feels like a Category 5 hurricane, but by noon, we're turning off 280 and rolling into Ben and Sabine's neighborhood, a quaint little pocket of houses and shops called Crestline. Their house is situated on a narrow street that runs up to the crest of Red Mountain. The streets below us are alive with lunch-hour joggers and stay-at-home moms walking the family dogs. Thankfully no one's home at the Flemings'.

Dele parks down the street, and we sit in the car, looking over our shoulders at the white shingled house with a dark-plum door and shutters.

"What now?" Rhys asks.

"We break in," Dele says.

"Seriously?" Rhys asks.

"You have a problem with breaking and entering? The guy who's running a massive criminal enterprise out of his bedroom?" Dele says.

"Hold your horses, Woodward," I say to Dele. "We don't have to break in." My eye on the little cottage, I climb out of the car, and they all follow suit.

"Woodward didn't break into the Watergate, FYI," Dele grumbles. "He just reported it."

"Come on." I motion them to follow.

The back gate's unlocked. When we enter the small backyard, which consists of a tiny stone patio, a gas grill, and a bedraggled vegetable garden at the far end of the fence, the only thing I'm worried about is Tiger. But he's nowhere in sight. He's probably crated inside.

And then, unexpectedly, bitterness coils through my gut. I spent countless summer nights running through this yard. Whenever Ben and Sabine had us over to grill out, or when Mom and Dad had to stop by on Jax business. I can't believe Ben would throw all of this away. I can't believe how little he values us.

I lead everyone around the back of the small shed, paint flaking and boards half-rotted along the eaves. The key's stuck in the space between two boards on the side of the cobwebby building, right where it's always been. It slides out easily.

Inside, Ben and Sabine's kitchen is cozy, nothing fancy, just the maple cabinets and granite they put in when they bought the place. In fact, the whole house is simply decorated, filled with comfortable, worn furniture, bright rugs, and simple art.

"No offense," Dele says, "but I thought you Jax people were millionaires."

"A valuation is hypothetical," I tell her. "Formulated for a fundraising round or an IPO. You don't get the real money until you sell the company."

"It's real money for Ben now," Rhys says. "And whoever his partner in crime happens to be."

Rhys heads to the front door to keep an eye on the street. I lead Dele down the hall to Ben's office. It's messier than the rest of the house. The only modern things in the room are the three sleek monitors and black keyboard. The desk is an oak farm table set against the double window that looks out over the front yard and the road, with a scarred metal desk chair on wheels and a couple of metal filing cabinets along the side wall. Dele flings open the file drawers.

I move to a bookshelf filled with rows of dusty books and frames of faded pictures. A curled, yellowed concert ticket rests against a picture of my mom, dad, Ben, and Sabine. It must've been taken back in their college days. Mom and Sabine have big hair and giant hoop earrings. Ben and Dad look apple cheeked and shaggy haired.

I pick up the ticket. *Ruffino-Vaughn presents the Ramones. Boutwell Auditorium, Birmingham, Alabama, December 17, 1989, Sunday, 7:30 p.m.*

"There's nothing in here that looks like a journal," Dele says. "Just contracts and stuff. I can't believe a computer developer keeps paper copies." She slams the file cabinet shut, heads for the desk, and opens a drawer. "Oh, look at this."

I move closer. She's holding up a tiny gold letter *M*.

"It's a charm," I say. "Layton wears a charm bracelet. It was her grandmother's. *M* for Marko."

We stare at each other.

"Just because he has one of her charms in his desk doesn't prove Ben's having an affair with Layton," Dele says. "But it is a little wonky."

"Yeah, wonky," I say. "Let's keep going."

"I'll check the bedrooms," Dele says, then yells, "Rhys? All clear?"

"Check!" he yells back, and I can't help but smile. I prop the ticket back in its place against the picture, which is next to a small, antique-looking book. *Leaves of Grass* by Walt Whitman. I slide the book out and open the front cover. There's an inscription on the flyleaf.

3/19/95

Ben,
Shall we stick by each other as long as we live?
I say yes.
Erin

I study the words. Mom and Dad got married in 1995, Ben and Sabine the very same year. But had Mom and Ben had some sort of relationship back then? Something more than just a friendship? It's hard to tell from this inscription, but something about the words feels significant.

In my head, I play out the *if-then-else.*

If Mom and Ben were always just friends, maybe they'd only recently started an affair. But even if that's true, why would my mother agree to skimming money from her own business, which she'd worked tirelessly to establish and ultimately to sell? It made no sense.

The *else* made more sense. Ben, pining for my mom—the one who got away—but unable to win her over, moved on. Maybe he'd even had his romantic revenge on Mom by sleeping with Layton and stealing from Jax.

Protectiveness wells up in me. For my father, my mom, everybody who's put any of their heart into Jax. And a feeling of hopelessness. I've always liked Ben, and even when I figured out he was cheating on Sabine, I never dreamed he would be capable of such vindictiveness.

"Shorie!"

I run to the living room, where Dele and Rhys are standing. She pushes something into my hands. "It was under the guest bedroom rug, under the bed."

A coffee-colored leather book. When I turn it over, I see the gold-stamped letters. *March.* My hands immediately start shaking, so hard I almost drop the thing.

He really took it.

Ben stole Dad's journal.

"I can't believe we found it," she says.

"I don't get why he didn't just incinerate the thing," Rhys says.

I close my eyes. I feel like I may topple over. The man I've known since I was a baby, who taught me to skateboard, to play lacrosse, to recite all the lines to Monty Python's *Holy Grail* before I was even allowed to watch it. Where is that man right now? What is he doing—laughing, eating, talking on the phone?—while I'm standing in his house, my whole world crashing down around me?

Ben Fleming is a liar, and I'm holding incontrovertible proof of it. He betrayed my mother and my dead father. And me. Ben has betrayed me, because Jax—not just the company, but the friendship it stood for—was the only thing I had left of my father. The thing that I got up in the morning for. And now that's gone.

I want to ruin him. Take the evil son of a bitch down. *I will.*

"Was there anything in it? Like stuck inside?" I'm trying to keep my voice steady, but I'm sure Dele isn't fooled.

"Sorry, Shorie," Dele says. "No letter."

My fingers lightly brush the cover. "I'm going to go look in the master bedroom. Just in case you missed something."

"You okay?" Dele asks.

"Yeah." But I turn away, my eyes burning. I need to be alone. Right now.

As I head down the narrow hallway, I hear Dele in the living room.

"Oh my God, a joint. Aren't old people so cute?"

"Do not smoke that!" I yell back at them.

"Check!" Rhys yells. Dele bursts into laughter.

I slip into the last room on the right. I've been in Sabine and Ben's bedroom before, but it was when I was much younger and wasn't really paying attention. This time I am. The curtains are green, the bedspread is eggplant and pink, and their room is painted a strange shade of blue. Yale blue, I think, picturing Arch's tie. The ancient sweatshirt he wore every winter.

Ben's side of the room is neat, but Sabine's looks like a very expensive flea market exploded. Her jewelry hangs from every available knob and handle and mirror corner. Hats adorn the bedpost, and a collection of strange art covers the walls from ceiling to baseboard.

A picture stuck in the corner of her dresser mirror catches my attention. I pluck it out. It's faded, taken a long time ago, when she was young. High school Sabine, with a boy's short haircut, dressed in her school's green-and-white track uniform. Tanned legs for days. And oh my God, the angle and the light . . . what the photographer did with the lens or whatever makes her look like a fairy princess.

I turn it over. Just a date, *1989*, and one word, *Hermes*.

Sabine was a senior in '89. I know because so were Ben and my dad. They were all seniors at Mountain Brook High School. Best friends, and they also ran track. I don't know if any of them were any good. Obviously Sabine would win for Most Like a Greek Goddess.

Stupid Ben. Stupid, horrible, selfish Ben's ruined all of it . . .

I hear the front door open, the scrabbly scraping of dog claws, and the clink of keys on a table. My heart throbs in panic. I peer around the doorway and down the hall, just in time to see a huge dog with a curly honey-colored coat bound through the entryway, toward the back of the house.

"Tiger!" yells a woman. "Oh shit."

I shrink back from the open door and listen, my fingers prickling with adrenaline. Is she following the dog back to the living room? What should I do, just saunter in after her like I was back here using the bathroom?

But then I hear the keys jingle and the front door open again. I hold my breath. She's going back out; she must have forgotten something in her car. I jam the photo back into the corner of the mirror and hurry down the hall and into the living room. Tiger, a frowsy goldendoodle, leaps on me, covering me in slobbery kisses, then does the same to Dele and Rhys.

"Guys!" I whisper. "Guys! It's Sabine! She's here!"

Rhys and Dele straighten, putting on their most innocent faces, and seconds later Sabine appears in the room, a neon-pink leash looped in her hands.

"Oh, hi there, Shorie." She cocks her head at Rhys and Dele. "Hello."

"Hey, Sabine," I say.

She doesn't look all that surprised to see me. For that matter, she doesn't seem perturbed to see a couple of kids she's never met sitting on her sofa right next to a saucer full of weed ash and a half-smoked joint.

I suddenly see young Sabine from the photo. The glowing, perfect goddess with the perfect legs and cap of golden hair from the picture in her bedroom. She's older now, a lot older, but she's still fabulously pretty, and I wonder how Ben could be cheating on her. But what do I know? Maybe when it comes to love, looks aren't everything.

She smiles her trademark Zen smile and tosses the leash onto a chair. But I notice her eyes are full of concern.

"Shorie?" she says. "Is there something wrong?"

37

ERIN

Jess settles back, eases out her legs on the stone floor. "My mom and dad met at a sit-in in Greensboro, North Carolina. Like it was not enough that they were making history sitting at a lunch counter, but also they were falling in perfect, fairy-tale love. And then they had my brother and me."

I nod.

"Both of us crush it academically. Both of us"—she sighs—"head to the Ivy League, then naturally, get our MBAs. And then, in no time, we're taking our rightful place in the Wall Street firms of our choice. Sister Jess, at J.P. Morgan in New York. Brother Matt, not at J.P. Morgan, but still a respectable bank.

"Things seem good. I'm moving up, up, up, but Matt isn't. He's just sort of stagnating in no-man's-land. For a while I feel sorry for him, until reality hits me. Or rather, I hit a ceiling of my own. I'm not going any higher; that much has been made abundantly clear from every executive I encounter on the top floor. So here we are, the golden children, disappointing our parents, the ones who taught us we could and should change the world."

"That's a lot of pressure to be under."

She nods. "All parents want their kids to do better than they did. But how do you top sticking your foot up the ass of Jim Crow?"

"Good point. So what happened?"

"Two years ago, we were back home in New Orleans. After dinner—and one too many drinks—Matt told me why he seemed so chill with his dead-end job. He had been stealing from his company for months. Little amounts here and there, accumulating quite a tidy sum. He dumped the money in an offshore account and nobody ever had a clue. And then he stopped."

Her eyes go unfocused.

"They never caught him, and, I don't know, I couldn't quit thinking about what he'd done. How smart he was, and what a fool I was, still thinking I had to play by the rules. Anyway, on that same trip, I happened to meet a woman. Married, in town on business." Jess hesitates. "She was stunning. Smart as hell and southern. Body to die for. I don't know. It was the right time, I guess. The perfect storm of where I was in my life and where she was in hers."

"Was her relationship an open one?"

She shakes her head. "I don't think so. And you can judge. I'm not proud of what I did; just know that I was in love, so to me, it felt right, at least on some level. Anyway, after that weekend, she went back home to her husband, and I went back to New York. But we talked every day. Texted, Skyped, the whole deal. I was overwhelmed . . . engulfed. In love." She sighs again. "And that's probably why I ignored all the warning signs."

"Warning signs?"

"She didn't want me to come to her. She always flew up to see me. And . . . I know I shouldn't have . . . but I introduced her to my parents.

I didn't tell them she was married. They would've hated it. I just wanted them to know who I loved."

The hairs on the back of my neck are standing up. Something is coming, I can feel it. Something very, very bad.

"I'm pretty sure she had somebody else, I mean, other than her husband, in addition to me. She was just that type—always scanning the horizon for the next best thing. But she insisted she didn't want us to break up. She told me if I'd just be patient we'd end up together, and I believed her. She'd come to town, and we'd have this amazing time. Then she'd go back to her husband—or whoever—and ignore my texts for a couple of weeks until she decided she needed to see me again."

"Seems cruel," I say.

Jess nods. "When we were together she was so attentive. Completely present. She had this way about her. Made me feel so safe and loved. I wanted to tell her everything. My struggles trying to be the good daughter. My drinking. I even told her what my brother had done." She laughs. "That got her interest. She asked some very specific questions. Like, she-might-be-planning-to-try-it-herself specific."

Alarm ripples through me for a second time.

"That was January. Spring and summer, everything seemed fine. Then, in late July, we had a fight. A big one, about her husband and the other person she was sleeping with. She made this crack about how I was disloyal because I'd told her about Matt's crime. I got scared, then. Made her swear she wouldn't say anything to anyone. She just laughed. She said why would she rat on Matt when she'd been implementing the plan at her own company since the spring. It was me, she said, who couldn't be trusted to keep the secret.

"About two weeks ago, she came to New York and everything seemed back to normal. She was affectionate with me, acting romantic, making promises. She wanted to go out to this new place, this bar in Tribeca where a bunch of celebrities were supposed to hang out. We went, had a couple of drinks. Then things got hazy. Next thing I know,

I'm waking up on Prince Street with nothing. My purse was gone, all my credit cards and phone and keys. Even my shoes were gone. And I didn't remember a thing."

My alarm has ramped up another level. "She roofied you. Did you report her?"

"I should have. I was angry. And it was so wrong, what she did. But I just . . . I couldn't bring myself to get her in trouble." She studies her blood-encrusted nails. "I called my parents. And in approximately twelve hours they were in the city, putting me on a plane to Hidden Sands. For my drinking problem."

I can feel the force of her stare, almost like a physical blow. But I don't want to meet her eyes. I can't. A strange chemical taste fills my mouth. The taste of fear.

"What's wrong, Erin?" Jess says quietly.

I don't reply.

"Aren't you going to ask me her name? The name of the woman whom I gave away my brother's secrets to?"

I can't speak.

"Don't you want to know who the blonde with the perfect body from Alabama is? Who that woman is, who is so talented—so incredibly adept—at drawing people to her and convincing them that she loves them?"

"I think I already do," I whisper.

"Yes. I think you do."

But I still have to say it out loud. I have to say her name. *My best friend.*

"It's Sabine Fleming."

Jess is quiet for a moment. "I would say this to you: if she did everything I laid out for her, everything Matt did at his bank, my guess is that she's stolen at least a quarter of a million from your company since March. Since your husband died."

38

SHORIE

I jam Dad's journal into the back of my shorts and pull my T-shirt out over it. It makes me stand up really straight.

"Shorie? Sweetheart," Sabine says. "It's the middle of the week. What in the world are you doing here?"

"What are you doing here?" I blurt out, then immediately regret it. This is her freaking house, hello.

"I had to run Tiger to the vet," she says. "But you should be in class, right?"

Her face fills with motherly concern, and I burst into a fountain of tears. It kind of surprises me. My first thought had been to play up a whole homesick act. Turns out I actually am homesick.

"Oh, Shorie," Sabine says.

"I'm sorry," I sob. "The key was where it always has been, and I thought it would be okay . . ."

"Honey, it's okay." Instead of hugging me, she turns her attention to corralling Tiger, who, at the sound of my crying, has started barking again.

"I was having a rough day. A rough couple of days, and I just wanted to see some familiar faces." I sniff, but the tears continue to flow. Mindful of the journal in my shorts, I lower myself gingerly to the sofa. Tiger leaps on me and sprawls across my lap.

"Is everything with school okay?" Sabine asks.

"Yes. I just really miss . . . everything. Everybody."

"Shorie," Sabine says. "You know you are always welcome here. And your friends, of course. Just give me a call next time. You kind of gave me a start, standing in here like that." She picks up the saucer with the joint and heads for the kitchen.

Dele punches my thigh and shoots me a meaningful look, but I can't focus. My phone dings against my butt—another email notification, maybe from Ms. X's account. From the kitchen, I hear the fridge open, drinks clinking in the door. I feel like I'm about to have a panic attack.

"Y'all want some kombucha?" Sabine calls out.

"Sure," Dele answers.

"Sure," I say too. I'm jittery now—sweating and jangly all over with the worst nerves I've ever felt. I wish I'd come up with a better plan before getting into this mess.

"Oh! I just remembered," she calls from the kitchen. "I have kale chips too!"

"Oh, *good*," Rhys whispers. "Kale chips."

"Go," I hiss to them. "I'm going to stay."

"No way," Rhys says. "What if Ben figures out you found the journal?"

I keep my eyes trained on the kitchen doorway. "I'll think of something."

And then, the front door slams open, and Ben and Layton walk into the living room. They're both dressed in running clothes, flushed and damp. Tiger starts his freak-out routine again, running around, barking at the top of his lungs, and Ben gives me a strange look. I give him one right back, then Layton gives me a hug.

Sabine bustles in, sets the tray down, and kisses Ben. I can feel the tension between them—or at least I think I can. Maybe I'm so freaked out, I'm imagining things. Over the din Tiger's making, I introduce my friends to Ben and Layton and repeat the homesick story. While I jabber away, I keep tabs on Ben and Rhys, watching for any indication that they know each other. But they both act pretty normal. That is, if I'm any judge of what normal means.

"So," Dele says to Ben. "Out for a jog?"

I widen my eyes at her, but she just smirks.

"They're training for the Mercedes Marathon," Sabine says.

Layton shows me a picture on her phone of Foxy Cat curled up on one of her chairs in the sunlight. She tells me how great Foxy's doing, then says she should be getting home.

"I'll take you," Sabine volunteers, and when they're gone, we all sit.

"So the Mercedes Marathon's not until February, right?" I say. "You're training already? And on a weekday?"

"We wanted to get an early start." Ben sits, stretches out his leg, and rubs his knee with a grimace. "So we don't drop dead in the process. You know how unpredictable the workweek can be. We take our opportunities when we can get them." He looks at me. "What's up, Shorie? It's good to see you. Surprising, but good."

"I just needed a break, that's all," I say. "Would you mind if I stayed here one night? I don't want to sleep at my house alone."

"You really shouldn't miss school this early in the semester."

Dele leans forward. "I'm in two of her classes, and they're . . ." She makes a *pshh* sound. "Shorie's so smart, a couple of days off shouldn't be any problem."

Then Rhys chimes in. "I can find someone to take notes for you in class. If you need me to." He's got this smug smile, which is funny—but sweet too.

Ben asks us more about school; then at last, Dele and Rhys say they have to go. I tell them not to worry about me, I'll be fine. Ben escorts them to the front door, and I hear him thank them for looking after me and tell them to be safe driving back. After they're gone, he walks back in the room.

"What's going on?" he says, and this time I can tell he means it for real.

"Nothing," I say. "I'm just tired. I'd love to lie down for a minute." That happens to be true. But also, I'm desperate to get this stupid journal out of my shorts.

"You can stay in the guest room," Ben says. "A day or two, if you don't mind a little Tiger hair on the comforter. But you know how your mom feels about you staying in school."

"I know."

He sighs. "Come on. I'll help you change the sheets."

While Ben is gathering the sheets from the hall closet, I hide the journal under a skirted chair. He returns, and we go to work on the bed.

"Talk to me, Shor," he says. "I can tell something's going on."

"I'm having a hard time," I say. "School's a lot harder than I thought."

His eyebrows shoot up.

"Not the classes, just . . . the other stuff. The people, I guess. I don't think I'm adjusting very well."

Ben examines the quilt. "Interesting. You know, I told your mom you aren't the kind of girl who's going to be easily distracted by things like football games and fraternity parties."

"You did?"

"Yes. You're a feeler, Shorie. It's your strength."

I go very still. Lots of people have made fun of me for studying too much or understanding a calculus problem just by looking at it, but never because I felt things too deeply. It makes me feel good. But mad, too, that Ben can break down my defenses with one stupid compliment.

I need to remember what he's done. I need to remember that he's the enemy.

I smooth the blanket and tuck it under the mattress. Ben does the same, but his side looks like crap. The next thing I say comes out of me in a rush. "Are you going to leave Sabine?" The words hang there, awkward and irretrievable. But I'm not sorry I said them. I'm curious to know how he'll answer.

He looks at me out of the corner of his eye, then lets out a bitter laugh. "Even the nurse who gives me my flu shot tells me right before she jabs the needle in."

"Sorry."

He shakes his head. "It's okay. You know, you are so much like your mom. When it comes to this kind of thing, she, too, has exactly zero tact."

He surveys the street outside the window. "Marriage is a funny thing, Shorie. Sometimes it's a partnership and a battle, all at the same time. I don't mean your parents—they got it about as close to perfect as anybody could. Compared to them, the rest of us are just wannabes and hopefuls. Sabine and me? We're not the epic love story I thought we were. That I wanted us to be. But that's okay, you know? That's real life, and it's perfectly fine."

He smiles at me. A fake smile, I think.

"I've never seen the point in shielding kids from the truth," he goes on. "But what do I know? I'm not a father. Anyway, I probably just said about five things your mother would shoot me for."

I don't say anything. Then after a few seconds, Ben claps his hands. "Okay," he says in this hearty voice. "Why don't you get some rest, and later maybe we'll pick up some pizza? Or maybe we'll cook. You could probably use a good home-cooked meal, right?"

"Okay."

He edges backward to the door. I think about my dad's journal, hidden under the chair.

"Get some rest," Ben says. He hesitates, like maybe there's something else he wants to say, but then he seems to decide against it, and he's out the door.

I slip off my Toms, retrieve the journal, and slide between the covers. The bed is really comfortable, and I burrow down the way I used to with Foxy Cat.

I think about Dele and Rhys, on their way back to Auburn. Will they stop for dinner and talk about me? They seemed to get along pretty well. We all seemed like friends today, and their absence feels like a dull ache right below my sternum. I suddenly wish I were with them, getting ready for class tomorrow. I miss all that: the books, the work, the energy of the classroom.

I lay the journal on top of the quilt and stare at it. I wonder for a second if it's wrong to read it. The notes and reminders Dad meant only for himself. Is it wrong to read someone's things after they're gone? Do they see you do it, from another plane? Someplace outside of the material universe? I hope so. I hope Dad is watching, even if it makes him mad at me.

I open the journal and slowly flip through it. Dad only filled out about half of it, which makes sense, since he died halfway through the month. On the back page, there's a list of seven phone numbers, each scrawled beside a first name only.

Barry L., Sandra C., Mason P.

There's a knot in my stomach as I turn back to the first page.

Perry Gaines, I read, and inhale deeply.

Friday, March 1

39

PERRY'S JOURNAL

<u>Wednesday, March 13</u>

TO DO:
- Finish Shorie's letter
- Buy floss

"What lies behind you and what lies in front of you pales in comparison to what lies inside of you." —Ralph Waldo Emerson (Shorie's letter?)

40

Erin

I know it's a dream, even as the events unfold.

Shorie and Perry are trapped in Ben's truck, sunk to the bottom of the lake. Their eyes, wide and scared, plead wordlessly for help, even as Shorie unaccountably flips through one of Perry's journals. I see them, but I can't swim far enough down to rescue them. Horror courses through me. I'm going to lose them—the two people I love most in the world—and I want to cry out, but I can't force the sound up and out of my throat.

The metallic *chunk* of the sliding bolt wakes me up. My face is pressed against the cold stone floor, and I push upright as the cellar door scrapes open. The next thing I know I'm squinting into the high beam of the flashlight, and something drops in front of me. My boots.

"Move," Lach says.

"Can we use the bathroom?"

"Outside."

He's got Jessalyn by the neck, and he grabs me, too, forcing us through the cobwebbed stone passageway and up the narrow steps.

We're behind the house, and when I look back, the place is lit up like a birthday cake. Women partying in every room, no doubt, stuffing their noses full of coke, pouring expensive booze down their throats.

"Do your thing." Lach shoves us both forward. He points to the gun in his waistband. He's removed the silencer, I notice, maybe to make it a little less unwieldy. Looks like we're going on a hike to a spot on the island where no one can hear him shoot us. The proverbial "second location."

"I don't have to go," Jess says, and circles back to stand by Lach.

I squat, right out there in the yard, the moonlight spilling over my bare backside, urine gushing for an eternity. I can feel him watching me, the asshole, so I keep my eyes on the ground. But it's not from shame. My mind is racing, linking the facts I know, filling in what I don't.

Sabine is cheating on Ben.

She's stealing from Jax.

The biggest question, though, is still unanswered. *Did my best friend also kill my husband?*

Then again, does it even matter at this point? There's nothing I can do, no matter what the truth is. And, right now, I've got bigger fish to fry. For instance, figuring out Lach's plan. My best guess is the waterfall. It's where I found Agnes's hair tie and the bone. Maybe it's where he keeps the bodies until he can dispose of them permanently later.

I'm just about to shake off and zip up when I notice Jess. She's moved behind Lach, her gaze boring into me, a white-hot bolt of pure, distilled intention. She raises her hand, her lips twisted into a smirk. Somehow, she's managed to swipe Lach's phone.

"Toilet paper would be nice," I comment as I button my pants. "Oh my God, what the hell is that?" I say, and point into the darkness beyond Lach.

He turns, and, just as nice and slow as a lacrosse ball you toss to your six-year-old daughter, Jess lobs Lach's phone to me.

Lach's phone in hand, I take off across the patch of grass and into an overgrown sugarcane field. Lach yells, but I don't slow. I scramble over the low rock walls that demarcate the borders, and before long I'm in dense forest. I don't hear anything behind me, but that doesn't mean Lach isn't in pursuit, so I speed up. It takes all my concentration not to face-plant on the sharp boulders or gnarled roots or to get tangled in the vines hanging like hair from the trees. And now clouds have obscured the moon. The night's no longer silvery, just plain dark.

Go, I tell my legs, *just go.* They obey, pumping faster and faster, carrying me up my path in time with the pounding of my heart. I don't know where Jess has gone, but I assume she's running, too, somewhere, in the opposite direction. I hope she is.

Breathe. Keep going. Stay alive.

I run and run, and when I can't run any more, I drop my hands to my knees, head down, gulping air. Sweat drips off my nose, runs down my cheeks and neck. I am beyond exhausted. I am . . .

I hear the roar and look up. Disbelief mingles with despair. I'm at the waterfall, just a couple of yards from the pool. Which means I'm going to have to set off in a new direction. I tell myself to stand, to choose a different path and just go, but tears rise to my eyes, constricting my throat. I can't move. I'm out of steam. And where can I go on this island that Lach's not going to know better than me?

Laughter rings out behind me. "Which way now, Erin?"

I spin to face the darkness.

It's Lach, hidden by the jungle. Somewhere behind me. But where?

"You could go right and follow the river. But I'll warn you, it gets really steep and rocky. Lots of places to twist an ankle. Break it clean through."

I hold my breath. But I am shaking now.

"You could go left, into the trees, but Antonia's sent every concierge she has in there. They will find you, Erin, and they will take you to her.

And trust me, you do not want to deal with Antonia after what you've done."

I squint into the darkness, but I can't make out a thing. No figure of a man. Nothing. I pull out his phone and check the bars. Only one. I dial Shorie's number, but it rings three times before the call drops.

"Why don't you make it easy for yourself? Join forces with me? I've been thinking about something. A plan I want to share with you."

I mop my wet face. I've been crying and didn't even know it. *Never*, I think. *Not in a million years.* He's lying. There is no plan. He's probably already shot Jess, and as sure as the river flows to the sea, the minute I give him a chance, he'll drop me where I stand.

"Erin," he says in a wheedling voice.

Before I've even had the chance to think rationally about what I'm doing, I'm turning, bounding into the pool, through the shallows, to the black rock wall beside the curtain of tumbling water.

"What are you doing?" I hear him yell.

I touch the rocks and scan the height of the cliff. Approximately a four-story building, give or take. I don't know what I'm doing.

"You planning on doing some rock climbing, Erin?"

My legs are already buckling from exhaustion and lack of sustenance, and the rocks are slippery. But, if I'm remembering correctly from our afternoon here, the face of the cliff should be sufficiently jagged for climbing. Not that I know the first thing about what makes for decent rock climbing. Not that I've ever rock climbed in my whole goddamn life.

Laughter rings out above the noise of the falls. "You're fucking crazy, you know that?"

Tell me something I don't know. I reach as high as I can, anchoring my fingers. The surface of the rock is more mossy than slimy. I can do this, I think. I reach up with the other hand, wedge my toe in between two rocks, and haul myself up.

"Don't do this, Erin," he yells. "I'm telling you, I figured out a plan."

I reach up, find another toehold, and pull myself up again. Water sprays my eyes and nose and mouth, and I turn away from the falls and hold my breath. Another rock lip to anchor my weight on, another ledge just big enough to grab hold of and pull myself up.

"A way for both of us to get what we want!"

I search for my next move, but water droplets cloud my vision, and I have to squeeze my whole face shut and just go by feel. *Hand, hand, toes, and up. Hand, hand, toes, and up.* My progress is excruciatingly slow, and through the constant stream of water, all I can think is how there's a technique to this, a better way than this pathetic scrambling I'm doing. But it's too late. I couldn't be bothered to climb that stupid, fake rock wall at the gym; I was too busy fast-walking on the treadmill.

I pause and press my body against the rocks. I want to look back at him to know for sure if he's holding a gun on me, but I'm afraid if I do, I'll catch sight of the ground and get dizzy. Or throw myself off. *The dizziness of freedom.*

I don't want to fall. I can't fall.

I have to get home to Shorie. I have to see my daughter again.

"Erin! You're making this so much harder than it has to be." His voice is fainter now, barely discernible over the pounding of the water beside me. But I can still hear him. Terror courses through me, making me feel like I'm not in my body. I tingle all over and cling tighter to the rocks. He hasn't taken a shot yet. I wonder if he's telling the truth about a plan.

There's a beat, then Lach yells again. "Erin?" he says. "If you don't stop, I'm going to have to do something unpleasant. Which involves shooting. But I'm not going to kill you, just slow you down, all right? So we're going to count to three, together."

A spasm of fear rockets through me, so hard and fast I feel my fingers slip the slightest bit. My eyes fly open. I've gone cold, and I can feel myself trembling.

"One!" he yells.

I blow air out and look up. *Do it, Erin. Go.* I grab the rock above me and to my right. Lift my leg and position my boot on a rock directly below it. I inhale and pull myself up.

"Two!"

I can't help it; I look back.

Oh, no. No, no, no, no . . .

I shift into high gear, grappling wildly for another handhold. I move up faster, higher and higher.

"Three!"

A shot rings out, but I don't stop, and if a bullet has hit me, I can't feel it. I keep going. *Hand, hand, toes, and up. Hand, hand, toes, and up.*

Another boom cracks the air, and this time I hear a small explosion to my left. My heart and lungs and every other organ inside me feel like they're going to burst through my skin. My head is ringing, throbbing with fear and exhaustion. But I have to keep going, keep focusing on the top.

I am on autopilot now. *Hand, hand, toes, and up.* The rush of the water is so loud now, I can't hear anything but my own thumping heart. No more cracks, no more bullets. Just the sound of the waterfall and the ache of my fingers and arms and legs. I'm no longer trembling; I'm out and out shaking, my teeth chattering.

At last, I feel soft dirt under my fingertips. I grab a great clump of it and give a final push with my dead legs and haul myself up. Up and over the edge, and finally—dear God, finally—I feel the level ground beneath me. I collapse, face-first.

41

SHORIE

Thursday morning I wake up in Ben and Sabine's guest room. Ten o'clock, to be more accurate, which means I was out for over fifteen hours. I feel hungover from all the sleep.

I check my email. There are thirty screenshots of Ms. X's account, but everything looks routine. No abnormally large balances, no new private messages. Both Dele and Rhys have texted, asking me if I'm okay. I say I'm fine, I'll fill them in later. Rhys answers right away.

Did you read the journal?

Yeah, I type. Looks like Dad saw the same error message that I did. It never showed up again, but it bugged him. He considered assigning it to me, even though he never did.

My phone buzzes with his reply.

Wow.

I tap out a reply. If I can get onto Jax's servers, maybe I can figure out how they did it. Gonna try to find a computer here. Maybe Ben's—or Mom's over at our house. I think she left her laptop.

So I find a computer, but then what? Copy all the information onto a hard drive and take it to the police? Or do I go to the FBI? There is a field office downtown, I think. I just don't know exactly how reporting a crime to the FBI works. My phone buzzes.

Badass.

I hesitate.

I'm talking about you. Your dad would be really proud of you.

And then he sends one more line.

I almost don't want to ask . . .

I type, Ask.

No letter in the journal?

No, I answer. Only a few sentences, things he was thinking about writing to me. And some stuff about Global Cybergames. He might've been checking into it for me.

That was the part that didn't sit right with me. But I wasn't sure why.

I'm sorry, Shorie.

It's okay, better than nothing. Also found a list of phone numbers in the back.

U gonna call them?

Not sure who they are or what to ask. Maybe should focus on getting into Jax's servers first?

Sounds good. Anything else?

Some dirty poetry he wrote for my mom—so now I need to bleach my brain, haha.

I wait a second, then send an eyeroll emoji, followed by a vomit emoji.

The three dots pop up, and I immediately regret the emojis. I wait. And wait some more. Eventually his message appears.

They were lucky to find each other, to be so in love. Not everybody gets that.

I stare at the words and feel the urge to cry yet again. That's the exact same thing that Ben said yesterday. I type one more line.

Can I ask you a question?

Sure.

If you're not working for Ben or anybody else at Jax, why were you really following me the other day at school?

I wait, but no answer comes.

There's a knock on my door. "Shorie? You up?"

I crack open the door. Sabine, looking like a teenager in a short yellow sundress and oversize jean jacket, stands in the hall. She's got a beat-up leather messenger bag slung over one shoulder.

"I left some fruit and croissants, and there's half a pot of coffee if you want. Ben's already left for work. I'm about to head out myself. Are you going to be okay here?"

"I'm fine." I smile at her. Thinking about Ben and Layton, what they're doing to her, makes me feel nauseated. "I can take Tiger for a walk, if you want me to."

"He'd love that. Thank you." She studies me. "You okay?"

I nod. "I'm good. Totally good. Thanks for letting me crash."

"I hate to leave you alone. You'll call if you need anything?"

Ben's desktop with the three screens should do just fine. And it doesn't even matter if he notices that I've been messing around in the servers. It'll be too late by then.

"I will," I say.

She touches my arm. "We'll do pasta for dinner. Maybe some veggies. Does that work?"

"Totally."

I'll make up some excuse to miss dinner and Uber over to the FBI office. I do wonder what actually happens when you show up in the lobby of the FBI with a flash drive of corporate fraud and embezzlement. Is what Ben is doing even called embezzlement? And do they take you at your word, that a crime happened, and let you speak to an agent? Or do they just take a message and send you on your way? The thought of it makes me nervous. I'm already jiggling my leg.

"Okay, bye." Sabine leans in and kisses my cheek. She smells like herbal shampoo.

"Bye."

After I hear the lock turn in the front door, I head to the kitchen and let Tiger in from the backyard. I eat while he sits beside my stool and stares at me.

"You already had your breakfast," I tell him, but I give him a pinch of croissant. He gobbles it up and inches his butt closer to me. "Oh my God, you are such a dingo." I give him a strawberry. "Does your daddy mind if I use his computer? Your stupid, asshole daddy?"

Tiger's tail thumps.

I put the dishes in the dishwasher and go shower. I put on my same clothes, make the bed, and find Tiger's leash. We walk a quick circuit of the neighborhood, and when we get back, he laps up some water from his bowl, jumps on the sofa, and immediately falls asleep in a block of sunlight.

When I open the door of Ben's office, I'm greeted by the sight of an empty desk. All the stacks of papers are gone and so is the computer. Well, not the keyboard or the screens, just the tower. I search the room, throwing open the closet, banging open file drawers, even looking behind the door. My email dings. Another screenshot from Ms. X's account. This one's from her messages. From Yours. Ben, I know now.

Working at the Grand Bohemian all morning. Meet me at 12:30pm. 522.

Ms. X hasn't answered yet. Probably because she told him not to message her over Jax. What an idiot. I check the time stamp. The message came in just now, right before my spyware captured it and sent it to me.

I feel a little lightheaded. They're meeting again, Ben and his lady partner in crime. I look at my watch. Eleven thirty. I've got plenty of time to get there and see if I can catch them together. Maybe then I don't need to find proof on the servers.

Then, my Jax dings with a message from Mom.

Shorie, it's Mom. Please se

It's dated two days ago but only coming through now? Surely a ritzy place like Hidden Sands has better Wi-fi than that. I click out, then refresh it. Nothing more loads. That's it. Just, *Shorie, it's Mom. Please se*

What's that supposed to mean?

Mom's not supposed to have a phone or computer or any electronic devices at the spa. Somehow she found a phone or computer because she needed to send me a message. But why me? Why not Ben or Sabine or Layton? If she was asking for something, a special favor, I can't imagine she'd reach out to me.

And what did *please se* mean? Please sell? Please see? Sew? Seal?

You know what she meant, my brain tells me. *You know.*

Please send.

Please send what, though? Money? Extra underwear? Trader Joe's Cookie Butter?

And then the answer comes to me just as clearly and plainly as the answer to a calculus problem.

Please send help.

Of course. Dele's words come back to me. *Don't you think it's more than a little coincidental that she had this random blackout and got sent away to a Caribbean island at the exact same time all this was going down?*

I hit the message tab. Mom, what's going on there? Are you okay? I type. But she doesn't answer. And the minutes continue to tick away.

I don't have time to wait for her reply. I need to go see who Ben's meeting at the hotel. I call an Uber, make sure Tiger's got plenty of water, then go out to the street to wait for the car.

༄

The lobby of the Grand Bohemian Hotel in Mountain Brook Village smells like gardenias, roses, and big piles of money. Even in the middle of a weekday afternoon, it's teeming with well-dressed businesspeople and out-of-towners. I arrive at 12:07 p.m. exactly and set up camp in a gargantuan wing chair, periodically checking my phone to see if Mom has messaged me back.

She hasn't. And of course, Jax is losing its tiny digital mind, pushing me politely hysterical notifications, one right after the other. *Unallocated Expense: the Grand Bohemian, Mountain Brook, Autograph Collection offers rooms at $211 per night! Alternative: Extended Stay America, 101 Cahaba Park Circle at $58 per night! Unallocated Expense: Habitat Feed & Social, Oysters Diavolo starter $15! Alternative: Brick & Tin, 2901 Cahaba Road, Fried Brussels Sprouts starter, $8!*

"Breathe," I advise the app.

And then I see Ben, striding across the lobby to the elevators, pushing the button, and then disappearing behind the sleek silver door. I wait a beat. It's only 12:10, way before the appointment time. But he's here, so I should probably get my ass in gear and follow him.

I hurry across the lobby and jump on the next elevator. When the doors slide open on the fifth floor, I creep toward the hallway and peek out. The left end of the hall is empty. Ben has turned right and is standing in front of a door, knocking.

Well, pounding really.

The door opens. There's a brief exchange, which I can't hear because I'm too far away. Then Ben steps inside the room, and the door shuts behind him. I duck back into the elevator bay. Should I wait here or leave? It could be hours before they come out. I mean, is that how long it takes for people to have sex in hotels? I literally have no experience with this.

It's been less than fifteen minutes when I hear the door open again. I peek out. Ben looks pretty normal, no mussed hair or flushed face or buttons undone. Just pissed as all get-out and stalking down the hall in my direction. I scurry in the opposite direction and around a corner, counting twenty *Mississippi*s and hoping he doesn't recognize the back of my head.

As soon as I hear the elevator ding and the door slide shut, I hurry back down the hall. I stand in front of the door that Ben came out of for a few seconds, my knuckles pressed to my mouth. Then, so I can't chicken out, I knock as hard as I can. On the other side, I hear the bolt slide open and the chain clank. Then the door cracks open.

Something yanks me back, and I yelp. Whoever's got a grip on me doesn't let go, just propels me down the hall. As I stumble, I manage to get a look over my shoulder. It's Ben, his face a red-and-purple thundercloud. He's making me feel like a naughty puppy, picked up by the scruff of the neck by its patiently disapproving mother, and I don't like it one bit. But he doesn't loosen his grasp.

"Let me go," I gasp, still trying to look beyond him and catch a glimpse of whoever just opened that hotel room door. But he shakes me so hard, pulling me to the elevators, it's all I can do to keep my balance.

"We need to talk," he growls.

42

ERIN

When I wake the next morning—midmorning, judging by the position of the burning, tropical sun—every muscle screams in protest.

The night before, I'd hiked about a half mile into the jungle, where I found another enormous tree sufficiently curtained by vines. I was about to pull myself up onto the lowest branch when I saw a narrow opening in the trunk. Big enough for me to squeeze in, small enough to keep Lach out.

Inside was snake and spider free, thank God, but most importantly dry. I curled into a ball on the bark-covered floor, Lach's phone powered down in my pocket. I'd kept the mobile data off last night so they couldn't track me, planning to try Shorie again in the morning. The night had passed slowly, the settling of my nerves even slower. I couldn't stop my brain.

I am a problem solver, I'd thought numbly. *A grade A, blue-ribbon problem solver.*

But maybe not.

Reality: A ruthless killer is after me.

Challenge: Outrun, outlast, outsmart him.

Twice already Lach had hesitated to kill me. Why, I didn't know, other than the plan he'd mentioned. It must have something to do with his son. But what? If I didn't have any idea what he was going to do, how could I plan my attack?

I stared up into the black thorax of the tree, and inevitably my mind circled back to Sabine.

She did this to me. To me and Perry and Shorie.

She put a contract out on me, like someone in an organized crime syndicate. Because she was stealing from our company, and I was about to sell it, which meant she couldn't keep up the skimming that easily. Taking into account our latest valuation—and about a half dozen other variables involved in formulating an acquisition price—if we sold in the next year, Sabine's share could be anywhere from under three million dollars to over five million. A tidy sum for most people, but not, apparently, the jackpot she was hoping for.

So, Sabine was angry. And wanted a bigger reward for all her hard work. But was it realistic to think she dreamed up this scam all by herself? I just couldn't see it. She's computer savvy, but she'd need help with the intricacy of the coding. So who else would get involved in a scheme like this? Scotty, our other developer, worshipped his wife and six-year-old twins—he'd never put their future in jeopardy. The truth was, I couldn't imagine any of Jax's employees doing something like this. Except the one person I'd never think to question in the first place. Ben.

Loyal, faithful Ben.

Ben could've been by Sabine's side every step of the way. Writing the code, putting something in my drink, then making sure I got in a car. Driving me to my house and forcing me into that sham of an intervention . . .

Kissing me right before he sent me to my death.

Safe inside the shelter of the tree, my mind had wandered back to one long ago June night. Perry, Ben, and I had driven down to Seagrove, to celebrate our impending graduation at somebody's parents' beach house. Sabine hadn't come with us. A family emergency or birthday or something back in Birmingham.

I'd had more to drink than usual, but when a couple of guys broke out the karaoke machine, that was my cue—I escaped to the balcony. Ben was there, stretched out on a lounge chair. I settled beside him.

"Come to contemplate the cosmos?" Ben had said.

"The world was two minutes away from being subjected to Perry and me ruining Elton John and Kiki Dee for everyone forever," I replied. "It was an act of mercy."

He laughed, and we contemplated the star-sprayed sky above the waves for a few quiet minutes.

"Is Sabine seeing somebody else?" he said suddenly. "Someone in Birmingham?"

I didn't answer right away. In the years since we'd first roomed together, Sabine had made numerous trips back home. Her mother struggled with mental illness issues, and her father needed extra help with her many younger siblings. I'd never questioned the trips, and I didn't think Ben did either. But in my opinion that wasn't what was really bothering Ben.

It was the way she treated him. She wasn't affectionate with him when others were around, never touched him or held his hand. While Perry and I were always stealing away to his ramshackle duplex on Glenn Street to get naked, Sabine always seemed perfectly content for the four of us to hang out together, day and night. In my opinion, she treated him more like a buddy than a boyfriend.

"There was this guy in high school," he was saying. "Totally in love with her. He goes to UAB now. Plays soccer."

"No way," I said.

"She had a thing for Perry once, too, you know."

"Ben. No she didn't." I laughed, then glanced his way. "You're not joking, are you?"

"*It was in high school. Ninth or tenth grade, before she and I got together. She told me she always thought marrying into the Gaines family would be like being in Birmingham royalty.*"

I rolled my eyes. "*It's so not, though.*"

"*My point is, she could still have feelings for him.*"

"*Ben, they were kids. We all had crushes when we were kids. They don't mean anything. She's not cheating on you. And definitely not with Perry.*"

"*What is it then? Is it me?*" He shook his head. "*I don't know how to explain it, but . . . it's like something's missing with us.*"

I chewed at my lip.

"*You see it, don't you?*" He sounded sad.

"*I don't know. I just think she's one of those people who's . . .*" I was floundering. I didn't know how to put my thoughts into words. How to say that I loved Sabine, but I thought she could be, at times, kind of distant. Cold.

"*Who's what?*" Ben pressed.

I inhaled. "*I think Sabine might be the kind of person you can never really . . . fully know.*"

He didn't reply.

"*Look,*" I said carefully. "*There are other people out there. Women who will open up and let you in. Women who want a relationship where both people let their guards down—*"

"*I don't want another woman.*" He propped himself up on one elbow. "*I want Sabine. And it's not fair to judge her by everybody else's standards. She's had it rougher than you know.*" He swung his feet around and started jiggling his knee. "*I know this sounds crazy. But I wouldn't blame her even if she was seeing somebody else. I just want to know, so we can deal with it.*"

I couldn't believe what I was hearing. "*Seriously? You really feel that way?*"

The knee stilled, and he stared at me, like it was a challenge. "*Yeah, I do.*"

"But what if it is Perry? What if she's in love with Perry and not you? What would you do then?" I couldn't believe I was saying this, but I felt like we'd gone beyond a place of politeness.

He stood up. "Before you say anything else, you should know. I love Sabine, and I'm always going to be on her side, no matter what. So don't push me. Don't make me take sides against her. You'll be sorry, I can promise you that."

I flinched. "Okay."

After he left, I had a good cry. But when we all woke up the next morning, bleary and hungover, he sheepishly handed me a mug of coffee and hugged me. Later, I told Perry about the exchange, but he shrugged off the whole episode.

"You can't get in the middle of somebody else's relationship," he'd said. "You have to let them work it out the way they need to."

But last night, looking back, the memory had chilled me. I should've listened to what Ben was trying to tell me that night. That when it came to Sabine, all bets were off. She was Ben's bottom line, his alpha and omega. Even if she wanted to screw me financially. Even if she wanted me dead.

What a pair of fucking traitors.

Sick of memories, I climb out of the tree, then move to the bank of the river, shaking the stiffness out of my legs and stretching my arms over my head. The ribbon of clear water has worn far down into the rock bed, cutting its way deep into the earth before shooting out over the cliff's edge to the pool below. The forest up here is much thicker. Quieter too. I need to decide what my next move should be.

I pick my way upstream to where the branch joins a larger river. It's wide and calm, a couple of yards across, and looks much deeper, like it might be up to my waist. There's no path along the bank, but this seems like the best way to go. At least I think that, until I see the bodies.

There are two of them, naked, bobbing in the current. A blue nylon rope, anchored to a palm tree on the bank, is lashed around their necks.

Their bloated greenish-black trunks, their arms and legs, are borne to the surface, again and again, like fish on a stringer. A kaleidoscope of butterflies flits over them, fluttering up and landing again. Feeding. I catch sight of a hand, the flesh eaten down to the bone. Several of the bones are missing.

I hear all the air exit my lungs in an audible groan, and turn away. I try not to collapse.

It's Agnes and Deirdre, I know it, even without taking a closer look. This is where Lach stores the bodies. Until he, or whoever's got the shitty job of disposing of them permanently, can take them to the volcano.

I unzip the pocket on my still-damp shorts and pull out Lach's phone. The waterproof case looks like it's done its job, because the device lights right up. I tap in the password *l-o-c-k* and study the thing. He hardly has any apps. There's the music he was playing back at the campsite. And an internet browser. An album of photos—most of them pictures of a beautiful, tattooed brunette woman with a chubby blond toddler.

I snap a few photos of the bodies, just in case I need proof later. Then I dial Shorie's number. Busy signal. Which means something's probably screwed up with the service provider. Or Shorie's phone can't receive international calls. Or the cell towers here are wonky. *Shit.*

I hit the browser. I can't sign on to my Jax account from someone else's phone—the multifactor authentication messages I'd need won't send to a non-remembered device. But I can create a new Jax account in Lach's name, a fake one, and contact Shorie that way. And it's just as well I don't get on my account anyway. In addition to tracking the phone, if they know what they're doing, Antonia or Lach could track me via the app's GPS metrics.

But they're probably tracking me right now, since I'm sure Lach's noticed that his phone has gone missing. So I'm screwed either way. I tell myself to slow down. To think. For now, it seems, this is the best plan to contact Shorie that I can come up with. I download Jax, and it immediately starts to autofill, dumping Lach's personal data from all his other social media and whatever else he's stored on his phone's account.

Excuse me. I mean to say, Lachlan *Erdman's* personal data.

I yelp out loud. Lachlan Erdman! Antonia's brother, it has to be. And it looks like he used to have a Jax account, which was why all the profile stuff filled in so nicely, including a profile picture of him hugging a little boy on a beach. All his profile info, except for his bank information. Those fields—the ones for his account and routing numbers—remain blank. Which means he probably deleted them before he shut down his original account. Well, there's nothing I can do about that—no way for me to know what they are.

When Jax requests a username and password, I comply.

Username: *Asshole*

Password: *Deadmeat*

As Lachlan Erdman, I request a connection with Shorie, then send her a message to call the US police or FBI, not Saint Lucia's force. But I can't help feeling pessimistic. What if Shorie's having so much fun at school that she's not paying attention to Jax? What if she never read the truncated message I sent her earlier, and all of this is for nothing?

"Shorie," I whisper fiercely at the phone. "You better have your Jax up and running. And you better ignore all the lectures Dad and I ever gave you about not responding to messages from strange guys."

She'd better answer Lach Erdman.

43

SHORIE

Ben and I ride down Montevallo Road in silence. The guy's face looks like it's chiseled out of granite, and I have to admit, I'm scared now. Back at the Bohemian, when he first tried to put me in his truck, I'd refused. My brain was clicking away, working its own private conditional statement.

> ***If*** *Ben is stealing money from Jax,* ***Then***
> *He will do anything to keep his secret safe,*
> ***Else*** *He has another motivation, like maybe trying to protect* someone else.

Ben swore to me that it wasn't what it looked like, that I was completely safe with him. But, he said, there was stuff going on, serious stuff, and we needed to discuss it. He said we needed to go somewhere private to do that.

And then, "I know someone's stealing from Jax," he'd finally said.

That's when I got in the truck.

But now he's turned into Granite Face Man, and my brain is jumping around between all the disconnected pieces of information. What was he doing at the Grand Bohemian? Who did he meet with? And who's having the affair? I can't seem to reconcile the facts I know. All I can say for sure is that I'm confused and things are bad. Very bad.

"We're close to Gigi's. Will you please drop me off?" I say in a shaky voice when he slows at the light near the golf course.

"I don't want you going there right now. We need to talk."

"We can talk at Gigi's."

"No. I'm going to take you somewhere else. Not Jax or my house. Maybe somewhere outside of town. We need to be alone."

I take a deep breath. "Is it you who's stealing from Jax? You and Layton?"

He laughs like he can't believe I've said that. "No, Shorie. It's not me. It's not Layton either."

"Then who was the person at the hotel?" I say. "And why were you meeting them?"

He shakes his head. "I'm handling this, Shorie, in the way I think is best for all of us. I need you to trust me. Can you trust me?"

And then my brain starts working again, and all the separate facts and ideas and pieces *chunk* into this one cohesive mechanism.

"Oh," I say, a tinge of wonder in my voice. "It's Sabine, isn't it?"

He presses his lips together. *Bingo.*

"It's Sabine, but you don't want to tell anybody. You're protecting her!"

"Shorie," he says. "This is a complicated thing. A complex, adult situation. There are implications that you haven't thought of, fallout that you can't predict. It's got to be handled delicately. By the people who are directly involved in it."

"That's bullshit."

"You don't have all the facts."

"I have more than you know!" I blurt out.

"What are you talking about?"

"Mom's in trouble," I say.

The truck swerves the slightest bit. "In trouble? What do you mean?"

"That place you sent her. Hidden Sands. She's gotten into some kind of trouble there."

He keeps staring at me, then back at the road. "What makes you think that?"

"She sent me a message on my Jax. It wasn't specific, it was only part of a message, but I think she was asking for my help."

I pull up the app, open my read messages. "Read it for yourself! She sent me a message, *please send*—I think she left off the word *help*. I don't know, maybe she's in danger or something."

"Here's what I think." He brakes at the red light at the Baptist church—almost to the turnoff to Gigi's house. "I think you and your mother have been through a life-altering trauma that has affected you both more deeply than any of us realized. And I think that what you really need is for all of us, your friends and family, to give you both the time and the space you need to get better. There is definitely something going on at Jax. And . . ." His jaw works for a second. "I think maybe Sabine has gotten involved. But like I said, it's complicated, and I will handle it. And hopefully get everything under control before your mom comes home."

"But what Sabine is doing and what's happening to Mom is connected. Don't you see?"

He shakes his head. "I understand you believe that, but I don't think you're right."

"That's why I want to go to Gigi's. Because she'll believe me."

"Shorie, you can't involve your grandmother. You've got to listen to—"

"Take me to Gigi's," I yell, "or I'm going to call the police!"

"Shorie, no." He turns to me, and I've never seen an adult's face look so scared. "Please. Promise me you won't call them. When it's time, I swear I will do it, but right now I need to talk to Sabine first. I think there's a way to handle this—"

Listening to him is getting me more and more confused. I feel like I'm underwater, drowning, bursting for a breath. And now we're at Montevallo and Church, and even though the light is green, traffic is backed up and we're inching along.

I claw at the door handle, jump out, and take off across the wide intersection, dodging the line of cars. A chorus of car horns fills my ears as I leap over a honeysuckle-twined picket fence and run through the yard of a little white house with a rain-faded Cozy Coupe on the front walk. I cut through backyards and side roads like some kind of fugitive from the law, keeping an eye out for Ben's truck.

My grandparents' house is a stately red-brick Georgian with a yellow climbing rose that canopies the front door. Two gas lanterns flicker on either side of the door at all times, day and night, and there's a thick slate roof. It's one of those houses that announces *I'm rich, but don't like to talk about it.* Still, when you look closely, you can see paint's peeling on the shutters, and the grass is patchy and overgrown.

I hunker down in the azalea hedge that borders the rise behind the house. It gives me the perfect view into Gigi's 1980s-era kitchen.

Sure enough, she's cooking away, wearing a white button-up blouse with the collar turned up, a pair of pink pleated linen pants, and a full face of makeup. She's done this, made supper five nights a week, every week of the year, ever since I've been alive. A meat, starch, and veggie, with a sourdough roll on a separate plate. Sweet lemon iced tea and maybe a glass of sauvignon blanc with one ice cube.

I open my Jax on my phone. There's a new connection request from some rando. But Mom hasn't responded to my message yet. And there's nothing new from Ms. X's account either, except she got gas and ate a roast beef sub sandwich at Subway.

When I look up, Gigi's gone. I stand, panicked. What if Ben followed me here, and now he's at the front door, asking Gigi where I am?

I run around the house and see Gigi returning from the mailbox with a handful of mail. Ben is nowhere in sight.

"Shorie." Gigi manages a hug and an air-kiss about a foot from my cheek. "It's the middle of the week. What are you doing here?"

"I got homesick," I say in my most pathetic voice. "My friends brought me up yesterday, and I stayed the night at Ben and Sabine's."

She ushers me in the front door and back to the kitchen. It smells like pot roast, and even though I haven't eaten in hours, I feel slightly sick.

"Why didn't you stay here?" she asks.

"I wanted to talk to Ben." I hesitate. "Gigi, I really want to go see my mom."

"Oh, hon. I know. But we don't want to interrupt her rest. We need to give her time, let her heal in peace and quiet. Soon enough she'll be home and we'll all go shopping and to Red Mountain Grill, okay?"

"Okay. I just really miss her."

"I know. But we have to buck up and be strong. That's what she would want."

She's talking as if Mom's dead. It makes my stomach hurt even worse.

I twist my fingers. "Hey, Gigi, do you mind if I use Arch's computer? Schoolwork."

"Of course not, hon. Supper's soon. I'll call you."

Arch's office is wood paneled, with a huge leather-topped desk at the far end against bookshelves packed with spy novels and a cushy leather chair that I used to spin around in when I was a little girl. I have no interest in that now. All I want is my grandfather's computer.

But his desk is empty, except for a few piles of paper and a fountain pen. I look in the drawers, but they're mostly empty too. Some files stacked in manila folders, old contracts and receipts for stock trades.

No computer.

I bang my fists on the desk, then grab my phone. I google the FBI, and right away a short form pops up—a tip sheet for anyone who wants to report a crime. I stare at it a minute, then quickly fill it out: name, address, and phone number. In the very bottom field, I tell them about the fluctuating balances on Sabine's account. I don't mention how I accessed it. Then I tell them I think my mother may be in danger at Hidden Sands. *I think whoever is stealing money from my mother's app is also trying to kill her,* I write.

They're going to think I'm a nutcase.

"Shorie," Arch says from the open doorway.

I hit "Send" on the form and put down my phone.

He grins, then lifts his crystal tumbler to me. As always, I think how dashing he looks, like he's stepped right out of one of those old movies where the men always dressed in slim-cut gray suits and the women wore dresses and bouffant hairstyles. I run to him, and he folds me in his familiar whiskey-aftershave-starch-scented embrace.

"What are you doing in my office, June bug?"

"I was hoping to borrow your computer. For research."

"A school paper?"

"Flannery O'Connor."

"I'm sorry, Shor. It was acting up, so I took it in for repair."

"It's okay." I give him a pat on the shoulder. "I can work on it later."

He smiles down at me. As a child, I never had to wonder what books meant when they said someone's eyes twinkled. I knew exactly what they meant because my grandfather's eyes did just that. But now they just look tired and old.

"Arch?"

He sighs and upends his glass. "Ah. I was thinking. How life is a constant ebb and flow. How we lose things and gain others."

"We lost Dad," I say. "What do you think we've gained?"

He cocks his head at me. "Time will tell, I suppose. Time will tell."

Right then Gigi calls us to come for dinner. In the dining room, the table glows, candlelight reflected in china, crystal, and silver. Gigi's gone all out for the guest of honor.

"Sit, everybody," she says. Arch has already settled at the head of the table, so I know she means me. I take the chair across from Gigi and drape a starched linen napkin embroidered with a *G* in the corner over my lap and wait for my grandmother to begin to eat. It takes her forever.

"Shorie?" Gigi says. "Would you like some lemonade?"

"Water's fine." I go to work on my dinner, but the roast feels like a rock in my throat, and my eyes start to burn from the effort of holding back the tears. I set down my fork, blinking.

"Darling?"

"I'm fine," I say, but I'm not, and they can both see it.

"Sweetheart," Arch starts to say, but I cut him off with a sob. A loud, strangled cry that makes them both sit bolt upright and stare at me, eyebrows nearly to their hairlines.

"Oh," Gigi says.

I plant my hands on either side of my plate and, surprising even myself, burst into a series of dry, cawing sobs. After a moment or two, the tears follow, and eventually my nose runs unchecked, all of it mingling in a giant mess on my cheeks and mouth and chin.

Resignation . . . flipped out . . . powerless.

I have so many emotions, I give up trying to list them because they're all in one roiling clump inside me. I am crying, but I also want to wreck Gigi's dining room. To smash her crystal and break her china. I'm out of control. I've become the Godzilla of emotion.

"Now, now," says Arch faintly.

"Shorie," Gigi says over him. "You have to tell us what's wrong if you want us to help."

"I want my mother," I scream at their stunned faces.

In thirty minutes, the pot roast has been Tupperwared, dishes stacked in the washer, and Arch's travel agent has the two of us on a flight to Saint Lucia first thing in the morning.

44

PERRY'S JOURNAL

<u>Saturday, March 16</u>

TO DO:
- Talk to Mom & Dad about their finances
- Send Shorie another Jax message???—do NOT let Gigi send extra $$
- Call Mason P. @ Global Cybergames

IDEA: New functionality for merchants—make corporate social responsibility (CSR) public/accessible to all users in real time?

- Pop-ups for participating merchants—nonintrusive, piggyback spending suggestions?
- Environmental, philanthropic, employee ethics, etc.—best practices
- Monetize?

~~Shor, you've got the skills, I've seen to that, just do me a favor?~~
~~Be careful how you use them. In life, it'll be tempting to use your~~
~~talents to get ahead of others, but your talent is a gift for the bet=~~
~~terment of humanity . . .~~

No, too preachy

45

SHORIE

At six thirty in the morning, the Birmingham airport is deserted and creepy, just like in a horror movie right before the zombies stagger out. I'm rolling Gigi's hot-pink carry-on with some toiletries and the few spare clothes we picked up from my house when I grabbed my passport.

It's no wonder I'm thinking about zombies. Everything feels off—inside of me and out. I don't know if Mom's responded to my Jax message yet, but if she hasn't, I'll send her another message anyway. Just to let her know I'm coming to help her. To let her know I love her.

I did, for one brief second, consider telling Arch what was going on with Jax and my worries for Mom's safety. But he's old, and he's been through so much already with my dad's death. He doesn't need more to worry about. Once we get to Ile Saint Sigo, I'll have to figure out something to tell him while I simultaneously search for Mom.

And then there's my message to the FBI. I wonder if anyone's read it, or if it just got dumped into a backlog file. Nobody's called me back, and I'm worried that means they laughed off the kooky teenage girl's message.

Arch and I have just gotten in the practically nonexistent TSA line when I see a kid race-walking toward us. It's Rhys, auburn hair sticking up behind a green bandana, cutoff sweats flapping around his shins, flip-flops slapping on the tile. He's carrying something strapped around his chest, and he's headed toward me. *Running* toward me, to be specific.

I step away from the line, nerves jangling. *This is it,* I think. The moment of truth. If Rhys is somehow caught up in this situation at Jax, this is the moment when he tries to keep me from going to help my mom. If not—if he's truly my friend, I guess this is when I find out.

"Shorie?" Arch calls after me.

Rhys doesn't slow down; he runs right up to me, wraps his arms around my torso, and puts his lips on mine.

"Ahhh," I gasp under his mouth.

The bag he's carrying swings around and thunks me on the hip, but we keep on kissing. I breathe him in. His lips feel like poetry. Like red velvet cupcakes and sweet tea cut with lemonade and sleeping until noon on Saturday. Turns out there is a movie moment after all, right here in the Birmingham airport. But not one from a zombie movie. More like a rom-com.

"Shorie." Arch is standing beside us. I disentangle myself from Rhys. My face is flushed, and my pulse has gone through the roof.

"Arch, this is my . . . this is . . ." I look blankly at Rhys.

"Rhys Campbell." Rhys holds out his hand. "Nice to meet you."

They shake. I look down at the bag Rhys is carrying.

"I brought your computer," he says. "Dele told me you were flying out this morning, and you mentioned . . . I thought you might want it."

"You drove up here from Auburn? At five in the morning?" Our eyes meet, and he removes the strap of my computer bag over his head and loops it over mine.

"Well, it was three actually when I originally left."

My face is flaming. I feel like I'm about to topple over.

"That thing you texted me yesterday," he says. "The question . . ."
I wait.

"I never followed you. But I did, maybe, drive around town to see if I could find you." His face is now so red it matches mine. "I know that's probably kind of creepy. And I'm sorry. But I wasn't stalking, I swear. I was just . . . hoping to run into you."

A woman announces the next zone of boarding over the loud-speaker, and a rush of sorrow engulfs me.

I feel Arch's hand on my elbow. "Here we go, love." He nods once at Rhys—"Young man"—and then pulls me into the security line.

The plane's full, and because Arch and I got our tickets at the last minute, we're not sitting together. Which helps me, because I can fire up my laptop and dig into Jax's servers without having to explain myself. Even before they close the doors, he's strapped in three rows in front of me and waving down the flight attendant for a drink. The flight to Miami is too short to get much done, and even though we got a rare direct flight to Saint Lucia and I'll have more time, I wonder if attacking the servers is the right approach. I'm starting to think that maybe I should focus all my efforts on getting in touch with Mom. Leave the tech stuff to Ben.

Once we're in the air, I pull out my phone, pay for the airplane Wi-Fi, and open Jax. There are no new messages from Mom, just that one from some rando dude I'm not even connected to yet. I angle myself in my seat so no one can see my phone and click over to my email to see if Ms. X—Sabine—has been up to anything. But the latest screenshots reveal nothing. Her balances have stayed level, and there are no new private messages.

And then something occurs to me: there are probably old messages that Sabine may have traded with Yours which she either deleted (if she was smart) or archived (if she was sentimental). I can't believe I didn't think of that. There could be a whole section of messages that could give me a clue as to who Yours is.

I'll just need to reconfigure the spyware to show me all of her archived messages.

I pull out my computer, and in less than ten minutes, I've modified the settings. I click over to email again, refresh, and hold my breath. Nothing.

The captain comes over the intercom, mumbling something about the wind speed or place in line for landing.

"You get your Flannery O'Connor research done?" Arch is standing in the aisle, looking down at me.

I tuck my laptop away and smile. "I can work on it later."

A flight attendant stops at my chair. "Sir, could you take your seat?"

"Just headed there now." Arch winks at her and goes.

"Seat up, please," she says crisply to me. But she's smiling. Arch always has that effect on women.

I raise my seat, check my phone again, and see a new email. I click on it, and a series of new screenshots downloads.

Oh my God. The archived messages.

There's a string of them, beginning in April, stretching across several weeks. *April,* I think, and feel jittery all over. One month after Dad died.

Grand Bohemian. Room 523. 1pm. Xx

I'll be there.

God, I've missed being with you. Why is it so good with us? Xx

Because we understand each other. We let each other be.

The next batch is dated a week later.

Can't make it today. Maybe tomorrow. xx

I have to see you, S.

S *for Sabine,* I think. But who's the person she's communicating with? I read on.

Sorry. Got to go to Atlanta for a couple of days. FaceTime at 9?

Not as good as the alternative.

We'll see.

Then three days later:

Just so you know, the strapless dress I'm going to be wearing tonight? It's for you. And whatever happens to be under it—or not under it—that's for you as well.

Yes. Go on.

Not now. B here.

B. That must be Ben.

I'm back . . . ready for more?

I'm ready . . .

I force myself to read the rest of the exchange, including body parts and what they want to do with them. I feel lightheaded, sick to my stomach, like I want to retch. I click on the next screenshot.

First deposit rolling in at midnight. Congratulations. We did it. xx

Okay.

Stop moping. Consider this your share.

Jax is going to sell at some point. You'll be rich.

One day. But I have to make plans for us now. And making plans costs money.

If you say so.

If Jax sold right now my share would be, might be, roughly $2.5mm, and that's if E doesn't have a breakdown. I'm not gonna sit here twiddling my thumbs, following the rules, to end up with fucking peanuts for a "might be." Another two years of this and, I swear, we're set.

And then we finally start living?

Like kings. xx

The next screenshot is from a week later.

Another deposit! Damn what a high. xx

You're brilliant, my Hermes, my golden girl, god with the winged feet. The god of thievery and cunning. I would follow you anywhere.

Good thing, it's my name on the bank accounts. xx

Don't joke. You're the most beautiful creature I've ever seen. I remember the first time I ever touched you. Eighteen and perfect.

Not 18 anymore, afraid.

Better, my love.

I love you, Arch.

I stare in frozen horror at the messages. I can't be seeing this. *Arch?*

Is that who Sabine is texting with? Arch, my grandfather?

I feel like I may pass out or die or start screaming right here in the plane. My lungs, my heart, my brain—they all feel like they've turned into molten objects, burning me from the inside out. My mouth has gone completely dry, so dry I can't swallow, much less even close it. The plane engines drone louder and louder until they seem to knock around my skull.

Sabine and Arch.

Sabine, Ben's wife, and Arch, my grandfather, are having an affair.

Arch is the one who said he had to see Sabine. He's the one who asked her to meet him at the barbecue place in Childersburg. Obviously, their plans changed. Or, who knows, maybe one or both of them recognized Ben's truck in the parking lot, and it scared them off. But, for whatever reason, neither of them showed that day, and Ben couldn't confront them. So he tried again at the Grand Bohemian. I don't know how he figured out that was their regular rendezvous spot, but he knew enough to show up early, before Sabine got there, to confront Arch first.

And I can see why. I don't blame Ben. All those messages, those raw, intimate words. Arch wrote those words to a woman who wasn't Gigi. I can't believe it. Not only that, they'd been involved for decades, ever since she was eighteen. Oh my God. She was Dad's friend. Ben's girlfriend. Ben must have been furious when he first figured it out. Heartbroken.

He must be heartbroken now.

I think of all those pictures Arch took of Dad at his track meets. I'd seen them years ago when I was flipping through old photo albums in his office. Did he take that picture of Sabine she kept in her bedroom? The sexy legs one, the one that made her look like a model?

Hermes.

My brain shifts into overdrive. Everything makes perfect sense now. Dele was right. Mom did get sent away to Hidden Sands at a really convenient time. *Right* after she announced she was going to sell Jax. *Right* after she blacked out after having one drink. Because, of course, selling would've ruined Sabine and Arch's plan. She would've gotten her $2.5 million, but she would've lost the easy access to Jax's customers' cash.

The timeline falls into perfect, chilling order: I don't know when exactly Sabine decided to steal from Jax's customers to finance her and Arch's new life, but she must've set up the process sometime in February or March, because Dad wrote about the error message in his March journal. She skimmed money at least twice in April and August. And probably also in May, June, and July. Which means she's possibly stolen upwards of two million dollars so far.

Then Mom announced that she wanted to sell, and it threatened to screw up Sabine and Arch's plan—so they had to get her out of the picture. They had to send her away. Far way. And to get her there they had to make sure Mom did something bad. Like drinking and driving. That's why they roofied her, just like she kept saying during that stupid intervention, to make sure it looked like they had a good reason to send her away. She said that's what had happened, but I didn't listen.

And now she's contacted me for help. Because she must be in danger. Which means Sabine and Arch weren't satisfied with tucking Mom away on a remote island . . .

They wanted her gone forever.

They wanted her dead.

Just like Dad.

I am trembling uncontrollably now, my ears ringing. I want to scream. I want to rush up the aisle and grab my grandfather and force him to answer every question that's running through my head. Did they kill Dad too? Did Arch and Sabine murder my father because he discovered what they were doing? There's no mention of it in their messages. But if my grandfather killed his own son—or even if he let Sabine do it—that means he's a murderer. And he won't hesitate to do the same to me.

My phone dings with a text.

We're descending, June bug.

I go cold, a chill running through me all the way up to my hairline. I want to cry. I want to die. I don't know how I'm going to do it, but I have to pretend everything is okay.

Or my grandfather may turn on me too.

46

Erin

I locate a small rocky outcropping that gives me almost a 360-degree view of the jungle below and a fairly long section of the river. After a day hanging around there, I spend one more night in the shelter of my hollow tree. But the next morning when I wake, it occurs to me I'll go bonkers if I spend one more minute just passing time—waiting for either Shorie to contact me or Lach to find me and put a bullet through my head. I need to be proactive.

Even if it means putting myself in danger, I've got to move.

As I walk, though, I wonder if I'm doing the right thing. I'm overwhelmed with the feeling I'm going in circles around this island, just using different paths. Eventually I stop to rest, collapsing on another high ledge at the crest of a hill that overlooks the lapping green ocean. My body is crying out for a real night's sleep, but I can't quit thinking about Deirdre and Agnes. Their discolored, bloated bodies tied to the tree, buoyed up by the river's current.

According to the spreadsheets on Zara's computer, this isn't the first L'Élu III Antonia's organized. So there had to have been official stories to cover the other missing women. *Julie? I heard she ran off to an ashram in India. Such a shame, deserting her children that way, but, if you ask me, they're so much better off. Rumor was, she was addicted to painkillers. And such a burden to her husband . . .*

Whatever the case, Deirdre and Agnes—and probably other women—will decay there by the river, and no one will know those bits of flesh and bone were real people. Actual women with lives and loves, hopes and fears, secrets and regrets and dreams. No one will even care, because their families will just tell their own lies.

My brain keeps rewinding back to the oddest memories, places I don't want to go. Shorie, two years old, gobbling up steamed cauliflower, all the while crowing, *Pah-corn.* Perry, standing in front of my study module on the third floor of Ralph Brown Draughon Library, two weeks after Sabine had introduced us. He'd been randomly matched as my calculus tutor, and we'd spent the entire hour saying how crazy it was and trying not to stare at each other in dazed insta-infatuation.

And then my mind fast-forwards to our honeymoon, in the seedier part of Florida's panhandle:

Perry, hair salty and stiff from swimming in the ocean, freckled shoulders peeling. His sunburned skin makes his hazel eyes the color of seafoam, and his lashes blond at the tips. We're tangled in the sheets of the thin mattress on the crappy bed of the beachfront condo he insisted on paying for himself. His parents were embarrassed we wouldn't let them send us someplace fancier, but he told them he wasn't going to start our marriage by mooching off them.

He smiles down at me, his gaze on my lips. May I, he asks. I say yes, and after he's done what he wanted to do, he makes another request. I smile and grant my permission. He continues, asking me again and again for my approval, a litany of delicious requests.

May I? Can I? Will you . . .

Every time, I say yes, over and over allowing him to do what he wants to, until the tension becomes unbearable, and I tell him I have a request of my own . . .

It's light now, and I'm in some part of the jungle I don't recognize. I'm out of plans and ideas and ways around this. Seems like the only plan I can come up with is to obsessively check my phone, like some mindless teenager. But Shorie still hasn't seen Lach's connection request or message—or at least she hasn't responded to either of them.

I open Lach's messages and type out another one.

I love you, Shorie. I always will. Mom

I stare at it for a minute. What else is there to say? There is nothing else. She'll either get it or she won't. But it makes me feel better knowing it's there, out in the universe.

I close my eyes, wanting a picture of my daughter to come to me, but all I see is Sabine, my best friend and betrayer. She looks at me, eyes half-lidded, mouth twisted in a mocking smile. She played me. She played Ben too.

I stand and immediately feel a rough hand close on my wrist, twisting me around. I find myself nose to chest with Lach. He is red faced, his wild blond surfer hair loose and blowing around his shoulders.

"Hi, chickadee," he says. "I thought I told you to stay put."

I yank away from him. "Where's Jess? What have you done with her?"

He grabs my neck. "Let's go."

He pushes me, and the next thing I know we're crashing through the dense thicket of jungle, him acting like a human machete, and me, stumbling behind. I know where we're headed—the French word reverberates in my head.

Volcan, volcan, volcan . . .

Whatever the reason, the best thing to do is to stall. I start talking. "Why are you doing this?"

He doesn't answer me.

"You're the older brother, but your father gave your little sister his favorite hotel. What did he give you? Couldn't have been much." I'm out of breath from trying to keep up with his long-legged strides. "You're out here, chasing me through rainforest and tying dead bodies up in the river. You got the shit detail, Lach. Why?"

He keeps marching.

"How many of these L'Élus have you done? Two, three? Ten? A hundred?"

He keeps walking, pushing me ahead.

"Tell me, Lach. What's your sister got on you?"

He grabs my shirt and, swinging me around, slams me against a tree. He pushes his face inches from mine, and I suck in a breath. He pulls me toward him and slams me against the trunk once more. I cry out at the pain that shoots down my back into both legs. Lach pushes my face sideways into the trunk, and the sharp bark digs into my skin. I squeeze my eyes shut.

"Antonia knows where my kid is." His voice is devoid of emotion. "So she offered me a deal. I do three of these jobs for her; she tells me where he is. So I can get my boy back."

"You don't need her. Listen—"

"No," he barks, holding me against the tree. "You listen to me. You have no idea what you're talking about. Who you're dealing with. When my sister was six, I gave her a gecko for her birthday. The next morning? Thing was dead. She'd stayed up all night, pinching off its legs, one by one, with a pair of pliers.

"When she was eleven, she stabbed our stepmother in the left eye with a pencil. There was a new stepmother after that, two months later. Then, when she was fifteen, she put a cigarette lighter to her boyfriend's dick. Third-degree burns. He was too scared to report her."

He releases me, and I stumble a few feet away. Out of arm's reach.

"She's psychotic," he says. "A fucking nutcase. The only thing my father could do with her was stick her out in the middle of nowhere before she either killed all of us or got herself locked up. She'll kill my son if I don't do her dirty work."

I fold my arms. "So why the hell are we still talking? Why haven't you killed me?"

He doesn't answer me, but his icy eyes look flat. Determined.

And then I see it, clear as the crystal Caribbean sea. "You double-crossed her, didn't you? You said if she didn't tell you where your son was, you were going to let me go. I'm the asset."

He doesn't answer, just lunges forward and grabs my arm. As he pulls me down the path, I can't help but suppress a small smile. I'm right, I know it. Lach finally got enough of Antonia, and he's turned the tables on her. He's going to set me free.

Free.

I try to keep my breathing steady. This is good news. Excellent news, in fact. No matter how things go down. Lach is negotiating with Antonia, and negotiations take time and involve emotion. Which can be a weakness, if that emotion is manipulated correctly. Even if everything goes sideways, there will be a million more opportunities to worm my way out of this situation.

"Where are we going?" I ask.

"Shut up," he snaps.

I let him drag me along, my mind clicking away a mile a minute. I don't know what I'm going to do, but I can't give up hope. Lach's decision to go rogue is good. And I still have his phone. This is the very best thing. Because it means I still have a connection to Shorie.

47

SHORIE

When we get off the ferry in Ile Saint Sigo, Arch says he wants to eat before we get a taxi and set off for Hidden Sands. They gave us oatmeal, yogurt, and fruit on the plane, and Arch had a couple of Bloody Marys, so this strikes me as suspicious. Like maybe he's stalling or something. And that fills me with a whole bunch of extremely negative feelings.

Foreboding, helplessness, pure fright . . .

At this point, I have no real data—no idea why my grandfather came with me, what his plan is, or if he'll hurt me if I get in his way. All I know is this: I think he and Sabine may have sent my mother down here to die.

But *I* will die before I let that happen.

For now, though, I need to act like I have no idea what's going on. And let him take the lead. There's a restaurant right next door to the ferry terminal, and we duck in. Every wall is painted a different color of the rainbow, and the ceiling is hung with silver Christmas tree garland. It's hot, only about a degree or two cooler than the air outside.

We choose a table near the back, and when Arch excuses himself to go to the bathroom, I whip out my phone.

Banana Crepes—US$3.50, Jax is recommending cheerily. *Coffee—US$1.00*

I open my messages. There's nothing from Mom, only that same request I saw earlier from that guy I'd never heard of, Lachlan Erdman. I'd have to approve his request to read the message, but that's not going to happen. I don't read messages from people I don't know. "Lach," if that's even his real name, says he's from Connecticut and has his arm draped around a kid. Bot account, probably.

I put my phone facedown on the table and peruse the menu. Of course, since Jax mentioned banana crepes, that's all I can think of, so I decide on that with a mango-strawberry smoothie. I drum my fingers on the table and sip the tepid water the server leaves.

My brain feels on the verge of exploding. It feels like I'm in a computer program, and all these hidden processes—previously unknown to me—have been running in the background all along and now they're shooting out notifications, and I don't know how to find the original function.

But I should be able to figure this out. At its heart, a program is nothing but a story. And a story is simply a problem to be solved. A progression of *if-then-else* in programmingspeak. So everything I know thus far—that Sabine and Arch are having an affair, that she's stealing from Jax's users, and Mom messed up her plans with her announcement that she wanted to sell the company—that's the *if* part.

The *then* is simple: Sabine and Arch need to get Mom out of the way.

I can't even think about the *else*, it's too upsetting. But I can't help feeling that there's something more. Some piece of the puzzle I'm still missing. That last bit of information I can't put my finger on. I keep mentally reaching out, trying to clear my head and balance the equation. But I don't think I'm going to be able to until I put some distance between me and my grandfather.

And something is niggling at me. I pick up my phone and stare at it. Strange that I just now got this message from some dude I've never seen in my life. A coincidence that happens once in a while—bots request connections—but Jax is pretty on top of that kind of thing. Our programs usually weed out the spam. But you know what they say about coincidences. They're all part of an improbable whole.

I grab the phone and tap on Lach Erdman's message request. Hit "Approve" and read it once, then again, my heart hammering against my chest and my mouth going dry.

Shorie, it's Mom. Someone is trying to kill me. This is not a joke. Call the police. Not Saint Lucia police, the FBI. Hurry.

I stare and stare, waiting for the words to shift and reconfigure themselves into something that makes more sense. But they don't. Nothing changes. Just those same horrible words, over and over again.

So I was right. It is the worst case, after all—someone is trying to kill my mom. And somehow, thank God, she must've gotten this guy Lachlan Erdman's phone and used his Jax to contact me.

With shaking fingers, I type back: Where are you? But there's no answer. I chew on my thumbnail, thinking, then type one more line. Mom, I'm here, on Ile St. Sigo. Just tell me where you are, I'll get help.

I dial 911 and wait for the connection.

"What's your emergency?" a woman finally says on the other end.

"Shorie?"

Arch is standing at the table, and I disconnect the call. He slides his phone into his pocket and sits. "I'm afraid I have some bad news."

I stare at him, my throat constricting even further.

"I called the woman who runs Hidden Sands. The spa where your mother's been. It seems she left a couple of days ago."

"She left?"

He nods. "Yes. Apparently, she took the ferry back to Saint Lucia, and no one's heard from her since."

I shake my head dumbly. "She went back to Saint Lucia? I don't understand."

"The director of the resort didn't know, exactly. She just said your mom seemed to be happy, complying with all the rules of the rehab, and then a couple of days ago, she didn't show up for breakfast."

"Why would she do that?"

"Shorie, your mom is a very troubled woman, I think. I'm sure she was upset about us sending her away, but instead of handling it in a responsible, adult way, she ran. I'm so sorry. I would do anything to spare you this disappointment. But I'm afraid we've got to accept that your mother isn't the person she used to be."

"You think she didn't just leave Hidden Sands. You think she left us?"

He laces his fingers together and looks down at them. "I don't know."

His face is so grave, so full of sympathy, that I think I'm going to vomit. It is a lie. He's lying to me. Mom is here on this island, and she needs my help.

And he knows it.

"I suggest we head back to the ferry, go back to Saint Lucia, and see if we can get a return flight back home."

"Okay," I say faintly. I feel like I can't breathe. I feel like I'm going to pass out. "I have to use the bathroom." I rise unsteadily.

"Shorie." He nods at my computer bag. "I'll watch that for you."

I pull the strap over my head and drop the bag on my chair. He catches my wrist and pulls me to him, kissing my clenched fist.

"Love you, June bug."

I smile and pull away. I walk toward the back of the restaurant, into the kitchen, and out the back door.

48

Erin

The path angles up steeply, slowing Lach and me down. We push through the underbrush and along twisting paths until I'm out of breath and bathed in sweat. Every tree and bush and rock looks the same, and I'm so unbelievably hot. I'm also starting to feel woozy, like I may pass out. I stop, swaying a little against a tree. Lach turns back with a frown.

"It's been two days, and I've barely had anything to eat." My hand falls against my pocket, covering the phone. It feels like it's as big as a concrete block. "And may I point out, if I die from thirst, then you've got nothing left to bargain with."

Lach tosses me his water bottle. I drink half, then he takes it back. "Let's go," he says.

"Can I just say, I think taking me to the volcano is a bad move. You're basically telling Antonia that you expect her to give in to your demands."

He doesn't answer.

"You're not playing this smart, Lach. You're saying you think she's going to cave, agree to find your son, and that you're ready to kill me, like she wants you to. You're insulting her and she's going to lose respect for you."

He shakes his head, like he's shaking off a swarm of pesky bees.

"You have to be tougher than that. Smarter. You should take me back down to the campsite. Or somewhere else."

"Just shut up. I don't need advice from you."

He yanks me back onto the path, but the water's brought me to life again, and my brain is buzzing. "I have a proposition for you," I say.

He doesn't answer.

"You know the FBI still puts rewards out on people? That's not just old-timey Jesse James shit; it's the real deal. Murdering four innocent women means several million on your head. At least."

This stops him. He plants his hands on his hips and fixes me with those spooky light-blue eyes.

I talk fast. "I'm sure cold-blooded murder must seem really badass to you until you realize that, with a jackpot like that, everybody you've ever crossed paths with in your entire life is going to be gunning for you. And then"—I shrug—"whoa, Nelly. The whole world after you is not good odds."

He mops his face with a hand. He's thinking about it. I feel a tingle, like an electrical charge zipping up my spine, the way I do every time I pull in another investor, every time I hit on a new idea. I have the best product, and I know how to make this sale.

"You know, right now, my company, Jax, is worth at least one hundred million."

Well, closer to seven, but whatever . . .

I take one step closer to him. "I'm the CEO. I own the highest percentage of shares in the company. I have access to a database of over ten million people . . ."

It's 1.3, but who's counting . . .

". . . a detailed digital trail of every single one of their bank accounts, tax filings, and financial decisions."

I lift my chin, my eyes never leaving his. "If you let me live, I will get you access to both the money and the data. Any of it. All of it. Whatever you need to find your son."

He snorts. "You'd never risk your company for me."

"Not just for you. For me too. For my daughter. Lach, listen to me. Antonia isn't the only person who can get your son back."

49

SHORIE

When I'm clear of the restaurant, I cut down a couple of side alleys. Eventually I find myself on a road, unpaved, that's lined with a series of small cinder block houses painted in pastel Easter egg shades. I duck around the side of one and check my phone.

Lach Erdman's preferences are set to public, so I'm able to see his transactions (minus the dollar amount) in real time. Although it doesn't really help me—he has exactly zero transactions as far as I can tell. But a public setting also means his location is traceable, even though after tapping the button, it takes a few minutes for the GPS signal to bounce back to me. When it does, I'm rewarded with a pulsing red dot on a map of green, all the way on the other side of the island.

Mom.

I shade my eyes. There are no cabs in sight, and the street I'm standing on is mostly deserted. A kid, a boy of ten or eleven, lolls on a banged-up moped on the sidewalk outside a pizza place. The moped's rack is wrapped with bungee cords for deliveries.

I amble over. "Hey. This your bike?" I casually eye the controls. Kill switch, ignition button, front and back brakes. Daisy's brother had a scooter, and I learned the basics on it a couple of years ago, but it's been a while.

He shakes his head, then inclines it toward the pizza place.

"You're watching it? For somebody in there?" He nods. I reach in my purse. Hold out a wad of bills. "I'll bring it back, I promise."

He takes the money and steps back, and I hop on, hit the kill switch, and push the ignition. The engine sputters to life, and the boy takes off down the sidewalk. I hear a voice from inside the pizza place— *"Arret!"*—and I open the throttle. The moped bumps over the curb and onto the street.

"Arret!"

He's too late. I'm down the street, swerving around a corner, maneuvering down another alley, and in minutes, I'm lost in the stream of people on a busier street. I feel bad about what might happen to the boy, but I feel worse about Mom, so I keep driving until I find my way out of town. I head down a dirt road, stopping periodically to check Jax's GPS, eventually whooshing past a long white building with a portico and fountain and a line of shiny black town cars in front.

Hidden Sands.

I don't stop. But I do think of something, the thing that's been tiptoeing around the edges of my brain all morning. Something Gigi had said at the beginning of the intervention. Arch had learned about Hidden Sands from a friend. It was his idea to send Mom there.

50

ERIN

I might not have closed the deal, but my pitch does seem to throw Lach off his game. At least just enough that he clams up and makes us start walking again. By the time we stop, I've reached a new level of exhaustion. But I don't sit. I can't. It's as if my legs realize what I'm seeing before my mind does.

We're standing at the edge of a football field–size crater of gray mud, half a dozen pools of bubbling mud belching plumes of white steam. The air is redolent with a funky stench that reminds me of two-week-old rotten eggs dipped in human excrement. It occurs to me I've never seen a volcano before. But I wish I never had.

If Antonia agrees to find Lach's son, he's going to throw me in that boiling-hot pit.

And then I do collapse, right there in the dirt. I hear a sound, low and constant, and after a second, I realize it's me. I'm saying no. Wailing it.

After a few minutes, I hear him beside me. "Get up."

I squint into the burning sun. He's a blobby black form above me. I think about all the articles I've read online about self-defense. How a woman on the ground has an advantage. And I might know how to implement the tactics if I'd just taken that stupid self-defense class with Shorie. But I was busy at Jax.

Too busy and now I'm going to die.

It's all so awful and pathetic and meaningless, I want to scream.

"Get up." He kicks me once, hard, in the side. Even though he doesn't use a fraction of his strength, it still hurts. I groan and roll away from him. But climb to my feet. "Go stand over there." He points.

My vision swims. He's pointing at a pool of bubbling gray mud, steam curling up from it. And his gun is out again, the same black pistol he shot Deirdre with.

"You never answered me. I made you an offer." My voice sounds pathetic, whiny.

"Go stand at the edge," he says. "Now."

"I can find him for you. Your son."

"Move," he growls.

I walk toward the pool, slipping on the gray scree that slopes into the billowing pit. The smell is so much stronger up close. The soupy mud is actually boiling. In addition to the heat, I feel something like pinpricks all over my body. They are sharp as needles. The physical manifestation of fear.

"It's almost two hundred degrees in that pit," Lach says. "It'll take a while, but eventually, they won't be able to find a thing."

"You want more? Fine. I'll help you find your son, and I'll give you cash. Right now."

He laughs.

"I'm going to sell Jax. Some giant tech company who's going to pay us more money than most people have ever dreamed about. And I'll cut you in. Whatever you want, the part of my take anyway. You won't have to depend on your father or your sister, for anything, ever again. You'll be free to go where you want, do what you want. And you'll have your boy back. I know we can make this work. Just please, don't do this."

I'm begging now. Pleading to be spared. I feel time stop, and I see not my life, but Shorie's, reel past my eyes. A squalling infant, sticky toddler, gangly adolescent. My grown girl, standing at her desk in her dorm room, arranging a cigar box in its precise spot. Shiny caramel-colored hair with random strands of honey and that one curly section. Her right shoulder hitched up the way it does whenever she's concentrating. She was so quiet in the hospital the night the doctor told us Perry had died. She waited to cry until we were home and she was alone in her room. I didn't go in. I wasn't sure she wanted me.

I drop to my knees.

"Jesus, stop it," Lach says. "Stand up."

I pull his phone out of my pocket and show it to him. But no words come out.

He stares at it, then looks at me. "Where'd you get that?"

And then the words come. "I downloaded Jax on it," I say. "You used to have an account, but you disconnected it. Lachlan Erdman of Old Greenwich, Connecticut. No financial transactions yet. Forty-six new connection requests from other users. Just one from you. To my daughter, Shorie Gaines."

He stares hard at me.

"I can't access my own Jax from this phone." I forge on. "But all I have to do is message her, and she'll deposit one hundred thousand dollars in your account—transfer it from mine to yours. One hundred thousand, just a deposit, the balance to come as soon as I return safely home. What do you say?"

He doesn't answer.

"How much is Antonia paying you to kill me?" I say. "Twenty-five thousand? Fifty?"

He presses his lips in a tight line. I'm close.

"Jax hasn't sold yet, but I don't care. I'll give you everything I've got right now. A hundred thousand dollars now. Nine hundred more when I get home."

He stares at me, but I can tell he's tempted. *Come on, asshole.* That's all of my IRA and most of Perry's insurance money. It's more than this guy will ever see stuck out here in the jungle working as Antonia Erdman's enforcer.

He points the gun at me, and instinctively I flinch.

"Do it," he says.

"What?"

"I said do it. Send the money."

"Okay, but how do I know you won't just shoot me then?"

"Jesus Christ, lady. I don't think you really have a choice here."

He has a point. I look down at the phone. A bead of sweat splashes onto the screen. I blot my forehead and open Lach's app, telling myself to stay calm. To focus on the task at hand. There's a new message—from Shorie.

Mom, I'm here, on Ile St. Sigo. Just tell me where you are, I'll get help.

Joy courses through me, then alarm. *Here?* What is she doing here? How did she get here? Is she alone? What if Sabine brought her?

I type as fast as my trembling fingers will allow me.

Shorie, find a computer and transfer $100,000 from my Jax to this account. ASAP. Mom

51

SHORIE

I zip up a series of dirt roads, past houses and fields and tiny little roadside shacks, following the little red dot on my phone. I'd feel like a badass female action hero except my body is shaking—literally shivering like it's the dead of winter. Maybe that's shock from all the horrible information I've uncovered in the past twelve hours, I don't know. But I bet Wonder Woman never peed her pants with fear.

Eventually I turn up a hill so steep I have to lean forward to keep from flipping ass over end. The dot is moving slowly, which makes me think Mom's on foot. That's okay, though. At least she's still moving.

When the forest opens up, I find myself on a large grassy field dotted with yellow wildflowers. To my left, crowning a high knoll, is a massive old white stone house. I shade my eyes. A shit ton of staircases zigzag up the leafy slope to the stone foundation of the house, then up to the wide front porch. Windows shaded with red canvas awnings stare blankly into the hot afternoon sky. It's been a while since I checked the GPS, so I stop.

But the red dot's gone.

I refresh the map, but there's nothing. Like Mom's disappeared. I spin around in a circle, shaking the phone, like that's going to help. I mean, how could she have vanished, just like that? There's no way she left the island. It must be an issue with the signal. I check the phone a second time and yelp. There's another message from Lachlan Erdman. From Mom. She wants me to find a computer and transfer money into this guy's account.

I chew on my fingernail. One hundred grand is a lot of money. And probably just the first installment. She has to be in danger. And where the hell am I supposed to find a computer out here in the jungle?

What am I going to do?

What can I do . . .

And then, it hits me, what to do. I place a call and wait. It takes forever to connect, but at last somebody picks up, and I practically scream into the phone.

"Rhys!"

"Shorie, is that you?" It's Lowell.

"Lowell? What are you doing on Rhys's phone?"

"He went out. Left his phone at the house. Oh man, he's gonna be pissed that he missed you. What's wrong? I can barely hear you. Where are you?"

"Ile Saint Sigo," I finally manage to choke out. "I'm looking for my mother. She messaged me to transfer money to this guy's Jax account, but I don't have my computer."

"Shorie," Lowell says. "Slow down. And you've got to speak up. What do you want me to do?"

"I need you to get to your computer and transfer one hundred thousand—"

And then the line goes dead.

"Lowell!" I scream, but there's no answer. I wave the phone over my head. "Lowell!" The signal's dropped. Tears of frustration spring to my eyes. I want to scream, to bash my phone against a tree until it's powder.

Now what?

I still myself, close my eyes. Breathe in, breathe out, and try to collect my thoughts. I can do this. I have to. My mother's depending on me.

Stop being a baby. Stop throwing a fit. Expecting somebody to ride to your rescue. You're wasting time. You have to do something. Now.

You're the only one who can save her.

I open my eyes. Turn to stare at the big house in the distance. Still myself and listen. Strains of trippy music and the occasional feminine "Woo-hoo!" drift from it across the fields. I don't know who lives there, but whoever it is seems like they're having a damn good time.

I hope they have a computer.

⟳

I ease open the heavy front door and slip into a wide hallway. It runs the entire length of the house, and at its far end, a massive staircase rises to an expansive landing where two young women are draped over an old-fashioned couch. They're giggling hysterically, but neither even glances my way.

I don't know whose house this is, or if they're connected to Hidden Sands, but just in case, I've got my story ready. I puff out a couple of nervous breaths, then edge my way down the hall, peeking into each room. They're all empty. I'm pushing open the last door on the right when it swings open, and a woman, not that much older than me, strides out. She is blonde and pretty and looks frazzled.

I smile brightly, and she stops.

"Can I help you?"

I keep my voice low. "Um, hi, yeah. I was wondering, would you mind if I hopped on your computer real quick? I just realized I forgot to send my housekeeper the new code to my lockbox, and my poor dog is trapped inside."

The woman studies me. "What was your name again?"

"Adelia Kent."

"Oh! Like on *The Lighthouse!*"

I blink. *Whoops.* I'd meant to say Foster, Dele's real last name. "Ha. Right. Um, look, I know we're not supposed to be on any devices, but, oh my God, my poor little puppers. He's trapped." My smile is starting to feel so fake that it's painful.

"Zara!" someone shrieks from somewhere above us, "I'm waiting!"

The woman lets out an impatient huff, but she points to the open door. "Computer's on the back desk. Make it quick. I'll be right back." She grins at me. "And don't tell. They'll kill me!"

52

ERIN

"Show me."

Lach snaps his fingers for his phone.

"It's going to take a minute. We're in the middle of nowhere."

I'm staring at the phone. The Jax icon, specifically. The way the lowercase *j* seems to be edging off the yellow background into oblivion. It's like I'm seeing the design for the first time. Really appreciating it. Perry, Ben, Sabine, and I had settled on the design for the app that same Christmas night. Drawn out a dozen iterations on Shorie's old art easel. It was actually Shorie who had tied all the pieces together.

It should file your taxes for you, piped up her high, fifteen-year-old voice from under the nest of fuzzy blankets on the sofa. *And you can call it Jax, because you get a jump on your taxes.* She leapt up, and on the easel she sketched out the icon. A mustard-yellow box with the *j* floating off to the side. *See? He's just this humble little guy, off to the side, quietly doing all your dirty work.*

We all stared, struck dumb by the perfectness of her proposal. I'd had another feeling too. One probably not that uncommon to mothers who are too busy, too tired, too pressed with things they think they need to do. It was intense shame and regret—because I'd had no idea how good my daughter was at design. I couldn't remember anything she'd drawn or painted or created since she was little, only the AP classes of math and science, the math competitions, the computer club. An inexorable, determined march toward becoming Perry 2.0. But my little girl had so many hidden talents. I needed to pay closer attention. But I hadn't. Not in the way I should have.

I know better now. If I survive this, I swear—I will be a better mother. I will pay attention.

Suddenly a little white bubble materializes on Lach's phone.

$100,000.00 Transfer Pending, No Bank Account.

I yelp. Shorie got my message and she's done it. I almost can't believe it.

"It's there?" Lach says.

I glance up at him, trying to keep my expression cheerful. "Essentially."

He lowers the gun. "What do you mean, *essentially?*"

"The transfer can't complete until you enter your bank data."

"You said a hundred K, done." His face has begun to transform from incredulity to fury.

"But when you suspended your Jax profile, Lach, it erased all your financial account information. It's a basic security precaution."

"Well, you built the app. Figure it out."

I feel myself beginning to lose it and clench my fists. "I can't just pull your financial information out of thin air, Lach. Neither can you, I suspect."

"No deal then," he says, and holds out his hand for the phone again.

"All you have to do is let me go, and you can go get your checkbook and enter the goddamn routing number in the blank space!"

"HAND IT OVER!" he roars, then chambers a bullet and aims the gun at my forehead. I push the phone at him. He places a call and puts it to his ear.

I hear something then. A low buzzing sound, far off in the distance. A four-wheeler or motorcycle, it sounds like. I strain my ears, wondering how close it is. I should run. But I'm frozen. And I can't be sure he won't just solve the situation by pulling the trigger and dropping me right where I stand.

"We're at the crater," Lach growls at the person on the other end of the line. "What's it going to be? You going to help me out, or do I let her walk?"

I stand there, dumbly, the barrel of the gun pressing into my temple, listening to the whine grow louder. And then he angles his body toward mine and gazes down at me, a beatific smile lighting his face.

A smile.

"Thank you," he says into the phone. To Antonia. Our eyes meet. "You won't be sorry."

"No," I say. "How do you know she's not lying . . ."

"I'll call you when it's done," he says.

I put my hands up. "Please . . ."

He shakes his head, and I close my eyes. Hold my breath.

I tried. I really did.

I love you, Perry.

I love you, Shorie.

The buzzing-whining sound is suddenly loud and close. Just as we both turn toward it, a dusty yellow moped bounces over the rim and down into the crater. A teenage girl is driving it, one of her sneaker-clad feet dragging for balance in the dirt. Her long brown hair is streaming behind her, and she's wearing jeans and a pink T-shirt.

She is screaming.

I start screaming too.

53

Shorie

When the moped crests the hill, I become every single emotion all at once.

Because standing at the edge of this gray bubbling mud pool is my mom. And a tall surfer-looking guy with long blond hair, who is pointing a gun at her. I start to scream, and just as I do, I hear the engine skip like it's going to stall out. I throttle up, the engine screaming, and head directly for them.

And then I'm screaming because I'm going to hit them; I can see it now. Even the surfer guy, who's turned around now, realizes it. What he doesn't see is Mom lunge at him and shove him hard, right in the direction of the steaming pit.

I lean to the left and go into a slide, the moped slipping out from under me on the gray rocks. Mom leaps back as I slide right past her. Steam from the bubbling mud envelops me. I open my mouth, suck in a huge, scalding lungful of it, and let go of the moped. It spins out from under me as I flip myself over onto my stomach. I flail, grabbing handfuls of the loose gray dirt to stop myself from going into the pit.

Then another person's screams replace mine.

54

ERIN

As Shorie and the moped slide together toward the sulfur pit, they kick up a cloud of gray dust, obscuring them from view. Everything slows down then, my thoughts crystallizing in a physically painful way.

I am the one who set all these events in motion. I summoned my daughter—my child who loved me and trusted me to always protect her, to always have her best interests at heart—to this island. But even before that, I'd been so selfish. I'd pushed her to keep going the way I did, insisting she go to school, brushing aside her pleas for my attention. And now I was about to watch her die.

All of this is my fault.

I sprint toward her, every cell, every building block that makes up my body, reaching for Shorie. Every day of my life, since the first moment that I held her, since I looked into her baby face, when I dried her tears when she was six, when I watched her draw that simple icon on her easel. The silent ride home the night Perry left us, the hours we cried, each of us hidden away in our separate rooms. Even the screaming match at the fraternity house—it has all led to this moment.

She's so close now, within a couple of feet of me. I can see her perfect Shorie hair, her freckled face and hazel eyes the same color as Perry's. They are fastened on me, full of all the hope and belief that a daughter has for her mother. Full of love.

I dive, a spectacularly awkward, Pete Rose headfirst thing, reaching for my daughter. But she reaches too, and our hands meet and clasp, just as the bike splashes into the mud. We scramble away from the pool and bear crawl up the slope, finally collapsing in the dust and rocks at the top.

By then, I can hear Lach's high, staccato screams ripping through the air.

55

PERRY'S JOURNAL

Monday, March 18

TO DO:
- Set up meeting with Sabine—Global Cybergames issue / next step?
- Drinks with Roy @ Epic—Columbus, GA—3/20, 8pm

> Love is not love which alters when it alteration finds,
> Or bends with the remover to remove.
> O no! It is an ever-fixed mark,
> That looks on tempests and is never shaken.
> It is the star to every wandering bark
> Whose worth's unknown, although his height be taken . . .

(for Erin and Shorie, William Shakespeare, Sonnet 116, no constraint because it's too damn perfect already)

56

SHORIE

Using my phone's spotty GPS to guide us toward the ferry terminal, Mom and I head through the jungle. As we go, I tell her everything I know about Sabine and Arch. How they've been carrying on a secret relationship for years and stealing money from Jax so they can run off together. How Ben figured it out, but that he seemed unsure how to handle Sabine, maybe even reluctant to blow the whistle on her. And how he definitely didn't want me involved.

"Does Gigi know?" she asks.

"I don't think so."

Just as I can see the glint of water through the trees, a river it looks like, Mom puts her hand on my arm.

"What?" I whisper, but she doesn't answer.

"Nice to see you all," comes a voice from the wall of leaves, and then a woman steps out, like the star actor from behind a stage curtain in a Broadway play.

She's blonde, tall, and pretty and wearing a sleek all-black hiking ensemble. Her hair is braided in this really complicated crown around her head. She has a gun holstered under her arm.

"Antonia—" Mom says.

The woman whips a walkie from her shorts. "I've got them," she says crisply. "By the river."

Mom puts her hand on my back.

A man's voice scratches back on the woman's walkie. "Copy."

She looks at me. "Hi there. What's your name?"

"Don't speak to my daughter," Mom says.

"Shorie," I answer.

"Shorie," she says. "I'm Antonia Erdman. Owner and operator of Hidden Sands. So nice to meet you."

"Antonia," Mom cuts in. "It's over. Let us go."

"And I'm so sorry to hear about your father."

I don't answer.

"I think he'd be impressed with what you've done today. What you've tried to do." She smiles. "Did you know, Shorie, that when my father turned Hidden Sands over to me, it was almost bankrupt? It was; then I took over and came up with the idea to turn it into a new kind of rehab. A *restoration*. I'm the one who came up with the L'Élu challenge, then L'Élu II. And finally, our premium service, L'Élu III."

I don't have to ask what she's talking about. I wasn't on Zara's computer for more than a few minutes, but it was long enough for me to see everything I needed. What's weird is that she's bragging about it.

"We've had sixteen women participate in L'Élu III. That's sixteen problems, solved. Your mother and the other woman are the only ones who've ever given us a hint of trouble."

"If you want to talk," Mom snaps, "talk to me."

Antonia regards her. Unholsters her gun and examines it. "All right, Erin, let's talk. I see you got away from my brother."

"Perceptive of you," Mom says.

"I have something to say," I interject.

"I gave you a chance," Antonia continues, addressing Mom. "I offered you a once-in-a-lifetime opportunity."

"And I told you, you can shove your opportunity up your sleazy, grifting, murdering, Executive Barbie ass," Mom snaps.

"I have something to say!" I shout.

Antonia raises her arm, points her gun at my mother, and ever so coolly squeezes the trigger. The jungle explodes with sound and light, but Mom doesn't fall. She just crouches over, holding her ear. It happens so fast I don't even scream, and it takes me a minute to realize she only shot in the air, inches from Mom's ear.

Antonia swings the gun back to me and tilts her head thoughtfully. "Next one's for real, okay?"

I'm shaking again, so violently now, I'm not sure how long I can keep myself upright. But I have to speak. "I have something to tell you. About your Jax account."

"My what?"

"I mean Hidden Sands' Jax account."

"What do you know about Hidden Sands' Jax?"

"Oh my God," Mom says.

"What the fuck did you do?" Antonia's face looks like a thundercloud.

"Shorie." Mom's straightened, and although she's still holding her ear, she's staring at me. "What did you do?"

"Just check your phone," I say to Antonia.

She pulls her phone out of her pocket. Taps, then squints at the screen.

"I just played around with the settings," I say. "Changed a few things."

"You hacked into my account?" Antonia says.

"Oh, Shor." Mom's eyes are wide, but there's a hint of a smile on her lips.

"You sullen little piece of suburban shit! You hacked me!"

"I didn't," I say simply. "Your employee, Zara, enabled the integrated password-saving setting on your computer, and I just opened it. You should really tell your team not to do that. It leaves your company vulnerable to all sorts of attacks."

Mom laughs.

"What did you do?" growls Antonia.

I glance at Mom. "It was Dad's idea, one from his last journal. A new feature he was considering, making merchant accounts public. I switched Hidden Sands to a customer account and made all its transactions public. It was pretty easy, then, to import everything from the files—your accounts payable and receivable and entire client list. And the link to your secret *Landscaping* file. Every fake company you've done business with, how much you pay them, and how much they pay you—I made every bit of it public."

Her face has gone gray.

"I also requested a few connections with a handful of key people. The US attorney general. Owner of the *Washington Post*. Somebody in the FBI's organized crime unit. Because they're really good at exposing shell companies. And murder for hire."

Antonia hurls the phone at me. I must be coursing with adrenaline, because I catch it. And then—I can't help it—I grin. Which is stupid, I know, an utterly boneheaded move, because this walking piece of filth nearly shot my mother and I'm pretty sure she'd love to shoot me.

So let her, I think. *Let her do her fucking worst.*

Dropping my hand back, I picture her head as a lacrosse goal, then whip the phone back at her, aiming directly for her head.

57

ERIN

The phone hits Antonia so hard on the temple, her head snaps back. She curses and stumbles sideways, clutching at her head. It's just the window we need.

We go together, hands clasped, crashing through the trees and underbrush toward the glinting river. I hear Antonia behind us, but I think we got a decent enough head start to make it to the waterfall before her. But then what do we do when we get there? Jump?

"Erin, I'm warning you!" Antonia screams behind us. A shot booms, then another, one hitting the tree beside me, splintering the wood. We duck our heads reflexively, but we keep running.

And then, as we near the river, something strange happens. An idea occurs simultaneously to us both—an unspoken but perfectly clear understanding between us—and we stop.

Our eyes meet, and I take in the beautiful sight that is my daughter. Her face is flushed and dirty, hair frizzed in the humidity. Her eyes glow with something, adrenaline or resolve. She smiles at me, and I smile back, and I realize what we are both thinking.

"Eeny, meeny, miny, mo," she says.

I nod to show I understand. And I approve. My daughter never did like waiting for somebody to find her. She's so much like me. We are so much like each other.

58

SHORIE

Our hands release, and Mom and I separate, each of us circling back to find a big enough tree to hide behind.

Please, please, please, please, I think as the sound of Antonia's footsteps grows louder. *Please let this work.*

I am praying, in a weird way. To my father, to my mother, to Gigi and Ben and Rhys and Dele. I'm asking for help. And hoping that when all this is over, in spite of everything, I will still have a family. Because, I realize now, family is the only thing that matters.

And then she comes into view, doing this mincing jog down the hill, blonde braids a halo in the sun. She's holding the gun straight out in front of her, cop-style, but she's got her eyes down, on the path in front of her. Behind my tree, I'm coiled—ready to go, just like I know Mom is—and when Antonia is inches from crossing the invisible line that connects the two of us, we let out bloodcurdling screams and spring at her.

We scare the shit out of her, just like I used to scare Dad. I can't believe how easy it is for us to pin her to the ground.

59

ERIN

By Thanksgiving, I'm living a life I barely recognize. I write it all down in my own slim leather-bound journal. My way of telling Perry.

Shorie's back at school, taking classes and doing whatever extra work I throw her way from Jax. Right now, she's working on the new merchant corporate social responsibility feature. I've agreed to let her work full time at Jax over the summer. Even though she doesn't like to talk about it with me, she and Rhys are dating. A little bird named Dele keeps me up-to-date on the general gist of things.

Ben's stepped back a bit from Jax. Not entirely—just enough so that we have the space to heal. I need to understand what he knew and when he knew it—and I need to know that I can trust him. He let his commitment to Sabine cloud his judgment. Now we just need to figure out how to move forward.

Jax is holding steady. We lost a good chunk of users after the story broke that Arch and Sabine were stealing money from accounts. But because we were transparent about it in the media, and because we recovered most of the money, I don't believe it will sink us. All we can do is let it play out and concentrate on winning back the confidence we lost. I'm still going in to the office every day, but keeping more reasonable hours, since we've hired some new developers, testers, product managers, and data analytics people. I'm going to hang on to the company and try to scale in the next few years. If we get an offer, we'll entertain it, but we're not in any hurry.

Dele wrote her article for the *Birmingham News*, and it was subsequently picked up by the AP. An explosive piece on Hidden Sands, the story laid bare the murders in crisp, vivid detail. She described the cabal of rich old men who were behind the scheme: Arch Gaines, William Monroe (Jess's father), and Edwin Erdman, all buddies since their college days at Yale, all with problems they needed to be rid of.

Dele set the scene well. The fusty golf club down in Augusta sometime in midsummer. The whiskey and cigars. Old jokes and new complaints. Drunken revelations behind closed doors in the wee hours of the night.

Arch told them about my plan to sell Jax. He confessed to his affair with Sabine, her skimming from Jax, and their plan to run away. If Sabine killed Perry when he became suspicious, as I suspect, he even may have told them about that too. At any rate, William Monroe had a confession to make as well. In a ghastly coincidence, his own daughter, Jessalyn, had become embroiled in an affair as well—and also with a woman named Sabine. Not only that, but William's beloved son had been involved in cyber fraud, and William was convinced that Sabine had somehow duplicated it at her own company.

As the two men compared notes, both realized they had unsolvable problems: I was jeopardizing Arch's romantic and financial future with Sabine. And Jess, if she chose, could bring Sabine's whole operation crashing down, destroying Arch and pointing a finger of blame at her brother, humiliating her family beyond repair. The two men agreed. Something had to be done.

Then Edwin Erdman spoke up, offering a solution. A secluded paradise, run by Edwin's daughter, that offered an experience to end all experiences. Edwin promised it would be the answer to their financial and family woes. Arch and William agreed on a plan to drug Jess and me to explain the need for a trip to Hidden Sands.

But I wonder what Arch's story was going to be beyond that. What was he planning to tell Shorie? That I'd inexplicably run off? That in my grief and addiction, I'd deserted my own daughter? I don't have an answer for that, but the lengths Arch was willing to go appall me anew every day. He is nothing less than a monster.

Now Edwin Erdman, William Monroe, and Deirdre's husband, who arranged for her death, are in prison. Antonia Erdman's locked up in a women's maximum security facility in Bedford Hills, New York. Hidden Sands has been shut down, and I'm not ashamed to say, I hope it rots.

After Shorie emailed the FBI, they contacted Ben, and he immediately cooperated, providing access to all of Jax's servers. The feds found hard drives in a safe-deposit box in Sabine's name, proving she'd implemented the cash-skimming program that automatically deposited money from customers' accounts into hers. As for me, I had my doubts that she'd written it all by herself, but it didn't matter. In her confession, she took full credit. Like she was proud of it.

What the authorities couldn't establish was that Sabine had any knowledge of Arch's plot to have me killed at Hidden Sands. While Sabine and Arch had traded numerous messages about their embezzlement scheme, they never discussed murder. That fact, along with Arch's connection to Edwin Erdman, has everyone convinced that he planned the L'Élu III thing without her knowledge.

But I have my doubts. I think she knew.

Sabine was released on bond and is now under house arrest at her parents' home, awaiting trial. I drove past once recently and parked outside. Just curious, I guess. And hoping for some kind of epiphany about who my best friend really was.

She'd started sleeping with Arch when she was eighteen, right before we met in college. She dated Ben. But she'd had many other relationships—Jessalyn Monroe, for one. I couldn't figure it out—who was Sabine Fleming? What did she want? Did any of her human connections have meaning? Or were they all merely transactional?

Had she ever loved anyone other than herself?

But that wasn't the question I wanted to ask her. There was really only one question I needed an answer to.

Did you kill Perry?

It wouldn't have surprised me if she had. She could've easily gotten to him that Monday evening after he met his friend and before he drove to meet Shorie and me at the lake. They did a toxicity screen on him at the hospital, but it was hours after his death. And I've read that GHB, the newest date rape drug, dissipates quickly in the blood and is often not recognized by emergency room doctors. If, somehow, Sabine was able to dose his beer, it's too late to prove it now.

I do think somehow, maybe with someone's help, she roofied me in Auburn. She—or a flunkie of hers—probably dropped some liquid or powder GHB in my wine glass when I went to the ladies' room. I also think that later that night she had someone call me, pretending to be Dele and saying that Shorie wanted to see me. Of course, the phone records show the call, from a local Auburn number to mine, but the phone that made it, a burner bought by Arch Gaines the week previously, still hasn't turned up. So impossible to prove.

At Sabine's parents' house, reporters swarmed the place like bees around a hive. I sat in my car for over an hour, but Sabine never showed her face. Not that I actually thought she would've told me the truth even if we'd had a face-to-face. I'll never know exactly what she did or didn't do.

There are other unanswered questions. Jess Monroe disappeared from the island, and no one's seen or heard from her since. Arch vanished, too, somewhere into the ether between the Saint Lucia airport tarmac and Ministro Pistarini International Airport in Buenos Aires, which was supposed to be his destination according to the ticket that was purchased for him from Antonia's computer at Hidden Sands.

But the feds are on it, and I will leave the old man to his reward. If he did have anything to do with Perry's death—and did it for nothing more than a woman like Sabine and a couple of million dollars—then having to wake up, day after day, with only his desiccated, empty soul for company is a good start to his punishment.

Gigi's experienced the biggest change of all of us. She's reinvented herself—a spunkier, more resilient version of Ruth Madoff—and made her grand reappearance into Birmingham society. Who knows if she's really okay or if she's tossing back all kinds of pills and potions to get her through the day. There's always the chance, too, that she's plotting some kind of Count of Monte Cristo–level revenge and that's what is giving her the extra bump. But I can't worry about that.

So here we are. November. Thanksgiving. The weather's been windy and gray for weeks, and I have to admit, I'm not looking forward to the rest of the holiday season. It's been eight months since I've held my husband in my arms, but that feels like an eternity.

After dinner, Rhys and Shorie and their friends head out, and Ben stops by on the way home from his parents' house. It rained during the day, so we spread beach towels over the Adirondack chairs by the clean, empty fire pit, and settle down to let our turkey and dressing and pumpkin pie digest.

After a while I speak. "I think I get why Sabine stole Perry's journal—she didn't want anybody to read about the error messages and put two and two together—but I can't understand why she held on to it." I sigh. "I think you were right about her, Ben. I think she had a thing for Perry. I think she loved him all along, and wanted to have something of his."

"Maybe she had a thing for him." Ben shakes his head. "But you're wrong about the other part. She didn't love Perry. She's never loved anybody."

He drums his fingers on the arm of the chair.

"I've been reading through the journal," I say. "Looking for something that'll explain what happened to him."

He sighs. "Oh, Erin. You'll just drive yourself crazy, you know that, right?"

"But I think I found something. Right before he died, Perry had put contacting the Global Cybergames on his to-do list."

"For Shorie?"

"I don't think so. One of the committee member's phone numbers was in the back of the journal, somebody named Mason P., and I called the guy. Turns out he and Perry had talked, specifically about a certain student who competed back in 2016. He sent me an email with some interesting information." I hand him the envelope from under my chair. "Check out the name and address on the last page."

His eyes go wide.

I go on. "Two days before he died, Perry set up a meeting with Sabine. Probably to let her know about this information. That a few things had slipped through the cracks on one of the background checks she'd run. Only, my guess is, she already knew about it."

Ben collapses back into his chair and shakes his head dumbly. "Holy shit, Erin."

"Yeah, I know. Holy shit."

We're quiet for a long time, watching Tiger sniff out God-knows-what in the shadows of my backyard. We can deal with all this tomorrow, report everything to the FBI. Right now, I'm just glad Ben seems to want to enjoy the remainder of the day with me. It was a good one.

He turns to me. "So tell me. What are you thankful for today?"

"Hmm." I think for a minute. "I'm thankful for my crappy garage door. And this fire pit."

Ben laughs. "Seriously?"

"Yes. Perry built it for me, but we never actually got around to having a fire in it. It's a good fire pit. We owed it better."

"Agreed. It's a very solid fire pit." Ben clasps his hands and gazes into it. "I could build a fire, if you want."

"I can build a fire, too, believe it or not. Among other things."

"Let's do it together," he says.

Ben gathers an armful of pinecones that have escaped the rain, and I pull out a few sticks of starter wood from the stack near the back door. The wood and pinecones catch and blaze up, and we throw a couple of logs on that. We sit there for hours, talking about nothing and everything and watching as the clouds flee the sky, revealing the web of stars above us.

60

SHORIE

After we finish cleaning up the Thanksgiving dishes, Rhys suggests he and I and Dele and Lowell all go for ice cream.

After a mere two days at home on Thanksgiving break, I'm pretty sure Rhys can tell that Gigi is driving me nuts. Since everything happened, she's traded her conservative Stepford Wife image for this wild new look with au naturel silver buzz-cut hair, giant cuffs, and hemp caftans. She keeps saying, "Girl power!" and trying to high-five me and Mom all the time. I'm happy for her and all, but it's wearing on my last nerve.

I run up to my room and shoo Foxy Cat, who is, as usual, hunkered down on top of all my important papers. I grab Dad's Caldwell Creamery punch card, and we all go. Using the last punch, Rhys gets Brownie Chunk. In honor of Dad, I get my free cone. Pralines and Cream.

It's still misting rain, so most everybody is crammed inside the shop. But we're outside on one of the soggy picnic tables, licking our cones in the semidark. Dele and Lowell skipped the cones and went straight out to the edge of the parking lot, where now I can see them making out hard-core behind her car.

"So," Rhys says, wiping his mouth with one of the tiny napkins. He's watching me closely. "How are you feeling?"

"Brave," I say. "Determined, happy . . ."

He grins.

". . . meditative, grateful, open minded."

"Good. Those are a lot of good words."

"How are you?" I ask.

"Good. Busy. Dismantling the business hasn't been as hard as I thought it would be. I told my mom everything, by the way. She wanted to kill me, but she was glad I told her." He hesitates. "You want to read it now? Or wait till later?"

"Now, I think."

I take a few deep, cleansing breaths—in and out, in and out—and open the folded papers I've twisted into a baton. It turns out Dad had finished his letter to me after all. Or at least the first draft of one. He'd composed it on his computer and saved it in a random file that Mom hadn't noticed until just a few days ago. A file labeled *SMS*—Shorie, my sweet.

And I'm ready for this, I think. Ready as I'll ever be.

Rhys flicks the flashlight on his phone, aims it at the first page, and I begin to read.

61

PERRY

. . . I'm proud of the father I have been to you, Shor. I think overall, I have been a pretty good one, and I hope you feel the same. One of the things I've tried hard to teach you is resilience. Get back up when you fall off the bike. Take another shot in lacrosse. Go all the way back to the very first error message . . . as many times as it takes.

I'm sorry to tell you this, but failure is the best way— sometimes the only way—we learn.

But here's what I've learned from my failures: it's not about the product, it's about the build. Jax is a great tool, but it's just a thing. And a thing will never be the true reward. My reward, what I gained from the past three years, is so much bigger than a little yellow square. My reward was the days and nights, hanging out at the office with you and Mom and Ben and Sabine, playing Ping-Pong and eating cupcakes. Creating something with the people I loved. Teaching you and seeing your eyes light up when you finally got it. It was all about the build.

And now, even after having built the product and accomplished the goal I set out to achieve, I feel sad—because the building days are over. Just like our building days are over, my girl. I'll miss those days, Shorie, but now the job is done, you're grown and smart and ready, and it's time for you to move on.

Do me a favor, will you? Take note of everything. The smell of the classroom, the professor with the heinous tie, the girl sitting next to you with nails painted like a van Gogh. The kid sitting in the back who's afraid to speak. Write these things down, all of them. You'll be glad you did.

I'll keep writing, too, about Jax and Mom and all my boring chores and how much I miss you. And I'll send you all my crazy Oulipo poems, okay? Maybe I'll write an epic poem without the letter s, in honor of your absence. At any rate, enjoy college. Learn everything. Make friends. Let yourself fall in love, if that chance comes along. But above all, believe in yourself.

Because sometimes, most times, you will be the only person who can fix the error.

Rest assured, I'll always be here if you need someone to talk to. My love for you is, in the words of old Will Shakespeare, an ever-fixed mark. It will never alter or bend.

Shorie, my sweet, I will love you until the day I die and all the time that comes after that.

Dad

TWO AND A HALF
YEARS LATER

Epilogue

ARCH

Some days when I wake up, I can't remember where I am. I don't know if it's a function of aging or that, after six decades in the same town, I'm living someplace new. Eventually, though, much like the persistent, unchanging tide, everything comes back to me.

Ah, yes . . . exile.

I did this to myself.

Made my bed. Sealed my fate. Nailed the coffin closed.

I live in a shack made of woven bamboo that sits just beyond a strip of white sand at the edge of a bay on a private island called Nosy Ankao. The island lies off the coast of Madagascar, at the edge of the deep, blue Indian Ocean.

There is close to a quarter of a million dollars stashed under the floorboards of my shack, which will last me until I die. My wife used to say I looked like Cary Grant, but I am beyond the age that even Cary Grant looked like Cary Grant, so I'm confident that the money will be more than enough to get me to the finish line. And anyway, I spend practically nothing here. They look after me at a so-exclusive-it's-nearly-always-deserted resort on the other side of the island, and in exchange, I eat most of my meals there.

Occasionally also, I sleep with one of the guests, wringing out every last drop of that Cary Grant advantage. I always try for the ones in their thirties, but invariably it winds up being a woman in her fifties or sixties, halfway around the world from her home, celebrating the conclusion of a nasty divorce. Even though I always give them some story about the source of my vast wealth—my imaginary homes in London, Milan, and Punta del Este—I can tell I'm not what they had in mind in terms of a rebound dalliance. But I couldn't care less. When I'm with them, I'm thousands of miles away.

I am with Sabine. My Hermes.

I gave up everything for her—for that glorious, amber-limbed vision of female perfection I first saw standing in my living room thirty years ago. Her otherworldly beauty—her *fantastic power*, Nabokov called it—set its hook in me the instant I beheld her. Later, the way she looked at me with that attitude of worship—an acolyte—that was what sealed me to her forever. I lived for her attention, dedicated myself to her only. Even though, as she grew and matured through the years, she changed.

I saw her wanting more. Saw the sociopathic streak emerge and watched her stray from our commitment. But I forgave her. I forgave her everything.

I remained married to a woman I didn't love because she insisted it was the best way, the only way, to continue our affair. Then, years later, when she finally said she had a plan for us to be together, I believed her. I trusted her when she said Perry was a problem and something must be done about him. What she intended, I never expected. And I'll admit, after he died, I convinced myself it was only a coincidence, that she hadn't been involved. But I knew I was lying to myself. The woman I loved had murdered my son.

So that is the truth I must live with. Some days I'm philosophical and tell myself we all die. But I know a father shouldn't cause his son's death, and so I'm filled with disgust for the man I have become. But then I dream about her, and I am restored.

This particular Nosy Ankao sunset has a slight green tinge to the usual lavender and pink, which gives me a melancholy feeling. I'm missing Sabine more than ever tonight. The curve of her cheekbones, the pout of her lips, the way her stomach sloped to the V between her legs. I'm desperate to see her again, but devoid of hope. I read it in the news. She disappeared over two years ago—skipped her bail and vanished, just like me. And even though I'm at the edge of the world, I think if she really wanted to, she could find me. She's that resourceful. But there's been no word.

I don't like to be alone so I've hiked over to the resort, parked myself at the bar beyond the pool, and started on the Glenfiddich. I'm dressed in a rumpled linen suit, a white shirt, and a pair of cobalt-blue Hermès suede moccasins I found under a chaise by the pool a couple of months ago. I knew whoever left them could afford another pair. The thing is, I treasure these loafers almost more than the quarter million under my floorboards. When I found them and discovered they were a perfect fit, I knew it was a sign. A portent that I would see Sabine again. That we would be together again one day.

I am holding on to that promise tonight.

There is more than the usual smattering of guests here this week, and the pool area is nearly full. The bartender is new, a rakishly handsome young guy with dark hair and pale skin. He must've talked to the manager because he slides me drink after drink without mentioning a tab. The whiskey eases my mood, and we talk for a while, casually, about the turtles and an algae farm he heard about on the western side of the island. Then he asks if I recognize him.

I chuckle. "What are you, a washed-up rock star or something? I'm afraid I don't get to many concerts these days."

The bartender just laughs. "You used to?"

"Oh yeah. My wife and I were always out and about. Concerts, art shows, charity dinners. In another lifetime." I laugh. I don't know why. The memories bring a sour taste to my mouth.

"You mean, before everything collapsed . . ."

A low thrum of warning switches on inside me.

He continues. "Before you personally guaranteed your mortgage on your last shopping center in Texas, but then it all went to shit and the bank came a-calling."

I stare at him. He has a slight southern accent. I feel like I've seen him before. But that's nonsense. It has to be.

He tsks sympathetically and wipes the counter in even, circular strokes. "I always felt sorry for you shopping center guys from the good old eighties. Those fancy outlets fucked up your shit something fierce."

"What do you want?" I say.

"Take it easy. I'm not going to alert the manager. Not until you make your decision."

"What decision? Who are you?"

"We met once, briefly, but we can reminisce about that later. Right now we have business to attend to."

I suck in air through my clenched teeth. "I'm listening."

"You have two choices. Choice A: I call the manager of this place and ID you as Arch Gaines, fugitive from the law, wanted for embezzling, computer fraud, and conspiracy to commit murder. The FBI shows up, extradites you to the States, and I'm a hero. But, guess what? You'll be pretty famous yourself, because you'll confess to everything, grovel before your wife, daughter-in-law, and granddaughter, and beg their forgiveness."

I feel lightheaded.

"Lucky you, you'll get a shark of a lawyer—a friend of mine—to represent you, so you'll do minimum time. Meanwhile, you'll go on *20/20, Dateline*. Give long, tearful interviews. Who knows, maybe even get a million-dollar book deal."

"And you?"

"Everything on my end's already set up. My guy's the new whiz-kid developer at Jax, hired by Erin and Ben. Been there for a couple of months already. When you resurface and freak everybody out with your dramatic tale of woe, he'll go to work cleaning out client accounts."

I laugh. "Not to burst your bubble, but that's been tried before."

"I know, old man, I was there. But I'm not talking pennies this time. And not just Jax. We've got more people on the ground this time, at dozens of apps. And plenty of international backup to handle the backend." He leans on the bar. "Do you hear what I'm saying, Arch? I'm talking a cross-platform, internet-wide, one-time deal here. Every account, every balance on every digital wallet app that exists. One clean sweep and then—poof—we all disappear."

It takes me a minute to process. Then logic kicks in.

"So you're telling me you write code?"

He smirks. "I write it, I hack it"—he holds up a sugar cube, then lets it plop into my whiskey—"and I get out before anyone knows what's hit them."

I lower my eyes to the little white cube and feel my gut twist. What exactly is this son of a bitch saying? Am I being offered an opportunity here—or being threatened with my life?

"Don't worry, Archie, old guy, I know what I'm doing." He rakes his hands through his black hair, squinting over my head like some kind of actor starring in his own western. "When I was in college I brought down a global cyber-hacking competition just for shits and giggles. Of course, I left that detail off my CV. To Erin and Perry and Ben, I was just another dumbass begging to grace the hallowed halls of Jax. Even though your boy, Perry, did figure it out, right there at the end."

His lips twist into a cruel smile, but I turn away, refusing the bait. I really don't want to talk about that whole awful subject, especially not with this ass-wipe. And we need to get back to the matter at hand.

"What's my other choice?" I ask.

"Your other choice." He looks thoughtful. "Well, let's see. In Choice B, all the above happens, only you don't get a cut of the deal."

Not that I need any more money, but . . . . I push the glass with the sugar cube toward him. "Just how do you plan to cut me in if I'm sitting in prison?"

He clears the glass. "Remember that great lawyer I'm getting you? He was her lawyer too, back when all the Jax stuff went down."

Her.

I straighten at the word.

"The guy knows how to get a person out of town."

My throat has gone dry. I'm not even thinking about the awful prospect of having some scumbag lawyer spirit me out of prison and then the country. I am thinking of one thing and one thing only.

Sabine.

And I don't even care if this prick sees my desperation. My love-torn heart. My sickness.

"Have you talked to her?" I say.

"Of course I talk to her. She's the boss, Arch. She's always been the boss, you know that."

I do. And I feel weak with joy at this turn of events. The blue loafers were a sign after all. My love is alive, and she has come back to me. I am in. I am all in, even if it means I have to go to prison for a while. Because it means I will see her beautiful face again.

"One more drink," I say. "If you don't mind, and then we'll talk details."

The guy refills my glass and extends a hand to me. "Nice to make your acquaintance, Mr. Gaines. My name, by the way, is Hank."

ACKNOWLEDGMENTS

This book sprang from a quirky seed of an idea—*"Lord of the Flies*, but with soccer moms!"—and while I'm still convinced that book would absolutely *kill*, I think we can all be grateful this one evolved past that point. Dreaming up Jax, Antonia's twisted L'Élus, and the smart, resourceful mother/daughter duo of Erin and Shorie was the most fun I've ever had with a book. And I have so many people to thank for contributing to that experience.

My agent, Amy Cloughley, listened to me pitch this to her over the phone and asked me some good questions that started me off on the right foot. Later, when things went off the rails (as they will), she had honest thoughts and practical solutions. Cory Johnson educated me on all things to do with tech and building an app and helped me make Jax a more realistic platform. Heather Lazare slogged through a rough early draft, sent copious notes, and spent hours on the phone helping me salvage the shiny bits. Alicia Clancy at Lake Union, a dream editor, was hands-on and encouraging at every stage. Shannon O'Neill helped me shepherd the book to its final form with her trademark grace, sharp eye, and humor.

As always, a shout-out to the regulars: My critique partners and general writer support, M. J. Pullen (who is one of the smartest people I know and always up for an emergency plot-fix meeting), Chris Negron (who offered invaluable tech expertise and insight into what it's like to be a person who's good with numbers, and didn't mock me), and Kimberly Brock (provider of amazing retreats, hilarious stories, and chocolate). Becky Albertalli, George Weinstein, J. D. Jordan (who spontaneously designed Jax's icon at one Happy Writers Hour), Ellie Jordan, and Jane Haessler. I am so thankful for each and every one of you. There were others who offered invaluable help: Elizabeth Maypoles (who helped me figure out Rhys's scam, though she's never done anything remotely bad in her life), Joy Garcia (who told me about hashes), Haley Herrmann (who gave me teen girl tips), Chelsea Humphrey, Rick Carpenter, Joanna Schuerman, the staff at Alessio's, my Lake Union ladies and lads, the incredible, tireless LU team (thank you, Danielle Marshall! Thank you, Gabriella Dumpit!), the Calamity Dames—Kimberly Belle and Kate Moretti (for brainstorming and making this sometimes-maddening process so much more fun), Ashley Taylor (a constant emotional support), Mary Alice Kier and Anna Cottle of Cine/Lit, and the Tall Poppy Writers.

Most of all, I want to thank you, my readers, for making another book possible. You are the reason I write, the reason I dream up new ideas, write them down, and get them out into the world. Your encouragement, affection, and generous promotion mean the world to me. I wish I could name you all here, but, alas, I have not compiled that database yet. I love you all!

Finally, to my family: Richard, Nancy, Karen, Jim, Mom, Dad, Henry, Kathleen, Danner, Jennifer, John, and Katy (book launch party helper extraordinaire and the best sister in the world—thanks for your continued support!). Rick, Noah, Alex, Everett, as you know, I love you.

ABOUT THE AUTHOR

Photo © 2018 Ashley Taylor

Emily Carpenter is the bestselling author of three thrillers, *Every Single Secret, Burying the Honeysuckle Girls,* and *The Weight of Lies.* A graduate from Auburn University with a bachelor of arts in speech communication, Emily has worked as an actor, producer, screenwriter, and behind-the-scenes soap opera assistant for CBS TV. Raised in Birmingham, Alabama, she moved to New York City for a little while to pursue her career before moving back to the South. She now lives in Atlanta, Georgia, with her family. Visit Emily at www.emilycarpenterauthor.com and on Facebook, Twitter, and Instagram.